Also by Daniel Maidman

*Theseus: Vincent Desiderio on Art*

# The Exile of Zanzibar

6·3·23

To Jess–

With such happiness
to be sharing a town
and literary life with
you–

D. MAIDMAN

# The Exile of Zanzibar

Volume I of Railroad to Zanzibar

written and illustrated by

Daniel Maidman

TOWER

Tower Books | Kingston

# The Exile of Zanzibar



Cover Art: Billy Norrby (Cover)
Illustrations: Daniel Maidman (Interior)
Book Design and Typesetting: Enchanted Ink Publishing

ISBN: 979-8-9875978-2-8 (E-book)
ISBN: 979-8-9875978-0-4 (Paperback)
ISBN: 979-8-9875978-1-1 (Hardcover)

Library of Congress Control Number: 2023900702

Publisher's Cataloging-in-Publication data

Names: Maidman, Daniel, author.
Title: The exile of Zanzibar / Daniel Maidman.
Series: Railroad to Zanzibar
Description: Kingston, NY: Tower Books Publishing, 2023.
Identifiers: LCCN: 2023900702 | ISBN: 979-8-9875978-1-1 (hardcover) | 979-8-9875978-0-4 (paperback) | 979-8-9875978-2-8 (ebook)
Subjects: LCSH Time travel--Fiction. | Bronze age--Italy, Central--Fiction. | Warfare, Prehistoric--Fiction. | Historical fiction. | Fantasy fiction. | BISAC FICTION / Fantasy / Epic | FICTION / Historical / Ancient
Classification: LCC PS3613.A349339 E95 2023 | DDC 813.6--dc23



TOWER

Tower Books | Kingston

To Charlotte

'Have you news of my boy Jack?'
Not this tide.
'When d'you think that he'll come back?'
Not with this wind blowing, and this tide.
'Has anyone else had word of him?'
Not this tide.

– **Rudyard Kipling,** ***Have You News of my Boy Jack?***

*Characters*

## Zanzibar

Claire, a patricia

Claire's mother (called Reason)

Berthelot Denys Vazhin, Claire's professor of metaphysics

Claire's aunt (called Moonlight)

## The Army of Florence

Units:

Second Morax, "The Wardogs" – the king's army, equivalent to a legion

Third Morax, "The Redheads" – the king's father's army

The Tagmata – the king's elite cohort

The Stonebreakers – a tenmen, or ten man unit, in the Second Morax

Semaion Fabius Albinus, the king's magister militum

Telamon, Semaion's lieutenant

Valerius Maximus Corvus, a warrior noble

Publius Decius Mus, a warrior noble

Marcus Irenaeus (later Marcus Irenaeus Diophantus), decanus of the Stonebreakers

Taranto, a Stonebreaker

Brindisi, a Stonebreaker

Varian, a Stonebreaker

Otho, a Stonebreaker

Cornelius, a Stonebreaker, victim of the storm's time fragmentation

Philo, a Stonebreaker, victim of the storm's time fragmentation

Titus Herminius, a runner

Egidio, a runner

Furius Nasica, general of the Third Morax

## The Genovans

Antiphon, a runner

King Pindar the Eighth, king of Genova

Dion Ambelokipi, scribe to the general logothete

## Florence: The Royal District

King Ambrosius the Ninth, king of Florence

Queen Antonella, queen of Florence

Domenico (called Bitsy Boots), prince of Florence

Ælius Pellucidus Ambrosius (deceased), older brother of King Ambrosius

Epida, a maid

Aeneas, a page

Lady Livia Faustina Varo, a disgraced noblewoman

Salvatorio Elegans Sestertius, chief judge of Florence

Cecilia Cluvia, overseer of begging day

Laurentius, captain of the royal district guard

## Florence: The Epicondyle

Flavius Papellus Reburrus, His Majesty's Own Ichneumon, high priest of Florence

Iacomo Antivola, Icht Most Capable, Reburrus's right hand

Ius Iunt (deceased), The Songbird of Pantokrator, previous high priest of Florence

Idomeneo Lucan, Ichneumon of the Hill, second to the high priest

## The Constantines

Cleon Tertius Constantine, older brother of Queen Antonella

Ineto Picolomini Constantine (called Barbarossa), cousin of Queen Antonella

Antonio Constantine, older brother of Queen Antonella

Tarquin Constantine, cousin of Queen Antonella

Ineto Tacitus Constantine, father of Barbarossa

## Florence: Serapetine Hill & misc.

Neander Federicus (called Nederick Frederick), mayor of Florence

Beno Thersites (previously Beno Tiresias), the king of the costermongers

Libra, butcher, and priestess of the low religion

Wanesa, niece of Libra and maiden of the low religion

Desiderio, proprietor of a public house

Caeso Barbutus (called Jackdaw), the master of Murderers' Blind

Vigiles, the police force of Florence

## Via Circumflorentia

Temet Nosce Ambrosius, magister equitum of Florence, cousin of King Ambrosius

Novacila, Ambrosius's personal groom

Leander Rigellus, a centurion of the Redheads

Lucius Vitus Pollius, a warrior noble

Marcella Julia Fortunatus, widow of Traian Fortunatus, a warrior noble

Nestor Fortunatus, son of Marcella and Traian

Rufus Quintus Ffidius, a warrior noble

Petrus Secundus Iustinius, a warrior noble

Sandor Pilvax Varo, a disgraced nobleman

Flaminia Pilvax, Varo's daughter

Gaius Pilvax, Varo's son

Geometer Modi Ambrosius, uncle of King Ambrosius

## Animals

Baldessaria, Queen Antonella's elephant

Fortis, King Ambrosius's horse

Boreas, Temet Ambrosius's horse

Polpetto, Claire's horse

Amicus, a hunting dog

## The Gods of Florence: High Religion

Pantokrator all-powerful

Reialia, Pantokrator's wife, mother goddess

Herostratus, light-bearer, a son of Pantokrator and Reialia

Myneia, goddess of the hearth, a daughter of Pantokrator and Reialia

Syrinx, god of justice

Andromache, goddess of love

Trypsomayne, god of sleep

Agathon, god of industry

Enantius, god of health

Vanadio, god of the hunt

Melpomene, goddess of the hunt

Belisarius, god of combat skill

Perenna, goddess of the spring planting

Tacita, goddess of just war

Heseveth,* goddess of sighs

Xorinirox,* god of total war

* inherited from pre-Florentine religions

## The Gods of Florence: Low Religion

The Maker of Hands

Master Rabbit, trickster god

Tacamo, his mortal grandson

Strypho, protector of homes

Sarai Ana Hen Hen Philomela, goddess of the harvest

Deianira, goddess of mercy

Coelestin and Iolanthe, the lovers

Claire, the sower of peace

*Contents*


Andropolis ..... 1

The Old King's Road ..... 71

Florence: The Royal District ..... 137

Florence: Serapetine Hill ..... 267

Ai Ctesiphôn ..... 407

The Tomb of John the Pilgrim ..... 519

# Prologue

## LEAVING ZANZIBAR

A CROWD HAD surprised her at the gate of the Aurillac. She might have expected her thesis committee, but de Staël, chairman of the Concordia? And the Twins? She'd begged the gang at Café Null not to make a big deal of it, yet here the Twins were, She and Her. All around, a rabble of philosophes and enthusiasts. At the back she glimpsed her mentor, Professor Berthelot Denys Vazhin, standing by her mother, called Reason – how were these two reconciled at last?

De Staël made a short fine speech. Listening to it reminded her how highly the Concordia valued her research. She had her own reasons to take it seriously – it was easy to forget others did too.

Surveying the crowd, she realized why so many came. It wasn't awe, but dread, dread on her behalf. She was excited to be off, and found herself impatient with them.

"Why the long faces, friends? What I'm doing here is safe – half of you reviewed the numbers, and the other half should know me better than to think...

"Look, go put on your finest, we'll meet on the Terrace this evening. You can buy me expensive drinks and I'll finally have a doctoral medallion to show off to you all. So much fuss over a thesis project! Go – get going! I'll see you in a few hours."

She stood aside with her mother and traded quiet words. Then she'd got back in her gold palanquin and Vazhin had, all unwilling, unlocked the gate. She'd ridden her car into the Aurillac, the sidereal garden, with its tendrils spread across the universe.

Almost immediately, everything had gone wrong.

# PART I

# Andropolis

# 1

## MARCUS IRENAEUS

*"ANDROPOLIS!" IT WAS their battle cry, but it was ours as well.*

Marcus Irenaeus had inflicted his share of death, but he rarely stopped to watch the dying.

The dying soldier sat in the dust, blinking dully around streams of blood. Marcus had hacked off the top of his head. It was a messy cut with a little notch in front. How could a man survive such a wound? Red brains wet and shiny in the sun.

The others had charged on. Marcus could hear fighting one street away. Were the king's skirmishers, the Tagmata, over there? That sounded like their war-bark. Marcus stayed where he was, lingering to watch the man finish dying.

The Genovan stared at nothing, emotions passing over his bloody face like the shadows of clouds. Marcus saw love and grief pass by, happiness, loneliness, the knit brow of confusion.

The Genovan craned his neck, looking around Marcus's legs. Marcus shifted and turned his head, but there was nothing there. He looked back to the Genovan, and had a thrill of horror: the man's gaze was climbing up to his face.

Marcus had watched as a god watches, above, apart. Now the Genovan met his eyes and Marcus shrank and became just a man, and the Genovan was another. Tears started in Marcus's eyes and streamed down his cheeks.

The Genovan blinked at him, and the confusion smoothed from his brow. All mortal woe smoothed from him. The bloody sword shook in Marcus's hand. The Genovan smiled, the most generous smile, without any reservation. He lifted up his hands and held them there a moment. Then they dropped, and the man was dead.

Marcus stood there, alone and trembling. The edges of his vision blackened, so that all he saw was the slumped head of the Genovan and his naked brain. Marcus ran his fingers along the sheared-off hairs on his helmet's plume, where he'd almost taken the same cruel cut the day before. His mouth formed a circle, and a wordless animal sound escaped him.

He turned and ran, up the street, toward the sounds of fighting, fleeing what he'd done.

## XXX

THE KING OF Florence ran away.

Wise King Ambrosius the Ninth sprinted down the narrow street with six and a half tenmen of the Tagmata, light-armored skirmishers, barking as they ran. Behind, the Genovans were gaining. Maybe five hundred strong.

His foot passed a chalkmark in the street, and he glanced to his *magister militum*, Semaion Fabius Albinus.

The Genovans were gaining – gaining –

King Ambrosius whispered a quick prayer to Master Rabbit, the trickster god of Florence. Semaion raised a gilded city horn to his lips and blew a loud clear note.

The walls on either side of the Genovans *erupted*. Stone and brick and wood collapsed into the street. Ambrosius planted the leather sole of his sandal and turned. He surveyed the scene: his engineers waiting in the weakened buildings had done their job, his trick had worked. Genovans vanished in their dozens, crushed beneath debris, lost choking in the dust. But the trap was sprung a little late. Too many passed before the walls fell. Ambrosius bared his teeth. Like all the men of house Ambrosius, he loved a good fight.

He called on the other god, god of gods, fiery Pantokrator. He felt Pantokrator firm his heart and arm. He charged into the foremost Genovans. His skirmishers followed him.

This was no phalanx battle, ranks neat and tight, shield against shield, spears seeking gaps. It was a street brawl. The gaze of Ambrosius turned red and his breast swelled. He slashed all around him, arm tireless and universal, foot dancing over paving stones. He was faster than the Genovans and stronger. He grew drunk on blood, flying amongst and through his enemies. His skirmishers fought well, but he fought ahead of them. He was bred and raised for war.

To his side, he glimpsed important motion: the long line of a spear. It transfixed Semaion, dear companion of so many battles, and lifted and flung him aside. Ambrosius roared and pressed direct into the angle the spear shot from, threshing all who stood against him till he came against the spearman, a giant man with arms like tree trunks. Ambrosius crouched and thrust upward and gutted the spearman and the spearman fell. Ambrosius moved on.

He turned and turned among the crush of men, smiting those who attacked, pushing away the ones who fell. His body read the jostle of bodies against him. It read how the fight was going, who prevailed, who grew heavy and despaired, how many remained to kill.

Now the poetry of battle shifted; somebody new had entered. Behind him, Genovans were panicking. The pressure at his back diminished. The king turned and beheld a Florentine, half his helmet's plume sheared off. His broad shoulders swung as his sword darted hawklike all around him. *He fights like I do,* thought the king. But there was no joy in this man's fight. He fought desperately, as if to redeem himself.

The battle bent around the man. Where he fought, the Genovans flinched and scattered. In his wake, the Tagmata was heartened, and they followed him.

The man's eye flashed to Ambrosius. The king shuddered with blood-thirst. *I want to impress him.* After a lifetime of war, he knew how to submit himself to battle, and never missed a pace. *He takes your place at my side, Semaion.*

From the time he spotted this man, one breath had passed, maybe two. Letting go the gaze of the young Florentine, King Ambrosius renewed his whirling assault, and Genovans fell before his mighty arm.

## XXX

WHEN IT WAS done, King Ambrosius the Ninth of Florence was black with blood, and he'd won Spring Street, the last of ten decisive streets.

The Pontus Sextus Trassinope sent streets out into Andropolis, like spokes from an axle. Ten on one side of the ancient bridge, ten on the other, radiating into the deadly midland of the contested city. Ambrosius finally held all ten streets on the west side. Now he could mass his army on the riverbank and try to take the Pontus Sextus Trassinope itself. It was the last surviving wide bridge across the Sinope. If he took it, he could enter the nation of Genova. If he entered the nation, he might reach Genova city itself. If he reached the city – he would win the war. The long, terrible war.

*O Pindar,* he thought, *I know you're over there. I wish you'd come out and fight, you coward. Just the two of us. We kings could end this in an afternoon.*

His lungs burned. His knees and shoulders ached. He had a wicked scrape across his ribs on the right side. His belly rumbled, but then, he was always hungry after battle. He'd survived to the age of forty-five and he could still fight, but the price grew steeper every season.

He scanned the scene, the hazy air, the ruined buildings, his milling skirmishers and engineers, the dead criss-a-cross in their heaps. Semaion lay at his feet, curled like a babe, around the spear that still transfixed him. The last of the field magisters. This season had been brutal on officers. He gazed at his friend a long while, and nobody disturbed him.

Finally he bent, and took the badly dented city horn from Semaion's belt. He reviewed the old heroes of Florence, sculpted in the gilding of the horn. He made an instant decision, trusting his judgment in matters of war. He tramped through the mud of brick dust and blood. He came to the warrior he'd seen, helmet off now, sandy hair plastered to his skull. The man stood hunched over, hands on his knees, back rising and falling as he breathed. He looked up as the king approached, and straightened. Ambrosius saw the pale clean tracks of tears in the filth on his cheeks.

The king clapped him on the shoulder. Heat broiled off the man and beneath the stink of gore, his sweat smelled sharp and youthful. Ambrosius said, "Florentine, you are stout chested, as am I, and born to murder. Do you love me?" The handsome young man recited the formula, "I love my king as I love my nation." The milling Tagmata slowed to watch.

Ambrosius gestured and said, "Yonder lies my magister militum, Semaion Fabius Albinus." He paused, but the young man said nothing. Ambrosius could see he was exhausted and unspeakably sad. He grandly pronounced, "Florentine, you will take his place for now in council and in field." The man went pale behind his mask of filth. With shaking hands, he accepted the city horn from his king. The crowd murmured.

Ambrosius continued, "Tomorrow we take the bridge. I will lead the Tagmata and the reserves. You will command the force already gathered by the river. In which morax do you serve?" The man solemnly answered, "Your own, my lord. The second." "What is your rank?" The man said, "I'm a decanus, ninth cohort. They call us the Stonebreakers." Ambrosius raised a brow. The soldier hotly added, "I've never lost a man!" One skirmisher shouted, "You've only got ten to worry about!" Laughter.

The king raised his hands. He said, "My friend, I create you tribune. Please your king and keep the rank." Then he smiled at the soldier, his famous smile of comradeship with his men. Those skirmishers who had, by martial instinct, followed this young warrior in battle, began to clap. The king clapped with them.

When it was quiet again, the young man stood dumb before the crowd. Ambrosius said, "My son, what is your name?" The man said, "I am Marcus Irenaeus." Ambrosius waited for the third name, but none came. He said, "You have a noble look, but you hide out at the bottom of the army. Black sheep of an ancient family? Rebel youth?" Marcus answered vehemently: "None, my lord. I'm a Florentine city rat. I was raised an orphan, picking pockets on Serapetine Hill."

There followed a long, long pause. The skirmishers looked at the king, and the man, and one another. Then Ambrosius laughed and said, "A new man for a new day! Victory, Marcus Irenaeus the Pickpocket! The bridge, the land, the city – victory!"

## XXX

THE KING AND his young tribune reeked of blood, and men parted for them as they passed through the camp. The Florentine army was on the move, pouring out of Wall Street and the Street of Roses and Water Street into the piazza on the west side of the mighty bridge. When King Ambrosius came to Semaion's tent, the dead man's staffers had only to see his face, and they slumped in grief. One brought a pitcher and a bowl, and the king and his man washed the gore from their faces and hands. Marcus looked round for his tenmen. Spotting his friends, he gave them a slight shake of the head; they kept their distance.

Ambrosius showed Marcus into the tent of the slain magister militum, and the young man scanned a bed and desk, scrolls and styli, fine cloths and trinkets from the war. He smelled roast meat and lavender. Then he looked at the king and said, "A councilor may speak freely to the king, and the king won't punish him?"

Ambrosius sighed and said, "The others do, and I don't even like them. I hope you'll level with me, Marcus Irenaeus the Pickpocket."

Marcus said, "We attempt the bridge tomorrow?"

Ambrosius said, "At last."

Marcus frowned and shook his head.

Ambrosius said, "Look at me, man. What have I missed?"

Marcus eyed him, then dared. He said, "I think it'll be another Daffodil Field."

The king sighed. Daffodil Field is a famous battle from the time of the Wanaxes. It was a proper phalanx battle. The two armies knit their shields, leveled their spears, and charged at one another. On each side, each rank was twenty tenmen wide and three files deep. It so happened that these armies were exactly matched, not only in number but in arms and armor, strength and bravery, luck and perseverance. Therefore when they clashed, neither side could break the other's line, and end it. They stood in place, nose to nose and brow to brow, trading cuts and blows. The god of war worked awful mischief in the world of men that day: the armies butchered one another, standing there in place. One by one the tenmen fell, and the soil swole with blood. At last the grunts and cries died down, and a silence fell on Daffodil Field. Nobody survived. The Wanaxes and their crowds upon the hill sat speechless and aghast.

The king tapped a map of Andropolis still flat on his general's desk. He said, "I know it."

Marcus said, "Then why fight?" The king heard a note of anguish in the young man's voice. He said, "My son, you see the truth of the thing in front of you. But the king looks at it from above."

Marcus said, "If you want my best counsel, help me see what you see."

Ambrosius said, "The bridge is a little Daffodil Field inside a bigger one. The entire war is a Daffodil Field." He looked at Marcus, allowing him to see he shared his anguish. Then he continued, "I don't want to to kill even one more man, my son. And to avoid it, I must kill as many as I can." Marcus flashed a disgusted face before he caught himself. *He fights brilliantly, how can he despise war so?*

Ambrosius said, "How comes a city rat to know about Daffodil Field?"

Marcus said, "Tiresias told me, when he was trying to convince me not to run off to war."

The king laughed and said, "So you're one of Tiresias's apple boys?"

Marcus smiled the first real smile the king had seen on him. It was a dazzlingly happy smile. *I chose well. All I need is someone men will follow. Men will follow this one.*

"Yes, my lord. Tiresias is as like as I've got to a father."

Ambrosius heartily joked, "Am I safe alone with you?"

Marcus said, "Wha – oh – yes, of course, my lord," blushing.

Seditious old Tiresias was called the king of the costermongers. He ran a produce empire in the market on Serapetine Hill. He would capture thieving urchins from the alleys, feed them and give them a place to sleep, and teach them to run his carts round Florence city, selling apples and quinces and so forth. He loved his army of apple boys. And he noisily detested the king and his war. It was no surprise he was telling his boys about Daffodil Field.

Ambrosius said, "Well then, pickpocket apple boy, invent you a family name. Consider it carefully. When we prevail, I will name you your name, and you will father a new ancient family."

Marcus sat heavily at the desk of Semaion Fabius Albinus. He whispered, "Why?"

Ambrosius crouched to look at his face and said, "The ancient families founded Florence. We are at the turn of the age. A new Florence approaches, I can smell it like the storm. Help me found it." He let it hang a moment. Then he stood and said, "I'm off to the Killinghouse to marshal the reserves. Get Semaion's man to knead the knots from your muscles. Give your blades to his smiths. Summon his staff, hear their report. Arrange the army as seems best. Eat, drink, and sacrifice to the god. You're a nobleman now, get a decent shave. Sleep well. March tomorrow with your Stone-breakers at your side. *We take that bridge.*"

He tussled Marcus's hair, hard enough to bend his neck. Then he swept out of the tent, war-glamor still inflating him, still making him larger than life.

## XXX

THERE WAS A brief heavy rain in the afternoon, raindrops cold and fat. But the strangest thing – the sky stayed clear. The brilliant sun shone down on the raindrops, so that they fell like jewels, raising clouds of dust in the streets.

The Florentines couldn't understand it. Their terrifying priest, the ichneumon Reburrus, was up on the Killinghouse, the western hill outside Andropolis, and there was nobody else to read the portent. Some found it disquieting, and others pleasing. After a hot day, it was good to feel a cool rain down your aching back. There was a lot of laughter.

Marcus Irenaeus poked his head out when he heard pattering on the canvas. He'd been sitting in the tent, examining a set of little clay figures: a woman and two boys and a girl. They must have been Semaion's family, back wherever he came from. The clay was dark from handling and the paint was worn. *The war has orphaned three more.*

The street was empty now except for Semaion's staff, looking up at rain falling from the clear sky. Marcus told them they could pack and move the tent. He ran up the street to the ruined temple he'd been sheltering in, to his tenmen. They were called the Stonebreakers because they'd once drawn a miserable job of work, breaking stones.

XXX

MARCUS'S MEN PATTED his smooth cheek and he winced because it stung. He'd never gotten a proper shave before, from a barber with a bronze razor. His Stonebreakers mocked him, Cornelius saying, "Nice nice nice, you've got a cheek like a nobleman," and Philo saying, "Like a sweet little baby's ass."

Once their mockery had made him one of them again, he told them the whole story while they passed the gilded city horn around. He finished it, saying, "...so I can't go with you. And you can't enter battle beside me, or you'll never get out. I'll tuck you away on the right wing. As soon as we advance, break ranks and head south. Down the riverbank and under the bridge. Stash your packs there tonight so you'll have them to take tomorrow. Follow the river to Traiana Road. After that, the plan is unchanged. Our smuggler friend in lawless Rhegium is expecting us."

They'd been planning to desert together. The Stonebreakers did not intend to die on that monstrous bridge.

Stout Otho grumbled, "Wasn't very bright of you, catching the king's eye today of all days." Marcus shrugged, "Nothing for it, brother." Wispy Varian said, "Why'd you do it?"

Marcus saw again the dying Genovan, bleeding from his opened head. He said, "Thank Master Rabbit I did, Varian. I can place you where none will catch you." He put his hand on his man's shoulder, as Ambrosius had done to him. He looked around at his men. He spoke steadily: "I'm going to trade my life for all of yours." Only yesterday, he'd craved escape as much as any of them. But he wasn't the man he'd been yesterday. They stared somberly at him. Taranto, hulking brute that he was, had tears in his eyes. Brindisi, just as big, said, "It's not fair."

He walked onto a terrible shore.

Marcus nearly blurted something, but when he opened his mouth, he didn't know what he meant to say.

## XXX

HE PASSED UP his chance at Semaion's comfortable bed. He slept on his mean straw roll, beside his Stonebreakers, on the red and yellow tiles that paved the ruined temple. Lying inside the temple was like lying inside a half-shattered egg. Marcus fell asleep looking at stars past the shards of the temple's dome.

He dreamt he was lying in the temple. Past the shards of the dome, the sky was the color of flame, and a hideous shade of yellow dripped down it, like melting butter. He stood and left the temple and walked onto a terrible shore. Behind him, the land was covered in dull reddish fire. The shore was scorched black, and the sea was black as well. Slow oily waves reflected the flaming sky.

He found he held a skull in his hands with the top hacked off, a messy cut with a little notch in front. He didn't look to his side. He knew who was there, hands raised in friendship, all mortal woe smoothed from his brow.

Marcus couldn't bear to look.

# 2

## ADVANCE!

AT FIRST, SHE panicked. As much as her palanquin was lost in the storm, she lost herself in fear and terror. But even in the depth of it, she registered the heartbeats of time and distance:

*Now I am out of the Aurillac.*

*Now I am out of Zanzibar.*

*Now I am over the sea; over the sea, or the desert.*

And this grim timekeeping calmed her, and she grew lucid.

She took stock of her reason and found she was still herself, still all of herself. She knew it wouldn't last. Her full nature was tall as a tower. Outside her home, only the base of it could stand.

She embraced her predicament. Her native vanity reasserted itself. She saw a way to use the storm. *You are great, Storm, but I am greater.* She rifled through the polytopes and chose one. She snapped her silver gaze to the chaos of the storm. She harnessed it, mapping the storm to the shape. Now the storm was a lens, an insect's eye, its overwhelming flow of information sorted in six hundred cells.

She looked through it at the entire Earth. A perpetual student, she knew everything, but only from reading books. She read the world, the land of Midnight, like a book: sea and land, forest and plain, tribe and nation, strife. *There*! Two proud free peoples – two armies – a bridge. *Mortal men, I could save you.* Her reason frayed. She set the gold palanquin on a course. It would navigate the storm, after she'd forgotten where she went and why. *Mortal men, you could save me.*

She aimed the gold palanquin toward the bridge. Toward the war.

## XXX

A BOY, NO more than eight years old, clambered around the rocky side of the great hill called the Killinghouse. Every stone, every flowering weed, every insect delighted him; he was at that magical age when the world is fresh and fascinating. He wore a soldier's uniform, reduced in size, complete with breastplate, pteruges, greaves, and leather boots. His name was Domenico, but the soldiers called him Bitsy Boots, on account of the boots. They treated him like a mascot, pinching his cheek when he passed by, giving him sweets when they had them.

The reserves were mustering this morning. Bitsy Boots took advantage of the commotion and slipped his minders. He left the camp and went straight for the high path. From there, the world looked flat as a game board: Andropolis hazy on the plain and the river Sinope a ribbon of silver.

His minders must be searching the camp for him by now, but he'd rounded the side of the crest, leaving view of camp and Andropolis alike. The minders wouldn't let him near the sacred caves on the backside of the Killinghouse. He made his way along the path, hot sun peeking over the stony heights above, green grass carpeting the slope below. The boy almost lost his footing once, and gravel hissed down from the path. Finally he came to a cave entrance, black and full of mystery.

He hesitated, wondering what King Papa would say, then firmed his courage and passed into the cave. It was cool and damp inside, and smelled of fragrant smoke, as from a fire in which herbs are burnt. He stood breathing, listening to echoes on the stone. The cave looked black from outside, but once he stood inside, it only took his eyes a moment to adjust. Cool light streaming in the cave mouth fairly lit the place. Bitsy Boots perceived he was in a room, big but not as big as the great hall back home. The walls were dusty stone, the floor engravelled like the path outside.

He crunched quietly around, giving himself shivers with thoughts of gods and ghosts. The farther he explored, the dimmer the cave got and the broader the dark shadows. At the back wall, he had a good scare: he almost stumbled into a statue of a man.

The statue was made from shiny white marble. It was a naked man, seated, and very skinny, so that you could see all his sinews and bones. He had a bald head and a stern face with great eyes, closed. When the boy got over his fright, he stood back and admired the statue. It seemed to him very ancient and sacred, just like this cave, full of all kinds of secrets. Little snakes crawled up and down its arms, and spiders wandered its chest. Following one spider with his eye, the boy's gaze came to the center of the statue's chest, where the breastbone ended in a jagged little triangle. This sculpture was very skinny indeed. The boy had only ever seen the most miserable of beggars so thin that you could trace the tip of their breastbone.

Now the aimless jangling of the boy's limbs grew still. The tip of the breastbone was pulsing very slowly, in and out, in and out. Horror filled Bitsy Boots, just like water poured slowly into a jug, freezing black water, the horror filled him. The sculpture had a beating heart.

The sculpture's great eyes snapped open, staring through the boy. Bitsy Boots screamed and fled the cave.

Back in the warmth and light of day, he stopped and caught his breath. He realized he was being very silly and childish. It was just a holy man, meditating in the cave. That's what sacred caves were for!

He thought about the living statue. His mind's eye summoned the statue's face. Seeing it again, Bitsy Boots realized he knew this man.

*Reburrus.*

Terror, blank and overwhelming, pierced him. He ran. He didn't stop running till he got back to camp.

ᚸᚸᚸ

THAT SAME MORNING, Marcus Irenaeus woke before dawn. The men were silent all around him, not even snoring. It was as if he were alone in the world.

He stared past the shattered dome at the sky. Gray light dusted the east; stars were still thick overhead. *The great unploughed field,* he thought. The Florentines and Genovans both called it that – a billion stars unploughed upon a million acres. *Maybe this is my last time looking at the great unploughed field.* His gaze sank deep into that numberless depth, and he felt liberated from a terrible burden. A cool breeze caressed his face. The scent of thunder filled his nostril, and a sweet smell of honeysuckles. A storm? A garden? Where?

The breeze shifted and took the smells with it. The light in the east brightened and turned yellow, and the stars faded and the sky pressed Marcus back down to Andropolis.

He shifted on his straw roll. He found his head unbearably heavy. His wrists and ankles were stiff. He was like a man with fever. He closed his eyes again, hoping to wring a little more sleep from the night. As soon as he closed his eyes, he remembered that scorched shore on a black sea, between the fiery sky and land, and his awful friend beside him.

*This is sin.*

*It was sin I fled yesterday, wading recklessly into the fight.*
*It is sin that crushes and fevers me.*
*It is sin I will remedy today, leading my nation in battle.*

As soon as he became aware of his sin, a soft astonishment blanketed him. For if the death of this one Genovan was a sin, then what of all his other dead? How many had he killed since he'd abandoned his apple cart? He'd heard some men survive an entire war without raising the sword in anger. If it was true, those men survived because of men like him.

*How many have died so that my tenmen might live?*

He turned his heavy head and looked at his sleeping Stonebreakers, indistinct in the dimness. If he carried a sin, they carried it as well. Each of them had proved himself in savage battle. Love for them filled him, it filled him so that he could scarcely contain it. *Yes, my friends, fleeing the war, you will leave your sins behind. And I will leave my sins as well, fleeing life itself.*

XXX

MARCUS IRENAEUS, SMOOTH cheeks still stinging, trailed by his tenmen and Semaion's staffers, crossed Platea Lux, the piazza on the west side of the bridge. A fog had rolled in just after the sun rose. Now it hung heavy and blue upon Andropolis. Marcus's cheek was damp and he felt the great force of the Florentines around him more than he saw it.

He came to the lip of the bridge. The bridge, the heart of the war. Stepping onto it seemed like stepping off a cliff. He made himself walk two steps forward, onto the massive paving stones. He squinted, but the fog hid the view ahead. He turned and faced Semaion's staffers. He said, "The second morax – we Wardogs – will take the center of the bridge. Two tenmen wide, fifteen men deep. That leaves room for one more tenman on each wing. But you will fit two tenmen on each side. March them diagonally. The entire army will advance like an arrow, with the second morax at its tip."

Semaion's lieutenant Telamon, a stern old man hacked up with scars, said, "I think I see your aim, but verify to me what you intend."

Marcus said, "Everything depends on punching through the line of Genovans right away. Therefore the front of us must be hard as bronze – tight-packed, unbreakable. If we do only this, the day is won. I will take the center of the first rank."

Telamon nodded his respect and said, "With your Stonebreakers to either side of you?" Marcus shook his head. He turned to his men and said, "You will take the front rank of the far right wing. I depend on you to hold the line tight from the outside edge." *May Master Rabbit bless our scheme, my Stonebreakers.* He turned back to the Telamon. "Who is like in discipline to my tenmen, to hold the force together from the left?" The lieutenant named him a tenman from the fourth cohort.

The staffers shouted orders. There was a good deal of stumbling about in the fog. Marcus sat himself cross-legged, dead center of the bridge's lip. He emptied his head. The sound of boots on gravel filled his ear, and later on, the sigh of wind in the bulrushes and the murmur of river water.

The wind grew stronger and colder and drove back the fog. There it was, emerging from the blue: the famous Pontus Sextus Trassinope. It looked bigger maybe than the city hosting it. It was as broad side to side as it was long. It was built of gray granite. Marcus knew its wide back rested on a dozen low fat arches crowning tremendous slime-streaked legs. When he'd seen it from the side, it had looked like a slow disastrous animal, heaving itself up from the mighty Sinope.

Marcus stood and rolled his shoulders and shook his ankles. He picked up his shield and settled its weight on his arm. Picked up his spear and judged the wobble of its long shaft. Lowered his grip a little. He touched his elbow to the hilt of his sword.

He scanned the sky. A flock of little clouds had gathered in the lower reaches. Larger darker clouds were slowly drifting in to make a solemn upper vault. He looked back down. The wind was still rising, driving back the last of the fog. Now the far side of the bridge appeared.

With a Genovan army arrayed for battle. They'd formed an arrow too.

Marcus's guts went cold and heavy as clay. *Daffodil Field.*

He looked to the men beside him, at the center of the front. He had a rude shock – here were Otho and Varian, apple boys like him. And Taranto and Brindisi, his thug stablehands from the Bætica.

He said in a low voice, "And the others?"

Otho murmured, "We had to force them to go."

Marcus nodded. He called out, "Noble Telamon, could we march this minute?" The lieutenant shouted back, "One quarter hour!" Marcus scanned the Genovans. They weren't quite ready either. He shouted back, "Quicker, Telamon!" and Telamon spread it through the army.

Marcus advanced from his rank, out onto the deadly bridge. He turned and looked at the force of the Florentines, a wall of shields and helmets, a forest of spears. He shouted over the wind, "Florence!" The army shouted, "Magister militum!"

He strode back and forth, as he'd seen great men do before battle. He called out, "King Ambrosius had a plan for today, but the god of war makes plans for all. He and his Tagmata and the reserves are back there somewhere. The Killinghouse? The streets? Too late, my friends, too late."

He smelled thunder and honeysuckles. The day was darkening. He looked up again. Flashes of lightning lit the upper clouds. Rain from clear skies yesterday, fog this morning, now this. Very strange.

Marcus turned back to the Florentines and cried, "The war spins round Andropolis. Andropolis spins round the bridge. And the bridge depends on us. It is only us, my brothers! We are the axis of the war!

"Semaion Fabius Albinus should have led you. He was a great man from an ancient family. Perhaps you've heard of me by now. I'm a pickpocket and an apple boy. I'm as low as the worst of you." He fetched the dented city horn from his belt and blew on it. It made a crooked, ruined note.

The crowd laughed, and he let them laugh. He could smell the sweat and piss coming off them as they faced the terror of battle. He thought of Tiresias, hater of kings.

"Today the god ordains that Florence rests on her lowest men. But remember always this: Florence is a nation of proud free men. Therefore the lowest Florentine is so much as the greatest."

The wind began to howl. Voice rising, Marcus went on:

"Prove it, Florentines! Prove that you are proud free men! This is the fatal hour – deliver your nation!"

Now he planted his feet on the granite bridge and roared their battle cry: "Andropolis!"

They roared back, "Andropolis! Andropolis! Andropolis!"

He took his place, and in the midst of noise, his soul went to a quiet inward place. Stained with sin and loath to live, he faced the mighty gods of Florence. *Pantokrator all-powerful, watch over me. Reialia, gather me within your sparkling hem. Have mercy, dreadful Syrinx, on my soul!*

*Save my nation!*

*Save my nation.*

Across the bridge, the Genovans began their march. The soul of Marcus Irenaeus came back from its solitude. For a moment, he was not out of the world or in it. A sweet despair filled him and he thought, *We must be what we are.*

He thought, *Must we?*

Then great Pantokrator hardened his heart. A dark valor filled him. His sins and fears slid loose from him like skin from the serpent. His naked heart joined with his fellows. His armored body became one of the thousand limbs of war.

"*ADVANCE!*"

## XXX

THE STORM CROSSED the bowels of heaven. It carried her gold palanquin with her inside of it. By now, her silver gaze was gray. Her reason was a fraction of itself, and she understood so little of what she'd been and known.

She opened up the smallest window of the great palanquin and stuck her face out. The storm attacked her face as if it hated her and wished to destroy her.

*Storm, you are alive*, she thought. *After what manner are you alive?*

The lightning lit up regions divided past deciphering. The sound was louder than she could bear. She felt her ears must burst from the sound, and yet she went on listening. Her reason expanded to meet the sound.

*You are alive after the manner of matter, and you are alive after the manner of mind. Storm, what are you?*

There was order hidden in the overwhelming roar. It was a gigantic order, written on the lightning and the clouds. Gazing deeply into this order, she was astonished: it was written on time itself. Time fragmented inside the storm, and flowed at different rates in different places.

For an instant, her reason was restored, increased even, and she *saw*.

*How did I think I was greater than you, Storm?*

The storm's order was the merest fragment, the tiniest arc, of Heaven's Ring. *My thesis was correct – it's real!* Glimpsing Heaven's Ring, she understood why she suffered, and would suffer. And she saw that it was good, and welcomed it.

Giddy with magnificence, she bade herself farewell. That

The storm carried her gold palanquin with her inside of it.

glorious creature set herself aside, even though a lifetime must pass before she met herself again. She shut the window. She fixed a shining city before the eye of her longing, called Zanzibar.

XXX

SOME TIME LATER, moments, days, a gust slowed her. She intuited to brace herself. The palanquin crashed. The left side screeched and rattled, settling lower than the right. Inside, she was unhurt.

She drew aside a curtain on the right. Rain and blackness. Lightning flashed. She made out human figures on a stone-paved square, and beyond, a raging river. She shifted and drew aside a curtain on the left. Lightning. The same view: square and river.

She was on a bridge.

# 3

## THE FURY OF THE STORM

MARCUS IRENAEUS LOOKED up at the gathering storm. *We will fight in the rain.* He started across the bridge, Otho and Varian to his left, Taranto and Brindisi to his right, the Wardogs of the second morax all around them, the fifth and seventh moraces on the wings, peltasts well ahead, two thousand Florentines panting for war. His entire body shook with the booming of their feet, the clanking of their metal.

The cold wind bit his flaming cheeks. It shoved his spear. He blinked. Heavy freezing drops began to fall. He roared, "*AT SPEED!*" Around him the army advanced to a trot. Two more orders – *Level Spears* and *Charge*.

The day dimmed nearly to dusk. The raindrops rang music on the helmets of the Florentines. The wind pressed against him and he could scarcely walk. Then it reversed and a gust yanked his shield. It broke him from his rank. He staggered forward. When he got his feet under him, he looked across to the Genovans. Their front line was breaking apart. A horrible sight: men at their far wings falling from the bridge. He felt his own formation softening around him.

Doggedly, he advanced, leading the Florentines. The paving stones seemed to ripple. The rain began to fall in sheets. Now it hid the Genovans entirely. Branching arms of lightning blazed paths down from the sky. The Florentine phalanx shuddered once, and again, and then it dissolved. Men scattered back toward the Platea Lux.

Marcus flung away his useless spear and shield. He bared his teeth at the storm. He felt hands clasp each of his, Otho's heavy paw his right, Varian's long fingers his left. Hunched over, hollow-chested, they turned him around and led him west.

They stumbled onto the piazza. Gaps opened in the blinding rain. Marcus saw gaunt Telamon, bent against the wind, retreating back to his tent. Then the tent reared up like a monster and he fell. Marcus understood it an instant after he saw it: the wind tore the tent loose from the street, and one of the pegs spiked the old man in the chest. The gap closed, and the scene was gone. He turned to his friends, and in flashes saw beyond them. He saw men falling, men slipping down the slick bank of the Sinope, vanishing in the frothing river. The speed and violence of it was astonishing. *Where are the rest of the Stonebreakers?*

Marcus howled like a beast. He tugged at the hands of his friends, and now they followed him, upland, away from the furious Sinope, away from the murderous grounds.

The shrieking wind drove the rain up, down, and across. They made for the ruined temple. Debris blocked the door, so they squeezed themselves into the narrow alley between the temple and its burnt-out refectory. The walls sheltered them a little from the storm, and they stood there, panting at one another in the night the storm brought. Water coursed over their feet to the level of the ankle. A horse slid past in the street. It caught on something and they heard it screaming and kicking, then suddenly it stopped.

Marcus and Otho looked at one another. There was a flicker and Otho's head jerked back. Masonry, falling, crushed his skull. Marcus and Varian fled the alley.

Panicked in the blackness, they fought the debris at the temple door. Lost shields clattered by in the street. Strange figures flapped past overhead. Shifting the debris at last, they opened the door. Marcus pushed Varian inside. Lightning flashed nearby. One hand on the door, Marcus turned. Behind him in the street he saw two men together, one of them pointing upward. Marcus shouted and beckoned to them. Neither moved.

Neither moved at all.

Lightning struck again, and held, so that Marcus saw the street clearly. Beyond the frozen men, in front of a wall, he glimpsed flickering. There were human figures milling there, faster than blinking, fast than heartbeats, faster than anything. The lightning went dark.

Marcus stood, incapable of movement. Lightning struck again. The flickering men were flailing on the ground, hideously swiftly. Darkness. Then lightning. The men were still. They were real men, he made out their bronze armor, their wet skin. Then the street went dark.

Terror eclipsed Marcus. He couldn't turn away. The wind tried to tear the door from his grasp.

Lightning flashed, and Marcus squinted toward the fallen men across the street. They were bloated and black now.

The door tore loose from its frame. Marcus lost his grip on it and it clattered away. He retreated into the temple. Varian sat huddled on a wrecked marble pew. Marcus splashed over and sat with him. He kept his gaze away from the door.

Even in this shelter, wind lashed Marcus. Rain poured through the shattered dome. Freezing water streamed down his skin inside his armor. He shivered and his teeth chattered. *If I had not Varian with me, surely I'd go mad.*

The storm went on, there was no cease in it: the firmament had broken open, and the elements themselves made frenzied war on one another. He glanced once out the door. The two men still stood frozen in the street, one of them pointing to the sky. *They aren't real. They can't be.* Formed by chance and fear from the shifting of the waters, mere ideas in the mind of the storm. *Only Varian and I are real, Varian and I and the storm.*

## XXX

ONE DAY. ONE night. One day. Or something like it.

Marcus and Varian sat slumped against the wall, laps beneath the level of the water. In the night, the stones flowed past outside. Here they sat now, skin cold and soft, eyes blind, ears deaf, a living death, and all the world only noise and mess.

Varian was drifting, Varian – *Varian, no!* Marcus shook the wispy man. *Live, Varian!* He sank against Marcus, and Marcus bent his legs above the level of the torrent and settled Varian's head on them, so that Varian could rest. Lightning sometimes lit Varian's eyes, and they seemed to glitter. Marcus held his narrow fingers, he squeezed his hand. He felt him shaking. Even in that sundered chaos, he saw the life leak out of him, till he was – *only stay, Varian, stay!* – till he was gone. Then Marcus wept hot and wretched tears of grief, and the storm stole them from his face.

He shook with his weeping some uncountable time, and finally he calmed. He dragged his hand across his eyes as if to dry them. He let Varian slip from him, and the waters covered his friend. Now he was alone, all alone before the terrible face of reality.

He stood. He left the temple. The two men still stood in the street. The one still pointed at the sky. Marcus stuck his face in theirs and shouted, but they didn't move. He tried to shake them, to push them. It was like pushing solid bronze. He gave up and crossed the street. The armor still lay before the wall, half-sunk, but the flickering men had gone.

No, not gone. There were bones in the armor.

*How? How?*

Marcus found his terror less now. He abandoned these grim miracles. He wandered without direction. He was careless of the effort of lifting his legs, careless of the hazard of losing his footing. He never met another living thing. The roar and spray never dropped.

His demolished reason began to rebuild itself. Alone against the world, he fell into himself. He asked himself strange questions. He asked:

*Does this storm scourge me for my sin?*

He asked:

*Is this the last day? Is the world ending?*

He thought:

*It is not ending – it has ended.*

He grieved again then. Not for Varian and Otho, nor even for himself. Marcus Irenaeus grieved for the world. No man should outlive his people, his nation, the world. To go on living thus was worse than dying. The last day had come and gone. This was afterwards and he alone survived to witness it.

*This is how I pay for my sin.*

He stopped guessing day and night. There were no more day and night. No before, no after, no here, no there. The great wheel of being had ground to a halt, and there was only roaring, as the sages tell us there was roaring before the world began. Looking blindly into the spray, he sometimes thought he saw faces, or heard voices; but he knew there was nothing there. Condemned to wander in this final wilderness, he tried to reflect on happier times. All dying soldiers recollect sunlit scenes of childhood. But he could not remember his parents. He'd lost them both when he was so very young. He nursed a fresh fear. So much as the world was not the world, maybe he was not himself. He thought:

*Am I tricked? Am I someone else? Am I no man at all? Was I ever?*

He thought:

*Am I the storm? Am I the world? Is my sin the sum of the sins of a ruined world? How can my debt be repaid, even at eternity?*

He was wandering thus, ensnared in fearful revelations, when he saw before his eye – something. Something that was not the same as everything else. It was a single point of light. It shone steadily in the depth of the storm. Therefore it was in the sky. Suddenly the wheel of being began to turn, spinning differences again: before the light appeared, and afterward. Marcus here, and the light there. The light above, and Marcus below. All the evidence of a world. Surely he was imagining this light.

It increased in brightness and took on a golden cast. It illumined a scene. There were clouds and vapors and spray. There was flat stone ground. And there were *men*. Scattered around the ground stood living men, men apart from himself. They were looking to the brilliant golden point of light. They could all see it.

Was he imagining the light? If these men were real, then the light was real. And if he was real, then these men must be real as well.

*This I know, perhaps only this: whatever I am, I am real.*

Therefore the point of light was real. But it was no longer a point. Rather, as it grew it took on form. The flashing of the lightning showed light and shadow on it.

The storm screamed its rage at this golden thing, this real thing. It went on growing, and resolved into a great and gold palanquin. Marcus's reason, so divorced from his senses, suddenly comprehended its increase in size. *The thing approaches*. This chariot was streaming down from heaven.

He was not wrong before. He had outlived the world. For what else was this gold palanquin, cast off from the shoulder of the storm, what else was it than the chariot of god? Who else could have ended everything, then sparked a new world? The gold palanquin hurtled toward the mortals and they scattered from it, screaming like bulls before the butcher's blade.

In the final moment, the raging wind caught the gold palanquin in its hand. It set it roughly down upon the flooded stone. The gold palanquin screeched and rattled, and its left side settled farther than the right. Then it was done.

The din of wind and rain diminished by some fraction. The new world had the same map as the old. Looking round, Marcus found he stood upon the Pontus Sextus Trassinope. The river rushed loudly not far below. The palanquin rested at the center of the giant square. Knees weak, beggared by what he had survived, Marcus shuffled toward that mighty golden car. He saw the others in the square approach it too. Through the thinning rain, he got a clearer view of it. Its top was sculpted like the feathers of a wing or waves upon a sea. It had a circular golden door, and circular windows down each side like glaring eyes, staring everywhere. It had no wheels. The heavy body of it rested on gold struts, attached below to curving golden sledge-rails. The struts on the left hand side had crumpled when it struck the Earth.

He felt the future pulling on him, he foresaw glory unendurable. He stood watching the golden door, waiting helplessly for it to open.

## XXX

SHE SAT SHAKING in the dim light, filtered golden by the curtains. There was silence in heaven, silence on Earth.

She was diminished now to mere humanity. She remembered only human things.

She remembered a day at Angoulème. She had to raise her arm to hold hands with her mother, so she must have been very little on the day that she remembered.

It was a fine hot summer's day, and they came to a vendor, and her mother bought her a spiral-wing. The smiling vendor leaned down to give it to her. Its red-and-white paper wing was wrapped around a stick.

Delighted, she let go her mother's hand, and took the spiral-wing and spun it between her palms. She let it go, and it rose up in the air. A breeze caught it, swinging it higher. She saw right away there was no catching it, and she serenely watched it carried aloft, out over the sea. The spiral-wing grew hazy in the shimmer of the day, far above the waters.

"Iss like papa," she lisped in her scratchy child's voice. Her mother said, "Yes, like papa." Then it was gone.

Seeking him, she'd become like him. Now she was an exile too.

She remembered only human things.

She remembered her mother's warning, the warning the mothers of Zanzibar tell their children as soon as they are old enough to hear: *All the Zanzibaris must come home at last, or die.*

She steadied her heart. She steadied her breath. The storm was gone, but she still smelled thunder. From where? She sniffed around, then raised her arm and sniffed the back of her hand. She'd always smelt of honeysuckles. Now she smelled of thunder too.

*This is not a story. This is happening to me. This is real.*

The exile sank completely into this dream people call human life.

She put her hand to the golden door.

# 4

## THE PATRICIA IN THE GOLD PALANQUIN

WHEN RAIN FIRST fell from the empty sky, the ichneumon Reburrus took it for the prodigy it was. He left his tent and made his way around the Killinghouse, to the cave of Quintus Martyr. He blessed the sacred cave and entered it. He took off his miter and robe, folding them carefully and setting them on one of the shelves Quintus had carved. Then he walked around to the back, to the demolished sanctuary. He sat naked in the dust, fasting and meditating. Spiders and little snakes crawled over his body and he knew nothing of them.

When the king's boy visited the cave, Reburrus saw him in a distracted way. When the great storm arrived, he stared half-blind at rain pounding mud in the mouth of the cave. His reason remained in his body, but his soul departed.

His soul passed through the region of unlikeness, and the region of likeness, until it entered the square hall of infinite length, and at the end of the hall the one god, Pantokrator. The one god was a furious god, a planet of flame. Like his god, the ichneumon was furious. His fury made him strong; his religion made Florence strong.

When Reburrus was still a boy – just saved from scrounging in the alleys off Serapetine Hill – and the priests had begun to train him to control and use his fits, his protector Ius Iunt, the greatest ichneumon of the last generation, had mocked the boy's superstition, saying, "What did you expect the god should be? A big man? A tall man? A man with a very fine beard?" This wasn't fair; like all Florentines, the boy learned his idea of the Pantokrator from the priests themselves. Ius Iunt was called the Songbird of Pantokrator, so beautifully did he speak about the gods: Pantokrator with his majestic beard and terrible sling and suns for sling-stones. His wife Reialia with great warm eyes like a cow, and a motherly figure, and a plaited himation, stars sparkling in its hem. Herostratus and his torch, Andromache and her seashell, Syrinx and the balancing pan...

"No," said Ius Iunt, "These are fables for the sellers on Serapetine Hill, for the freemen on their farms and the soldiers doomed to die. They are true, but only in a simple way. The ichneumonoi see the last nature of things. Our discipline is the circle inscribed in the square."

And so it was: in time the superstitious boy became a true ichneumon, mastering his fits, summoning and banishing them. He used them to penetrate the scrim of the world, and perceive the Absolute. The infinite hall with its square cross-section, and the blinding sphere of the Pantrokrator at its end: Pantrokrator Imminent and Radiant.

In the sacred cave on the north flank of the Killinghouse, he returned to the almighty god. In the flames that blazed from the ineffable surface of the Pantokrator, he squinted out details of the present, yes, the present and the future. But the storm was not pictured there. The Pantokrator had nothing to say about Andropolis. It shook the ichneumon, and he came back down the endless corridor. He returned to himself and sat in his cave, among the spiders and the little snakes. He made his prayers, and his eye wandered the rain, that his god, *the* god, did not speak of.

## XXX

The clamor quieted. The rain stopped. The without-form took on form.

There was a sound of rushing from the flooded Sinope, and a trickling and gurgling of waters draining off the square. The heavy darkness paled. The clouds of the lesser regions broke in one place, and far above them, the clouds of the greater regions showed thin and filmy.

A new world in the shape of the old.

The circular door of the palanquin clattered aside. At this very moment the clouds of the greater regions broke, so that a single shaft of sunlight fell all the way to Earth, striking the figure in that open door. Marcus's eyes streamed at the shining of the figure and the gold. Painfully blinded, he turned his head. Through his tears, he saw other mortals cringing from the brilliance. Squinting, he turned back.

It was a woman. Standing in the shaft of light, she seemed herself made from the light. She was a river of light, in the shape of a woman, ablaze in an ocean of light.

Slowly, slowly, his dark-accustomed eyes learned light again, and picked out details from the light. The woman wore a white gown, tied about her hips and waist, beneath her breast and at her throat by threads and bands of gold, and her plaited hair was a gold almost white in the overflow of light upon her. In despite of her brilliance, she was not entirely of white and gold. Her eyes were a calm pale gray.

A world in the shape of the old, but new: clean, unruined.

This was not a woman like the women he had known in the filthy world that was. They were broken by the fierce masters of war, that are called terror, rape, and death. This woman, this womanly pillar of light, was unbowed, she was somehow complete. Seeing her, Marcus understood no man survived the storm. The orphan of Florence recognized her.

She was the mother of the world who is in heaven. When Marcus as an infant entered wailing in the world, he forgot her face. Now he'd left the world, and so soon as he saw her he remembered her. All his life he'd longed for her, without knowing what he longed for. Returning to his mother after many sufferings, he saw she wished to forgive him, as she was forgiving all her sons, gathering them into her arms that spanned the seas and stars. He craved to press his brow to hers and sob.

The soldier of Florence caught movement in the corner of his eye. Other men were crowding near. Protector of the good, Marcus scanned them, but their faces were open and innocent; they recognized her too. They remembered her and knew her, Genovans and Florentines alike. The sons of the two nations got mixed up among each other in the storm. Now they stood together on the Pontus Sextus Trassinope, in awe before the prodigy.

The clouds shifted again. The sky grew lighter and patches of blue appeared, but the woman was no longer bathed in radiance. Instead, she solidified. Marcus could feel his understanding of her melting away. He knew how he felt about her, but he forgot why. He had thought her ancient, but now he saw she was young, hardly a woman. Like the goddess of just war and her twin, the goddess of the spring planting, her left breast was shockingly bare. She was paler than Florentine women, and shorter and narrower than them. She carried her back straight and her chin up, like a noblewoman.

His thirsty eye marked everything about her. She had no paint on her face. A filigree of gold kept her hair from her brow. Her white hands had long fingers that tapered like well-made candles. Her fourth finger on the right side had an inlay of emerald in the nail, and on the left, an inlay of ruby. She wore sandals of white leather, and her fourth toes were inlaid with sapphire and amethyst.

This solidified woman took on the qualities of living things. There was gooseflesh on her arm, and her chest rose and fell, and being near her, Marcus heard her breathe. She raised her clear gray eye to him, and he felt a squeezing in his chest. He felt joy and terror both. Knowing not what else to do, he took the knee. The woman's gaze roamed to his neighbor, and this man also knelt. His own neighbor knelt in turn. She was like the wind that bends the wheat, and spreading outward from her, the ragged survivors of Andropolis knelt.

Because he was near to her, he heard her whisper. She said, "Let all men bend the knee, then, until all men shall stand." She wasn't speaking Florentine. She wasn't speaking Genovan. He didn't know what tongue she spoke, and yet he understood. He looked up to her. She stood there breathing, and she slowly turned her head round about, so that all the world fell into the gray depth of her eye, the land and the clear sky both.

Again she whispered, saying, "How many leagues are we from Zanzibar?" There was silence until somebody stuttered, "We don't know any Zanzibar." She turned her eye to that one. Looking up at her, he explained, "We are in Florence," and another said, "We are in Genova." Then they laughed. They all laughed. She tilted her head at the sea of armored men, and thought it through, and when she understood, she smiled.

Her gown flared around her and she sat. She sat at the foot of her fearful machine. She sat on the wet stone, comfortably among them, and folded her hands on her lap. A warm breeze from the west calmed the gooseflesh on her arm. She looked after Marcus's gaze, and when she caught it, the corners of her eyes crinkled. She was smiling at him.

She spoke again, but not in a whisper. She used the ordinary voice of speech. Her voice carried far on the quiet of the day. She said, "I know what you are. You know what I am. If there was a war, there must be kings. Sons of Florence and sons of Genova, send for your kings. Tell them I am here. Tell them to meet me here."

The sound of her voice was clear and pure, like a fresh bronze bell. Her tongue was transparent to all. It was not accented by the northern waste, nor the fertile heartland or its great cities, nor the southern swamps and deserts. It had no east or west in it, no toil or occupation in it. It had no smell to it, no history. It was a new voice for a new world. Her words rang in the sweetest tones of reason, as if no other words could be wanted, or needed, or possible.

# 5

## THE MADNESS ON THE BRIDGE

KING AMBROSIUS THE Ninth of Florence couldn't parse it. The runner might as well have spoken nonsense. The storm was one great mystery. This runner's message was a mystery no less great. What had happened down there in Andropolis?

Ambrosius was mustering the reserves when the storm began. From atop the Killinghouse, he'd seen the storm clouds of the lower reaches gather, and the storm clouds of the upper reaches. The rain up here was miserable, but not the out-of-nature madness that had struck Andropolis. Through the rain, they'd looked toward the contested city. They saw the pale buildings vanish behind the dark wall of the waters. They'd seen the flooded Sinope bursting from the heart of the storm.

Surrounded by his Tagmata, amongst a force of thousands, Ambrosius stood in the freezing rain and stared down toward Andropolis. What men were suffering there was unimaginable. Would anyone survive? Finally he gave the order to break formation and shelter in the tents.

When the rain thinned, the men emerged. The ichneumon came back from whatever sacred cave he'd been hiding in. On the green slopes of the Killinghouse, rain-soaked, wind-chilled, they watched Andropolis. King Ambrosius weighed his choices. Wait for the land to dry, and lead the cavalry? Strip heavy armor and march the reserves over mud? Could he take the bridge before Genova knew he was there? What was King Pindar thinking, standing across the river, east of the city, on top of Butcher's Ridge?

King Ambrosius had five thousand reserve on his hill. They were fine loyal veterans of the second morax, war-hardened like a spear shaft from the coals. But if he lost them, he could not replace them before Genova broke out into the heartland. Looking down into the catastrophic city, King Ambrosius hesitated. His gut clenched as his council gathered round him: the ichneumon, and two warrior nobles, Valerius Maximus Corvus and the venerable Publius Decius Mus, and that wretched merchant Cleon Constantine, the queen's oldest brother. How he hated council.

He said, "I am of a mind to march down there right now and take my chances." Corvus said, "Chance favors vigor." Mus, a generation older, said, "I favor waiting on dry land for the horse, but I will follow you." Of their support, Ambrosius had had little doubt. He turned to the Constantine, and Cleon started, "The venture overruns your purse –" Ambrosius growled, "I *know* that." His debt was like an open wound in his side. Cleon smiled faintly, continuing, "– the Constantines will underwrite, a third forgiven upon victory of course." Humiliating, but nothing Ambrosius could do. He turned to the ichneumon. He made himself ask, "How tends the god?" The priest, face bounded in the red cloth of his miter, said nothing. His fearful great eyes stared at the king, and he raised his right arm. His extended finger pointed to Andropolis, and Ambrosius looked where it pointed.

A single shaft of light was falling to Andropolis from heaven. The king's eye traced its path until it vanished in the murk; it struck

Earth somewhere round about the Pontus Sextus Trassinope. The king squared his shoulders. He walked a little ways to address the reserves. He spoke in his loud voice of command:

"Prepare an immediate expedition! Light armor. Horsemen dismount. Every man will march. I take the front rank."

The reserves chanted: "Andropolis! Andropolis! Andropolis!" Thus Ambrosius turned the awe and fear they felt at the storm, to hot blood in his cause. The Tagmata barked their war-bark. The knot in Ambrosius's belly eased.

They were ready in an hour, leather-armored, ranks well-made, eyes bright for war, for final victory. He prepared to speak, but there were shouts and he saw men looking down the hillside. He turned from his army and looked as well. Pale against the soaked grass, there climbed a man. Pale? Aye pale, he was covered head to toe in pale Andropolitan mud, he looked like something creepy from a fable. King Ambrosius only knew him by his gait. This was one of Semaion's runners, Titus Herminius. So mortals had survived down there.

Titus loped up panting, and it was the strangest thing, he was light with joy, his white teeth gleamed as he grinned through the mud that coated him. "Hail Ambrosius," he gasped, then panted, then got out in one rush, "Good-news-from-the-city."

Ambrosius, astonished, said, "By great Pantokrator, Marcus Irenaeus took the bridge?"

Titus said, "Took the bridge?" He brushed his sopping hair from his eyes, and shook the mud from his hand. He turned and looked at the city. Then he understood and laughed, a startling familiar laugh, as if he and the king were equal of rank, as if they were friends.

His laugh dissolved into a runner's cough, then he collected himself and said, "You were poking fun. No, of course not."

He was not so drunk on joy he missed how the men around him stiffened. He scanned the scene, as if trying to solve a riddle.

Looking at King Ambrosius with his living eyes set in his pale mask of mud, he said:

"She's arrived, my lord. Certainly the new world has begun up here as well, but you haven't seen the mother of it all. She's down there right now with the men. All the men. She's on the bridge, come quick to the happy meeting."

It was as if familiar Titus Herminius, taciturn like all his western clan, a moody clan of shepherds, had been replaced with some confounding stranger. King Ambrosius said, "My good man, what madness is this?" Titus pinched mud from underneath his nose. He shrugged in frustration. Then the ichneumon finally spoke.

Flavius Papellus Reburrus was generally acclaimed the most frightening man in Florence. Even his voice inspired fear. He said, "It is not madness."

Those there with him stood back from the red specter of the king's ichneumon. Ambrosius grated, "Explain me this."

Reburrus said, "Don't go down there. Andropolis has slipped out from beneath the hand of Pantokrator."

## XXX

MARCUS SENT THEM Titus Herminius, but he got the king's runner Egidio back, bounding staglike from the west. Something had gone wrong.

Egidio called out, "Florentines, ho –" but then he stopped. Marcus watched him notice it. Florentines wore segmented armor, and Genovans leather with little plates. Egidio was scanning the armor of the crowd. He blinked stupidly and tried to reckon it some other way and couldn't. The Florentines and Genovans were mixed together. A tiny blossom of dread bloomed in the back of Marcus's heart. *This shouldn't surprise him.*

The runner said, "What madness takes place on this bridge? Why is everybody all together?" The crowd shifted uncertainly. Marcus saw Egidio's first sight of the woman and her golden vehicle. The runner's eyes widened. *Can it be he doesn't know her?* Egidio grew tense and still, full of terror and awe.

The woman addressed the runner, "I am not more than you. I am not less than you. Fear nothing from me, and I will fear nothing from you. Ask me questions."

A runner is not only a soldier with swift legs, he is a diplomat as need be. Egidio tilted his head to one side, then the other, then he calmly said, "Who are you?" and he said, "Where did you come from?" and he said, "Are you a mortal or a god?" Questions Marcus had not thought to ask, because he did not need the answers. Questions from the world that went before.

She said, in her bell-like voice, "My public name is Claire. I am a patricia of Zanzibar. Like all mortals, I've got a shard of the god lodged somewhere in my breast. Now do I ask one question in return: will your king come and greet his guest properly?"

Egidio didn't answer her. He looked over the head of the crowd, and Marcus followed his gaze, and saw him trading glances with a runner of the Genovans. He was, like Egidio, not the man who was sent.

His opposite did not aim his words at the woman; it was as if he hid his face from the brilliance of the sun. Addressing the crowd, he said, "I speak for good King Pindar of ancient Genova. He leads reserves about five thousand strong. They will meet you and support you. Prepare for battle. We take the bridge."

There is a tale of Tacamo the Vagabond, where Tacamo sneaks onto the high road. He is walking along, chewing on his reed, when he sees the Prince approaching with his princely retinue. Because Tacamo is on the high road, the Prince assumes that Tacamo is also a prince. He stops and they have lunch together beside the road, discussing princely things. Warming to the conversation, Tacamo forgets he is a vagabond, and invents the most elaborate tales of his principality. It is only when he stands and turns, accidentally showing the patch on his bum, that the Prince realizes he's been deceived. He says, "You tricked me, vagabond!" Tacamo, dismayed, recalls himself. The Prince's men give Tacamo an awful thrashing before Tacamo wriggles loose and escapes into the tall heather. This ending always has the children gasping in fear, then laughing, no matter how many times you tell them the story.

The runners made Marcus feel like Tacamo rebuked by the Prince. In the company of Claire, he forgot his world, his history, his sin. The orders of King Pindar reminded him. His cheeks flushed hot with shame, shame to flaunt his filthy war before this queen of peace.

*Must we be what we are?*

Egidio dismally called out, "Wise King Ambrosius of mighty Florence leads the same. He orders the same."

## XXX

King Ambrosius picked his way down the sodden slope. To either side of him the warrior nobles Corvus and Mus. Behind them five thousand Florentines. They did not run, and therefore never fell, and so they grew pale only to their ankles with the mud.

It was an uncommonly beautiful day. When the men grew hot with their exertions, the breeze cooled them. When the men grew cool from their motion, the breeze warmed them. The blue sky was clear and forgiving. The sun was moderate. Somewhere, a bird made a sound one time. The army found itself happy. Ambrosius could feel their happiness at his back, pressing him forward.

He led them down the Killinghouse, across the fields and past the ruined outworks, heading east toward Andropolis. He led them into the gigantic midland. He strode confidently down the western boulevard, where the old King's Road turns into the Via Mercaturae. The place was pale with mud. Soon he slowed, confused. He couldn't understand what he was seeing. Slowly, his eye picked out details from the mud. He gasped, then clapped his hand to his mouth.

The storm had slaughtered everything. Man and beast and stone and tree lay all conjoined together in pale ruin. Here a man, back arched, neck snapped. Two more in the street, crushed beneath a column. In the corner between these buildings, the twisted body of a horse. Over there a dead man still sheltering his dead goat, no wound visible on either one. In the square, bodies woven in a fallen sycamore. Half the dead were naked, so violent was the storm. Clothing, tools, and bones were strewed before the feet of the king. Even after a life spent at war, Ambrosius had never seen killing so indiscriminate and absolute. His eyes grew wet and blurred his vision. Andropolis was tangled white death.

Filled with horror and despair, he turned to his friends, to his men. He saw they felt what he felt. Soldiers in the rear were stumbling against those ahead who had slowed. The king felt a twinge of shame at the sword he carried. He did not name this feeling to himself. He drew the sword and raised it into the kind blue sky. He spoke without conviction.

"To the bridge."

## XXX

Marcus Irenaeus, decanus of the Stonebreakers, felt two massive figures at his back. The patricia Claire looked up and past him, impressed at their size. The runner Egidio looked as well. A shiver went through Marcus: his tremendous bruisers, Taranto and Brindisi, had survived the storm. *I haven't lost them all.*

Taranto stooped and murmured in his ear, "Decanus, you heard the runner. Nothing's changed." Brindisi in the other ear, "This is no place for a woman, sir. The war's still on." Taranto again, "Let us take her down the river. What's one more to your smuggler in lawless Rhegium?" Brindisi implored Marcus, "Come with us. Let someone else get the second morax killed." Then they straightened up.

Marcus considered Egidio. *I can overpower his will.* He looked over at the Genovan runner. More of a man, to be sure, but not so much as him. He called out, "Genovan, join us – what is your name?" The runner approached. He walked lightly, a cat to Egidio's stag. He spoke in the more guttural language of the Genovans: "My name is Antiphon." Marcus addressed them both, speaking loudly so that the crowd could hear, "My men here want to spirit off the foreign woman. They know a way. What say you, Claire?"

Egidio kept quiet. Claire shook her head and said, "I cannot be separated from my vehicle, and I must get me home to Zanzibar. Therefore do I need more than two with me against the world, even such a mighty two as these." Marcus couldn't see them, but he knew his men were blushing.

Still speaking loudly, he said, "O Claire, I have a question for you. The answer changes all. Therefore I desire your answer to be well informed. Listen what you need to know."

The crowd grew quiet, except the new arrivals. Every minute, more survivors came. How does rumor cross empty streets and alleys? It must, for a rumor of Claire seemed everywhere now in Andropolis. The survivors were gathering at the famous bridge. Because these men had endured the storm, they recognized the golden woman. Each man let out a breath like a sob when first he saw her. They took their places in the crowd, and sat and looked at her and listened.

Marcus spoke:

"This is a wide and fruitful land, bounded on all sides by a ridge of mountain. We call this land the valley of the world, and little care what lies beyond. Half the valley of the world is Florence, and the other half is Genova. We are two proud free peoples. We have been at war a hundred years. There are several gates between our nations, and this place is one. We meet here to decide who shall have this gate. The city is Andropolis. The river in it is the Sinope. The bridge we stand on even now is the only proper bridge across the Sinope. It is the Pontus Sextus Trassinope. Who controls the bridge must win the war, and destroy his enemy from out the world."

The beautiful patricia turned herself then. *How comes it the seat of her gown is dry and clean, though she sat on wet and dirty stone?* Claire looked up at her own great gold palanquin. Then she looked to the corners of the bridge. *She's measuring the distance.* She realized what he'd already noticed: her palanquin sat in the center of the bridge. She smiled over her teeth. It was a sad angry smile, such as some very old wolves sometimes smile, and looked strange upon her.

She said, "What is your name?"

He said, "I am Marcus Irenaeus. I have no family name to give you, though soon I am to choose one."

Claire said, "Marcus Irenaeus, what was the question with the answer that changes all?"

Marcus said, "If you could have things as you wished, what would you wish?"

The look of gratitude she shot him made his heart lurch. Then she told him what she wished, and how she wished to get it.

Marcus turned to Egidio. At Claire's words, the runner's eyes had filled with tears.

Marcus gently said, "Friend, you see what madness takes place on this bridge."

Egidio nodded. Marcus addressed both him and Antiphon.

"Let us figure out how to get the patricia what she wishes."

## XXX

THE KING AND his army faced a long and slippery march to the bridge. Long before they arrived, Ambrosius saw Egidio bounding back to him. "Hail wise King Ambrosius the Ninth! Hail mighty Florence of the impenetrable walls!" the runner called as he approached. Hearing the formalities, Ambrosius thought, *This can't be good.* The king said, "Are the survivors ready for war?"

Egidio was lit by that same joy that made a stranger of Titus Herminius. He said, "My king, I have seen the foreign woman, and she is very fine and noble. Here is the account she gives of herself:

"She is a daughter of the loveliest of cities, far off in the west, where the desert meets the sea. Her name is Claire, her rank is patricia, and her city is Zanzibar. When the storm overtook the world, it found her riding in a city garden. It heaved her vehicle upon its mighty shoulder. She passed many fearful hours carried on the shoulder of the storm. When finally it shrugged her off, she landed on the bridge.

"There is no army at her back. She does not aim to conquer or to plunder. She wishes only to return to Zanzibar.

"Because she represents a mighty state which is not allied with either of our warring nations, she will play no favorites here. She calls again upon the ancient rights of hospitality. She bids both kings to greet her."

Ambrosius grated, "Egidio, what is going on on that bridge?" Egidio swayed, but as a sturdy oak sways, only to allow the wind to pass.

The runner concluded, as if the king had said nothing, "Because she claims her right of greeting from the lord, the men have set aside their arms. They respectfully perform your hospitality till you and good King Pindar assume the duty."

Ambrosius said, "Speak no more nonsense to me. This girl can be nothing other but a dolled-up Andropolitan. On this fatal day, she may not interfere in matters of the state. Tell my soldiers this: execute her, destroy her cart, and form ranks. I will not ask again. We arrive within the hour."

# 6

## CALL ME DIOPHANTUS

FLAVIUS PAPELLUS REBURRUS paced atop the Killinghouse. The priest never paced. He was the master of stillness and of silence. His pacing spooked the remaining men.

Reburrus paced, and struggled to keep his hand off his nose. As he'd survived the vigor of his manhood, and graduated nearly to old age, he'd developed an irregularity of the organism: the bridge of his nose always itched, as if a single long hair had fallen on it. He was disciplined in all things, and in this as well, and never scratched the bridge of his nose. It tormented him all day long.

When wise King Ambrosius mustered his reserve, Reburrus accepted defeat and prepared to go with them. But the king put his gentle hand upon the ichneumon's wrist and said, "Stay." Reburrus said, "Ignore the word of god, but do not spurn his support." The king said, "Did god foretell the storm?"

He left the ichneumon behind. Reburrus paced.

Ambrosius and his five thousand reserve had rumbled down the slope. They left Reburrus in a nearly empty camp. Horses stamped, tents flapped, poles creaked. The wind ruffled the grass. Little Bitsy Boots played in his yard, under the stern eyes of his minders. The runner Titus Herminius was out of sight, sequestered by order of the king. Reburrus paced.

After a while, he could not bear inaction any longer. He resorted to mean old devices, primitive theatrics and signs. Returning to his own tent, he grabbed a handful of corn and went to consult the holy doves. At the dovecote, he found the dovekeeper clammy with terror. The head of one dove was torn off, and her crimson guts spilled out, and the other doves were pecking at her innards. The stammering dovekeeper explained he'd just now driven off a fox. *How like ordinary men*, Reburrus thought in annoyance, *he dreads punishment more than he regrets error*. He said, "Give me your bowl and your sandals, and be gone from before my face. You are no icht." Thus he sent the man out to the barren land, barefoot and penniless, to scratch out what living he might, away from comfort and the god.

There was no error here. There couldn't be. Dovekeeper – fox – dove and doves – all had their parts to play in one perfect omen. Old devices had their uses. This hideous omen explained the silence of the Pantokrator: the storm was outside His dominion. A divine invasion of Florence. War among the gods.

## XYX

CLAIRE STEPPED BACK from Egidio's grim face. She breathed in sharply, and a single tear spilled from each of her eyes. She wrapped her arms around herself and shivered. She whispered, "So that's it then."

Marcus turned from the awful sight of the young patricia's terror. He scanned the mix of Florentines and Genovans on the bridge. These men thought they were a crowd. But Marcus recognized what they were: an army. In the years since he'd left Florence city, he'd gotten to know what armies are and how they think.

He felt his soul slipping its bounds. It joined with the men all around. Their thoughts were his thoughts. His heart was their heart.

*Do we hope by some means to return to town and farm, and hold again our wives and children, bid farewell our aging parents, pray to our familiar gods? Behold, we do not: the tears of the patricia show us where we are, at our extremity, in the fiery mouth of war. Our lives are forfeit. She gives us hope, but not that we'll survive. The hope she gives us is hope for a worthwhile death, with her, for her, by her. Let our example educate posterity:*

*There was another world, and there could be again.*

This army would fight.

His soul came back to himself alone. *No, I need not be what I have been. I can choose again.*

Marcus Irenaeus said, "O Claire, he may not have you, except he go through each of us. Let him try."

He looked at Egidio. Egidio moved into the crowd, taking his place with the army. He looked at Antiphon, returned from conference with Pindar. He said, "Choose, man. Join us or leave."

The Genovan stared at him a long time, then he said, "A porcupine is our best chance. We will beg the kings to speak" – he rolled his eyes – "then their lines against our porcupine. If the Genovan line breaks, we make for Genova. If the Florentine line breaks, Florence." Somebody called out, "And if neither line breaks?" The Genovan flashed his teeth and said, "Then we'll have ourselves a little Daffodil Field."

Those who understood the reference explained it to their fellows. The crowd grew heavy with dread. Marcus saw how it was going and clapped his hands and said, "My friends, time is short. We've got enough men for three ranks. There's a litter of weapons all over Andropolis. Split in three groups and go find the arms of your rank." They went.

They were about a thousand men. They went out from the bridge into the streets, harvesting muddy arms from the pale face of the Earth. Marcus gathered up a round shield with the strap good, and a sword. The blade was nicked all up and down it, but the size was right. He was proud to hold it. He found a dented cup, and collected it as well.

When each man had what he was looking for, they came back to the bridge. Marcus proposed a libation. There was no wine for it, so he dipped the cup in one of the clogged gutters of the bridge. Claire's eye followed him, and stayed on something in the gutter, marking where it lay. Marcus offered praise to fiery Pantokrator, and poured out the water, and the men sang the hymn. Florentines and Genovans, they all sang the same hymn. They worshipped the same gods.

When it was done, they formed the porcupine around Claire and her gold palanquin. It was a circle, three ranks deep, at the center of the square. The men in the inner rank leveled spears through narrow gaps between the men in front of them. The men in the outer rank held swords and round shields. And the men in the middle rank held curved greatshields aloft, two handed, against the archers and slingers. When they had rehearsed it, they sat to save their strength, and waited on ten thousand enemy. The bridge, though broad, was narrow yet enough to deny their numbers the advantage. A stone bridge was not a bad place to stand and fight. It is as Angry Pius roared upon that western hill, "One arrow for the queen, a second for humanity." And the dogs tore him to pieces, after all.

Claire walked slowly round the inside of the circle. Marcus walked with her. She spoke so that the men could hear:

"You have welcomed the storm-borne stranger. You have consoled the fears of the weary traveler. Zanzibar does not forget her friends." She brushed with her palms the fingertips of those who reached up to her, completing a circuit of the army.

Then she spoke quietly, so that only Marcus heard her: "If I am to die – if I am to die, I say – if I am to die upon a foreign shore, unremarked by my countrymen, if I am to die, I am grateful to die with such fine men." She swallowed and finished meekly: "A spiral-wing upon the breeze. Thus I submit me to the deep."

She climbed up her palanquin, limbs all capable and mannish, and sat atop it keeping watch to east and west. She looked down at Marcus, with that gentle forgiveness he first saw in her. She said, "Let me tell the men when it is time to stand." He nodded up at the tiny foreign girl, then made his way to the front rank, facing Florence.

After some dream-like interval, he heard her scramble to her feet. She called in a mighty voice, "*Arise Genova!*" The hairs on his arms stood on end. Now he understood why she wanted to give the order. Her war-voice was loud as a trumpet. It portended only victory. All those facing east heaved themselves up from the paving stones. Another moment passed. Marcus's blood galloped.

Claire roared, "*Arise Florence!*"

## XXX

AFTER HE'D CHOSEN the brutal course, a terrible loneliness swathed King Ambrosius. His men trudged beside him and behind him, but he felt utterly alone, far from man and god. In this awful place, the world's pulse had stopped. Everything was an idea of itself. *Why am I here? What is to be gained from Andropolis?*

His passions clashed when he approached the bridge. At the end of the path of death, he found living Florentines, and the joy of it lifted him. But these Florentines stood alongside Genovans, bronze flashing, defying him, and the fury made his cheeks burn and his eyes start. He spoke loudly from the riverbank. He said, "I told you I wouldn't ask again. Drop your weapons. Step aside and wait upon the punishment. Florence passes here."

A helmeted soldier stepped forward from the front rank of the porcupine. The king recognized his new tribune, battered but alive. Ambrosius said, "Marcus Irenaeus, what does this mean?"

Marcus said, "My lord, you asked me a question when we met. Do you remember?"

"I asked you if you loved your king."

Marcus Irenaeus said, "I answer you again. I have never loved my king or nation more than at this hour. I speak for all of us."

Ambrosius knew how to read a man. Softly, he said, "Step aside, son. We will sort this after."

The tribune shook his head. He said, "Remember my answer, and hear what we all say."

The nostril of Ambrosius flared. He hissed, "What do you all say?"

Marcus Irenaeus said, "We are your loyal soldiers. Our part is to fight our nation's enemies, and yours to host our nation's guests. We do not wish to shame you by outdoing you. Therefore do we set aside our quarrel, until you and King Pindar meet upon this square, and make a greeting to this patricia in manner duly befitting of her dignity."

Ambrosius snorted. He said, "So much my runner has already told me. He's given you my answer. Step aside." Marcus Irenaeus went on firmly:

"We have made this compact all together, Florentines and Genovans mixed as water with water. We are like a hound that was confused, and has finally caught the scent. The scent we caught is death, and we chase death with joy. We are a thousand men. Fling at us your five thousand. Let Pindar do the same. We make the porcupine round the patricia Claire. We will bear her on our back, from the pillar to the post. We will defend her every hour, at every price, scornful of our flesh, for we have found our souls."

Ambrosius stared hard at Marcus. It is no small thing to take a hard stare from the king. But the tribune gazed steadily back. When it became embarrassing to go on staring without result, Ambrosius looked away. Only then did Marcus move. He bent his head and took off his helmet. Bare-faced, he looked at Ambrosius.

He said, "As you commanded me, I've chosen the name my family shall have."

Ambrosius goggled at his tribune. Marcus said, "Call me Diophantus, for I have seen the god."

*I am not that which I was. When she remade the world, she remade me too.*

## XXX

King Ambrosius nearly drew his sword and ran his tribune through. But Marcus Irenaeus surprised him again. The soldier knelt. He invited the king's sword.

The king was shocked, as if by a blow. Suddenly he understood. His vanity had blinded him. There was no sedition here.

Eyes cleared, Ambrosius saw only loyalty on its knees before him. He thought of Bitsy Boots, his last surviving son, to whom he dearly wished to leave a better world.

He crossed the short distance to Marcus. He put a hand on the man's shoulder. He thought to find him shivering, but he was still as stone. Fearless.

The king said, "Diophantus, I will speak to your patricia."

# 7

## I WILL FOLLOW YOU

ZANZIBAR IS BUILT on the ruins of Trebizond.

There are many stories of the Viri people, who conquered old Trebizond. In one story, a force of the Viri has got far off from their desert haunts. Betrayed in a foreign land, they are surrounded by an evil army. Their general has been lured outside the palisade and killed. They wait upon the morning, when the final blow must come.

It is well into the second watch, and the men have gone to sleep. In the tent of the officers, the lieutenants have all got drunk and passed the hours playing warjack on the Villain's deck. The youngest of these lieutenants is Katalin. Young Katalin folds his cards, disgusted with his fellows and himself. He thinks - *I am too young to seize command. But how much older do I expect to get, if I hand myself to the enemy in the morning?*

Therefore Katalin stands up, and delivers a very persuasive speech to his fellows. They acclaim him general. Sobering up, they all go out and quietly wake the men. They form up the army in the moonless, misty dark. Silently, they leave the palisade. Carrying oil and glowing rushes, they spread throughout the camp of the sleeping enemy. When they are dispersed, they douse the tents and light them, everywhere at once. Before the enemy can get his wits together, the Viri make a great noise, shouting and whooping and banging their swords on their shields. It is a glorious night: the Viri rout their enemy, and elbow their way to freedom.

Claire reflected on this story as ten thousand men converged on the bridge. *The blood of Katalin flows in my veins as well,* she thought, *and I too lead an army.* The thought calmed her fear, and she climbed down from the roof of her gold palanquin. Life promotes all mortals to general, when first they understand nobody is coming to save them.

She listened to the testimony of Marcus Irenaeus Diophantus. When he chose his name, her heart surprised her: it fluttered.

She listened to King Ambrosius say, "I will speak to your patricia." Claire's thousand men whispered it around the porcupine, till Antiphon spoke loudly in his harsh Genovan. He said, "My lord, your opposite will speak to the patricia." There was a pause, then a deep, muffled voice answered, "Genova ne'er stand in Florentine shade. We speak to her as well."

From the declaration of Ambrosius to the answer of Genova, no more than a minute passed. Claire closed her eyes, then opened them, then spoke clear and crisp enough to let one thousand hear:

"*Stand aside, my Thousand, let the kings approach.*"

With a practiced stamp, the force of men divided, forming three ranks to the north, and three ranks to the south.

The young patricia displayed herself proudly. She looked west to wise King Ambrosius, and saw a compact man somewhat past middle age, abundant in vitality and strength, beard silver, neatly trimmed, right cheek scarred, eyes the palest blue. There was something unusual about his eyebrows, but she couldn't parse it at a distance. He wore light armor, mostly leather with a little bronze over the soft parts. Claire was raised in the shadow of war, and understood how to read what she saw: this king moved swiftly on a battlefield, sprinting from one part of the fight to another, visiting all and leading in person. He had a square white cloth draped on his breastplate, embroidered with a tall rectangle outlined in blue. The interior of the rectangle shaded from white at the bottom to blue at the top. It was a strange coat of arms.

She looked east to the king of Genova, the one they called good Pindar – but she didn't see him. She looked at the dark filigree of a screen, the front of a sedan chair. Twelve men carried it. It had gold tracery painted on black lacquer, and it was large and fine. But it was not so fine as Claire's gold palanquin, that loomed behind her. *Good*, she thought. *Know before whom you stand.*

She spoke in her tones like a bell, calmly saying, "Come." She could not read King Pindar. But she could read Ambrosius. She saw his thought on seeing her majesty and beauty, that all of this made sense now. And she saw his second thought, that kings cannot fling aside the nation for every pretty woman, as soldiers might. He nodded to her and approached. The sedan chair approached as well. Ambrosius stopped some paces back. She saw his eyebrows clearly now: they were notched with scars. The sedan chair turned as it slowed. The footmen set it down and one of them opened its door. Claire glimpsed a face floating in the gloom inside.

Claire made the great bow, sweeping around from west to east to west again.

She swung her hips: *I am entirely a woman.* And she showed to them her naked shoulder and delicate collarbone: *I am a girl in your care.* Her forehead touched the stone: *I submit.* Then she stood splendid and noble: *I command.*

It was one of the bows she'd learnt in etiquette class at the Lycée, years before. It dazzled the kings. It dazzled her too. *I am this.* By the motion of the sun, a moment passed, but a world turned over, in the numberless timekeeping of the soul.

Now she spoke:

"I am Claire, a patricia of Zanzibar. I am today an exile in your land. Therefore I throw myself on your protection and the hospitality of your persons, which is to say your nations. Treat me

The patricia faced the kings.

in accordance with the ancient bond of guest and host, and earn the gratitude and high regard of mighty Zanzibar. My nation will repay its debt the day it learns what has become of me; and one way or another, it will learn."

There was a long silence. The porcupine was dissolved. The kings and their men stood all the way to the foot of the patricia. There was no defending her. The metal of the Thousand tinked uneasily. Claire stood straight, demonstrating her noblewoman's posture. Fear flapped his violet wings above the garden of her passions. She thought, *I will not tremble.* She cast her gaze beyond her present troubles. The sun was starting his fall toward the west. *What a fine color the yellow sunlight makes on this pale city.* Though Andropolis was ruined, it was still beautiful.

A throat clearing summoned her back to herself. She turned east, toward the sedan chair. The face leaned forward from the gloom into the yellow afternoon. Good King Pindar had long dark hair and a thick dark beard. His skin was pale like a man who doesn't go outside enough. A diadem pressed his brow. He had a very serious brow, but under it, a twinkling eye. He would have looked mischievous if he had been their friend, but he was not. So he looked menacing.

"Verify how you came from afar, rather than being some Andropolitan sorceress."

Claire coolly said, "What language are you speaking?"

Pindar answered, "I am speaking Genovan of course."

She looked to Ambrosius and he said, "I am speaking Florentine."

She said, "And each of you can understand the other?"

Ambrosius growled, "It is difficult, but we can make it out. The languages are similar, and written down, they are the same."

Claire said, "What language am I speaking?"

There was a long, long silence.

Pindar stuttered, "What – what language are you speaking?"

Claire said, "I am speaking the human tongue."

Pindar whispered, "There are a thousand languages."

Claire said, "There are a thousand languages, but only one human tongue, and I am speaking it."

The kings shrank back.

Her lip curled.

"'Andropolitan sorceress.' I am a patricia of Zanzibar. I am the last daughter Reason bore."

A wave of smell rolled off her, her native scent of honeysuckles and of thunder. She knew it was a strange perfume. Pindar's nostrils flared. He looked past her at Ambrosius, then back at her.

"Come in my royal car now, both of you. We will talk."

## XXX

MARCUS STARED AT Pindar's car, as if he could hear better if he widened his eyes. But he made out only murmurs. Everyone edged forward, straining to hear. Gradually the voices rose, until they could hear the kings shouting. They could almost see the spittle flying.

This was bad.

Then they heard a single word, a woman's voice, furious. Claire.

"Enough!"

A shocked silence. The soldiers drew back from the car. Her voice again, more softly.

"Enough."

The car jolted with a shift in weight, and the door burst open. Claire blinked at the soldiers, and they at her. Then she turned and spoke into the interior.

"Fathers of your nations? You've forgotten who your children are. Come with me and I will show you your son."

She faced the soldiers again and jumped down lightly. They stared questions at her and she raised a single finger: *wait*. She half-smiled.

The kings emerged. They squinted at the orange light of afternoon. They looked shaken, humbled – what had she done? Did they recognize the new world yet? They climbed down unsteadily, dazed, almost embarrassed. Marcus heard the Genovans gasp. *They never mingle with their king, so close you could touch him.*

## XXX

Claire led them from the car to the place that she remembered at the clogged gutter. The silent thousand parted where they passed. Claire took off her sandals and set them on dry stone, then gathered the skirts of her gown up in one hand, showing her shapely calves to everyone. She climbed down in the gutter, so that her feet got pale mud on them. Leaning over the gutter, both kings saw the thing she pointed at.

It was a jagged white bowl. It once had been the head of a man, but weather and time had reduced it to bone. It had lost its top, in a messy cut with a little notch in front. It lay there buried to the sockets of the eyes in muck. She picked the skull up in her hand and held it tenderly. Mud in the spine-hole plugged the bottom of the bowl. Therefore the rainwater that nearly filled the skull didn't drain, and those nearby could see the water was a thin clear pink, like wine too heavily mixed.

Claire spotted Marcus Irenaeus staring stricken at the skull. *He recognizes the wound. Was this a friend of his?* He looked up to her face and saw her looking at him. He flinched away in shame. The blood in her breast turned to ice. *He killed this man.* She had planned to say a certain thing. She took a moment to revise it. Then she addressed the kings.

"This was a man. And in this very bowl once swarmed the passions of a man. There once were found inside this bowl the arches, halls, and towers of reason. Once inside this bowl there lived a soul which knew itself an elemental piece of an innumerable wonder that fills up all the world. All these things, the passions and the reason and the spirit of a single man, once made their homes inside this puny bowl, and there was room enough for each to have its realm. Therefore this pathetic little bowl once had in it a region greater than the world, with all its lands and seas. This was your son, Florence and Genova."

She let her gaze slip from the kings, as if to the crowd, but it came to rest on Marcus.

"You have another son, still living maybe, who bears the sin of having done this thing. No mortal can relieve him of this burden. Grace may come to him and say 'Follow me,' and he will follow her, and raise his burden to the mountaintop. On the last day of his life, he sets his burden down. Thus he lived in bondage to his sin, and death alone restores his freedom."

She stepped up from the gutter, feet and ankles white with mud. She offered the skull to Marcus Irenaeus Diophantus, murmuring, "Carry this for me." He took it and held it against his breast. She gazed at the skull, protected by his strong hands.

"These two men, the living and the dead, were destroyed to feed a war with no beginning and no end."

Her eye returned to the kings.

"Your war."

She gestured at the skull.

"The precious contents of this nameless bowl were spilled so that one or the other of the two of you could satisfy the honor of his nation. Honor?" – she spat – "So that one or the other of the two of you could call the other's piece of land his own and compel all those surviving there to do his will. Therefore now this glorious planet has been shrunk to such a pitiful size, the only thing the world tries to fit in it is several mouthsful of pink water. If you have no shame, you may share equally between you this bitter wine got at so dear a price. Both of you have earned it."

Then there was silence in Andropolis.

Ambrosius looked from the skull to the army of the rebel thousand. Their living eyes shone brighter than the setting sun. He stared at them; they stared at him. Then the king repeated the gesture of his tribune Marcus. He got down on his knees.

For a moment only, Pindar looked down at his enemy. Then he knelt as well.

Claire had been rehearsing something like her speech for years. This was not the audience she'd hoped for. She'd hope to tell it to her mother, her mother and all the generals who led *Guerra Domestique*, the civil war in Zanzibar. They'd nearly unleashed Midnight on the happy republic. They'd nearly ruined Zanzibar. *Look what you've done to yourself, Mother. Look what you've done to me.*

Packing years of pain and vehemence into her words, she spoke their own doubts to Pindar and Ambrosius. Younger than the war, she helped them see the new world in the ruins of Andropolis.

Their armor dropped off from their hearts. An arrow pierced the anger in their naked hearts. They could have died for weeping from it. The arrow was shame. She gave them back their shame.

Therefore did they listen when she spoke, as they could not have listened even to their souls, and the fight went out from them. The gazes on them were the gazes of their sons, and the skull before them was their son as well, dead by order of his father. One of the kings, Ambrosius or Pindar, said in a hoarse and breaking voice, "Somebody – somebody come here with a cloth and water – a bucket of water, a cloth and a stool – somebody come clean the feet of her, the patricia is our guest, she shouldn't have dirty feet in the mud of our country."

The war was over.

## XXX

IN FRONT OF his opposite and the thousand men, King Ambrosius of Florence pressed his brow on the paving stone of the bridge. The world fled from him, and he perceived only the damp cool of the stone, that soothed the pulsing heat in his head. Opening his eye, he saw a crack in the stone, and in the dimness of the crack, a pebble, and a twig, and a tiny beetle caught in a drop of water. The twig in the crack reminded him of the withered oak in the window of ai Ctesiphôn, and of his older brother Ælius Pellucidus, who would have been king, except he went searching for the oak. He missed him then, missed terribly the laughter and high spirits of Ælius Pellucidus. He should have lived to see this day.

He heard a clinking near his ear. He realized it was the two half-coins of greeting. In Pindar's sedan chair, each king had given one to the beautiful alien woman. His was silver and Pindar's was gold. *Pick one*, they'd said, *and be forsaken of the other nation.* She kept both and now they clinked against each other, hidden in a fold of her scandalous gown. He looked up from the stone and saw Claire's left hand, with the long white fingers and the dark ruby inlaid in the fourth fingernail. The hand reached for him.

He took her extended hand, and she raised him up, and he stood. With her other hand, she raised up King Pindar.

## XXX

STANDING, THEY ROSE from shadow into light. The falling sun was giant and orange now, and the sudden glare of it overwhelmed the kings. Their grief shook them and their mouths hung open in self-horror. Blind and trembling, they clutched at the hands of the beautiful patricia. She stood with them and waited the right interval, then cast her gaze around. Her gray eye passed over the silent close-ranked soldiers, and the soldiers saw what she intended, so that a great cheer went up.

The noise penetrated to that solitude each king was lost in, and they came back from the grove of their grief. The first thing they saw was Claire, whose smile seemed the wellspring of the uproar. Then they looked around at the men, banging their bronze and hollering, and each inclined his head.

Claire said, "Do you noble kings Ambrosius and Pindar negotiate a treaty of eternal reconciliation between Florence and Genova."

And they weeping said, "We will do it, we will do as you say, O Claire, we will do the very thing you say."

## XXX

AMBROSIUS SAID TO Pindar, "My tent on the Killinghouse? Yours on Butcher's Ridge? Your sedan chair?" Pindar thought it over and said, "Right here, I think, beneath the open sky." Ambrosius understood: the hidden king was making a show of being seen. This was to be part of the legend of the peace.

Ambrosius had brought soldiers only, but his opposite seemed to have brought his entire court. From Pindar's retinue emerged the general logothete, with his toolbox and his scribe, and the hexagon logothete, also with a toolbox and a scribe, and finally the royal cartographer, who did his own writing. Men conjured a table and chairs. The kings and their staffs gathered. Everybody settled down, realizing only at the end that Claire was missing. They turned to look, and saw the patricia standing where she'd been, looking at the sky.

Ambrosius stood and returned to her and she turned to him, gray eyes wide, their depths unfathomed. He offered her his hand and said, "Come," and she answered, "I cannot."

He said, "How should we conclude the peace without that you watch over us, O Claire, the very sower of the peace?"

Claire answered him, "This thing you do, you do sovereign. No foreign power dares to oversee it."

He nodded his respect at her diplomatic prowess. He gestured to his Tagmata and three stepped forward: one with a stool, and a second with a bucket, and a third one with a cloth. They rounded on Claire in an intimidating way. The one twizzled her into his stool, and the second set up his bucket, and the third one seized her foot and scrubbed it with his cloth. Ambrosius wagged a finger at her and said, "If you won't sit with us, you'll sit and get your feet clean," and she grinned at him, as any of his daughters might have grinned, if they had lived. How fine her teeth! He grinned back. Glancing down, he saw the scrubbing cloth was royal. It had thread of silver woven in, that kept catching on the dainty knuckles of the woman's toes. She didn't put up a fuss.

He left for the table of the peace.

Around her, some among the soldiers sat and tended their feet as well. They were rubbing the blisters where the flood had softened their skin. Some watched the kings at their table, fascinated. The reserves shared their food among the rebels, and the starving rebels ate. Many slept. Stunned and relieved, their fatigue was catching up with them. Waters bubbled as they drained from the bridge, and the flooded river sang its chorus below. The setting sun faded from orange to red, like the desert sun at Zanzibar. The voices of the kings never rose. The hushed crowd reminded them of their purpose and their dignity. When it was done, those at the table stood. The army, startled, stood, and Claire as well.

The general logothete held up a parchment. He read it in a rich storytelling voice, like a father to his children. The crowd hung on the tale:

"The hostilities, at every place they are ongoing, will be concluded, nor one last blow in vengeance will be traded. Horsemen will be dispatched to spread the news, to east and west and north and south.

"The prison camps will be opened, and the surviving captives returned to their native capitals of mighty Florence of the impenetrable walls, and ancient Genova of the flowering paths.

"The nations will return to the borders they had before the war, to teach the children of the valley of the world, now and forever, that a century of war accrued no benefit to Florence or Genova.

"Finally, this lesson will be sealed by construction, paid from a common fund, of a new tower at Andropolis.

"This black tower will be named Epikrition, or The Monument to the Futility of War."

One thousand rebel soldiers roared. Ten thousand reserve heard the word, and roared.

The heart of Claire swelled with joy, she who so loved peace.

XXX

WHEN IT WAS calm again, the two kings crowded Claire and said, "Youngest daughter of Reason, surely we must get you home to Zanzibar." She began to tremble. She couldn't control herself. *This entire mummery worked.* She thought she'd stop trembling now, and found she couldn't. *Stop, Claire. You'll shake yourself to pieces.* Pindar touched her chin and raised her face to meet his eye. She gulped and held his gaze and stammered, "I – I would be very grateful for it." He said, "We owe this much to you at least. How far is Zanzibar?" Her trembling faded. Pindar dropped his hand. She said, "I was waiting on the sunset, when I could reckon it. Let me take my leave of you a minute, then I'll know."

She nimbly climbed on top of her gold palanquin, the highest place on the bridge. The setting sun shone on the river; beyond the glowing mist of the city, she saw the lay of a green and empty land. Her westward gaze turned south, and raised up to the heavens. Her sun-dazzled eyes calmed and she saw it – there it was.

*Oh no.*

XXX

SHE WAS SILENT up there a great long time. Marcus looked down from the palanquin to Ambrosius, making his way over. The king spoke in a low voice – "The Stonebreakers?"

Marcus looked woefully at him and said, "Two died with me, two I have found alive, and five I lost in the storm."

Ambrosius squeezed his arm, and they stood together mourning for a minute. Then Ambrosius gestured at Marcus's stubble and said, "Keep that cheek smooth, Diophantus."

XXX

THERE WAS A rich man once in Zanzibar, who had a private garden full of exotic animals. Famously among them was a tiger, imported from a snowy land. The tiger got to walking the same path, all day long, padding a bare circle in the grass of his fenced plot. Around and around he went, brow furrowed, eye vacant, getting thinner every month, and finally he died. He wore the grass away, seeking some road home, and he died an exile, of an exile's broken heart.

Claire's mother told her the tiger's story. That's how the mothers in Zanzibar introduce that terrible warning: All the Zanzibaris must come home at last, or die.

*How did you leave, Father? How could you?*

## XXX

EVERYONE BEGAN TO wonder why the patricia didn't speak. They looked at each other, and at the hulking palanquin, trying to see her up beyond the sculpted feathers, or waves.

Finally Claire called down, "Yon bright reddish star, south of west – you see it? We call that the snout, in the constellation of Fat Bear."

Somebody called up to her, "To us it is the boot of the Wealthy Man."

She said, "I know its distance along the horizon from the evening sun in Zanzibar. Therefore, measuring the different distance here, I can compute the distance west, from Andropolis to Zanzibar."

Ambrosius said, "How far are we from Zanzibar?"

She climbed wearily down, and when she faced them, her skin was gray and there were tears in her eyes. She said, "One third. I am one third part of the world away from home."

The red sun swelled and fell behind the ruins in the west. Marcus recalled a black shore, between a burning land and a burning sky. He clutched the dead man's skull and swore a silent vow.

*I will bring you home. You said 'Follow me.' With my sin on my back I will follow you, all the days of my life.*

# PART II

# The Old King's Road

# 8

## THE GAP IN TIME

MEN CAME AND went from the Killinghouse. The story of the peace spread around the camp. Cleon Constantine's men packed his tent and carried it behind him to Andropolis. Even little Bitsy Boots went down there with his minders. But Reburrus never got his summons from the king. The ichneumon thought, *How much does he want to punish me?*

Reburrus watched the crowds and fires in the center of the white field of the dead. When the wind shifted, he faintly heard their songs and celebrations. He could not see the alien, the woman made of light. He imagined her with his king, and the part of him that was a man burned with humiliation and resentment, and the part that was a priest feared for Florence.

The rebel army on the bridge, *the Thousand*, men were calling them, doused their fires about midnight. Reburrus watched them bed down open air on the bridge. On either bank the ten thousand reserves, who would have tried to kill them, laid themselves down. Eleven thousand men with the whisper of the river for their lullaby.

An hour later, sleepless Reburrus first saw her, a white pulse in the deep of midnight in the valley of the world. He had no way to know it was Claire, but he knew. She was awake. She persisted before him, a splinter of the moon's illumination in a field of indistinct dim shapes. He could not tell if she was walking, or if she merely swam against the darkness his hawk-like eye was squinting into.

Soon she came to the edge of the bridge; she'd been walking. She stood on the edge, almost out over the water. What was she looking at? Slips of moonlight rippling on the Sinope? The places of the stars in a strange sky?

*What are you thinking about, alien?*

His eye lost her in the night, and then found her again, returning from the edge of the bridge. The white smudge winked out, and he understood she'd laid herself back down and covered herself. He marked exactly where she lay.

*This is my only chance.*

## XXX

THE ICHNEUMON MOVED slowly, because he wished to move quietly. His sandals squelched softly in the thin, slimy mud. He stepped carefully among the rubble and the dead. Here were naked bodies, bleached by death, by icy water, by the setting moon. Even their wounds were bleached, honorable wounds in front and shameful ones behind, all white and empty in the moonlight. Here were two horses with their ribs out, gleaming, still harnessed to an upturned war-car. Here was a public garden with every tree broken.

*Grieve, man,* thought Reburrus, negotiating the hectic ruin in the last light of the moon, planting each footstep so as not to snap an ankle. When the sun got up this place would turn into a city of flies and crows. The gases of corruption would become unbreathable. Tonight there were no wolves, no flies, no crows, no awful smells. Peace reigned tonight, but tomorrow peace must drive the last men from Andropolis. *Which god did this thing?* Reburrus grieved. He mourned the dead of Florence and Genova. But he never forgot the wars of men were little things, set against the wars between the gods.

This is the cruel fate of the ichneumon, intercessor between men and gods. He occupies two worlds and is not at home in either. *An ichneumon must burn, serving fiery Pantokrator.* Reburrus burned with grief and fury. He held the osculum in his right hand. It was a weapon to be used carefully, at intimate range, specialized to penetrate the heart and hold fast. Instant death for a sleeper, yielding a body that could be moved without leaving a bloody trail. An assassin's weapon. The stains on this one were decades old. Reburrus gripped it tightly as he picked his way across the boneyard of the midland. Not even crickets sang.

The moon set. Starlight showed him his path. After the terrible pale silence, he came to the Florentine reserves. They were black mounds on the riverbank, but he knew his way among them. They'd settled themselves by the map of an army's camp, the same in every place an army rested. The river muttered in his ear, and the great bridge spread out before him. He took off his muddy sandals, so that their distinctive prints would not show on the paving stones. The ichneumonoi announced themselves, but not tonight.

Sandals in his left hand, osculum in his right, he padded out over the Sinope. He passed between the sleeping rebels. Nobody stirred. Crossing the midland had taken him a long time, and now it was the darkest hour before the dawn. He went toward the place he'd seen from the hilltop. Then he followed the reported smell, of thunder and honeysuckles. Finally he came to her.

Her face was half-covered by a dark fur. Squatting, he set down his sandals. He gently lifted the fur and folded it aside. Once he saw her, clear beneath the stars, he shrank back, standing. *Am I doing right, Antivola?* Only Antivola could moderate his violence; only he could moderate Antivola's violence. But Antivola was in Florence where he belonged, and Reburrus was alone in the night with eleven thousand men and the pale harbinger of a divine invasion.

Reburrus shivered at the sight of her. Her god was a wily god. He preyed on kallotropy, the weakness of men for beauty. Asleep, scarcely lit, her beauty still dazzled: in this dimness he could see only the broad shapes of her, like an old sculpture with the paint scoured off and the details worn away. She had a wide brow and a strong curved jaw. Large eyes lay at dreamless rest behind smooth eyelids. Her throat was long and graceful; she had delicate shoulders and collarbones. He could count her ribs at the sternum.

Squatting again, he counted to the fourth rib, hefting the osculum in his right hand. He primed its scolex and centered it over her heart. He raised his left hand to strike its ball. His right hand ached; his jaw ached; all the muscles in his left arm jumped.

Her eyes snapped open.

Her gaze was simple and direct. Reburrus froze. Or rather, he was frozen.

It was like being trapped inside a bronze idol of himself. He nearly missed it. His mind wished to leap to the next moment. *Don't miss this.* He wasn't in an idol. His breath was frozen. His eyes were frozen. *Don't miss this. What is this?* He pressed his soul to meditate, and it told him where he was. It was not bronze that froze him, but time. He was inside a gap in time. The wind was silent. The river was silent. The patricia stared at him.

*What is this?* The patricia's eyes scanned down herself, staring at her breast, at the osculum poised right above it. She looked back up to him and slowly tilted her head and whispered something. He didn't know if he heard her in his ear, or in his reason only. She said, *I know your name: Enemy.* How was she moving, though time itself had stopped? *What are you doing, alien?*

Claire looked past him. Was she studying the stars, bright and motionless? No, something close. She was looking at something right behind him. A soft smile formed at the corners of her mouth.

A rising smell of thunder penetrated him. It was like her smell. It was the smell of the storm. She smelled it too. Her eyes widened.

*She's afraid.* The smell scorched his sinuses, and started on his mind. His vision began to blur.

She looked back to him, and rudely shut her eyes, as if to say she feared nothing from him.

The gap in time closed. Flavius Papellus Reburrus slammed his left hand down –

– but his palm halted sharply, striking only air. A band of force crushed his wrist. First it reversed his arm, then it lifted him. He was not a heavy man, but it would take a very strong man to lift him by the wrist. And so it did. Twisting as he rose up from the alien woman, he found himself facing grim Decius Mus.

The warrior nobles slept lightly, ready to attack and be attacked. Now that he was an old man, Publius Decius Mus hardly slept at all. Claire had awakened him with her nighttime wanderings. Unnoticed, he admired her as she passed between him and the moon, the edges of her gown rippling white in the wind. The black passage of Reburrus awakened him as well.

# 9

## WHAT PRECISELY SHALL WE DO WITH CLAIRE?

AMBROSIUS WHISPERED TO Reburrus, "O my brother, what have you done?"

Reburrus answered him. Ambrosius sucked air through his teeth. He resigned himself to meeting in council.

He lit a lamp and sent those he had, to summon those he needed. He told them to meet at the big tent of the merchant Cleon Constantine, because it would fit everyone, and he'd been wanting to see inside it anyway. Marcus turned up first, fully armed, still shrugging off sleep. Ambrosius asked him, "Any more from your six Stonebreakers?" Marcus shook his head, saying, "I don't think we'll hear from them again."

They swept past Cleon's angry guard into the tent. By the flicker of the lamp, Ambrosius took in patterned cloths and gleaming wood. It was nicer than his own tent, and it smelled of myrrh. Cleon Constantine lay snoring underneath his covers. Ambrosius gleefully shook him awake.

Cleon pulled a blade, and Ambrosius danced back. Getting his wits about him, the Constantine sat up and said, "Wake me again, *my lord*, and I may quit your council." Ambrosius said, "I'll schedule every meeting at midnight." Cleon snorted and said, "What do you want?"

Just then Corvus filed in with King Pindar, hair all mussed. A thick brute entered with Pindar, hovering around him, a roving shield of bronze and muscle. Behind them came a tall thin man like a water bird. It took Ambrosius a second to place him: he was the scribe of Pindar's general logothete.

Cleon's tent was indeed big, but it was getting a little crowded. Pindar's eye settled on Reburrus, face hidden by his cowl, feet bare. He blinked at this strange apparition, then turned to Ambrosius and said, "Six Florentines and only three Genovans; perhaps I should summon some friends." Ambrosius said, "I've heard you have opinions enough for four men." Pindar said, "I've heard that between you and any one of your councilors, there is opinion enough for one." Cleon made a sound not unlike a laugh.

Ambrosius colored and said, "My high priest has an urgent policy to advocate. Reburrus?"

The ichneumon rubbed his bruised wrist and waited for calm. Then he said, "Good my king, Pantokrator spoke me nothing of the storm. A foreign god invades the valley of the world. He plants his foot on pale Andropolis. What else is the girl but the foot of her god, the foot and finger?" The faceless dark inside the cowl swung toward King Pindar. "Doubt she has a plan, an alien who ends a war?"

He paused. Ambrosius understood the Genovans were unsettled at the sound of Reburrus's voice. It was thin and high and twanged like a bowstring near snapping. His words seemed to swim around and mean hidden things.

Finally Pindar realized he was meant to answer. He said, "I think it likely Claire has intentions."

The cowl nodded and said, "Good King Pindar, do you think her capable of following her intention?"

Pindar said, "I have not seen the limit of her capability."

The blackness behind the cowl looked back to Ambrosius. It said accusingly, "Have you mapped her giant plan? Hazard she wills only good?"

Ambrosius spoke softly, "I cannot know."

Reburrus hissed, "Protect the valley of the world from her!"

His bony hand gestured toward the tentflap.

"Let them remember her for a miracle. A god came once to save the nations, then she vanished. She left a gift, her golden chariot." The cowl scanned the room. "Murder her and sink the body."

The room seemed to darken. They stood there aghast. None of them had thought these things, but once Reburrus said them, they seemed inevitable.

Ambrosius watched Marcus drift to the tentflap, where none might reach him instantly. He saw the tribune's hand was on Semaion's dented horn.

Cleon broke the poisoned silence. He said, "I am of one mind with Reburrus on this." Ambrosius could scarcely fathom how much the peace would cost the Constantines. *Feed war, feed a Constantine.* The Genovan scribe said, "I concur as well," and turned a serious eye to King Pindar, who acknowledged it. Ambrosius grasped that the logothete was a puppet, and his scribe the power.

Reburrus said, "We must all act together. I tried just now –"

He paused as some muttered oaths.

"– tried, and failed."

Mus rumbled, "Of course you failed, I stopped you."

The black cowl seemed suddenly uncertain. It said, "You did, but something – something else happened. It passed like a dream, and I cannot now say what it was."

Anxious muttering. Ambrosius turned slightly and stared at Marcus until Marcus noticed. Then Ambrosius glanced at the horn. Marcus understood.

The young tribune took the horn from his belt and spoke quietly and slowly, and there was a terrible force behind his words. He said, "I repeat what I said before. Fling your ten thousand at my Thousand. We will make the porcupine round the patricia Claire. We will bear her on our back, from the pillar to the post. We will defend her every hour, at every price, scornful of our flesh, for we have found our souls."

Reburrus said, "Who are you to speak against me?" The armored man looked down at him and said, "Ichneumon, I am one who has seen the god. If you or any mortal here resolves on harm to Claire, then I will have a thousand men awake before you reach her. They may not live, but certainly you die as well." And he raised Semaion's gilded city horn, dented but still loud.

A pause followed. Ambrosius heard the current of the mighty Sinope, lapping at the pillars of the bridge beneath him.

Finally Pindar said, "I would have counseled saving the patricia."

Ambrosius said, "Noble Valerius Corvus – venerable Decius Mus – escort Reburrus to the Killinghouse. He will not oppose you. When he is situated there, do you ride home. Ride home at last, my friends, from weary war. Southward, Corvus, to the green fields of Mantinea – northward, Mus, to the bluffs of windy Apaphon. I ask you only this, that you will stop with every ancient family, with every warrior noble. Last night was the full moon. Spread the word: at the full moon after next, we host the *familia cenoam* in Florence. I will tell them in the west. Ten score of our breed, the founders of the nation. Land holders, horse riders, the shield and spear of mighty Florence, gathered in the great hall for the Family Dinner. As they once feasted to kindle war, so too speedily, in our own day, we feast to celebrate peace."

Corvus and Mus understood his meaning, which was not exactly what he said, and stood. Reburrus stood with them. Reburrus said, "I am ever faithful to you, my lord, and to Florence, and to the Pantokrator." The fury boiled from him. He went on, "She is a thing of her god, made hastily of living clay. She will lack a navel or a womb, menses or bile. Time and age will not flow naturally for her. I foretell you this – you will never see behind that gown of hers."

The nostril of Ambrosius flared; they might mock his infidelities in the street, but not to his face, not even the priest. Reburrus withered under the king's glare. He muttered, "No mortal may see behind her gown. To see her naked would be to die. Her god will not permit exposure of his tricks."

Ambrosius waited a long time to answer, and when he answered, he spoke dangerously softly. He said, "The Pantokrator loves you, Reburrus, and Florence loves you, and I love you. I beg you wait upon the soothing counsels of Antivola. Wait at least so long. Then you will know what to say, and I will bend my ear to it. Stay far clear of Claire till then, and of ourselves as well." All eyes turned from Ambrosius to the priest.

The shadowed cowl was still a moment, then the priest mumbled something.

Ambrosius rasped, "Repeat it."

Reburrus said again: "I left my sandals by the alien."

Ambrosius said, "Mus, get him the boots of a dead man on your way."

So saying, he dismissed them.

When the ichneumon was well away, Ambrosius addressed Marcus. He said, "Reburrus will seek a side road to his purpose. I will protect one flank of the fair patricia. You and your Thousand guard the other." Pindar said, "He will disobey his king?" Ambrosius hotly answered, "He will obey his god." Marcus said, "Every Florentine understands implacable Reburrus. We will do the thing you say."

Ambrosius said, "Very well. Now we resolve a question I had wished to put off."

King Pindar placated him: "Brother king, speak."

Ambrosius said, "If we do not mean to kill her, what precisely shall we do with Claire?"

After a short silence, the Genovan scribe spoke. He said, "Your priest was right. It is imprudent to maintain her here. You have promised her passage back to Zanzibar. I suggest you do it promptly."

He looked to his king, and Pindar nodded.

Marcus said, "What sort of expedition would you consider?"

King Pindar said, "Tribune, you have a proposal?"

Marcus spoke slowly and carefully. He said, "Of my loyalty to Florence, I have no doubt. Likewise the Thousand. But I can see reason. There is no way you –" looking to Ambrosius "–or you–" looking to Pindar "–can rest easy with the force that defied your orders. Therefore I propose you provision us and send us. We will see her home."

Cleon Constantine immediately added, "Constantine is prepared to underwrite it."

Ambrosius, queasy at his debts, replied, "Once you leave the valley of the world, your expedition must feed itself."

Marcus said, "We'll find our way."

Cleon spoke a little too eagerly: "Constantine is interested in concessions obtained in the west. We might be prepared to buy a share in the expedition."

Ambrosius snapped at him, "If we permit it." Then he noticed Cleon's posture and snarled, "Get out of bed, man." Cleon scrambled up, baring his pale legs.

The Genovan scribe said, "Perhaps, in time, the Constantines might research opportunities in Genova." Cleon said, "The bonds of commerce are the sinews of peace." The scribe said, "I am Dion Ambelokipi." Cleon said, "Dion Ambelokipi, I or mine will look forward to breaking bread with you in Genova." The tall scribe bowed. The entire exchange disgusted Ambrosius. This was the price of promoting low-born men of talent: they immediately got to thinking they did all the real work, showing the most transparent contempt for their betters.

He commanded, "Everybody out." The startled council looked

at him. He said, "We have need of private conference with our opposite." With a flourish, he handed his blades to Pindar's giant bodyguard, repeating, "Everybody out." Cleon said, "But –" Ambrosius said, "Out." Cleon shrugged angrily, and shuffled out of his own tent. The others followed.

When they were alone, Pindar raised an eyebrow at Ambrosius.

Ambrosius said, "All the preening got to me."

Pindar said, "I had heard you were weak-willed in council."

Ambrosius said, "It's true that between me and any one of my councilors, there is opinion enough for one."

Pindar shook a finger at him and said, "But it's your opinion, and the councilor finds himself speaking it."

Ambrosius said, "What does it matter, as long as the right thing gets done?" But he could see he'd impressed Pindar, and this pleased him.

He said, "We do have one last matter to settle."

Pindar said, "Only one?"

"Only one tonight, and it is this. If we mean to get Claire back to Zanzibar, it's too late in the season to set out. She's aiming west, so she'll have to cross the mountains through the Massilian Gates or the Brigantine. Snow already blocks both passes. Leaving aside the problem of Kharkhade raiders. So we have to wait on springtime in the mountains. That's six months in the valley of the world. Are you quite sure our nations can hold out six months against a tiny little girl?"

Pindar laughed, and made himself comfortable in Cleon's cushioned chair. His fingertips pushed papers around on Cleon's desk. He said, "They never told me you were funny. What's your name, King Ambrosius?"

Ambrosius sat himself down on Cleon's bed. He blew his nose on the cover. He said, "If I hadn't been king, I'd have been Manfredi. Manfredi Ambrosius."

Pindar said, "I am Khrysanthos Pindar."

Ambrosius said, "Golden flower."

Pindar nodded, "I'm told I had fine golden hair as an infant."

Ambrosius said, "What are we to do with her all winter?"

As if taking care of her were some objectionable chore. Pindar saw right through it.

He said, "No deceptions now, Manfredi. I'd like to host this prodigy in Genova. You have special need of her in Florence?"

Ambrosius sighed. He said, "I do. You've heard of the red sword?"

Pindar knit his brows and said, "That's real?"

Ambrosius said, "I held it as a child. My brother took it with him when he went into ai Ctesiphôn. What became of it, I doubt I'll ever know."

Pindar said, "What has this to do with Claire?"

Ambrosius said, "The war is over but I've got to win the peace. I've heard you have weak noblemen in Genova, and sometimes I envy you for it. Ours are proud warriors. I've just now sent my councilors Corvus and Mus to secure the nation. All the warrior nobles will be at Florence in two months' time, with orders to refresh their loyalties to the throne. We'll see how well that goes. Meantime I've got to secure the city. It's full of factions seeking an angle, and they'll move quickly in the chaos of peace.

"The red sword was the strong arm of my house. Everyone's been circling since it went. I'm going home with peace, but no victory. I need her, Khrysanthos. I need a trophy to demonstrate my strength.

"I must dominate Florence."

Pindar stood and walked to face Ambrosius. He squatted till he was level with the seated king. Ambrosius looked him in his wide-set northern eyes, now twinkling, now guileless. He found he liked his ancient enemy very much.

Pindar said, "One condition. Protect her from your Florentine zealots and knifemen. I will not forgive you if she comes to harm." He bared his sharp teeth, and Ambrosius nodded.

Pindar said, "Other condition. I will share the cost of provisions, but if you take her, you take her Thousand too."

Ambrosius sighed.

Pindar smiled savagely. "Your Marcus Diophantus is a handsome young man who's sure he's right about everything, and he's got an army." He clapped Ambrosius warmly on the shoulder. "May Pantokrator save you."

# 10

## SHE SHOULD HAVE TO BEAR HERSELF IF SHE WANTED TO GET BORN

IN CLAIRE'S DREAM she was back in the birth canal of her mother.

It was a rosy tube, with a soft light pulsing in its walls. It had a smell she knew from long ago, like the sea but more urgent. Claire was bigger now than when she was born. The birth canal had grown since then as well, and curved far above her, and she could not tell where it ended. Looking closely at the pulsing walls, she saw, growing here and there, hard knobs of a darker crimson color. These knobs were fit to serve as hand- and foot-holds. Reckoning nobody was coming to bear her, and she should have to bear herself if she wanted to get born, she began to climb. The knobs were warmer than the walls, and every sound she made as she climbed seemed damp and muffled in her ear.

She climbed a long time, and as she climbed, the canal kept its curve above her, and her climb seemed to have no end, and finally the irregular placements of the knobs came to seem familiar. Her foot slipped one time, her sandal scraping over the knob. Later she found in the same spot a bleeding knob. It was as she suspected: the growing tube had curved into a circle, and no longer had an exit.

For a while she sped up her climbing, reasoning like a dumb beast that if she went faster she might somehow escape the curve. Her calves burned and her thighs burned, and her arms and shoulders ached, and her fingers grew stiff. A terror seized her, that she should catch up to herself. In the eye of her imagination, she saw herself glance up and come snout-to-heel with the sandal of the beautiful patricia. But this imagined patricia was not quite the same as herself. Her gown was red, and she had a different face and character, and mind. If Claire were a formidable power, then this imagined patricia was in some unnamed way a terrifying overpower. Claire knew she'd once known how to name this overpower, but she did not remember it anymore. This was a real knowledge, and not a knowledge invented by the dream.

Fear halted her. She heard a distant sound, wet and crackling. Looking far, far down the curve, she saw the tube clenching and constricting. It was closing up beneath her. She couldn't descend, she couldn't stay where she was much longer, and she was terrified to rise. Her only path was through the pulsing rosy wall.

She clenched her fist. She foresaw the wave of blood, her mother's agony. Teeth chattering, she struck the wall. A piercing pain shot through her womb. Abruptly she awoke.

Clutching her belly, she found herself in her palanquin, underneath a warm fur that smelled of sweat and sandalwood. She couldn't remember where she was. The phantom pain receded and her mind spun and cleared. She thought, *This is Pindar's fur, he lent it to me.* Slowly and in parts, as if it were a dream, she remembered the storm and the rebel soldiers and the kings and their war and its peace. She remembered her enemy and his clawed murder-thing, and how his hand was stayed in the darkest hour of the night. She remembered retreating to the safety of her gold palanquin, which no other mortal could enter.

She remembered that as soon as she'd unfolded time, the storm found her again.

She saw only shades of peach, dawn's light passing through her eyelids. Reflecting on all that had come to pass, she stole herself, anticipating a surge of sorrow at her exile. But she didn't feel it. Free of the sealed tube, she was elated. She was out on her own in the wide world. Whatever this place was, it was hers to learn and master. She had nothing but her wits and charm to save her. A wild delight surged in her youthful breast.

*This is real and it is mine.*

She opened her eyes and looked out the window at the cool light of dawn. Her vast pupils retreated into the sea of gray around them. The men outside were just awakening.

She turned her attention to the muddy sandals. They smelt of cedar oil, and cut in each wood sole was a circle inscribed in a square. The symbol reminded her of something, but she couldn't say what. Her enemy had left them behind.

# 11

## TWO ROADS LEAD INTO ZANZIBAR, BUT ONLY ONE LEADS OUT

THE LAND WAS broken. War had broken it.

From a window of her gold palanquin, Claire watched the valley of the world roll past. Right beside the old King's Road she saw a pile of wood and tangled leather; scavengers had taken the bronze parts of this armor. Passing by a stream, and then a stand of alders, she saw people hanging from them, and the children turning sleepily one way then the other, in the autumn wind. There was a town, that had an empty square, where leaves rattled against a body, bigger than a man and smaller than a bull. Claire saw wolves, prowling the rubble.

Passing out again from that empty town, a stink of gases rose from the water along each side of the old King's Road, and the corpses in it, that were some of them bloated, and others burst. All the box turtles had died from the filth. Claire breathed lightly through her mouth. Farther from the town, there were fewer corpses, and less stink.

In her ear there was the rumble of the giant cart her gold palanquin sat in, as it bumped along the awful road. There was a constant clap of hooves on stone and dirt. Ahead, men shouted, and behind as well. But beyond the royal party, there was silence.

The clattering of traffic, the cries of vendors at their road-side stands, the music of clapboard entertainers, the shouts of children, the bells and groaning industry of towns, the complaints of sheep, the songs of farmhands sweating in the fields: all these sounds were missing. Sometimes crows cawed, out over the forests.

## XXX

AT DAWN, THE two kings had explained their plan to her: she, a guest of Florence for the winter, would travel west in springtime with the Thousand. She heard more from them about their mountains and their scary mountain-men and their snowbound mountain passes.

Her broad-chested champion, Marcus Diophantus, approached her and the kings. He said, "Leave me and the Thousand behind a few days." He scarcely dared look Claire in the face while he said it. He went on, "Let us collect the dead. We'll build proper pyres for them." He upset and frightened her. Why was he doing this?

Claire deciphered it: the rebel was working to earn these kings' trust. And abandoning Claire to them, Marcus was declaring his trust as well. Ambrosius said, "Be blessed of the gods for attending on the dead." Marcus raised his downcast gaze and said, "I send only my surviving Stonebreakers, Taranto and Brindisi, with the patricia." With a sparkle in his eye. *O you impetuous youth, you just couldn't resist, could you? The kings are right to be suspicious.* But she was pleased to have his giant friends for protection. He turned to his work without addressing her. Everything was so exact now, so proper.

Pindar watched the young man go, then looked at Ambrosius and grinned. Ambrosius scowled. Pindar turned to Claire and said, "I won't see you again. Know this, daughter of Zanzibar: you did what king and state could not. You sowed peace." He took her hand and stooped and kissed it. His dark hair brushed her wrist. Then he stood and said, "If Genova should hear of your distress, count on her to answer." He nodded gravely to the beautiful patrica.

He turned to Ambrosius and said, "You I'll see again." He clasped Ambrosius's hand and said, "Manfredi." There was no guile at all to it. Ambrosius said, "Khrysanthos," similarly true. The king of Genova made his way to his sedan chair.

The Florentines loaded Claire's gold palanquin in a great cart. The palanquin had smooth rails, not wheels, and it didn't work outside of Zanzibar. She'd warned them it was heavier than it looked, heavier than could possibly be explained. They hadn't believed her till they'd tried to get it up on the cart's open bed. Laughter turned to curses. The work gang called friends to the task. In the end it took ropes and planks and logs and men and horses to load the massive thing.

XXX

THE CART JOUNCED over the road, dragged by a team of eight tremendous draft horses with shaggy fetlocks and ox-like shoulders. It rolled with the forward party: the king and his staff and their carts and near a thousand men from the king's army, the ones they called the Wardogs. Taranto and Brindisi drove her cart. Claire sat in the gold palanquin, looking out one of the eye-like windows.

In the muddy fields alongside the road, great divots were ripped out, as if some enormous beast had fought the land. In the divots, pools of stormwater reflected silver ribbons of the freezing sky.

Later she smelled fire. She looked all around, and finally behind. She saw a fat column of black smoke rising from Andropolis.

Aside from the men who traveled with her, Claire never saw a living human being. Florence was empty.

XXX

THIS MADMAN SAID, "I think I know you."

He said to King Ambrosius, "I think I know you, for your father came here once, and you have something of his look. You'd have been a boy then. Could you be Ælius Pellucidus, grown up to king of Florence?"

Claire saw the jaw of Ambrosius clench. The king waited on himself, then gently answered, "You have it nearly right. He died, and I am the younger brother, that became king. And what do men call you?"

But the madman only nodded and gnawed the salted lamb they'd shared with him. The staff held their tongues.

Ambrosius tried again. He said, "Florentine, I'm passing through with happy news. The war is over."

The madman pulled the lamb back from his mouth, revealing an uncertain sneer. He looked at the king, then idly scratched his beard, then looked around among the men as if they might be poking fun at him. Finally he turned back to King Ambrosius and said, "No, no, I believe you must be playing tricks with me. Let us reason together on this. There is nothing but the war, nor has there ever been. That's one point for war. Then, if the war is over, where is the evidence? The town is still empty, and the fields still lie fallow. The dogs are in the streets and the birds are in the barns. That's four more points for war. There are points enough for war to fill my honest right hand. No, it cannot be true the war is over!"

Ambrosius said, "Florentine, put away your hand, for these are true tidings. The war is over quite so much as I am your King Ambrosius."

The madman tilted up his nose, and a light lit his eye. He said, "Scoundrel! Trick me? I must have been mistaken when I thought you looked like the prince. Perhaps instead you are the headman of a band of players. Perhaps the pack of you have nothing better to do than taunt a madman who has lost everything to the war, everything! - even mortal memory of his name. Or perhaps, perhaps" – and a great fear came over him – "perhaps you are not the younger brother after all, but the ghost of Ælius Pellucidus. They said he was high-spirited, like his father. He would never end the war, but his shade might roam Florence, mocking those who suffer."

Claire saw a tremor pass through Ambrosius. She recognized a man whose burden is lifted from him, and feels his life redeemed. His cheeks puffed in and out with his ungoverned breathing. Nobody else saw what Ambrosius underwent, and Ambrosius did not see Claire.

The madman beat his brow and blinked and looked around again. In a pleading tone he said, "A king of ghosts and his strange ghost-subjects. I see through you now! False word – false hopes – false men – false meal – I am alone! Always alone!" He looked down at the salted lamb and threw it on the ground. His high smell got thick with terror, and he stood and backed away, striking his breast and barking at King Ambrosius and Claire and all those there with them.

Now Claire did a thing which astonished all. Separating herself from her fellows, she came toward the madman. His birdlike eye settled on her, and loudly she said, "Hey – hi! Stop you! Stop!" And he stopped. So she approached him, and when she came to him, she laid a hand upon his arm. They conversed quietly with one another, the patricia and the madman, and then she returned to the Florentines. Behind her, the madman stood and wept, but peacefully.

## XXX

SHE SAT SUNK in thought behind the closed gold curtains of the gold palanquin, staring without looking at the gold thirty-two clock hanging on one wall. She considered what she'd learned about Ambrosius. She considered ruined Florence. Her adventure in the wide world wasn't so appealing as it was, before she'd seen the price this nation paid for war. *I'm nowhere*, she thought, *I'm lost in a ruined land, at the start of history, at Midnight. How will they ever get me home?* She began to feel very sorry for herself.

She didn't pull her curtain back again till much later in the day. The white and blue of the icy sky had settled into bands of faded yellow and violet. On the western verge, the sun was partly hidden in a little theater of piled-up clouds. He had lit them peach and rose, as if he were giving a private performance of his glories for his favored friends, in the far-off province of the gods.

*The cart rolls west. Every hour brings me closer to Zanzibar.*

## XXX

THEY BUILT CAMPFIRES in the evening. Prince Domenico, called Bitsy Boots by everyone, ran around with a flaming stick. He wore a soldier's uniform, adorable in miniature. Later he came and sat by Claire and looked up at her in open-mouthed awe, as children do around beauty.

He said, "Is it true you ended the war?"

Claire said, "Have you ever picked up a very heavy rock, and your father helped you out a little bit?"

Bitsy Boots nodded vigorously.

Claire said, "Who really lifted the rock?"

He said, "I did it almost by myself."

Claire said, "That's exactly how the war ended. Your father did it almost by himself. I only helped him out a little bit."

The boy's face lit up. He was delighted to understand. Then his face fell and he said, "But I won't get to fight." And he waved his burnt stick around, like a sword.

She smiled at him and said, "Fighting is a terrible thing, and nobody should want to fight if he can help it." Bitsy Boots became quiet and embarrassed. He looked at her, then looked away.

He said under his breath, "May I ask you a question?"

She said, "Anything you like."

He worked up his courage and said, in a small voice, "How come you've got your bubbie out?"

She almost laughed, but caught herself. She said, "I come from very far away, and this is how my people dress."

He thought it over, then said, "The men too?"

She said, "The men have both out, or none."

Bitsy Boots stared at her a while longer. He said, "Shall I call you Auntie Claire?"

She said, "I'd like that very much."

He grinned and jumped up and ran off. *He'll remember this evening.*

Not long after, she spotted a minder carrying the boy away, fast asleep.

Claire recklessly drank unmixed wine. She felt her face hot, and her back freezing, and remembered bonfires on the cold night desert, not so many years ago. The wind shifted and woodsmoke blew in her face. Her eyes streamed and she was filled with a warm conviviality: alone in the world but tipsy among friends.

A buzzing filled her head, and when it hushed itself, she realized Kimg Ambrosius was sitting with her, and the others were carefully apart from them. *First the son, then the father*, she thought.

The king looked at the fire, as if trying to see in it how to say what he meant. When he spoke, he spoke to her, but he faced the flames. He said, "I don't doubt Zanzibar is real. There is not wealth enough in the world to make only one of you. If there be one of you, there must be five hundred more, and not patricias only, but the men that govern them, the lands that nourish them, the mines that yield them coin, the arms and treaties that protect them, and the drudges that support them. By god, it must be the finest city in the world! And yet – I've never heard of it. We are not entirely provincial here, O Claire. We receive ambassadors and travelers and the wandering Ottolenghi. No one has ever breathed a word about Zanzibar."

He fell silent. Claire's heart raced. Staring at him, she tried to blink away the smoke and drink. Finally, he sighed and turned to her. Eyes glittering, he said, "*What is Zanzibar?*"

She wiped her tears with the back of her hand, stealing one last moment to frame her thoughts. For the law of Zanzibar is clear:

none shall tell what it is. But there was nothing to stop her edging around the law.

The wind shifted, clearing the smoke. Ambrosius stared avidly at the patricia. Claire squinted into the fire, and spoke as if reporting what she saw there. She said:

"Two roads lead into Zanzibar, but only one leads out.

"Zanzibar, my Zanzibar, lies far off in the west, where the desert meets the sea. Draw you near to Zanzibar on the high road, and first you see the ancient outworks, walls and towers with horizontal stripes upon 'em, the lighter tan between the darker brown. The outworks have the look of striped mud in the day, and striped gold in the evening. On the high road hear you but the sighing of the hot wind, that never stops its sighing, and the little rattle of the sand against the outworks, that has blown against the walls a thousand years and more. My Zanzibar is younger than the morning, but in the years of men, she is near half so old as the world."

Her voice was like a low song, rising from the crackling of the flames.

"Now come you off the high road, inside the mighty gate. This is what you wish to see. What do you see?" Claire paused, and Ambrosius stared at her, mouth a little open. She turned and looked at him, gray eyes blooming, depths uncountable. She said, "Are you a good king?"

He shrank from her. He knew this question. He had asked it of himself. He said, "I hope that I am."

She said, "Then surely you have often dreamt the dream of the good king."

He started a little, for she spoke of a thing close to the hearts of kings, and known to none but kings. Then his eyes widened and he got a happy look to him. She saw he'd comprehended: only good kings dreamt this dream that he had dreamt. He must be a good king.

She turned back to the fire and recited slowly. She said, "In your dream you saw your city. But it was not quite like your city.

The crumbled parts were made whole, and the filth was washed off, and the crooked road was straightened, and the sunken road was leveled. The burnt district was rebuilt, and the blighted orchard was replanted. Beyond these general improvements there were changes more difficult to comprehend. The whole geography seemed larger somehow. Each street was longer end-to-end. There was room on them for fine new tenements and markets. There were new public buildings. Some were temples, or gymnasia, or libraries, but others were inscrutable. It all seemed so beautiful and true, in the strong clear light of day. Raising up your gaze, you saw towers taller than any of your squat familiar towers. There were gleaming bridges joining them, soaring far above your familiar heavy bridges.

"There was a music of the happiness of men, and turning your eyes back to the long clean streets, you saw your people, who are like your children. Every day you strive for your people, and wish only good things for them, as a father wishes for his children. Now you saw your people had grown up into fine men and women, as you had wished and striven for. You saw your people feeding the pauper, and comforting the widow, and clothing the orphan, and soothing the madman. You saw the blind, the deaf, the lame raised up. You saw your people competing in the theater, and the footrace, and the team sports, and the dance. You saw them throw their backs into their work, in the field and at the forge, in trade domestic and foreign. You saw them studying great books and writing them, and pushing back the ignorance of man. And you saw your wise children taking joy in life, that lasts a little while, and preparing in good time to go out from underneath the sun, so that when the joy of life was done for each, they went serenely where they must.

"All these things you saw in your dream of the good king, and then you felt peace, for you had done what the god lays on his king to do, which is to be the good father of the people, and the good custodian of the city. But when you woke the peace fled from you, for the dream dissolved, and you saw the wretched squalor and the misery of the world as it is, that can be kicked in the front, and in the back, but stubbornly keeps its shape.

"You ask me what is Zanzibar, and I tell you that the law of Zanzibar seals up my lips. I may not tell you what is Zanzibar. But I need not tell you. My dear, dear king, know you that the dream of the good king is no dream. That strange city that you saw, that started as your city but became another city, is Zanzibar. Therefore do you already know what is Zanzibar. Turn your inner eye upon the temple of your soul. A word is written above the temple door, in letters that burn bright, so that they can be seen at midnight, and even from a great distance. You have always known the word was there, but couldn't read it until now. The word is *Zanzibar*."

She looked from the fire to Ambrosius. He saw the tears were streaming down her cheeks. He spoke in quiet awe, "The word is there, and written as you say. O Claire, this city I love, and the love for it sears me, yet I have never seen it. For you who have seen it..." He bared his teeth a moment at the fire, and they glittered in the crackling light. "No mortal can have loved his nation as much as the Zanzibaris."

She put her hand over her mouth and her knuckles were white. She stood and hurried off unsteadily, her white gown billowing in the cold night. She climbed up on the cart and into her gold palanquin. He heard her weeping, for a moment only, then she shut the door.

## XXX

IT WASN'T ONLY the thought of Zanzibar that upset her. The wine propelled her down a path of logic she'd been avoiding. Now she couldn't help but face the fact she couldn't bear: what her exile was doing to her mother.

Her mother must have been frantic since her youngest daughter vanished. So strong in all things but helpless in this alone, perhaps that woman stumbled now along the shore, seeking for the surf to raise her baby's lifeless, gleaming crown. Or maybe she was pacing and haranguing the Sûreté-Metro, hair disheveled, eyes red-rimmed, voice hoarse. Or they might have sent her home to wait on word, and she was sobbing at the kitchen table, where the closest neighbors might hear her through the open window.

Claire rubbed her burning eyes and stared at the awful hands of the ticking thirty-two clock.

*Was it worth it?*

She tormented herself.

*I didn't know.*

# 12

## DO YOU HAVE THE HEART TO GO ON BEING KING?

THEY CAME TO the place where the Euxis River joins the Selene, which flowed at that time to the Sinope, and thence to Lake Lethea. They crossed a picket line just before they arrived. It was well fortified, and Claire puzzled out the desparate, hardened feel of the line: if Andropolis had fallen to Genova, Florence would have made her stand here. Now it would never happen.

The weather was like summer again. It was warm in the shade, and hot in the sun, and the cicadas took turns buzzing in the willows. Tall grass choked the flooded riverbank. Upriver on the Euxis, the waters were cool and slow. It was a famous swimming hole. The soldiers and staff laughed and ran as they approached the place. Everybody likes a bath.

When they reached the water's edge, they eagerly stripped off their armor and their linen; the staff unpinned their stained woolen chitons and set them down, women and men alike. Claire studied their bodies in the wash of daylight, building up by glances what it was rude to learn by staring. The human beings in this place were lean, as starvation and hard work breeds. They had pale skin, bronze where the sun touched it, and fine hair. The men were long from nipple to groin, but short in the forearm and leg. They were all sinew; to lie with one must be like to lie with a pile of rope. The women kept a little fat in the thighs and ass. Their hips were broader than Claire's, and their breasts larger. Their bellies were flat till middle age, when they turned round.

Naked, they ran to the water, hard soles pounding over pebbles and thistles, mud and grass. Bitsy Boots went with them, hair streaming, little red circles flaming on his cheeks, ass as pale as a toadstool, shrieking laughter.

The heart of the patricia went out to this people. The high did not hide their nakedness from the low, nor the woman from the man, but all went down together to enjoy the pleasures of life. They stormed into the patient Euxis, then howled at the coldness of the water, laughing and shivering and splashing one another.

The king remained a little ways behind with the patricia. Her heart beat slightly faster in her breast. *He's not done testing me.* She waited.

Watching where his people had gone, Ambrosius spoke idly, as if to himself. He said, "Go with the Florentines if you wish, O Claire. We aren't stuffy like Genovans: at the riverside, nobody is ashamed."

Smiling, she said, "It were best I didn't."

Idly still, he said, "All tribes have their story of the fearsome beauty, that no man dares to witness bathing."

*Who put this idea in his head? It's very sharp, and not at all how he thinks.*

Claire said, "I have heard one or two such stories along the way, my lord."

He said, "Some have the witness changed into a stag, so that his own dogs tear him."

*Ah well, let's have fun then.*

She said, "There is another where a bear comes out the woods to savage him."

Ambrosius said, "Just so, and one where he feels the slimy grip of the river god upon his ankle."

Claire said, "This one I have not heard, but I have heard one where the swallowtails carry him off to their house in the clouds."

Ambrosius looked around at her and said, "Perhaps you are some such fearsome beauty, Claire."

She looked at him and said with a straight face, "Who sees me naked certainly must die."

They looked silently at one another a long minute. The sun beat down on her pale breast, and on his furrowed brow. She noticed that the scar on his right cheek was not one scar, but several, from several deep cuts in almost the same place, made at different times. The cicadas buzzed, and the water lapped, and the men and women laughed a little ways away.

Finally Ambrosius said, "O Claire, is this the truth?"

## XXX

SHE SMILED HER strange smile, so that her mouth was full of mischief, and her gray eyes flashed. Then she turned and gazed along the river. The half-coins of greeting clinked in her gown as she turned.

The word of Reburrus was true then. No mortal eye might see behind that gown. Was Claire a god? A human girl? He considered she herself might not know. Such tales are common enough. There was the son of Ilyrion and his human lover, who lived three-score years before surviving a mortal wound and discovering the truth. There were the twin daughters of Pasiphae, one of whom grew old while the other remained young. There was even the time that Pantokrator, turning himself into a bull, forgot he was a god. He lived out a bull's life, thinking bull-like thoughts, and only remembered himself upon the pyre. *What have you forgotten, Claire?*

King Ambrosius looked at the back of the patricia's head. The short hairs at the top of her neck stirred in the summery breeze, and beads of sweat shone in the groove below them. Whatever she

She turned and gazed along the river.

was, or was not, her beauty was beyond nature and above reason. In one light it was so gentle as forgiveness, and in another light as fierce as battle. The will of men must fall before it. She would be able to unstitch the world, so long as she lived.

Claire turned and looked at him and he saw she'd understood everything. She knew that he was seeking to discover what she was. Her eyelids were still red from weeping the night before. His years at war had cost him most of his married life, but he knew women well enough to recognize this in her look: she was about to pay him back.

She eased into it. She lifted her hand and softly touched the scars on his right cheek. She dropped her hand and said, "How came you by these scars, Ambrosius?"

He touched them and said, "*Ultima cicatrice.* When a warrior noble thinks he is about to die, he may cut his right cheek. Not clean through of course; enough to bleed and show."

She said, "Why?"

He said, "It is a message to his fellow nobles, should they find the body – *I died with honor. I died well.*"

He saw her trying to count the faint lines. He said, "Four. Four times I was certain I would die."

She said, "With honor?"

He said, "I would not die without it."

She said, "My lord, do you have the heart to go on being king?"

He blurted, "How dare you ask me such a question?"

It wasn't how he wanted to answer – he'd tested her, and meant to give her her turn. But she startled him. He saw fear shove her, and he saw her steady herself.

She said, "When that madman took you for your brother, and then said that your brother never would make peace, I watched you. I watched you and I saw you, my lord, and I saw a burden lift from you. I have revolved this scene many times before the eye of my reason, and I have told myself a little story what it meant. May I tell you this story?"

Ambrosius controlled himself and spoke warmly, "Guest of Florence, for sure do you tell me this story."

He saw her read his intentions. She spoke cleanly and simply: "This is the story I tell myself. I tell myself King Ambrosius here had an older brother called Ælius Pellucidus, who was to be king.

"Ælius Pellucidus was high spirited, joyful and warlike, like his father. Therefore, like all warriors who take after their fathers, he fought ferociously with his father. But like all warriors whose sons take after them, his father loved him best. Everyone loved Ælius Pellucidus best. He cast his younger brother into shadow, but his younger brother worshipped him. Fine Ælius Pellucidus loved the chase, and the hunt, and the kill. He loved to tilt and lunge. He was excellent in all the arts of war. It is true he would have been the better king of war. But that madman was right. High-spirited Ælius Pellucidus never would have made the peace.

"That nameless madman told you a true thing, and you saw you were the right king for the hour, and the god was wise in taking your beloved brother. His death was redeemed in that very minute, my lord, and your life as well. This was the burden which lifted from you."

She stopped. Ambrosius blinked back tears. She said, "Have I got that story approximately right, my lord?" He growled, "Slowly, Claire." She studied him frankly, like a child, and he meekly submitted to it.

After a long patient time, his eyes dried, and she went on. She said, "I have studied great men, my lord. The lives of great men are like stories, and they reach their crisis, and then they are done. There is no great man without his story.

"These many years, you defended your nation and you warmed your brother's throne. Now both stories have reached their crisis, and are done. Therefore you have earned your rest, and perhaps you have spent all the strength of your arm.

"When I ask if you have the heart to go on being king, I ask if you will set aside your rest and your reward. You may take them now with honor. Leave them and perhaps you lose the chance. One story is done. Soon you must decide upon the next one."

Ambrosius stood in awe of her. She was the kind of fool permitted, like a madman, to say true things.

Her gray eye penetrated him. She said, "I do not ask from any charity toward you or Florence. Consider my position. I am at the farthest exile, a helpless woman in a vast uncertain world. I depend upon the good intentions and firm abilities of those who shelter me."

Sudden anger took him. He felt cheated, as a man is cheated. He said, "Haven't you got your Marcus Irenaeus and his army? Aren't they enough?"

She tisked dismissively. The sound made his heart rich with joy. She said, "You are Florence, and he is your hand. You take me for some girl who loses her head over handsome lads?"

He swallowed and said, "What are you?"

She said, "I am nothing but myself."

They glared at one another a while. Then she held out her hand. He took it and held it, as if he were a boy, and she his mother. They walked together on the spongy ground toward the riverbank. Ambrosius had the rolling gait of a long-time rider of horses, and his footfalls on the right hitched a bit from some old wound.

# 13

## AN EATER OF THE LIVING, AND AN EATER OF THE DEAD

WHEN THE SUN rose on the fifth day of Claire's exile, Claire scanned the eastern sky, as she had each morning on the old King's Road. But this morning, she couldn't see the thread of smoke rising from distant Andropolis. Was Marcus Irenaeus Diophantus on his way? She was discovering she was exactly the kind of girl who loses her head over handsome lads. *Where is he?*

XXX

ON THE SEVENTH day of Claire's exile, they called the halt just east of Rusadir, a very old forest, with a name inherited from the people who lived there before the Florentines.

Claire had figured out the map of the war: the front along the Sinope was soft, and each side had ravaged the other beyond it. But the picket lines contained the destruction. Beyond the Euxis, life was almost undisturbed by war.

The king's party was no distinct thing any longer. Riders clopped past them east and west, hurrying on business. A mass of refugees had caught up with the king's party. Some went on, and some stayed. Tenmen of the picket reserves joined them, though Ambrosius had the generals keep the main line intact. Camp followers cluttered the road, dragging along their carnival of tents and wares. One soldier killed a whore; two gamblers stabbed each other; and somebody beat a miserable Ottolenghi till he was like to die. The surgeon told the bailiff they should pay the liquorman a commission, but the bailiff didn't think it was funny. When this messy company halted on the seventh day, they rested in a town called Mœnia Rusadir. It still had some open public houses. The fields all round were cultivated.

Word of the peace was rapidly outpacing King Ambrosius, and reached the mighty walls of Florence itself in the morning of that seventh day. At the very hour the king's party halted in Mœnia Rusadir, Barbarossa Constantine heard of the peace. A messenger disturbed him where he prayed at the tomb of Eiuenos il Waidhor, though of course he knew it as the tomb of John the Pilgrim. The messenger bore a letter from his cousin Cleon. Barbarossa was not the strategist that Cleon was, and Cleon hinted in the letter how peace must ruin their design. It took Barbarossa a little while to figure out what Cleon refused to set in writing. When he understood, he flushed as scarlet as his beard. One part of the flush was anger at the peace, and the other part anger that Cleon had to point it out to him. This demonstrates why they worked well together: Cleon provided the phlegm, and Barbarossa the blood. Barbarossa picked a fight with the messenger, right there in the holy place, and pummeled him. Rage still blazing, he hastened from the bower and summoned the others.

To return to Mœnia Rusadir, rumors of the peace had preceded the king's party here as well. Therefore the burghers of the town, and their wives and children, came out on the King's Road to greet them, blowing trumpets and strewing autumn flowers. Claire rode a tall white horse with a well-combed girly look, just behind the king, as they processed down the muddy street where the King's Road crossed the town, and the running children tugged her hem and she smiled down at them, so that their necks tingled at her thrilling radiance. Then they fell back to suck their fingers, and others replaced them, reaching for the exile on the horse.

XXX

IN THE MORNING they hitched fresh horses to Claire's enormous cart and traveled west into Rusadir. The cool damp air and dappled light delighted her. The forest was like a vast room, floor soft with litter, walls red and yellow with autumn leaves.

Presently she noticed that the road, which had been rising since they left Andropolis, was dipping again, and concluded that the land behind had drained into the Sinope, and the land ahead drained into whatever river ran through Florence. So much for east and west. To her left the southern land was always higher, and to her right, the northern land was always lower. It seemed she was indeed inside a giant valley, slope so gentle as to be invisible. She supposed the river behind, and the river ahead, both emptied into Lake Lethea, which they'd said was nearly an inland sea.

By midday, the king's enormous party stretched out far along the narrow forest road, and it took messengers an hour to walk from the front of it to the back. In the afternoon, even near the front of the party, Claire heard the thundering behind them. Soldiers started running east. She soon heard cries. She listened intently for battle, but made out cheering instead. Then she realized what it was, and called out to Taranto and Brindisi to stop the cart, to let her down.

XXX

MARCUS WAS SOOTY and gaunt and looked weeping tired. The Thousand behind him the same. They'd all painted an angled pale stripe on their breastplates, the symbol in their writing for "one thousand." It served now for emblem of a separate army, one more bit of provocation. It looked like they'd used Andropolitan mud.

When he spotted her, a shadow of anger and fear crossed his face. She was aghast. *What's happened?* She timidly nodded to him. He looked from her to someone behind her.

Claire turned. There was Ambrosius, looking mystified. He'd seen all and been confused as well. He swept past her and put his hands on Marcus's shoulders, heavily, and said to him, "Florentine, you have honored our dead," and kissed his brow. Marcus shut his red-rimmed eyes and clenched his teeth.

They let as many of the exhausted Thousand as they could ride on in carts.

XXX

A HAND TAPPED softly on a window of the gold palanquin.

Claire woke with a start. The hand tapped again. She was frightened anybody got past Taranto and Brindisi. She'd been trying fruitlessly for days to find her enemy with the missing sandals. She couldn't just report him without admitting she could unfold time, and this she didn't dare to do. Now it was the dead of night and someone was tapping softly on her window. She could see the glowing fires of little hand-lamps through the curtain.

She steadied herself and tested the speed of her arm. When she felt ready, she drew back the curtain. She faced Marcus Irenaeus and several of the Thousand.

No other mortal could enter the palanquin. So she had to come out. He had that look that had shadowed his face when he spotted her before, anger and fear. He said, "Come."

XXX

IT WAS A chilly night in the damp wood. Claire made her way among the Thousand in their camp. They were all awake and looked at her warily. Taranto and Brindisi shielded her on each side, as confused as she was.

Marcus led them to a clearing. There was a low fire in its center, more glowing coals than flames. Two old men sat by the fire, the diagonal mark of the Thousand daubed on the breasts of their ragged tunics. The older of the two looked senile and fidgeted with a clay winecup; the younger one drank calmly. When the calm one saw her, he smiled and set down his cup. He was the only man she'd seen who seemed happy to see her. He rose and said, "I live to meet you." He approached her and stiffly knelt and took her hand and kissed it. All this she permitted, with a questioning look at Marcus.

The old man stood. Taranto said, "What is this?" The man looked at him and said, "O Taranto, don't you know me?" Taranto squinted at him in the red light of the coals, then a tremor shook him. He said, "Cornelius?"

The old man flashed a smile. He gestured at his ancient companion, saying, "And Philo."

Taranto said to Claire, "They're Stonebreakers," then turned back to the old man and said, "But – how? What happened to you? Some curse? A witch – ?"

He realized what he was saying and his gaze shot to Claire, then Marcus. He shut up. Without noticing what he was doing, he took a step back from the patricia. Brindisi did as well. She felt the forest wind brush her naked arms.

Marcus said, "We found them living by the river, south of the bridge."

Claire said, "Tell me what happened to you, Cornelius."

The old man said, "Marcus says the storm lasted two or three days only, with very heavy rain. I can't understand it. It caught us near the bridge – me and Philo, and Valens and a lost Andropolitan girl who was following us. Philo and I got separated from Valens and the girl. We were on the riverbank. The rain grew slow and thin, and we found we couldn't leave. The river fed us. The current was choked with fish. The riverbank fed us. The bulrushes were plentiful. The storm lasted a lifetime. Now the storm has passed, and Marcus is still young young young. He tells us you came from the storm, and brought peace to the valley of the world. This is true?"

Claire whispered in a choking voice, "It is true."

Cornelius closed his eyes and sighed a sigh of great satisfaction.

Marcus said, "Claire, I have gathered and arranged six thousand dead. There was a little forest south of Andropolis, and I have cut it down and burnt it, to give the dead their pyre.

"In the heart of the storm, I saw men frozen in their place. I saw – I saw bones where bodies had freshly fallen.

"Some of the Thousand were young men when the storm began, and now they are grown old.

"What have you done to my friends? *What are you?*"

Claire turned to him and spoke, voice breaking, but clearly, so that all could hear, "O my champion and savior, I am not the storm. The storm did not come from me. In the valley of the world, you must have your stories of the way the world was, before the god brought order to the cosmos."

The crowd murmured and Marcus said, "Chaos begat Time, and Time begat Pantokrator, and Pantokrator slew Chaos."

Claire said, "The storm, I think, is a living tooth of Chaos, surviving age on age, down to the present generation. The roaring of it is the fury of old Chaos. The death it wrought is the destructiveness of Chaos. And what happened to your friends –"

Marcus said, "Yes?" Cornelius and the whole crowd leaned in.

Claire said, "I am a student of a kind of meditation, which allows me to see time direct. When the storm carried me, I looked at time in it, and..."

She gestured with her hands. She found she had difficulty explaining.

Senile Philo abruptly dashed his winecup on a rock. The crowd jumped. The clay cup was reduced to shards. Philo looked at Claire, eyes sharp, mouth slack.

She said, "Yes. That is what the storm did to time."

There was a long silence.

Finally Marcus said, "Is the storm chasing you?"

Claire pressed her lips together and shook her head and lied, "It was passing through our world."

Marcus looked around at the Thousand. They whispered back and forth among themselves. A consensus slowly formed. Marcus read it and turned to Claire.

He said, "Take the blood oath with me, Claire. You for Florence, me for Zanzibar."

She winced and said, "That one I cannot take."

His expression darkened and he said, "Are you a false ally?"

She said, "I am your true ally, Marcus Irenaeus Diophantus."

He said, "Then why won't you share blood with me?"

She startled everybody with a grin. She said, "Because in Zanzibar, the blood oath is for marriage."

The Thousand laughed. Marcus blushed and studied his feet.

Claire said, "For the oath that you describe, we share saliva. Will you take the oath of saliva with me?"

Marcus looked at her and said, "How – um – how –"

Cornelius offered his own clay winecup and said, "You spit in the wine, you fool."

Claire said, "Yes, that."

So he spat in it, and she spat in it, and he drank, and she drank.

## XXX

REBURRUS KEPT CLEAR of the king and the patricia, but he shadowed them, with his staff of ichts. If he could not undo Claire yet, he could undo her works. He learned the story of the nameless madman she had soothed. The ichts sought him out. The madman raged at the ichts, but when they dragged him to an abandoned temple, and he saw the ichneumon in it, he grew meek and deathly, like a little animal pinned by a big animal. Claire understood the madman, and the madman understood the priest. Reburrus sat the madman in a chair and put the Lucarnian Sleeves on him. He was no crueler than he had to be.

One icht slowly poured water in the sleeves, and another warmed more at the temple's rekindled hearth. The madman sat before Reburrus and tried to answer his questions. The bloody water dripped from his fingers into bowls on either side of the chair. Reburrus spoke ardently to him, saying, "My brother, I am a teacher of men. I have resigned my knowledge; I speak to you with tears." He said, "Help the god to see me. The ichts place the dry bowls, and you make the bowls wet. I am a teacher. My hands are empty and I invite you." He said, "Dear my brother, my hands are sick, but I appeal to you." And he showed the madman his hands. They had grown dry and scaly.

The madman said, "The patricia from Zanzibar came to me and smelt of thunder; she is terrible of eye and hand. She smelt of honeysuckles; she is kind of eye and hand." He said, "The tower of the city will fall to her. She will walk the highway of the saintly conqueror. The waters and the soil whisper their secrets to her. She is an eater of the living, and an eater of the dead." The ichts could not make heads or tails of the strange conversation of the ichneumon and his dying captive. The madman's speech grew slurred and drowsy near the end, and finally he slipped out from underneath the sun.

Reburrus rested his hands in the bowls, but their water did not soothe his raw skin. So he set the bowls before the sacred doves and they drank their fill, and he had the ichts congeal the rest. Dread consumed him.

## XXX

CLAIRE DIDN'T SEE Marcus after that. He had the Thousand to attend to. Taranto and Brindisi went back to treating her as they had, like a little sister they'd appointed themselves to protect. The forest seemed to last forever. When they called the halt next dusk, they were still beneath the trees. Claire climbed down from the cart to stretch her legs. She was less anxious than she'd been, so she gave Taranto and Brindisi the slip and roamed along the line alone. She was hungry and had some vague idea to beg a little food somewhere. But when it came to it, she found herself bashful, and simply greeted those who greeted her. Under the fading light of twilight, the shadows in the forest seemed impenetrably black.

Claire thought of an aunt of hers, called Moonlight, a younger half-sister of her mother's. Claire's grandfather was a lady's man, and her mother had half-siblings everywhere. Aunt Moonlight, like Claire, did not smell human to animals. She was a forest hermit, a solitary huntress. As a child, Claire had thought her very beautiful: dark eyes flashing, smile giddy, thighs rippling muscle. But there was a repellent madness to her too, and Claire understood why she had to live alone.

Walking in Rusadir, Claire recalled a discourse of Moonlight. She'd said, "Little Claire, first the huntress will learn to ask the forest for the prey, and will listen only to the answer. If she never grows wiser than this, it is enough; she will not starve. But the true huntress will learn to hear the forest, and the forest will speak to her of many things, and possibly all things."

Moonlight had a given name; Claire's mother Reason did as well. And Claire had her own name-of-the-soul. But these were tender names, and she wasn't about to tell hers to the Florentines.

Night fell, and the forest seemed to lighten. Moonlight silvered the trees and shone off the leaves carpeting the forest floor. Claire caught a smell of roast rabbit and drifted toward it. As she got closer, she made out herbs mixed into the smell.

She caught sight of the warm glow of a fire, a little ways from the road. She quietly approached it, steeling herself to ask to join the feast. She heard chanting, and saw men and women surrounding a great flat stone. Rabbits were burning in a small pyre on the stone.

"Fearful Strypho!" they cried out. "Strypho, blade and berries! Strypho!"

A maiden passed a gray rabbit to an old woman with a big curved knife. The woman cut the throat of the struggling thing and stretched it, front legs in her knife hand and hind legs in the other. Its blood spattered the flat stone. The woman skinned it expertly and wrapped oregano around the carcass and flung it on the flames.

Not a feast at all.

The crowd chanted, "Fearful Strypho! Strypho protect our homes! Strypho hone the blade! Strypho string the berries! Strypho!"

The crowd finished its repetitions and fell silent. A wind shook the trees overhead. Claire heard voices and the clink of implements from the king's party on the road.

The crowd started a fresh chant. They cried, "Beautiful Claire! Claire, Sower of Peace! Claire!"

A thrill scurried up Claire's spine. The maiden came forward with another rabbit, a white one. The old woman cut its throat and stretched it, pouring its blood on the altar. She skinned it, wrapped it in thyme, and flung it on the flames. The crowd chanted, "Beautiful Claire! Claire bring us peace! Claire!"

She felt like she stood outside herself. The crowd turned toward the place she was hidden in the darkness of the woods. *How? How did they perceive me?* Immediately she felt the honeysuckles and thunder pouring off her. *They smelled me.* She stood there, poised between choices. *Should I flee?* Her heart fell. *Should I play the part they've written for me?* Pleasure touched her entire body like a dress of metal.

She stepped forward, her white gown brilliant in the firelight. They cried out, "Beautiful Claire! Sower of Peace! Claire!"

The old woman turned from the fire and looked at her. She waved Claire over, saying, "Come." Like her sacrifices, she did this in a practiced way, as if a lifetime of experience and repetition guided her. Claire obeyed.

They faced one another. Close up, Claire could smell the old lady smell on her. It must be the same across the face of the Earth. *Will I smell like that someday?* The old woman leaned forward and kissed her softly on the mouth. Claire somehow knew to bow her head, and the woman put her hands on top of the patricia's head, on the gleaming hair, behind the golden filigree. The woman addressed the gathering of men and women, "The goddess blesses Florence, and Florence blesses the goddess." The crowd renewed their chant. The old woman let Claire go, leaving rabbit blood in her hair. Claire looked up at her.

The woman said, "You look hungry." She turned and stuck her hand right in the pyre and pulled out the rabbit that had had white fur. She handed it to the maiden and said, "Prepare it."

Claire looked around the crowd and absorbed their adoration and understood she didn't dare refuse what came next. She turned back to the old woman and the woman said, "You'll eat."

Claire ate.

# 14

## WE ARE NOT PIECES ON A GAMEBOARD

THEY BURST FROM Rusadir into sunlight. Two days they rode across the rich fields of Sasso-Indaco. The patricia hardly saw Ambrosius or Marcus.

She often rode in the seat of the cart with Taranto and Brindisi. She was getting accustomed to the company of soldiers. She enjoyed the attention of these hard men, enjoyed playing a tiny waif sandwiched between two giant brutes. Sometimes they told her war stories.

When she wanted solitude, she took her leave of them and lay on top of the palanquin, hidden by the golden waves, or feathers. She was seeking solitude from herself as well, from the branching maze of analysis which cluttered her reason and stole her enjoyment of things and made her feel empty and unreal. On top of her palanquin, she banished men and thoughts alike. Stretched out beneath the open sky, she absorbed sunlight like a plant.

From the start of the second day, she heard the cry of geese flying south. It was an unsettling, excited, sorrowful sound. The land was crowding up. They were approaching Florence.

# XXX

THE OLD KING'S Road bends suddenly in Altamira, correcting a northward defect. The view around the corner is blocked by tenements two and three storeys high. All you can see are yellow clay walls and dark irregular windows and washing, hanging out to dry. This is how the elephant snuck up on Claire. The king got a good laugh from it, and the queen, who was riding the elephant. Where they got an elephant, Claire could not imagine.

It was a great she-elephant with gilded tusks and patterns painted on her wrinkled hide. Her ears seemed to twitch in pleasure at the cheering of the crowd, and her vast eye smiled at the petals and the colored bits of paper they were throwing. The queen, a pale matron, rode in the jeweled tower, rising and falling with the gentle tread of her beast. A parade of well-carved chariots followed. These were not the stern warrior nobles. They were city dandies from Florence, come to greet the king.

The elephant-master lifted his hook and gently tapped his charge's lip, and the elephant halted her slow stride. Attendants scrambled up the ladders to the tower, throwing wide the door and helping down the matron. In the light, Claire saw her gown was hyacinth purple, but the weak shade, made from plants. By this means she understood the Florentines had no trade with those who lived by saltwater, or the queen would certainly have worn rich snail purple. As it happened, Claire was very good at purple. She could see the difference between mixed red and blue, and true violet. Few mortals have accomplished this, but no matter, it is a fairly useless skill.

Bitsy Boots ran to the queen's ladder, crying "Mama! Mama!," sounding even younger than he was. Claire thought, *Seeing our mother again returns to us the gestures of our childhood.* The insight was like a blow to the gut, and she missed her mother terribly. The queen reached the ground and picked up her boy, armor and toy sword and all, and spun him around, eyes closed, nose buried in his hair. She put him down and he wrapped his arms around her waist and leaned his head on her belly and said, "Mama, Mama, the war is over, King Papa ended the war." She tussled his hair and tears spilled down her cheeks. Ambrosius approached her. She touched his lined cheek and his dry white hair. She said, with loving dismay, "My king, you've grown old." He wrapped her in his arms, with the prince buried between them.

For a long moment they were a family alone. Then their solitude dissolved, and the king took the queen's hand and led her a little ways to where the beautiful patricia stood back. Ambrosius said:

"My love, I present you Claire. The titles she claims are these – patricia of Zanzibar, and the last daughter Reason bore. The title we give her is – Sower of Peace.

"O Claire, I introduce to you my beloved wife, queen of queens, soft Antonella, scion of Constantine, mother of mighty Florence, vessel of kings."

Claire made another bow from her class in etiquette, deep and modest. With her head still bended, she kissed the proffered hand, feeling it was soft and warm and thick, so that the knucklebones lay in little furrows of the flesh. There was a lapis ring on the fourth finger, and a faint perfume of lilac on the smooth skin. The hand rose and touched the chin of Claire, and gently raised it, and Claire looked up, and a quiet bloomed from the queen while they looked at one another.

Claire thought, *You are nothing like my mother. Your hands are nothing like my mother's hands.* Her mother had big hard hands, with fingers like pillars of stone. "Strangler's hands," the baker used to joke, and her mother would look ruefully at them, and Claire would get a sickening thrill, thinking of all the things her mother did when she was young and the war was on.

One summer a tree was dying in the olive orchard out back. Claire's mother dug a little ditch around it, baring the top of the root ball. Then she made a sling of rope and wrapped it round the trunk. The trees were too closely planted to get an ox between them, so Claire's mother bundled the ropes over her own shoulder, and grasped the ends in her mighty hands. She set her feet and pulled on the twisted olive tree, its old wood hard as iron. Claire saw the muscles bulge in her mother's long golden arms. Sweat darkened her thick lion's mane of hair. She grinned at Claire with her blinding teeth and pale gray eyes. Then there was a cracking in the earth, and the tree leapt from the ground, and Claire's mother went rolling. Little Claire stood over her where she lay gasping and laughing in the black soil, and thought there was no woman in the world more beautiful than her mother. She was half a man in aspect, and liked to say Claire must have got her girlish ways from her father.

Antonella was nothing like Claire's mother, except in this: she was overwhelmingly a mother. Therefore lonely Claire's heart went out to her, and she took a step toward that understanding only infants and adults have, that things which look different are often the same.

Antonella smiled at Claire, softly, like her elephant. Claire glimpsed worlds more to the queen. She blinked, and Antonella's quiet folded away, and the cheering throng and autumn petals on the breeze closed in.

## XXX

A FESTIVE CROWD milled in the streets. Claire got the itch for wandering alone. So she asked Taranto to fetch her cashews, and Brindisi mead. Hard men they might be, but they were trusting stable hands beneath it all. While their backs were turned, Claire gave them the slip again.

Walking along, remarked and unremarked, she observed the swarming dandies. It slowly dawned on her their number, finery and simpering told the king how his interest went in the city. She had started the morning confident where her allies stood, but now unease fluttered in her passions.

Meeting up with the king, she said, "My lord, how long since you were home in Florence?"

He smiled, pleased at her understanding, and said, "It's been three years. Worry you no worries today, dear Claire. This is perhaps our last day of peace."

"Our last?"

"The war is over, but when we reach Florence, then the war inside the nation begins. What the sides are, we cannot yet say. But sure it will be, now you've killed the war with Genova." And he grinned a predatory grin at her and made his way among the throng.

Claire stood where he left her. She looked after him, then when she lost his back, she stared down at the earthen street. She reasoned on his words and grin. She told herself this little story: that the king grinned his grin because he knew how to war. And in fact, this was his strength, that he was a warrior. But his eagerness to war betrayed a corresponding deficit, which lay in his ability to govern. And this was the first Claire understood that Ambrosius was a fine warrior, but a weak king.

The unease in her passions beat against her ribs. She calmed her unease, and as she calmed herself, her eye turned from the inward to the outward. She was still looking down at the dirt. Now she realized that some of the footprints in it had a mark in them, of a circle inscribed in a square, like the sandals of her enemy, that first night in Andropolis. These ensymboled footprints magnetized her. She followed where they went; there was more than one set of them, all walking together.

Looking only at the ground, she came to the faction that wore the sandals, without thinking to approach them stealthily. She saw a flock of sandaled feet, with long dirty toenails, and amongst them one pair of feet shod in a soldier's leather boots. Sweeping her gaze up, she saw all the sandaled feet belonged to men in black robes, and they all fluttered around the man wearing boots – the one who had lost his sandals. His robe was red, embroidered with a bronze serpent on each side. He held a bronze bowl. He wore a red miter with a shining bronze disk upon the brow.

She'd found him at last. Her magnetizing attached to him. She was compelled to him. She stared frankly at him in broad daylight.

His face was bounded all around by his miter, so that she saw neither hair nor brow nor neck, but instead a stony face as lonely as the moon. The moon bears scars from age on age of pummeling by rocks; so too this man's face was pocked and lined. His fleshless face reminded Claire of some old women lunatics she had once seen, when she was visiting a friend in hospital. His eyes were lunatic as well. Pale mixed purple, they were pitted here and there with dark craters, and the tiny pupils were like rotating locks of tremendous ingenuity, which constantly changed their shape to deny every key. Claire looked into these cold alien eyes, and they looked into hers.

She whispered, "I know your name." The ichneumon heard, and slightly bowed his chin. Before she could poke this wasp's nest any more, she found Marcus Irenaeus Diophantus at her right hand. He spoke quietly, but he made himself heard. He said, "This man is Flavius Papellus Reburrus, wanderer, intermediary, bearer of light, His Majesty's Own Ichneumon."

A high priest then.

Claire put her hands together in front of her, and dropped her right foot back to make a little bow, eyes closed, throat bare. Then she opened up her eyes again and faced the ichneumon.

Reburrus slipped his bronze bowl into a fold in his robes, and took her white hand in his reddened hands. She felt the scaly rashes on his palms. His hands were feverishly hot. He kissed her hand and said to her, in a frightening, twanging voice, "O Claire, Sower of Peace, how good it is to see for myself, to see, indeed, and smell and touch, that alien who has discovered to us the undiscoverable peace." The skin on her cheeks went tight at his lie. *We've met before, but you don't know that I know. I can unfold time and you cannot.*

He kissed her hand.

She held his bright locked gaze and whispered again, so softly it wasn't clear she spoke at all. But she knew the ichneumon would hear her, and he did. *I know your name: Enemy.* Reburrus absently scratched the bridge of his nose. She was magnetized to him, and he to her. She saw fingers scrabbling for throats, and teeth filmed red. Under the fearful glare of the ichneumon, she became what the madman foretold, an eater of the living.

Then Marcus took her hand and even though she didn't know what to say to him, his touch was like a sweetness on her tongue.

## XXX

MARCUS STEERED THE patricia from the nest of ichts. His arms shivered and grew weak, and he realized he'd been ready to fight. He led Claire through the crowd, through shafts of sunlight sharp-edged in the floating dust. He found a lonely staircase to a higher part of the city, the yellow walls of buildings on either side glowing in reflected sunlight. He sat them in this narrow place, and got out clementines and leathered veal for them to eat.

They sat a while, staring out into the slice of Altamira they could see between the walls. He sensed Claire's stiff shoulders softening. He looked over and saw the bunched muscles on her naked shoulderblade had settled. He looked back out into the street. A troupe of children bundled by, shouting and throwing litter on the gravel walk.

Claire said, "I love cities, Marcus. I've only seen a few, but I think each had a soul to it, a glorious soul. Each city seems to me a world with its own heart, beating, and every limb alive." He experienced a startlement of recognition. He turned to her and said, "I've got to know a few, and loved them just as you describe, as living worlds. Soon you will see my Florence."

She smiled at him, but the corners of her mouth turned down. She said, "I did quite a stupid thing back there, didn't I?"

He surprised himself and laughed, as one laughs after dodging a blade: relieved, aghast.

He told her about the religion of the Florentines, about Pantokrator and his society of gods, and the ichts who guard the virtue of the state, and the ichneumonoi who bridge men and gods. Her told her about the legendary visions of Reburrus, and how all Florence trembled at his anger. He started to tell her about the Correction of the Weights and Measures, but the episode was so horrific that it shamed him to repeat it, and he stopped. Instead he told her about the Icht Most Capable Iacomo Antivola, the only man to tame the fury of His Majesty's Own Ichneumon. He didn't mention Reburrus's attempt to butcher her, that first night in Andropolis. He wanted to warn her, not terrify her.

Claire said, "The last night in the forest, I came upon an ancient altar, and there were men and women there, making sacrifices to the gods of Florence."

Marcus said, "Was it a man or woman who led them?"

She said, "A fine old woman and her maidens seemed to be in charge."

He said, "This was the cult of the Maker of Hands. The religion of the poor people. The ichneumonoi and ichts are all men."

She stole herself and finally she blurted, "They named me in the number of their gods."

He paused a long time. Finally he said, "Were they right?"

She looked at him. He felt a distance stretch between them, a distance of the soul. *What is she?*

He said, "Did you eat of the sacrifice?"

She blushed and looked down.

Dismayed, he said, "O Claire, these are your people now. The ichneumonoi tolerate them as long as they stay faithful to the gods of Florence. Reburrus may name you *a* god, but not *his* god. He will persecute these people if he learns of their impiety. Do you understand?"

She heaved a sigh. She seemed so childish to him then.

He said, "War, peace, faith, heresy. We are not pieces on a gameboard, Claire. Real men and women stand to die."

Still looking at her lap, she firmed her mouth. She muttered, "I understand."

She looked up to him then, strangely, with her cool gray eyes. His were just as pale, but blue.

She said, "I'm going to steal something that isn't mine to take." He knit his brow. She leaned forward and kissed his cheek. It set his heart trotting, as if he'd run up a steep hill.

She said miserably, "I don't own anything."

When he saw Taranto and Brindisi later on, he berated his Stonebreakers for letting the patricia out of their sight.

## XXX

CLAIRE HID HERSELF in her gold palanquin and glared at the thirty-two clock. She listed to herself her failures and missteps. Marcus was right: she was failing because these people and their land were still unreal to her. She considered her mentor, Professor Berthelot Denys Vazhin.

Her craving for her father drove her to metaphysics, and metaphysics led her to Vazhin. She'd worshipped him from the beginning. It seemed to the young patricia that this dignified academic knew everything. It was only as she studied with him that she understood herself a pilgrim, and him her guide, and their way a path toward a beach. Each grain of sand, each shell, each dune-grass was some prize of knowledge won by mortals. But they reached the beach at last, and Vazhin spread his arm over the sea. The sea was the great mystery of things, and mortals standing only at its shore. Young Claire had raged against this sea a while. When she was ready to perceive wisdom, she saw the spread arm of Vazhin was benediction: *he blessed ignorance*. From that day, Claire began to be a scholar.

When she became a scholar – a perpetual student – she set down the world. She let go the agony of her mother's generation, the generation of the civil war. A day after her mother had torn the dying olive tree from the earth, Reason had fallen into one of her black moods. She couldn't leave her shuttered bedroom for a week. When Claire had tried to feed her, she'd screamed at her terrified daughter. Her episodes had shadowed Claire's childhood. Now, accepting Vazhin's benediction, Claire shook free of the damaged side of her mother. She could think of love and beauty when she thought of her, without also thinking of terror and grief. A detached brilliance, Claire devoted herself to learning.

She considered Marcus again, who turned out to see cities as she did, as world-beasts, fascinating, terrible, and lovable. She tried to imagine his Florence, but she couldn't, quite.

*Florence is real. Marcus is real. King Ambrosius is real. I need to believe in them, or I'll die here.*

# 15

## TRAITOR'S GATE

THE ACTUAL FACT of Florence, however, tested her resolve. She nearly ruined the king's triumphal entry into the city. This is what happened.

On the day after they left Altamira, in the later afternoon, their company came in sight of the city walls. Everybody who'd mentioned them to Claire had called them "the impenetrable walls, tall as a mountain and wide as a plain." She took this for a fanciful epithet. It turned out it wasn't far from the truth. At a distance, they were confusing to look upon. As her cart approached, she made out three walls, forming concentric rings around the city. The outermost was shortest, and it was four men tall. Each wall had its own towers. It was an astonishing great set of walls, much more complicated than the striped walls of Zanzibar.

A giant eastern gate was open. A crowd of Florentines streamed out of it. The king's army and the camp followers and the city dandies and the Thousand slowed and spread along the plain. The king advanced on his horse, and the queen on her elephant, and Claire atop her gold palanquin.

At some point she was able to make out details on the outer wall, the short one, to each side of the gate. There were big hooks there and they weren't empty. She climbed down from the gold palanquin, then from the cart, and stood on the plain trembling, her hands on her cheeks and her mouth open in horror.

The cheering crowd drew near to her and she said: "That man there, hanging from a hook, with his hands and feet cut off, why did they do these awful things to him?"

- He walked away from the fifth morax many years ago and fought for the Genovans, and we only just now caught him.

She said: "And this one with his head missing, what had he done?"

- That one sold the plans for the city walls to Genova.

- How could anyone possibly know that?

- Many people said so.

- Did he deny it?

- All men deny their guilt.

Somebody else remarked:

- I heard he was innocent.

But the first one vehemently said:

- Not at all, there were witnesses.

The second one shot back:

- Florentines?

And the first:

- Genovans.

Claire said: "And this one here, with the stain running down the wall between his legs, what crime did he commit?"

- He was a poisoner.

- And who proved it?

- His customers, they got sick from the pies.

Claire stood there shaking, until somebody said:

- He didn't do it.

And another said:

- No, it seems clear he didn't do it.

Claire said: "That one with his guts torn out and his hands sewn together over his empty belly, what did he do?"

- Oh that one was a speculator caught hoarding wheat and barley.

- Was he guilty?

- Yes, he admitted it himself.

- Practically pinned himself to the wall.

Claire stood in the violet shadow of the mighty city. At the base of the wall was mud, and in the mud were bones and scraps of cloth. A pair of dogs was grappling for a long bone they had pulled up from the mud beside the gate.

She said: "But *why*? Why is Florence chopping up her criminals and pinning them around the city gate?"

Somebody said:

- O Claire, this gate is Traitor's Gate. It faces Genova.

The horrendous scene was all at once replaced, and before Claire stood wise King Ambrosius. In a voice as cold as the city's violet shadow, he said to her, "Daughter of Zanzibar, this is the justice of Florence."

She said, "How, Ambrosius? How is this justice?"

He half-turned and gestured at the bodies, saying, "That one was an enemy of house Ambrosius. That one crossed the Constantines. Those two over there drew down the wrath of Valii, one of the ancient families."

She hissed, "This is how you settle *feuds*?"

He said, "Watch your mouth, girl, you're not thinking clearly –"

She interrupted, "Swear me you will end this savagery, or I won't go in your bloody city. I'll *walk* to Zanzibar before I'll treat with you. Barbarian." But she said it quietly, so that he was not humiliated before his people.

XXX

AMBROSIUS STARED MURDER at the patricia and considered his options. King Pindar would not take her death kindly. Maybe he should pack her off to Genova and let them deal with her. Or he could send the Thousand west right now, winter in the mountains be damned. Neither choice pleased him. Her insult stung. He wanted to punish her.

She stood there with her lip trembling and her jaw stuck out. She seemed more adult already than she had when she'd arrived. She made him wish his daughters had lived.

He breathed deeply, calming his temper. *She is like a madman. She cannot help but tell the truth.* As he breathed, his gaze broadened. He saw the sun still shone on those who stood a short ways off to either side of her, and the shadow of the wall was on her alone.

His heart hurt in his chest, as if a strong hand squeezed it.

It could not be the wall that cast this narrow shadow on the patricia. Only ai Ctesiphôn might cast it, and only if it were right now standing behind him, peering over the mighty wall. He dared not turn to see the fearful tower, that had come to welcome Claire to Florence.

Now a splintered square of sunlight started climbing the patricia. The sun, the other sun, was dropping past the window of ai Ctesiphôn. Its rays were splintering through the branches of the withered oak in its window, the tree of kings. Perhaps the bones of his brother Ælius Pellucidus lay at the foot of the tree. No mortal could reach the tower and climb it and reach the tree, and live.

The splintered sunlight sparkled on the golden bands of Claire's gown, and in the emerald on her fingernail. It crawled up her belly and her breast, and climbed her throat like flames, so that she was flickering and brilliant.

If Ambrosius had met her when she fell to dull Earth at Andropolis, the sight of her would have been familiar. But he wasn't there that day. Only the Thousand had already seen her in her guise as a womanly pillar of light. Therefore the Florentines stood back in fresh awe as the alien was greeted by the tower.

The sun rose to Claire's face, and her wide pupils nearly vanished, gray eyes blinded by ai Ctesiphôn, that glared at her above Traitor's Gate.

Ambrosius knew when he was facing powers greater than himself. Eyes still locked on the patricia, he raised his voice, so that the Florentines could hear him. He said, "We unpin the dead from Traitor's Gate. We make the pyre and burn up what remains of them. We set up a pension for the widows of the dead, and a fund for bringing up the orphans of the dead. As for those still languishing in gaol, we bring them speedily to trial. The innocent we free. The guilty we punish humbly.

"Traitor's Gate faces Genova. It is the gate of war. The war is done and peace is come. No more traitors will we pin at Traitor's Gate."

He turned his gaze and scanned the crowd and roared, "I am Florence!"

The crowd answered him, "Hail Florence! Hail Ambrosius!"

Then he looked at Claire and murmured, "That will cost me." The sun was fading from her face, and her blindness was clearing. She wavered and he caught her by the tops of her bare arms and held her up. She weakly said, "I know the chasm you have crossed for me, my lord." Then she closed her eyes and her brow wrinkled and her chin pocked, as if she were about to cry. He whispered, "What is it, Claire?" She breathed twice, then opened her eyes and looked at him and said, "By the time I get home, my mother won't recognize me." Her voice was high with grief.

He said, "You are too young to know what parents know –" She looked to him, desperate for consolation. He said, "We always recognize our children."

She blinked against her tears. He let go her arms. She stood herself upright and rubbed her cheeks and blew out a breath. She said, "I understand you face intestine war. By your side do I endure the coils of the serpent. I survive in you, or perish in you, as fate may decide."

He watched her walk shakily back to her cart. *I am helpless before her.* She climbed up to the seat and stood herself between Taranto and Brindisi. They gently supported her. She looked above Traitor's Gate, perplexed. He turned and looked; the tower was gone.

The procession started up again. The king entered Florence.

# PART III

# Florence: The Royal District

# 16

## BEFORE THE STORM

SHE BUILT THE baleful thirty-two clock on her own. She was a tinkerer and turned a corner of the kitchen into her workshop. She had the knack from her mother, who had set it aside early in her career. Her mother would cook, and she would tinker, and sometimes they'd trade places.

The morning of the storm, it was clear skies in Zanzibar, rich dark blue toward the desert, and hazy green-blue toward the sea. The dawn chill gave way early to the blazing heat of day. She checked the clock, hanging now inside the gold palanquin, and rode to the Aurillac.

Protected by locked gates, the Aurillac is a sidereal garden on the grounds of the Académie. Claire rode the palanquin because the garden is gigantic, and the hedges move, and she had to be at just the place, at just the time. If she was correct, Zanzibar would be passing through one node of the universal map, and her father through another. At the double transit, she'd be able to summon her father from the depths of the cosmos. Not his flesh, of course; only his soul. She'd built a life-sized doll for him to animate. It was made of gold and iron and it was wildly handsome, just like she remembered him. It had thick gold hair, and a flowing golden beard, and high broad cheekbones like her own. The eyes were colored glass, but they were shut. Her mother had smiled bitterly at the doll and said it looked as her father must have seemed to a tiny girl, before he left.

When the hour drew near, Claire sat the doll beside her in the palanquin. At the gate, she met up with the startling crowd of academics, city officials, and friends. Berthelot Denys Vazhin pleaded with her one more time, not to challenge the garden. But this was her thesis. Ridiculously self-serving as it was, it tested profound claims. The committee had approved the math, and Vazhin could no longer stop her. She stood aside and traded quiet words with her mother Reason. Then she rode into the Aurillac.

She glided along the surge and roll of the sidereal garden. The hedges moved as the universe moved. To enter them was to invite disappearance. All branches of knowledge have their own aesthetics, and Claire was sensitive to the aesthetics of her branch. It wasn't her facility with numbers that protected her, but her intuition of their nature. She was the one who felt, and then proved, that her father could be summoned. Her childhood ache at bedtime never went away, wishing her father would kiss her goodnight one more time.

When she reached the place, she brought the gold palanquin to a halt. Opening its door, a sound of wind rushed over her. She hadn't heard it from inside the palanquin. She paused. She should have heard it. The palanquin didn't muffle sound that much.

She climbed down and squinted along the path. The hedges rustled urgently. She smelled thunder. A storm was coming. Nothing in the Aurillac could be taken for granted. She hauled out the doll, and set it on the spot, one eye on the strange weather in the hedge maze. Leaves scattered past her.

She was in the right place, at the right time. Communication would only last an instant, but she only needed an instant. Back in the palanquin, the thirty-two clock ticked down to zero.

When it chimed, Claire unfolded the present.

Time around her opened like a rose. The hedges' rustling slowed to lake bed undulations, then their motion was extinguished. Even an ordinary Zanzibari would have flowed to stillness.

But not Claire. The tinkerer had tinkered herself. Every day for many years, she'd meditated on time. Finally, she learned to see time directly. Now she continued awake into the expanded present.

The sky turned dull and flat. The doll faced her on the path between the hedges, a dark shape in the dimming light. Behind it, the storm had formed a wicked funnel, spinning leaves and dust from Zanzibar to heaven. She'd have to flee before she set time loose again. But for now, she had eyes only for her father's effigy.

The iron eyelids of the doll sprang open, and its glass eyes stared at her. It was *him*. He *saw* her. She gasped, "Daddy," and her eyes filled with tears. The doll raised its hand, and opened its mouth –

Then it vanished.

The storm's advancing funnel swallowed her father. Before grief, before terror, she felt only confusion. All physical processes stopped in hyperbolic time. Only motions caused by consciousness could persist. *What was this storm?*

She collected herself, and retreated from the slowly spinning funnel, backing up against the gold palanquin. Running her calf along its cold smooth rail, she found the stair. She raised herself into the carriage and shut the circular door. Silence. She turned the palanquin to escape the storm, and still it came through time toward her, and she felt it lift her, she felt her heavy palanquin lurch free of the ground. She rose as if through honey, and silent lightning flashed lazily before her eye. She screamed as the storm pressed its snout to her window, and the instant collapsed. The clock completed its chime, then thunder deafened her. Water sprayed across the windows, and the storm whirled her away she knew not where.

XXX

THUS FROM ZANZIBAR she fell. She knew history from books. Now she was inside it. She fought against despair at being trapped at Midnight. She relished being thought a god, but what good did it do her in the blood-drenched basement of civilization? What good could she do anyone? They called her the Sower of Peace, but what was peace to the hands that wrought Traitor's Gate?

She entered the city held up between two brawny soldiers, at the front of the giant cart. Evening was falling and they'd lit torches along the route. There was something in the torchwood to give them a sparking white flame. *I must look pale as death.* The Florentines applauded and leered till they got close enough to read her face. Then they shrank back from her, and she saw it was fear that moved them. *I hope I'm the trophy you were looking for, Ambrosius.*

The city unrolled in a stinking, smoky pageant of stone and brick and wood; now a ripple of light off a river, now a glimpse of long avenues and distant walls; everywhere a noisy crowd, throwing herbs and coins. Her head throbbed and sometimes she swayed. Taranto and Brindisi cared for her.

Progressively she recovered herself and began to hear the words they were singing:

Home is the warrior, home is the father
Home from the mountain, home from the plain
He brings his far-flung spear
He brings his blood-stained sword
He brings his shield unbroken
He covers the nation in gold
He covers the nation in glory
Home is the warrior, home from the field.

She and her palanquin were the front of the procession. *Just like a captured enemy queen. Go ahead, stare. I belong to him, the one who rules over you.* She turned back to look at Ambrosius. He rode atop a tower-chariot behind four excellent stallions. His gaze immediately turned from the crowd to her. She felt a pang of guilt; he shot her such a look of love that she had to turn away. It was the way she wished to see her father look at her.

The whole route was lit up like day. Trumpets and bells and kitharas blasted and jangled, and sometimes the cheering of the crowd took on a pulsing rhythm, like the waves of the sea crashing ashore on a rising tide.

Her strength returning, Taranto and Brindisi let her stand on her own. She waved to the passing crowds and smiled, and their cheering and screaming took on an aspect of madness in its vigor. Taranto shouted to her that they were processing down the Via Floribus, then back up Lata Via, to end atop the Epicondyle.

Claire studied the texture of the crowd's mood. Anyone who has performed on the stage understands how closely a player can read the feelings of his audience. Thus Claire, reader of men, read the Florentines: she read their joy to see their king, and their fascination with her own person, and their celebration of the peace. But she also read their mistrust of the war's end, and the privations they had suffered, and the anger they harbored for their absent king. This was a city that could go one way or another, on an omen, on a chance killing, on a rumor.

A storm was gathering in Florence.

## XXX

The Epicondyle was a hill, and they took a winding path up it. The horses strained and slowed as they hauled the gold palanquin. Claire looked back from a curve in the path, curious about the procession behind the king and queen. As the she-elephant moved from blocking her view, Claire was shocked at what was revealed: thousands of soldiers in neat formation, filling broad Lata Via. The king's Triumph was the march of an army. Had they gathered so many on the long road from Andropolis?

Standard-bearers among the soldiers held up standards of their houses. Claire saw the sign of the yellow rooster, and of the grappling lions, and of the hedgehog with his trident, and of the murd'rous snail; she saw those who march under the sign of the green mermaid, and of the scarlet rhinoceros, and of Polpo the Mysterious, and of the spiny urchin. She did not see the tree of crows and apples, but she saw the legends of the houses represented by stones and blackbirds, and by an army of pelicans, and by a beehive, and by square blocks stacked one atop the other. She saw the sign of the circle, and the sign of the cross, and the sign of the crooked cross, and the sign of the triangle with three sides all the same. The Académie of Zanzibar had trained Claire in the skill of total memory. Each banner that she saw, she inscribed upon a tablet in the palace of her memory, and she could trust she never would forget it.

She turned back ahead. The bad smells of the city - rotten fruit and sweat and grease, hot piss, damp shit, boggy water, dead rats - cleared up here. There was just the woodsmoke of the torches and a hint of juniper on the night breeze. She squinted through the haze at the white building at the summit of the Epicondyle. As it came closer, she made out long wings either side of a projecting center. The center was two angled walls that came to a point. What this was, she couldn't say, until the angled walls swung wide, each pushed by a team of white-robed men. She saw a long room with a giant golden statue shimmering in firelight at the end, of a bearded man carrying a sling and sling-stones. More men came out from the room onto the porch, all white-robed except the one at the center, who wore red.

The building was a temple.

Taranto and Brindisi drew up the team of eight and they snorted to a halt. The king in his chariot and the queen on her elephant came behind, and the soldiers after, stopping in their places on the winding path. It seemed to Claire the entire city fell silent. She heard crickets in the hill grass. Bruised of heart, exhausted, overwhelmed, she knew what to do and how to do it. Taking the hand of Taranto, she gracefully climbed down from the cart she rode. She spared a glance for her beautiful palanquin, a little crumpled on the left. She waited on the king, and together they approached the knot of priests with Reburrus at their center.

Reburrus intoned, "Hail Pantokrator! Hail Ambrosius! Hail Florence!" And Claire and the king, and all those behind them, repeated, "Hail Pantokrator! Hail Ambrosius! Hail Florence!"

Reburrus did what she anticipated, improvising a greeting to her that dripped with implication: "The gods of Florence welcome the mortal from Zanzibar." In her overtaxed reverie, she knew exactly what to say. She answered, "The gods of Zanzibar acknowledge the greetings of the Pantokrator and his god-friends." She saw the ichneumon suppress a reflex to step back from her.

There were sacrifices, led by men, to gods she didn't know. Then there was a feast. It ended not long before dawn.

# 17

## THE ART OF ADORNMENT

THE THOUSAND SETTLED themselves on the plain called Campus Iucundum, just northwest of the city walls. While they were setting up their camp, Marcus sent a runner to the castle. The runner carried orders for construction of a great warehouse, to collect and store supplies for Claire's expedition. Marcus was testing the crown's commitment to the project; Cleon Constantine, the king's councilor for finance, controlled the budget, and he was known for his tight fist.

When Marcus's runner came back, he had with him a fancy-looking fellow. Marcus sized him up. He was about fifteen years Marcus's senior. He had a long sword on his hip and tight clean clothes that sparkled with metal clasps. He held his back so straight that Marcus looked at the bottom of his chin, though the two men were the same height. His jaw was clean-shaven and he had a dark thick mustache, waxed to points.

This man was not here to make a warehouse.

Marcus drawled, "Can I help you?"

The man extended a stiff hand and said, "I am the *magister equitum* of Florence." His diction was crisp and haughty. He clicked at the ends of his words. *The master of the horse.* Marcus had heard of the office, but wasn't sure exactly what it did. He clasped the magister's extended hand and said, "Marcus Irenaeus Diophantus." The magister nodded gravely. He answered, "Temet Nosce Ambrosius." Then Marcus saw it – the prominent brow, the harsh angles of the cheekbones. "You're a cousin of the king?" The magister briefly inclined his head. Every movement precise.

Silence fell again. The magister seemed content to stare at Marcus, nose wrinkled in a permanent sneer. Marcus's fingers flew through the pickpocket's warmup. The magister's gaze shot to the motion. Marcus hated to give away his anxiety like that. The corners of the magister's eyes wrinkled – a smile. He clicked, "You're from Serapetine Hill." *You're a street thief.*

Marcus clenched his teeth. *And from the stick up your ass, you must be from Linthicum Heights.* He said, "I am."

The magister said, "I was raised in Linthicum Heights." Marcus said, "You have the accent." Temet nodded crisply again.

Finally Marcus repeated, "Can I help you?"

Temet said, "Tell me what makes a nobleman."

Marcus frowned and said, "I'm sure you'd know better than I."

Temet said, "Blood and deeds."

Marcus found this fairly moving, and said, "I beg you will unfold this further for me."

The magister said, "The king ha' made us brothers, Diophantus. On our shoulders he rests the honor and the fate of Florence."

*Honor makes the king supple, but it makes you stiff as a wooden doll. Very strange.*

Marcus said, "I love my nation before myself."

Temet said, "This is the correct sentiment. Validate your blood with deeds."

Suddenly, heat flared in the eye of Temet Ambrosius. He stepped toward Marcus, and Marcus twisted, ready to fight. But the magister embraced him, wide flat ribs hard as stone. It was the fierce embrace of an older brother welcoming a younger one home.

He said, "Warrior noble, we shall live out our lives together."

Then, just as abruptly as he'd embraced him, Temet broke the embrace and stepped back. He gave a faint uptilt of his chin and said, "Your interest in a warehouse has been submitted to the treasury."

## XXX

ON THE CHAIR that faced the vanity, she smoothed down a white linen shawl stitched with that strange Florentine emblem, the shaded blue rectangle. She looked closely at it. Individual lines of thread, the space between them diminishing, crudely made a gradient from white at the bottom to blue at the top. It seemed like a lot of work for an effect ill-suited to needlework.

Her apartment was a nice one in the women's dormitory, high up in the younger castle. It had several rooms, but little light or air. The majordomo meant well and he went all out with it: rich curtains smothered the windows, chairs and half-couches crowded the floors, the bed was too big, and a flock of rugs and knickknacks looked ready to trap dust. As soon as Claire saw the place, she vowed to empty it.

She sat down on the shawl and drew the two half-coins of greeting from her robe. The mutilated portraits on the coins looked pathetic to her. She turned the half-coins over and over in her palm, clinking them against each other. The Florentine coin had the shaded rectangle on its back. The Genovan coin had a branching pattern that looked like a tree's branches or a leaf's veins. She put the half-coins on the tabletop of the vanity, beside all manner of perfumes and paints. There was a mirror of beaten silver, recently polished. Claire spotted the mirror as soon as they showed her in, but resisted looking in it till she'd slept. It would be her first view of herself since Zanzibar. Now she sat at the vanity, not looking at it. Her belly clenched.

Of beautiful women, they are two in kind. The one kind grows beautiful late. To her, beauty is an alien thing, forever startling. If misfortune stole her looks, she would not cease to be herself. The other kind is beautiful early. She grew up with her beauty, and it is not a thing she has, but what she is. Her beauty is like all things of nature: it has no interior. It merely exists.

Claire was of the latter type, that is inseparable from her beauty. In fact, being beautiful was one of the few ways the voracious student felt at ease and all one thing, united with herself.

Like all early beauties, she had a faint terror of looking at her image after time away from mirrors. She blushed and pressed her lips together. She leaned forward into a patch of daylight slipping past the curtains. She looked.

Immediately she slumped, relieved.

*I'm still me.*

She drew herself back up and examined all her parts, as carefully as a domestic choosing beef at market.

Her hair was still a gold nearly white. Her brow and cheek were still smooth and milky, her eye still clear and gray, and her teeth still good. When she raised her hand to brush away a hair, she saw her hand still pale, and the fingers long and tapering still, like candles. The ruby was still inlaid in its place on the fourth fingernail. She turned her face to one side then the other, and her gray eyes never left the image in the beaten silver. A cloud broke, and the daylight brightened. Light flooded the gray eyes of the patricia. She looked into the blackness of her tiny pupils. Calming herself, she went indoors from the world.

She climbed the vast inland. She crossed the place the bulrushes grow, nor did she suffer a single rush to touch her. She came to the little city of herself. She looked up to the square palace of her reason, where light blazed from a thousand windows. She passed through the garden of her passions, full of girlish butterflies and flowers. She shied from the circular palace of her memory, that stored the life she'd lived; it was filled with painful longing now. Outside the city of herself, she came to a particular hill. Atop the hill, there was a temple. In the temple was her soul.

Beside the temple was a second vanity, the inward vanity, which is dedicated not to being seen, but to seeing. Claire sat at the vanity and filled her eyes with coals and her ears with cotton and her mouth with sand. Then, hand on the temple wall, she approached the temple door. It opened only to a four-faced key. Claire alone had the key. She used it now to open up the door.

In despite of her protection, facing her soul nearly undid her. It was singing its single Word, that began before Claire and the world, and will go on forever. Her soul was what it ever was, a point of light, blinding her through coal and tears and flesh. She fell to her knees before her soul, hugging her shoulders, vomiting sand.

*I'm still me. I'm still me. I'm still me.*

## XXX

THE WOMEN'S DORMITORY was staffed with maids who went rounds room to room. A timid slip named Epida came by to tell her she was summoned to the great hall of the main castle opposite. This landscape of kings and queens and castles still delighted Claire and she fluttered with excitement.

Epida conducted her out of her apartment to a hallway, that was nearly dark, for it had only a little window on each end. In the hallway they met a page who didn't introduce himself. Eyes wide in the dimness, Claire saw he was hardly more than a child, like the maid. But she herself was hardly taller than either one of them, or much older. She followed the page down the hall. In the punctuated dimness, she formed impressions of stately passages and gilded decorations and paintings of adventures of antique heroes. She smelled wood dust and stone dust, mold and incense and boiling cabbage, jasmine and amaryllis, mouse droppings, and the urine of dogs and cats and men. Sometimes she heard voices and clangs, but she didn't see a soul. The castle was probably smaller than it seemed to her, because she didn't know where she was going. She mapped it in her reason as she went. They came at last to the outside, a colonnaded courtyard with trees in the middle.

They crossed the courtyard, and Claire got a moment with sun and rustling leaves. Then she entered the older castle, which was mainly a great hall.

High windows let daylight into the tremendous echoing room of stone. The hall was empty underneath the gaze of ancient kings and queens, depicted dimly on tapestries hung between enormous buttress piers. A faint breeze was cool and moist and there was mist near the ceiling.

A dark figure walked toward them from the far end of the hall. Claire could tell by the footfalls it was a woman in wood-soled shoes. The page slowed. Claire slowed behind him. The woman approached, and when she arrived she dismissed the page with a wave of the hand, and the boy gave a rude little flip of a turn and scampered off.

The woman frankly studied Claire, so Claire took her measure too. She was much taller than most of the Florentine women, and had little in the way of bust or hips. She wore a linen chiton and cloak, dark blue patterned with red. Like the queen, she wore a wimple, baring dark hair at the brow, parted in the middle. She had thick dark eyebrows and large dark eyes. Powder on her cheeks and long proud nose covered what appeared to be a sunburn. She held her mouth rigid like a scold, but her eyes were intelligent and sad. Her neck was very long.

Claire could not have said if this severe-looking woman was young or old, or pretty or plain.

The woman nodded and said, "I am Livia Faustina Varo; you may call me Livia in private, and Lady Varo in company." With a sweep of her arm she offered her hand to Claire.

Lady Varo's posture was stiffer than Claire's, and Claire adjusted hers to match it. The patricia echoed the lady's sweep of the arm, offering her hand in return. They clasped hands. Livia's palm was surprisingly rough, and Claire found herself envious of it. She said, "I am Claire."

Lady Varo tilted her head and said, "Say something else."

"I am Livia Faustina Varo; you may call me
Livia in private, and Lady Varo in company."

Claire knitted her brow and said, "I'm not sure I understand."

A smile lifted Lady Varo's entire face. She said, "It's true then."

Suddenly Claire understood. She smiled and said, "Yes, I'm not speaking Florentine."

Lady Varo shook her head. Claire watched her catch herself, patching over a look of wonder with a mask of skepticism. She said, "Daughter of Zanzibar, the king has summoned the warrior nobles to Florence. In two months' time, they and their families – the ancient families – will fill this hall. You will adorn House Ambrosius. I will instruct you in the art of adornment."

Claire blurted, "I don't think I should like to wear a wimple, if that's alright."

Lady Varo frowned at her. Claire explained, "You seem a noblewoman to me and you wear one, and the queen wears one as well." Lady Varo sneered, "The *queen*," but didn't elaborate. Instead she said, "No, Claire, anyone can see you are both well-born and foreign, there is no need to follow our way of dress."

Claire said, "I'm glad I seem well-born to you; I hope I bring credit on my family with my bearing."

Lady Varo said, "Yes, perhaps more credit than they deserve."

It was as if she slapped Claire. Claire's mouth dropped open and she said, "Wha –"

Lady Varo mirrored her an instant, mouth circled and brows raised, then composed her face and said, "You're well born but not well situated, I think. You're missing your father. Run off, has he? You walk like a woman's idea of a man, you get that from your angry mother, and what else are women angry about?"

Claire blanched.

Lady Varo went on, "Your mother brought her own name to the marriage, so she's kept it and raised you in it. She hasn't got a lot of money, though, and doesn't care for it. But you do, don't you?"

Claire knew her naked face was admitting everything. Lady Varo explained, "You've got the fine posture and gestures of your breeding, and yet the minute you meet me, you copy mine. You lack confidence in your inheritance. You want to ingratiate yourself among high people wherever you go."

Claire shot back, "So what if I do, you horrid woman?" Lady Varo grinned. Claire went on hotly, "I'm a third part of the world from home. I have nothing. I'll use what I can to get where I have to go."

Lady Varo said, "Excellent. We establish the stakes of your education in adornment. Do well, and Ambrosius may get you home. Fail, and he most likely dies."

Claire was startled again. Lady Varo ducked her chin, looking at her expectantly. Claire didn't trust her tongue to out-sharp this strange woman, so she said coldly, "Go on."

Lady Varo seemed pleased. She said, "Good. If you cannot speak well, speak little." Claire colored. Before she could answer, Lady Varo said, "Has anyone explained the red sword to you?" Claire grated, "I've heard it mentioned." Lady Varo said, "Briefly, this is the story. The kings of Florence have always gone into battle with a particular red sword –"

Claire made a point to interrupt her, "It's painted red?"

Lady Varo nodded her appreciation at Claire's move, and when she spoke again, her voice was a little kinder: "No, there's something in the metal, the blade itself is red."

Claire loudly said, "Do continue."

Lady Varo favored her with a look that was almost warm. She said, "King Ambrosius the Ninth – your King Ambrosius – has never had a chance to wield this sword. His older brother had it with him when he disappeared. Now this wouldn't matter much, except we warrior nobles are very superstitious, and a pack of wolves. Without the red sword to verify his claim, we've always shown a little doubt he belongs on the throne."

Claire said, "What has this got to do with me?"

Lady Varo said, "The sword *adorns* House Ambrosius."

Claire riddled it. Lady Varo nodded with her, saying, "You

see." Claire said, "He's got them all coming to Florence." Lady Varo said, "Indeed. He plans to use the peace to squeeze a declaration of allegiance from them." Claire said, "Has he really got reason to worry?"

Lady Varo got a pinched look for a second, like an old wound was hurting her. Claire thought, *You've got a keen eye and a quick wit, but you can't hide your emotions.* Lady Varo said, "He has reason."

Claire nodded without speaking. She let the silence drag, until her opponent was forced to speak. She said, "You will help him by adorning him. Perhaps he lacks a red sword, but he has a blonde patricia." She looked at Claire, and Claire read the ardor of her gaze. *She really worries for King Ambrosius.* Claire said, "I understand." Lady Varo's posture relaxed a fraction. She said, "From now to then, we will meet on occasion, and I will instruct you in history and manners."

Lady Varo was cordial now, but Claire perceived a danger to herself in leaving this woman's aggression unanswered. So she said, "Where is your husband, Lady Varo? Your palms are rough and you wear no ring. Where are your children?"

Lady Varo stared Claire right in the eye and said, "They are nowhere, nor ever will be." Claire said, "I don't understand." Lady Varo folded her hands over one another and said, "The family Varo has been sentenced to extinction. I am among the last to carry our name. We may not marry or sire or bear." She turned to go.

Claire hazarded a hand on the woman's arm. Lady Varo looked at it, then looked at Claire. Claire said, "I'm eager to like people. I'm eager to like you." Lady Varo twitched her shoulder, shaking off Claire's hand. She said, "I am not eager to be liked." Claire made a hurt little moue. Lady Varo looked at her in disgust and said, "Earn my respect."

She started off the way Claire had come, toward the colonnade exit of the great hall.

Claire stood where she was. When Lady Varo was already far down the hall, Claire petulantly shouted, "I'm the Sower of Peace!"

The dark-robed noblewoman stopped and turned back and shouted, "Smartly done! Always announce yourself to the king! He's waiting for you at the end of the hall!"

Then Livia Faustina Varo continued on her way.

# 18

## THE QUEEN'S HOUSE

WHEN AMBROSIUS WAS able to control his laughter, he gasped, "Leaves a mark, doesn't she?"

Claire said, "Have I angered you, my lord? Are you punishing me?"

Ambrosius managed to get out, "Not at all."

Claire said, "Then perhaps I've angered her somehow."

Ambrosius started laughing again and said, "She does that to everybody."

Claire said, "I'm not sure I understand why you set her to meet me."

Ambrosius pulled himself together and said, "It's – it's important for a guest of Florence to understand her. There is perhaps no more sincere partisan of Florentine virtue than Livia."

Claire bared her teeth. At her loom, the queen raised an amused eyebrow. Claire noticed and said to her, "She doesn't fancy you either. What could she possibly have against you?" Antonella combed down a thread and said, "I'm not of an ancient family." Claire's eyes widened and she said, "I knew that but I forgot."

Antonella smiled at her a little more affectionately than Claire expected. *I must not forget I'm high born and she isn't. They care about that here.* Antonella searched around and picked up a spool of yellow yarn. She casually said, "I'm a dirty Constantine." Suddenly no one was laughing.

The king stood and went to the queen and caught her hand, trapping the spool in her grip. He kissed the back of her hand, eyes shut. It went on so long the tension dissipated.

He let her go and opened his eyes and said, "It's good to be home." Antonella said nothing, but she smiled to herself, winding the yellow yarn onto a shuttle.

They were in a house at the far end of the great hall. From the outside, it was a hulk of dark wood with a few pale windows in it. When Claire had opened the door, she'd found a room with heavy walls of polished wood and its own low ceiling. The windowpanes were parchment and let a bony light; the Florentines did not have glass. The room's back wall was the stony wall of the great hall, most of it a fireplace. Just now the fireplace held only enough fire to heat the little room. Rugs covered the stone floor, tapestry portraits of Ambrosius and Domenico hung on the walls, and several chairs were heaped up with pillows. The queen sat by her little upright loom weaving a fresh portrait, spools of colored yarn all around her. The king had a comfortable chair by the fire, and the prince arranged little wooden soldiers in formation on the floor. It felt so much a home Claire had a pang when she entered it.

Now she considered the place again: the Constantines were prosperous merchants of some sort. Antonella made this house on her model of right living and kept it ready for her absent men. By the standards of royalty, she supposed it was quite mean.

Claire said, "Whence this sentence of extinction on Lady Varo and her family?"

Ambrosius and Antonella traded a glance. Ambrosius said, "I take it you've gathered two of the marks against my reign: the missing red sword, and the missing elder brother. Varo has had its eye on the throne for generations. Not long after I took the throne, Livia's uncle Catiline made his play. He put assassins inside the castle and marched an army on Florence."

Bitsy Boots, his toy soldiers abandoned, breathlessly said, "What happened then?"

Ambrosius smiled at his son and said, "The assassins were discovered. I threw one out the north tower myself. As for the army, Catiline wasn't much for planning war. He should have waited on a market day when the city gates are open. His army couldn't best the impenetrable walls."

The boy glowed with pride in his father. Ambrosius turned back to Claire and said, "The sentence was extinction of the family name."

Claire said, "And *this* is the woman you give free movement in your house?"

Antonella leveled a pointed look on Ambrosius. The king said to Claire, "What means do you think we use to enforce the extinction?"

Claire said, "I don't know."

Ambrosius said, "None."

Claire frowned and said, "None?"

Ambrosius said, "None at all. They're free to marry and have children if they wish. The children wouldn't carry the name Varo, but there's nothing forcing any Varo to live lonely and barren, and in fact, many of them do not."

Claire said, "But not Livia."

Ambrosius encouraged her, "Not Livia."

Claire said, "I think I understand, but confirm it for me."

Ambrosius said, "The virtue of the ancient houses is stern and cold. Nation before family, family before self. No Florentine has greater virtue than our Livia. The one Varo I would like to see make babies, and she's married to Florence. That, Claire, is why I keep her around, to remind me and my court what we aspire to. I'd put a blade in her hand and sleep like a lamb."

Antonella rolled her eyes. Claire said, "Your opinion?"

The queen didn't answer right away. She shedded the warp ahead of her shuttle and Claire perceived the labor of her hands helped her think. Finally Antonella said, "Proteros Kai Hysteros and the other founders were hard men, brave and resourceful, and they did what it took to get themselves a nation. It was poets and philosophers who made up all these so-called virtues afterward. Force of will is a living thing. Virtue is a dead thing. Livia worships the dead. She's got the charm of spoiled milk and the temper of a viper. I will concede, however, that she's no assassin. And if that's all it takes to find a place in the castle, then I can lodge no objection to her residence here."

Ambrosius sighed. The queen glanced at him, then completed her line of weft. The shuttle came free of the loom.

Claire asked, "Why are her palms rough?"

Antonella brightened up and said, "That's the one thing I like about her. She sneaks out and does a little smithing."

Claire said, "*Smithing?*"

Antonella said, "She's prone to melancholy. Swinging the hammer balances her humors." She held up the shuttle. "I like to see a woman with a craft." She smiled. "If you're nice to her, maybe she'll make you a horseshoe."

## XXX

THEY SENT ORDERS round the kitchen for their lunch, and Florence found out what Claire preferred to eat. While they waited, they played a selection of those insipid games that noblemen play at court: rustler on the Landsman's Deck, and a fancy version of knucklebone, and chain-of-beads, and Temperance. Given all the time involved, Claire deduced the king had some purpose here apart from hospitality. She waited for him to introduce his subject.

Lunch arrived. The king and queen said a prayer to Myneia, their goddess of the hearth, a daughter of Pantokrator and Reialia. Thus even the descent of gods breeds mediocrity: Chaos begets

Time, Time begets Pantokrator, and Pantokrator, slaying his ancestors, settles down and begets gods of gadgets and hearths, who beget, no doubt, gods of twigs and squirrels.

Claire ate the food she had desired of the kitchen, being the lighter things of the world that were in season in Florence then: dishes of cooked apples and beets and raisins, and clear sauces drizzled on salted trouts, and fresh water, that never goes out of season. She was always hungry and always grateful for food. She didn't admit to the Florentines it would not have starved her to eat nothing at all, should she be favored now and then with a sip of fresh water.

The only thing the meal lacked was quinces. The kitchen didn't have any.

## XXX

WHEN LUNCH WAS done, the king sat down in his chair and stared into the fire. The queen patted the grease from her hands and settled herself back at her loom. Bitsy Boots gathered his soldiers in a stripe on a rug. He split them in two facing groups, with a hollow square of soldiers in the middle, facing outward. When he got done, he said, "Auntie Claire, is this how it was on the bridge?" Claire said, "The Thousand stood in a circle." Bitsy Boots rearranged the square of soldiers. He said, "What shall I use for the gold pala – pal –" Claire said, "Palanquin," and fetched out the half-coins of greeting from her gown. She glanced at the king for permission, then handed them to the boy. Bitsy Boots, delighted, said, "Palanquin," and set the half-coins clinking in the center of the Thousand.

The king stood and began to pace. He winced now and then with a spasm in his back. When he came near the queen, he would set his hand on her shoulder, or pick up a peg or a spool and put it down again. Finally he spoke.

He said, "O Claire, it is true that we'll do everything to get you home. But before you set yourself upon it, we beg you consider our proposal." Claire noticed the queen tuck her shuttle in the warp and clasp her hands on her knee.

Ambrosius went on, "Instead of chasing dreams across a third part of the world, you could make a home in Florence. You have saved our nation from ruinous war. You could further weave your fate with ours." He looked at Bitsy Boots, entranced by the Genovan half-coin. He looked at Claire, and she understood, and turned white. He said, "It will not be so many years before he's of age. Join your house with house Ambrosius. Inherit the purple. Bear kings." Claire's glance shot to Antonella. The warm queen's eyes crinkled at the outer edges.

Claire stood and walked to the king and knelt. Bitsy Boots sensed drama afoot and put down the half-coin and paid attention. On her knees, Claire clasped her hands and put her brow on her thumbs. Head bowed, eyes shut, she spoke. She said, "Under the ancient trees of Rusadir, I faced the Thousand and swore myself to Florence. I swear again eternal loyalty." She looked up to him, eyes bright with tears. Her voice trembled and she said, "If I cannot get me home to Zanzibar, I will die. I will not be put out. I will not be aggrieved. I will die. The children of Zanzibar must come home again, or die. Therefore, though I would, I may not, accept the crowning honor that you offer me. My lord, I would die."

Bitsy Boots began to cry and said, "King Papa, is Auntie Claire going to die?" The king squatted and the boy ran to his embrace and Ambrosius patted his head and said, "She will not die."

Relief filled Claire. She put her fingertips to the rug before her and pressed herself to standing. The king lifted the prince and said, "Oh! You're getting heavy, Domenico." The boy's shoulders shook as he calmed, face still buried in his father's shoulder. The king sat in his chair, situating Bitsy Boots on his lap. Bitsy Boots turned and looked at Claire, wiping his eyes, and smiled shyly.

Ambrosius looked at her over the top of his son's head and said, "If it is not to be him, it cannot be another. You understand? If the Sower of Peace used her time in Florence to make a child with, for instance, the Florentine general of her army, the people might acknowledge that child's claim on the throne. I will not permit it. The father, the mother, and the infant would face the ultimate sanction."

Claire's stomach turned to lead. She said quietly, "I understand."

Ambrosius said, "If you will not be queen, you must be Lady Varo. Marry Florence. Live in chastity."

In the bony light of the windows, Claire could see Bitsy Boots's ears turn red. He understood more than his father knew. He turned away from her.

Claire did not look at Antonella. She didn't want the king to think she appealed his order. She didn't want to see the hard look on Antonella's face.

XXX

A SMALL CROWD of professionals turned up on the Campus Iucundum. The surveyor and the architect greeted Marcus. Behind them came a Constantine warehouseman, and the quartermaster of the second morax, and the master of the city granaries. These three had a short, intense argument about dimensions, then gave the architect his orders.

The architect and the surveyor walked the chosen area, lining up their gazes with notches on sticks, and placing stakes and strings in a giant rectangle. When they got done, they conferred with their work gang. They left, and the gang started grading the land.

XXX

THE PATRICIA STILL wasn't sure how seriously she took Florence and everybody in it. But she found herself sad all afternoon and her sadness thickened at dusk. She told little Epida she was going to go sit for a spell in the colonnaded courtyard. Epida insisted on summoning the boy page, though Claire remembered the way. The boy page came, and Claire dutifully walked behind him down the faintly glimmering halls and dimly glowing marble stairs. In the courtyard, everything was a ghostly white in the failing twilight, except the shadows of the trees and porticos, which were inky black.

She had intended to have a proper wistful yearn, but as soon as she got outside and glanced to the right, the perpetual student forgot her intention. Looming over the north wall was an enormous tower. This tower seemed at first so tall she could not credit the Florentines had built it. She looked down to the page, and then back up, and now the tower seemed a little to the right of where it was, and a fair ways smaller, so that she could see a single window at the top of it. She realized this was the same tower that she'd seen at Traitor's Gate. She looked away again, but when she looked back, the tower's size and place remained. Therefore she took her first impression for some confusion of the light and angle. She spoke to the back of the page: "I beg you tell me what is that strange tower." He turned back, so that his little face hung in the dimness, and followed where her finger pointed. He looked to the diminished hulk, then spoke to the patricia.

- That's ai Ctesiphôn.

- Did you say Aictesiphôn or ai Ctesiphôn?

- I said ai Ctesiphôn.

- Where's the other one?

- What other one?

- The other Ctesiphôn. Your Florentine word "ai" is between *the* and *a* – it tells us this instance is one of two, doesn't it?

- Oh, yes, I suppose so.

- Is the other one in Florence?

- Surely not, or someone would have noticed it by now.

- Perhaps the other one stands in the land the name comes from.

- O Claire, now I'm confused.

- I mean only this: Ctesiphôn does not sound like a Florentine word, wouldn't you say?

- Perhaps not! I never thought of that, or of the tower really. Hardly anybody does.

- Why should nobody think of a great big tower like that, right in the middle of Florence as it is?

- There's a good reason, but it's a long story, and if you're going to have a nice sit down in the courtyard, you need to stop running your mouth and get on with it. It'll be night soon and time to go in. Ask any Florentine, they all will tell you why it boot you nothing to consider ai Ctesiphôn.

He led her to a bench and told her he'd leave her as long as he dared. Then he vanished in the gloom.

She sat herself down and faced ai Ctesiphôn. *What Art made you?*

She squinted at the tower a while. The sky turned violet around it. Not a mix of red and blue, but true violet. She felt a wretched ache in her breast, a mix of lost hopes and shame. *Why am I ashamed?* But a rebuke shames an honest player, deserved or no. Claire had got herself a fine rebuke from the king, and the shame ached in her breast. As for Marcus...

*O my savior and champion, this is the end for whatever we might have become.*

The stars were coming out, but no stars shone in the vicinity of ai Ctesiphôn.

She squeezed her eyes shut. *Why should I care? My life here is a dream; these are not my people. He cannot be mine, I cannot be his.*

She listened to the crickets a long while, and the wind in the grasses, until the ache in her breast dulled.

She opened her eyes. The tower was gone, leaving only a gap among the stars.

## XXX

THAT SAME NIGHT, Reburrus and Antivola finally found leisure to sit properly with one another. They spoke in the flickering light of a little clay oil lamp set on a table between their chairs. They kept the table and the chairs atop the temple complex on the Epicondyle. The complex was called Massafra, the House of Pantokrator Undefeated, and it was much bigger than Claire had understood. Its central chamber was the public hall of prayer that she had glimpsed. But its wings projected far back from the front. The left wing was cells and common rooms and kitchens of initiates and priests, and the right wing was administration and records, the library and scriptorium. Reburrus ruled the left, and Antivola the right. It was nearly its own town, atop its hill, above Florence.

The two men first met on the roof, when they were youths. A humid summer's night chased sleep off from young Antivola, and he heard weeping out the window of his cell. He could tell from the hoarse adolescent tone it was a boy his own age. The hopeless sound tugged his passions, and he padded to the hall, looking for its source. He crept barefoot around the left wing, catching the sound and losing it again, till finally he came to the kitchen in the back. The kitchen had a skylight to let out heat and steam. It was usually shut at night, but Antivola found it open, with a cutting table dragged over to it. He clambered on the table and put his hands on the lips of the skylight. He heaved himself up, gaining the roof with his elbows, then his ass, and finally entire.

A bony boy sat on the roof, facing away from him, his head between his knees, his body wracked with sobs. Saying nothing, Antivola went and sat beside this boy. He sat with him a long time, till he was sure the boy had grown aware of him. Then he put his hand on the boy's back. He could feel his ribs. A long time after that, the boy had spent all his sobs, and lifted his head up from between his knees. In the starlight, Antivola recognized him: he was the favorite of the ichneumonoi. They said Pantokrator spoke to him, that he was a new prophet. Antivola had an intuition not to ask him what troubled him. So he didn't, and they sat, and eventually they talked, about life in Massafra, about their boyhoods, about myth and doctrine. Young Reburrus didn't tell him why he'd been sobbing.

They took to meeting, up on the flat roof of the temple, enjoying the night breeze, drinking pilfered wine, slapping at mosquitos, arguing the fate of god and nation and man till the sky turned pink in the east. Reburrus shared his vision with Antivola, opening the vast territory of the cosmos to him. It made Antivola swell with awe. It was like a music that lent sense and structure to eternity. Antivola gave lonely Reburrus the world beneath the sun: day and night, the smell of soil and grass, the joy of food and drink, the poignant weaknesses of men. Reburrus felt his cold blood thaw in the mortal warmth of Antivola.

Eventually, the ichneumon told his only friend why he was sobbing, that first night. Sharing the knowledge awakened a genius for violence inborn in each youth. By careful degrees, they gave their genius its head. They devised between them the Correction of the Weights and Measures. They planned each step, then followed their plan. When they had done it, Florence quaked, and none dared oppose them.

Now they met again. Antivola said, "I have your letters, Flavius Papellus – and I saw ai Ctesiphôn shine on her at Traitor's Gate. Let me see your hands." Reburrus shuddered, breathing his woe raggedly, and held up his hands. Antivola took them gently, and squinted at them closely in the dim light of the oil lamp. There was no other mortal who would treat Reburrus so, and none other from whom he would take it. He said, "I soaked them in the madman's blood, but the god didn't relieve it." Antivola drawled, "Perhaps we'll try a little chamomile." Who else could chide the fervor of Reburrus?

Reburrus said, "Dear my Antivola, we stand before the turning of the age. I went to the god and I said, 'My god, what is she? What does she intend?' I searched the forest of the god's flame and read every leaf, and the god had nothing to say. There is a crack in heaven, Antivola. I am afraid – I am afraid –"

Antivola listened calmly, but his guts froze with terror. It was a sympathetic terror; he had not judged for himself the alien from

Zanzibar, but he knew Reburrus better than he knew his own soul. Furious Reburrus always had the god at his back. He lived in terror of the god, a perpetual and devouring terror. It enforced and clarified his holiness, till he was himself the deadly sling of Pantokrator. He had always scorned to fear any thing beneath the sun: no man, no weapon or disease, no privation moved him. All men were nothing to Reburrus, dust and nothing in the blazing face of the Almighty.

Thus if Reburrus said, "I am afraid –" then Antivola froze with terror. But he didn't act on it. Terror and faith were his friend's domain. His own was proof and patient reason. He listened calmly, spoke coolly, and soothed the passions of Reburrus. Reburrus let him do it, as the king had begged him. Antivola demanded leave to verify the threat. Reburrus let him have it. Antivola knew Reburrus needed him. Only working together, unified in purpose, did the two friends show the discipline that served them during the Correction of the Weights and Measures: understanding, and then planning, and then action. They were working on understanding. It was not time to plan or act, not yet.

# 19

## THE KING OF THE COSTERMONGERS

MARCUS IRENAEUS DIOPHANTUS woke before dawn. A voluptuous feeling filled him: anticipation of departure. He'd left Florence at dawn to join the war. His Stonebreakers always broke camp at dawn. He'd planned to flee the war at dawn. He'd spent his life leaving everything behind at dawn. The poignant sweetness of dawn filled him like honey.

Then he remembered the war was over, and he was back home for the winter. A youth when he left, light as innocence. A man when he returned, heavy with sin. He opened his eyes.

XXX

HE SPENT THE morning working on his census of the Thousand. In fact, they were one thousand fifty-six. One by one they came to Marcus's table, and he sorted out whether they could go on expedition to Zanzibar – whether they had family to get back to, whether they'd suffered injury or premature age in the storm, whether they had the spirit for marching on. Marcus recorded everything. As an apple boy, he'd learned from old Tiresias how to run a business. He knew his numbers and letters.

Marcus set up his table beside the broad rectangle marked in string, well out of the way of the builders stacking beams and planks. He put the dead man's skull, with the notch in its brow, on the table by his papers. It reminded him of his purpose. It reminded the Thousand who it was sowed peace and what they owed her. One by one, the Thousand came before his table. He met the eye of each. He refreshed his brotherhood with each.

Of the ones who had no family or injury, and had the spirit to march west, he asked regarding special skills: this one knew some medicine, and his friend knew surgery; this one sharpened blades; this one hunted; this one could make salt from lake and land.

The mad venture was starting to take shape in Marcus's mind. It would be the biggest departure of his life.

## XXX

HE INTERVIEWED THREE score of the Thousand and justified it as a good day's work. He left his papers to his staff and made for Shepherd's Gate. His legs carried him and his eyes scanned for threats, but his mind was somewhere else. He was rewarding his day's work with thoughts of her: her gown flaring at the hip, her smell filling his nostril, the touch of her lips on his cheek. She seemed to him like the beam of light that lit her in Andropolis, a thing fallen from a higher, brighter place.

He hadn't a lot of experience with women. Orphan, pick-pocket, apple boy, soldier: a life spent among boys and men. He reckoned he'd done well by the beautiful patricia, but he feared each further meeting with her, shamed by his awkwardness, his poverty, his brute humanity. Like all the Florentines who met her, he adored her and was terrified of her. But alone among the Florentines, he craved companionship with her.

He entered the city and hurried toward the east end, taking quiet side streets. His feet remembered the feel of the streets as soon as he walked them: worn marble paving slabs, strewn with pebbles and stones, mud and straw. He surprised himself with the surge of love he felt for the city, his city. He'd forgotten how happy he'd been here, wild and rebellious and street smart. *She understands cities too.* He adjusted his plan for the day.

He came to Primavera Circle. Royal district workers were coming and going at the wide Golden Gate, under the eye of the guard. The royal district had its own wall, shorter than the city wall but still good for a siege. The wall enclosed perhaps a quarter of Florence city: bustling crowds outside it, the king's quiet preserve inside.

The district guard noticed him carrying a sword and waved him to the front. He unbelted his scabbard and handed it over and explained who he was. He felt no need to confess to the blade in his boot. They verified his story and gave his scabbard back and saluted him and let him in.

He'd never entered the royal district as a youth. Now he had full liberty of the place. He left the path, walking on the soft grass of the bailey, circling past the stables and the royal granary. Everything smelled good. The gardeners wore colored surcoats and held themselves with pride. He spiraled in toward the two castles at the center of the district, the old one and the larger, younger one.

When he got close enough, he followed the smell of baking and roasting. There it was: the kitchen. Marcus entered. The cook dared not turn him away. The pantler dared not turn him away. He intended to start making up for all the days in his life that he'd starved. He mostly wound up stuffing his face with warm wheat cakes, dipping them in syrup and leaving crumbs in the pot.

Finally she came in.

He used a little of his thieving skill to keep her from noticing him. Unseen, he admired the gleam of her clean hair, the confidence of her stride. He finished his cake and licked his fingers and wiped them on his chiton. She was asking the pantler for a quince, and the pantler was explaining he didn't have any. Finally Marcus detached from the confusion of shadow and steam that hid him and said, "Come with me, I know where to get the finest quinces in Florence."

She looked at him, startled, and said, "I didn't see you at all."

He said, "You weren't looking for me."

He knew faces, and he read hers: joy first, by reflex, to see him – then the shadow of a woe, and a gate shut on her open look.

*Something has changed. What?*

She said, "Were you looking for me?"

He said, "I was." She said, "Why here?" He said, "Daughter of Zanzibar, you are always hungry." She couldn't help but smile, and said, "It's true." He said, "It's a long walk to your quinces, try one of these delicious wheat cakes before we go."

## XXX

MARCUS LED THE Sower of Peace past any number of fruit carts, insisting that the finest quinces were to be had up Serapetine Hill. This wasn't necessarily true, but after his morning walk, he needed to share Florence with her, and he wanted to show her off to his man on the hill.

He led her on the same route as the Triumph, west along the Via Floribus. This is the name the old King's Road takes inside the impenetrable walls of Florence, crossing from Traitor's Gate in the east to Jubilee Gate in the west. With the triumphal crowd dispersed, he got Claire a better look at the city. Narrow streets opened off the artery of the Via Floribus. Tenements sagged against each other. On the first storeys, humble signs hung above open shutters. He watched her scanning them. A crudely painted picture of a horse's head on one, a sword and breastplate on another, a barrel on a third. Each street had its own species of establishment: goldsmiths, armorers, notaries, scribes, the dust-clouded yards of the masons and carpenters. Marcus knew them all.

In open places, her gaze rose to the top of Florence. He saw the city with her fresh eyes, its angled roofs and forest of narrow steeples, red and gray. Farther off, the hulks of scattered larger buildings: the half-collapsed amphitheatre of Statilius Taurus in the north, the curve of the hippodrome hazy in the southwest.

She made a big show of looking around, not saying much to him. He could see whenever her fascination passed, her misery returned. He couldn't riddle what had changed. Had he done something?

They drew near to the Liliana and Marcus had to stop and collect himself. When he blinked away his tears, he saw Claire looking curiously at him, with an almost savage lack of sympathy. For all the cruelty of her look, it thrilled him: he often felt he wasn't quite real to her. Right now, he was. She spoke quietly, and he had trouble hearing her over the daytime clattering and shouting. She said, "You were raised in Florence." He said, "I ran these streets till I was old enough for war." Bitterness creased her face and the exile said, "You've finally come home."

They climbed the Pontem Spe Bona. The Liliana flowed lazily below, full of turds and garbage and dead birds. The smell made Claire gag, so he handed her his nosegay. She pressed it to her face, eyes bulging, and Marcus cracked a grin at her. Behind the nosegay, he could see she smiled back. Then the fœtid river was behind them.

When the stink settled, Claire stopped a moment. Marcus waited. She looked around the city. The span of her vision seemed larger than him and her, wider than Florence, longer than human life. Her cool gray eyes returned to him, and her far look made him feel very small.

After that, her spirits lifted. Florentines shyly greeted her, and she greeted them back warmly. It was fair to say she grew delighted. This was what Marcus had craved: the glamorous alien delighted with his city and he the first to show it to her. He gently took her hand to lead her round the crooked paving stone at the corner of Via Strocchia, the one everybody trips on, and she let him, though she reclaimed her hand when the danger was past.

XXX

THERSITES LEFT THE boy up front with the bins and customers, and retreated to the back to run the numbers. The problem was the same for all the autumn produce: the crop was good but the demand in Florence city, swelling with returning soldiers, was out of hand. Scenting an opportunity, great farms and small were marking up their prices. Thersites was the biggest wholesale buyer on Serapetine Hill, which is to say in Florence, so he was in a spot, and all of his competitors were looking to him to set city policy.

If he flat rejected the markup, the farmers were happy to send their carts up north to Tyana, to Victumulae, to Novaria – everybody wanted the same apples and pumpkins and squashes. On the other hand, if he passed the markup on to his customers, he risked their anger. They didn't have any extra coppers in their pockets. He was seeking numbers for each fruit and vegetable: nudging the farmers down enough, and sharing the pain with the customers enough – that the farmers sent the goods, the customers understood that he suffered too – and the volume compensated for the skinny profits. Anticipating volume was the trick of it. Each guess justified a different price. He scratched his sunburned head, and as much as his reason worked the tables of numbers, his passions roamed the city, his city, dwelling on the people and their mood. Mood, as much as need and budget, determines shopping.

He was going in circles with this speculation, and the sound of his name was welcome distraction from it. He set aside his tablet and stood and stretched. It wasn't much of a stretch, he was bandy-legged and lame of one foot, with his two shoulders rounded and hunched over his chest. Every joint cracked. Then he made his way out front to find out who was calling, and shortly he was sobbing.

XXX

Here he was, "the ugliest man in the third morax," still living, shuddering with sobs. The top of his pointy head was level with Marcus's chest, he'd grown so short. He blubbered, "My boy, my boy, back from war, home at last – unharmed? Are you unharmed?" – Marcus hastened to reassure him – "Unharmed – home at last" – and he lost his words a moment, then Tiresias blew his nose on a rag and stuffed it in a pocket and stood back and looked Marcus up and down and said, "Look at you, a man! I sent you away a boy, dear swift Marcus Irenaeus, and you've come back a man!" He thumped Marcus on the chest with the back of his crooked hand, bursting with pride.

Marcus felt his face crumple, because there were so few left amongst whom he could still be weak, still be a boy. Tiresias, smart as a whip, said, "I sent three of you away." Now the tears rolled down Marcus's cheeks and he said, "I lost them, *pater*. I lost Varian and Otho in the storm." Tiresias sobbed anew and beat Marcus on the chest, and Marcus wrapped his arms around the old man and held him and absorbed his blows. When Tiresias calmed, Marcus let him go and he stood unsteadily on his bandy legs. He looked as old as the hills, but then, he always had. Tiresias dropped his fists and said in a low voice, "You've killed men?" It wasn't really a question. Marcus pressed his lips together and nodded, and Tiresias said, "A terrible thing, terrible for the soul," and he clasped Marcus's hand in his and his love flowed into Marcus through the palms of their hands.

Then his eye turned to Claire.

Marcus said, "Pater, this is Claire, the patricia from Zanzibar, who ended long-lived war," and he said, "Claire, this is Beno Tiresias, who is like a father to me. When I was a starving little boy, I stole apples from him, till finally..."

Then he faltered, because this was where Tiresias always took up the story. Studying him, Marcus saw he had a cold look for the beautiful patricia. Suddenly anxious, his fingers flew through the pickpocket's warmup. He continued the story himself:

"...till finally he caught me, the 'king of the costermongers' caught me, and I expected a good thrashing from it. But the old softy said, 'Children need fruit to grow up big and strong,' and he gave me to eat till I was full, then put me to work, right where that boy is now, selling to the cooks and wives. When I was old enough – right, pater? – you let me join your costermonger army, you gave me my own cart and my own street to walk it on..."

There was a long silence, and finally Tiresias said, "That's a nice shave you've got." Marcus's hand darted to his smooth cheek. Tiresias said, "New men both. It's Thersites now."

"What?"

Tiresias stood up as straight as he could, in all his ferocious ugliness. He said, "My name is Beno Thersites. My father's grandfather was a Genovan from Colophon, but he changed the family name when he fled to Florence. Now the war is over, I can be Thersites and nobody will tack me up at Traitor's Gate."

Claire made a deep and respectful bow. She had such a way with bows. This bow was not like the dramatic one she offered the kings in Andropolis, or the insulting little dip she bestowed upon the priest Reburrus in Altamira. This was a bow of respect for a free man, and Marcus could see it mollified Tiresias – Thersites – a little.

Marcus clapped his hands and said, "Pater, have you got any quinces today?"

## XXX

SERAPETINE HILL IS the great market of Florence. A hill is a stupid place for a market, because the vendors have to haul the goods uphill, and the buyers have to haul them downhill, and if anybody drops anything, it rolls away. By the time the ancient Florentines figured all this out, they'd got in the habit, and on the hill the market remains.

Once Marcus got Claire her quince he showed her around Serapetine Hill: a maze of stalls with food so varied and rich the smell of it overpowered the stink of the city. Fruits and vegetables – herbs and medicines – spices – flesh and fish and fowl – grains and milled flour and beer – milk and cheese and wine – cooked foods and bread and snacks. There were sellers of cloth and soap and idols and flowers, and a puppet theater. Marcus didn't know this, and Claire had only an intuition of it, but there is an innocent joy to food markets in all nations. Every mortal grows hungry, and it is no sin to eat. To see all foods at once, in all their colors and smells, in their bins and baskets and casks, makes people happy, even those who haven't the money to buy. Therefore Claire was happy with Marcus on Serapetine Hill, among the ducks and salmons, saffron and sage, grapes and lettuces and sweet potatoes.

Children ran around the place, and the wives of poor men rubbed shoulders with the kitchen staff of rich men. Veterans lounged around the corners, and ichts kept an eye on public morals. Claire said, "Who are these women in the undyed wool himations, with the white veils covering their faces?"

Marcus said, "Those are the war widows."

## XXX

"NOW LET US consider the asymmetry of killing." He ignored the confusion of his congregants. They didn't know what *asymmetry* meant, but they'd understand what they needed to. He went on, "The day comes that it is your turn to be killed, and his turn to kill you. On your way out to the blade, the unfairness weighs upon you.

"For you, this is the day of days. Of course it is: his birth, the birth of his first son, his death – these are the most important days in the life of a man. But for the one who killed you, it is no important day at all. The sun will go on shining on him. When he has done with you, he'll wipe the blood off his hands and start thinking about lunch. By evening what troubles him more, his upset stomach or the fact he killed you?

"No, it is unequal, and therefore unjust. How can we abide it?"

The veterans nodded. They knew what he was talking about.

"Dear my friends, I am a teacher of men. This knowledge was given to me, and I give it to you: the man who dies is not alone on the day of days. His killer does not know, but the god knows. Pantokrator watches all, and every death is precious to Him. We come from Pantokrator to the world, and when we leave the world, we return to Pantokrator. He welcomes us as if His heart had been torn out, and now returns to Him. Our god is a jealous god, a furious god, thirsty for our deaths, because each one of us is part of Pantokrator, all-seeing, all-embracing. Yes, the day we are killed is a day of lamentations in the world, but in the world beyond the world, it is a day of celebration. The importance is equal. There is justice for the killed."

The widows wept, imagining their lost men. Reburrus stood from his place on the porch and walked around among them, touching his hand to their veiled heads where they knelt. They tinked coins into his bronze bowl, and the veterans did the same. There was a decline in ordinary city folk among the congregants, and this disturbed him. The evil gods of Zanzibar, sapping the faith of the Florentines.

The lesson done, Reburrus led some of the crowd into the prayer hall of the temple. Others turned and walked themselves back down the winding road from the summit of the Epicondyle.

## XXX

ONE WIDOW STROLLED along the temple grounds, a veteran at her side. Around the far end of the left arm of the temple, they came to a garden. It was like a kitchen garden, but very large and well-tended; young ichts worked the cabbage and turnip patches even now. A corner of it was walled in by a hedge. Grief evidently did little to dull the curiosity of the widow, for she drifted toward the hedged corner. Peeking through the opening, her eyes behind her veil scanned weather peas and weeping bridesmaid and snakeroot, white trumpet and deadly nightshade, wolfsbane and buttonbush.

Then her view was blocked, as if a door had closed. There was no door: a man as big as a door moved into the opening in the hedge. Even this little effort made him wheeze. He had wiry hair and ruddy cheeks and little squinty eyes. He squinted at the widow and her veteran companion. He wheezed, "Good wife, this is a garden of the temple, and only ichts belong here." The young ichts looked over from their work. The veteran said, "We apologize, holy icht. I speak for this woman. My friend took an arrow meant for me, and she was his bride. She has vowed silence for a year, and I look after her. Obliged as I am to my friend, when she completes her mourning I will marry her." The veiled widow turned to look at the veteran, but said nothing.

The giant icht leaned toward them both and squinted again. He had the hesitating, careful motions of a man nearly blind. But beneath this gentle movement – metal. He said, "The god will smile on your virtues, each of you. Do not dishonor the dead. Resist temptation till the year is out. Come back if you prevail, and shine your virtue on me: I will marry you." The veteran and his widow bowed their heads. Looking up, the veteran said, "For whom shall we ask?" The near-sighted icht said, "Ask for Iacomo Antivola."

## XXX

NEAR THE BOTTOM of the Epicondyle, out of sight of the temple, she tore off the stifling veil. A gust of thunder and honeysuckles struck Marcus, as if she'd held her breath the whole time, keeping her perfume in. She said, "So this is Antivola." Marcus said, "Be not fooled by his mild look; he is the other half of Reburrus." She said, "It is good I heard Reburrus speak. I took his cult for a superstition, but it is a real doctrine." Marcus thought of answering this insult to Florence, but decided not to. Instead he observed, "The crowds were thin up there." She answered, "I will not marry you." He shot back, "Who's offering?" This brought her up short. Good. She said, "Perhaps – perhaps I misunderstood the drift of your tale." Marcus laughed in her face and said, "I'm sorry, do I owe you something? Did your husband take an arrow meant for me?" She looked at him as if he were quite an interesting sort of a fellow.

## XXX

ANTIVOLA WAS AN icht through and through, and untroubled by visions. Likewise he did not dream, or if he did, he did not remember what he dreamt. But he was not entirely locked in the house of reason. He had mastered the art of dozing, and from his dozes, he achieved his insights.

His cell, on the top floor of the administrative wing of Massafra, had a little vent down to the fireplace. That night, after the rushlights winked out, and his room was cold and dark, he sat in his chair by the vent and let it warm his legs, fat as they were, and ridged with burst veins. He stared at the dull yellow glow of the vent, and sometimes the indistinct flash of a spark. He reflected on his encounter with Claire – it had taken him a moment, but he'd recognized her.

Soon Antivola dozed.

The eye of his imagination showed him the patricia. She was a pillar of light, blurred in his imagination as she was in life. Female, certainly, and shining, but he wouldn't know her features till she'd come close enough unveiled for them to breathe in one another's face. Therefore she was blurred.

She stood fearfully motionless, like a statue. The rest of Florence moved at its normal pace, or even faster. Sometimes it bumped up against her, and he could not make out where she was or wasn't. Near-sighted Antivola encountered this problem all the time: that things slipped in front of and behind each other in his vision, and he couldn't make out what was where. He was a man of scrupulous orderliness, and this constant shimmer was to him like an ache that never eased. In his doze, the shimmer dominated Claire. All things passed through her, and she passed through all things.

Deep in the night, Antivola started from his doze, and spent a long time staring into the dimming yellow glow on the stone wall of the vent. Finally he got up and lay himself down in bed. He drew a big fur over his big frame, and thought about Claire. She was a menacing cipher. The space she filled was somehow less because she filled it. She presaged an unnamed passage of destruction. In his way, he saw her as Reburrus saw her. Now he'd met her, he shared the great man's dread.

# 20

## THE UGLIEST MAN IN THE THIRD MORAX

BACK TO THE king of the costermongers: why was Thersites so cold to the patricia? There is a simple explanation – the storm that brought her to his land cut short the lives of two of his beloved apple boys. But no one thing explains everything. It is worth learning a little more about the sentiments of Thersites. He was a strange case, and in a way condensed in himself the tragedy of his entire generation.

When he was young, having inherited little, not even his own name, he couldn't afford armor or horse, so he served as light infantry in the third morax. This was the morax of the king's father, Ambrosius the Eighth. The war had lasted over a century, and in that time repeated several forms. When Claire arrived in Florence, it was the-war-of-the-Sinope, a fixed clash at one crossing of the Sinope or another. But in the day of Ambrosius the Eighth, it was the-war-of-the-north, a roaming exchange of destruction among the border towns at the base of the mountains.

Thersites campaigned with the third morax for two years, ravaging the Genovans at Chalkis, at Sicyon, at Aegira. It was a good time, but the losses were mounting up. The king should have sought a victory for Florence and then gone home but, intemperate as he was, he turned his eye to the fearful mountain people.

Thersites was there on the plain when Ambrosius the Eighth got the idea in his head to storm Ēnu Šarr-im. This was an unusual Kharkhade stronghold just up the hill in freezing Petrobi province. It was surrounded by an especially impressive wall. The wall rose and fell with the hillside it was planted on, so that from the plain below, it looked like a black wave standing in the snowy forest. Ēnu Šarr-im was smaller than a city, but larger than a hunting camp. No Florentine knew why the Kharkhade had built it, or what they did in there.

The survivors of the third morax wore tattered furs and red kerchiefs. It was around this time they started calling themselves the Redheads, on account of the kerchiefs. They'd grown informal with one another. Ambrosius shared his plan with the men, and only young Thersites objected, saying, "O brave king, what more glory could you want? What serves it Florence that we open our veins for Ēnu Šarr-im? Perhaps we don't have enough enemy in Genova and need to challenge Kharkhadia as well. Or maybe I'm behind on news – has Kharkhadia allied with Genova? Does taking Ēnu Šarr-im buy us Ancomia? Does it stand between us and the Vextal Road? Have you got reports the Kharkhade keep all their gold and women inside yon sturdy walls – are you still lacking gold and women, king?"

He had a terrible speaking voice, shrill and squeaky. His hair was thin even then, and his posture already hunched, and his cheeks and jaw were cratered with pimple-scars. They used to call him the ugliest man in the third morax, an epithet he tried to take with good humor.

Now he shamed King Ambrosius. It would have been impossible for the low to shame the high quite thus in peacetime, but this was war, and the front makes brothers of all men.

Ælius Pellucidus, the hot-blooded firstborn of King Ambrosius, stood up and said, "Check your glib tongue, Tiresias, and babble not a word further. How dare you stand alone against the king? There is no viler creature come to Petrobi with the sons of Florence! If I have to listen to your nonsense again, I will forfeit my own crown and be called no son of great Ambrosius, or I will take you, strip you naked, and whip you out the morax till you run off freezing to the snowy wastes." All of fifteen years old, Prince Ælius Pellucidus, but so handsome and so sure of himself, so well-spoken and loved by all.

He raised his staff and beat Thersites about the back and shoulders till Thersites dropped and fell weeping. The staff raised a bloody weal on Thersites's back, so he sat frightened and in pain, looking foolish as he wiped the tears from his eyes. Finally he stood and, wordless and red-faced, turned his back on his companions and retreated to the tents. Just as Ælius Pellucidus had said, nobody stood with him. The men were sorry for him, but they laughed heartily and clapped the darling prince on the back, telling him what a great thing he had accomplished for the Florentines that day, finally shutting up whiny Beno Tiresias.

They stormed Ēnu Šarr-im that afternoon. Four thousand men went up the hill. Eight hundred came back down.

That was the worst day of Thersites's life: the most humiliating morning, and the saddest evening. The seeds of many of his later actions and opinions were planted between its sunrise and sunset. When he faced a quandary in life, he tended to understand it in terms of one of the forces present on that day. This was what made him such a king-hater.

So did he see the old King Ambrosius in Claire, whose crown permitted his vainglorious ambition to destroy his men? Certainly he did – she too was high-born and made shocking moves, answering to nothing but her own will. Her deeds were good, and even great, but he could not trust them.

Did he see Ælius Pellucidus in Claire, the handsome, silver-tongued youth whose arrogance had long since doomed him, somewhere in ai Ctesiphôn? Of course he did. Thersites understood the cruel entitlement of beauty as only the ugly really understand; understood it and resented it.

Did he see his companions of the third morax in her? Even this, a little bit, he saw. Those who should have stood with him, from the bonds of brotherhood, forged in marches and tempered in battle, from the dignity of free men, from reason and self-preservation – they too had abandoned him, sending him off to the chorus of their laughter, as they marched uphill to die. From that day, Thersites was alone. His army of costermongers salved his loneliness, because they were sons to him, and he was a father to them. But Claire was no son of his; rather, she had cost him two of his boys and charmed a third, his favorite, away. Therefore her company made him lonely.

Yes, he saw in Claire the king, the prince, and the army, and as he reviled them, so he reviled her. But above all, he saw in her the black wall of Ēnu Šarr-im. The Florentines and Genovans understood one another. Their war was like a war between kin. But the Kharkhade were inscrutable. Their history, their tongue, their nature and their numbers were unknown. Who were their gods? Where were there cities? They were aliens to Florence.

The Zanzibari girl was like the Kharkhade, a stranger. She might be kind or true, but she did not talk his talk. Thersites saw her face and eyes and mouth, but he would never know the soul behind.

# 21

## THE RUMOR OF THE CRIMSON KNIGHT

THE LIGHT IN the jade office was like swimming in a murky river, and sounds seemed very close and quiet. Marcus had had trouble finding the door, nestled against one of the giant columns of the great hall. He had been reluctant to send Claire off, so he was a little late. When he opened the door, he found the council already meeting. They turned and looked at him. The king sniffed the air and coolly said, "How is the fair patricia today?"

Marcus turned his head and took a little whiff of his right shoulder. It was true, he smelled of thunder and honeysuckles. He said, "I showed her Florence, and the city delighted her."

Reburrus tilted his head and said, "Was she on the Epicondyle?"

Marcus looked the fierce priest in the face and said, "Not today. I took her up Serapetine Hill and fetched her a quince." Reburrus stared at Marcus without answering for such a long time that the king was obliged to continue the conversation: "How does Tiresias like her?" Marcus felt his cheeks heat. He turned to Ambrosius and said, "Come to find out, my lord, his distaste for the high-born is not limited to Florence." Ambrosius laughed and said, "Don't tell him you're a Diophantus now." Marcus had the sense to laugh with the joke. Ambrosius waved at a seat and said, "Tribune, join us."

## XXX

THE COUNCIL SEEMED to be a very loose grouping of eligible men, summoned as the agenda required. Temet Ambrosius was there, mustache perfectly groomed. There were two Constantines present – Cleon, whom he'd met, and another one called Barbarossa. Like the queen, they had oval faces and warm hazel eyes, but apart from that, they resembled neither her nor one another. Cleon Constantine was trim and sober, with thin blonde hair and a high brow, lined with worry. Barbarossa was thick and solid as a roof beam, with brown hair and big pores on his cheeks and a messy beard dyed an absolutely ridiculous shade of red.

Ambrosius said, "Barbarossa, repeat to Diophantus what you have been telling us."

Barbarossa turned a surprisingly hostile eye on Marcus and rumbled, "I have heard a rumor of a Crimson Knight. He flies a white banner with a crimson horse on it. He is raising an army. The rumor does not say why."

There was an expectant silence. Marcus said, "Where did you hear this rumor?"

Barbarossa said, "When I was young, I served with the third morax –" Marcus heard the pride in his voice, and noticed how the king bristled at the Constantine's preference for his father's army over his own Wardogs "– since the second and the third came back to Florence, I am hearing whispers of recruitment from my friends among the third."

Marcus turned to the king and said, "You credit it?"

Ambrosius said, "I expected it, or something like it. The warrior nobles have ever doubted my place on the throne. The only question is – which? And what is his plan?" He looked to his magister equitum.

Temet clicked, "It's House Ambrosius, my lord. One of ours, still smarting you took your brother's place. No one else would dare."

Ambrosius wrinkled his brow and said, "I wish you were right, cousin. Corruption restricted to a single family. But I can think of at least seven Houses that might try it. I can even imagine them combining in their effort."

The magister hissed. He said, "How do they mean to pull it off?"

Ambrosius sat back and pressed his fingertips together. He looked around the table, his gaze lingering on Marcus a long moment. Marcus thought, *He's preparing to be very clever.*

Ambrosius said, "I have summoned the warrior nobles. In six weeks we celebrate the peace. That's when the Crimson Knight will strike. He'll have his army ready by then. He'll smuggle his men into the city among the crowds. This is his plan: smite me at the banquet, and announce himself. Open the doors of the great hall. Show the other nobles his army. Win their pledge and take the purple."

Silence. Temet Ambrosius said, "What will we do?"

The king spoke in his stony voice of war, "We will seek him first. Temet, I'm afraid I must ask you to leave Vestoria and the boys a little while; I need your loyalty and wisdom."

He turned to Cleon and said, "Cleon, how many riders can I afford to send on expedition?"

Cleon said, "Armored, with staff and a provision train?"

The king said, "Let's say they'll get provisions as they travel."

Cleon said, "Which budget are you drawing on, private funds, the public treasury, or your account with House Constantine?"

Ambrosius paused and said, "Private funds."

Cleon said, "Right now, you can afford twelve riders."

The nostril of Ambrosius flared, but he calmed himself and said, "Temet, take twelve men. Ride north up Ligusticum Street. It's two days out to the Via Circumflorentia. Turn west on the

Via and sweep its great circle around Florence. Question every warrior noble with an estate on the circle. If you find nothing, we will broaden our search. I'll have General Nasica canvass the third morax. Whether or not we find him, we'll be ready. I'll prepare the Wardogs for the fight. Today – tomorrow – two months hence – we will crush the Crimson Knight."

## XXX

AMBROSIUS WAITED TILL the room was emptying, then singled out his newest tribune: "A word, Diophantus." The others glanced over in surprise, but said nothing. Marcus sat back down.

Ambrosius studied him. He was not the youth who fought ferociously in Andropolis. The storm, the mutiny, burning those thousands on the dreadful pyre – the worries and loneliness of leadership – all had speedily weathered him. He had the gravity of a man now. But he hadn't lost his charisma. Men would still follow him.

Ambrosius was not at all convinced the Crimson Knight, if he existed, was a warrior noble. There was another obvious possibility.

Marcus looked at the king, and looked down. He opened his mouth, and shut it.

*How much guile has he? Can he paint lies up to resemble truth?*

Ambrosius said, "About Claire."

Marcus looked up, startled.

Ambrosius said, "I told her this, and I will tell you. You will not be lovers. You will not be wed."

Marcus blushed and said, "My lord–"

Ambrosius said, "Hold your tongue, Marcus. You have been loyal to Florence, even when I failed the nation. You have been candid with me in the face of destruction. Therefore will I be candid with you now. It is plain to see you venerate her, and I think she is much taken with you. Worship her if you must, but love her nothing. If the Sower of Peace made a child with her mutineer, that child could compete with Domenico for the crown. Your child and his parents…" he paused. Marcus furrowed his brow. Then he went on: "…would be forfeit."

Marcus bent away, cheeks flaming now.

Ambrosius continued, "You have a thousand, Marcus Diophantus, but I have fifty thousand. Do not think to defy my will."

Marcus sat there a long moment, eyes blazing in the gloom of the jade office.

Ambrosius said, "Speak."

Marcus began to say something, and stopped himself. Then he began to say something else, and stopped himself again. He breathed in and out in careful, measured breaths. Ambrosius watched the color cool from his cheek.

Finally Marcus said, "Is your order universal, or does it end at the border of the valley of the world?"

This was so unexpected, so daring, that Ambrosius slapped his knee and laughed. Marcus flinched, eyes downcast. Ambrosius said, "My boy! My inventive boy! You must have Master Rabbit for a grandfather!" Marcus continued to look down at his hands in his lap.

Ambrosius stood and walked to him. Marcus looked up at the king. Ambrosius said, "Trade places with her, Marcus, exile for exile, and what you do with her is no concern of mine."

Ambrosius gestured him out.

When the young tribune had gone, the king paced around the jade office. His back and hips were sore, so much sorer since the war. He ignored them. He circled the table, walking through the scene again and again. No matter how he sifted it, he could not separate the truth.

*Marcus Irenaeus Diophantus, are you the Crimson Knight?*

## XXX

COME EVENING, CLAIRE sat at a window in her emptied-out apartment. The majordomo had a hard time believing she wanted nothing. He left a sack of feathers for her to sleep on. She was glad to be alone with stone and old wood in her rooms. If she wanted comfort, she could hide in the palanquin and have the comforts of home.

She sat at her window, massaging her sore calves and looking out at evening. Clouds had gathered, and a drizzle was falling. A marvelous earthy smell was rising from the well-tended grass of the bailey.

She considered the day. She'd started out well resolved to tell Marcus of the king's order. Immediately she lost her nerve. Failing that, she hoped to ward him off with a frosty demeanor. In the steady warmth of his companionship, that had melted away. She badly wanted to touch his hair.

Clearly, she was going to have to start over, and tell him of the king's order.

As for Florence, now she knew: these ancient cities were very little. The entire place would probably fit inside Belazion Park, in Zanzibar. She'd walked it east to west, and west to east, with time left over for Marcus to hurry off and sit in council.

And yet, though Florence was little, it was great. She'd had a vision in the street, after crossing the bridge over the stinking river: she saw the city as the carcass of a pilgrim.

He once had reason, and it governed his breast, that rose and fell, and his stomach, that churned, and his limbs, so full of harmonious motion. But when he died, he went on living, and his empty breast sheltered a flowering plant, and moss furred the girdle of his hips, and poppies blossomed in his eyes. So too she saw a mighty Florence that once was, fallen into ruin, still protecting a reduced people, stunted by war, ceaseless in their activity, as restless men must be.

Her spirits lifted from there. This new city, too poor to think of building up fresh monuments or great halls – this new city, elbow and shoulder to its work, its citizens hustling value from the useless things of the Earth – this new city, this Florence – pleased Claire. For Claire knew that great halls and noble monuments are fossils of the will. They are symptoms of decline. She preferred the ugly noise of humble industry, which marks the start of things.

She remembered a sentiment she had felt toward these people – *I could save you* – and its complement – *You could save me.* She couldn't remember when or where she'd felt this sentiment. Most of her was missing.

Claire leaned out the window into the drizzle. She felt the tiny drops on her face. There was little rain in blazing Zanzibar, and only torrents when it fell. This fine cool dampness was enchanting to her. She sat and let her face slowly soak. She emptied out her reason, and thought of nothing. She soothed her passions, and felt nothing. She wished to be quite alone, even from herself. By dark, she was nothing more than a serene pleasure in the feel of gentle rain.

## XXX

MEN TAKE RARE events for miracles, but other men, in whose lives the same events are common, hold them in contempt. Therefore Barbarossa cursed the rain, which was ordinary winter weather in Florence. When his beard got wet, it dripped red dye on his shirt; he tried to wear a dark shirt when it rained, but his shirt today was light. His cousin and partner in all ventures, Cleon, kept a straight face, but Barbarossa could tell he thought it was funny, and this incensed him further.

The streets were blue and empty, and firelight, where it flickered, glistened on wet stone. Partway to the Counting House, Barbarossa's anger got the best of him, and he smashed up a rack of herbs outside a shop: fists, then feet, till it was dirt and stems and broken lengths of wood on the curb. The shopkeeper opened the shuttered window and popped his head out and Barbarossa roared at the poor man. Cleon hastened to offer silver. When it was done, Barbarossa fought his ragged breath. Cleon dryly remarked, "May I take it you have more on your mind than your shirt?"

Barbarossa glared at him and said, "Diophantus."

Cleon said, "Aha."

Barbarossa said, "Hundreds of years we Constantines serve Florence, and he picks some– " he waved his hand around "–some *alley rat*, a decanus nobody ever heard of, to elevate to ancient name?" Barbarossa's nostrils flared. "Our wretched king is like a bone in my throat, cousin."

Cleon wiped the drizzle from his brow, keeping quiet.

Barbarossa warmed to his theme: "He hands out Names to pretty boys. Calls this disgraceful peace a victory. Throws himself a Triumph! For what? Did he defeat Pindar? He keeps a foreign slut for a pet. He's taken down the traitors from Traitor's Gate. He doesn't deserve to wear the divided rectangle."

Cleon said, "Constantine will take its rightful place, cousin. Patience."

Barbarossa bared his misery, saying, "I can scarcely bear it, Cleon. Kissing this disgusting coward's ring."

Cleon nodded. There was no answer to make.

## XXX

HIS BEARD WAS good and soaked by the time they reached the Counting House, and his shirt looked like he'd met up with assassins. The Counting House was a Constantine establishment on the south side, where the river and the air were cleaner. They were late, but Barbarossa had calmed down. He waved Cleon on ahead and searched around the stable till he found a brown cloak. He wrapped himself in it before going inside. A dirty shirt tempts ridicule, and Barbarossa was a vain man.

The stable was a late addition to the building. The old front door, set in a brick wall, opened into it. The wooden stairs had long since rotted out, so the door hung awkwardly high up a naked wall. Barbarossa hoisted his bulk up it, cursing the miserliness of the Constantines.

Everybody else was already in the meeting room: Cleon had settled in with his and Barbarossa's peers, Antonio and Tarquin.

The four of them, scions in their prime, were the public face of Constantine. A committee of the old men was in charge, and a flock of youngsters attended to observe and learn. It took a long time to gather so many Constantines in one room, but this was their strict practice, pooling their strengths and passing them down, old heads to young hands.

The room was low and dim, and the pattering of rain was steady now. The place smelled of sour paper, ink, and greasy coins. The counting tables were shut for the evening, with some meager food laid out on their lids, and a pitcher of water to mix with wine from the amphora. A cheap wine the Constantines kept stocked, harsh and full of sediments.

Cleon was saying, "...even now, he's planning how to fight a phantom, who may never appear, instead of scheduling his debts, which will certainly come due." Barbarossa saw how Cleon's report pleased the old men. The end of war presented many reversals to the family. The obvious loss was in revenue from the armaments trade. But the more serious loss was this: without war to drain his coffer, the collapse of Ambrosius might drag on forever. The Constantines had been patient in their project, generations long, to seize the crown. They'd impoverished the Ambrosii. They'd got one of their own for queen. The next Ambrosius was already half-a-Constantine. But the name of Constantine was still spat on as a rabble of merchants and syndics, their very wealth sneered at among the warrior nobles. They craved their name on the throne. For Barbarossa's part, he craved respect.

He made the same proposal he made at every meeting: "Raise an army - overthrow them!" He was the only Constantine in generations who had marched against Genova. The family had a tradition of buying off their service.

As always, Barbarossa was voted down.

He raged a little bit, then filled a cup and buried his face in it. His great uncle, skin like parchment, croaked, "Our policy of bankrupting Ambrosius – or, rather, being patient while the fool bankrupts himself – will surely slow with peace, but it cannot halt, so long as Florence is Florence and Ambrosius Ambrosius." Another of the old men took up the thread: "We must show patience in the face of misfortune and continue as we've done. At the king's next loan payment, we'll have New Forest for ourselves, rich with game. Surely you'd like that, Ineto Picolomini?" Using Barbarossa's real name, as if he were still a little boy. Barbarossa growled into his cup.

The room waited on him. He put down his cup and said, "Ambrosius is weak and poor. The Crimson Knight, if he exists, may be strong and rich. If we will not act now, perhaps the enemy we face tomorrow outmatches the one we face today. Give me leave to organize among my men in the third morax."

Cleon was shocked. The cousins planned everything together; but Barbarossa hadn't discussed this with him first. One of the old men said, "Organize – to what end?" Barbarossa said, "To defend Ambrosius." Jaws dropped around the table. Ordinarily Barbarossa played the buffoon, and it was Cleon who talked sense. Murmurs back and forth. Barbarossa took his chance and spoke softly to Cleon, "I'd have told you first, cuz, but I only thought of it in the stable. I didn't want to miss proposing it to everyone." And he took Cleon's thin cold hand in his strong warm one, and Cleon grasped his hand in return. Thus they presented their customary unity to the meeting.

Barbarossa's motion passed.

He said, "I have one more proposal. What to put in that warehouse we're building for the march to Zanzibar."

He told them. There was a long pause. A very appreciative pause. Barbarossa's father broke it.

Ineto Tacitus Constantine said, "My troublesome son, you are finally growing up."

Barbarossa felt an emotion suffuse him, dark and cloudy as the wine.

Barbarossa's second motion passed.

Cleon said, “Should we weave Claire into our expectations and arrangements?”

Pale-eyed Tarquin said, “Must we?”

Barbarossa said, “Again with this woman. Here, let me repeat the wise words a woman offers.” He let out a loud meaty fart, a protracted scorcher with a little zip at the end. “Ahhh, my belly was tight with foolishness, and this wisdom has relieved it.” Those near him wrinkled their noses and waved their hands. Barbarossa grinned toothily at Cleon, then all around the table: *you bastards haven’t domesticated me yet.*

# 22

## BEGGING DAY

CLAIRE DIDN'T WANT to be washed or dressed or waited on. This was strange and upsetting to the women's dormitory maids. She noticed that Epida, the lowest and youngest of them, wound up almost alone on Claire duty.

The next morning, finding the maid in a hurry to finish tidying, Claire gently said, "Have you something fun to get to, Epida?" Epida looked over from across the apartment; she tried to stay as far from Claire as she could.

She said, "No, my lady. It's begging day, and I work at the food line."

Claire said, "Is that a duty of yours, or something you choose to do?" Epida said, "I choose to."

Claire said, "Surely you haven't much of your own – why do you choose to give away your time, which is to say your labor, which is to say your money?"

Epida thought that over for a minute, then she said, "All the more so should a poor person care for the poor."

This pleased Claire very much and she stood from the vanity

and said, "I'll help you finish up here, Epida. I beg you'll let me join you working at the food line."

Epida stopped dusting a moment and said, "Why should a noblewoman want to help out with begging day?" Claire said, "I am born of good name, but I haven't my father, and my mother doesn't care for riches. So I lived simply enough in Zanzibar, and own nothing at all in Florence."

Little Epida's mouth actually opened in surprise. She said, "You're poor?" Claire smiled at her and said, "I have only what is given me. I think I would do well to learn virtue from somebody of like station, and none is more like me than you, Epida."

Epida narrowed her eyes and said, "That's kind of you to say, my lady, but we aren't alike at all. You're special, and I'm not."

Claire, being young and naïve, didn't realize that when Epida said her words were kind, she meant the opposite.

## XXX

HER ARMS BURNED and her hands were sticky. It was past noon and Golden Gate didn't shade her table anymore. She could hear the clink of coins at the copper table to her side. She was cutting bread at the feast table.

"Claire! Take a rest!"

Wordless and exhausted, she handed Epida the knife. She stood and walked away from the table. One of the women handed her a bronze cup of tepid water and she gulped it down. She retreated to the shadow of the gate, fanning her sweat-soaked work smock out from her chest.

Back here, she had a clearer view of the line of beggars: widows, paupers, veterans. Children. The unbearable sadness of it bent her over. Hundreds still waited for their food and coins.

She breathed in and out till she felt steadier, then approached one of the women ladling soup and said, "I'll take soup a while." The woman nodded and finished ladling a bowl. That emptied the pot; the men ferrying supplies lifted it and replaced it. The woman handed her ladle to Claire, and Claire took her place at the table.

She ladled soup into a woman's bowl; the bowl was fired clay and its rim was chipped. When the bowl was full, the woman balanced it in one hand and reached out with the other. She softly touched Claire's cheek. Claire hadn't understood right away, but she soon realized it was no small thing to be served by the Sower of Peace, and have a gentle smile from her, and see her gleaming hair fallen past her golden filigree and sticking on her brow.

Claire wasn't only chasing virtue. She wanted to find that cult which had worshipped her and fed her a white rabbit in the forest. It had been dark and fiery when she'd met them and she didn't think she'd know any of them on sight, except perhaps the priestess with the knife. But Marcus had told her they were poor people, practicing the religion of the poor, and so she hoped if she put herself in the way of the poor, they might make themselves known to her.

They didn't.

All day long she served the beggars. Many wanted to touch her, softly, as the woman had. One of them looked Claire in the eye and said, "What sin are you working off?" Claire swiped at her tears with the back of her hand and said, "I don't know."

## XXX

When evening fell, she washed her hands with the others. She was satisfied to find blisters on her fingers. It made her think of Lady Varo's enviably rough palms. Work was real, here or in Zanzibar. Rough palms were real, her mother's or Varo's.

Epida came over and bumped Claire on the shoulder and said, "Well done, for a noblewoman. Will you finally let me bathe you?" Claire ignored her question, saying, "How often is begging day?" Epida said, "Every week." Claire said, "I should like to go on lending a hand, if I'd be welcome here." Epida frowned at her and said, "You're queer, Claire, but you pull your weight." She turned and put her hands to her mouth and hollered, "Cecilia! Cecilia Cluvia!"

A stout woman, middle aged, came forward from the staging area far back of the table, wiping her hands on a rag. Claire knew her on sight. Of course she did; this woman had been in the front row of the worshippers in the forest.

Epida said, "The Sower of Peace here hasn't learned her lesson. May she come and serve again next week?"

The woman crinkled her eyes at Claire and said, "Our mistress of the curved blade makes her living as a butcher. You'll find her up Serapetine Hill on full moon market day." Claire curtsied respectfully. The woman said, "You still want to come back and work the food line?" Claire said, "If I may."

Big Cecilia Cluvia hugged her, and her feet briefly left the ground.

## XXX

When she was working the food line, and one of the Thousand came before her, he hardly needed to identify himself; Claire would stop and clasp his hand and thank him. She was developing a sense of who was who – her Thousand, the loyal kingsmen of the second morax, the pirates of the third. She had the impression there were many soldiers in the line, and she was correct. This was the problem, in those first weeks: the Florentine armies, scattered over the valley of the world, found themselves without employment.

Those who had homes to return to, went. As for the rest, it was too late in the season for sharecropping. Some men found work as hands on the autumn harvest. Some took up where their soldiering left off, turning to banditry. The warrior nobles put these gangs down, each in his demesne, so well as they could. It became unsafe to cross Rusadir and the other great forests.

The remaining veterans drained into the cities. Thousands swelled Florence city. At the start, the grateful burghers of Florence took lodgers gratis. The price of flour soon spiked, and the hosts quickly tired of the extra burden on their pantries. Their guests were dirty and menacing. The arrangement was like an unmown hayfield at the end of a dry summer, waiting on a spark.

# 23

## OUR LADY OF THE POISONED TEARS

SENSING THE CITY sinking toward violence, the king restricted Claire to the royal district. Pampered and protected there, Claire eavesdropped one morning on two charwomen performing their rounds. She heard one say that the Sower of Peace could as likely be just one more Mathilda. She went back to the colonnaded courtyard and sat herself down on a bench beneath a tree. She waited there, tapping her foot and wondering where ai Ctesiphôn had gone, until she saw her young page hurrying past. She called to him, and when he reluctantly came by, she said, "Who is this Mathilda?"

Without preamble, he recounted a strange story. He said, "Mathilda was a great sinner, and Deianira, the goddess of mercy, punished her by poisoning her tears. They were harmless to Mathilda, but if they moistened anybody else's skin, that one would die. Mathilda went around constantly shedding her black tears, and nobody wanted to have fun with her.

"Half-blinded by her poisoned tears, lonely and alone, she was begging in the street. This was how she met Tacamo, who was passing through Florence. He shared his bread and cheese with her, and she told him her story. Tacamo had a fine nose for money-making schemes, and straightway asked Mathilda if her tears were poison to men only, or to all animals. Mathilda wasn't sure, so they caught them a pigeon, and Mathilda wept on it, and behold the pigeon died. Therefore Tacamo proposed they go into business together, and she, having nothing and no one, agreed.

"Tacamo decanted her tears into little pots and sold these to the burghers of Florence. They sprinkled the poisoned tears around the floors of their homes, and the tears killed all their pests and vermin, being mainly mice and cockroaches and bedbugs. This business was such a success that Tacamo and Mathilda found themselves atop a small pile of gold, and began to wear fine clothes and keep good company, notwithstanding Mathilda's constant weeping.

"Now in order to renew the fury of Deianira, Mathilda had to commit fresh sins every so often, such as making love to bravos, sometimes two or three at a time, or giving the chop chop to old misers and dowagers with her little axe. As her fortunes improved, these chores became loathsome to her, for everybody knows that wealth breeds virtue.

"One day her tears dried up, and she admitted to Tacamo she had no stomach for sinning anymore. He stamped and pleaded, but there was nothing for it.

"Mathilda went off and married a duke of splendid name, with much land and many men to till it. Tacamo should have husbanded his share of the candy, but he was Tacamo, after all, and soon spent everything on drink and gambling and presents for his ungrateful friends. The day came that his last good pair of trousers sprang a hole in the bum. He sewed on a patch cut from the torn sleeve of his last good coat. He piled up his possessions on a cloth, and made the cloth into a bindle to tie on his fancy walking cane. He sold the bronze head off the cane, and hefted the bindle over his shoulder. Thus impoverished, he left Florence as he entered it, alone on the low road, but happy all the same."

This was the first tale Claire ever heard of Tacamo the Vagabond, and she would have enjoyed it under other circumstances. As things stood, she found her jaw trembling. She felt ashamed of her pride in finding work on begging day. She felt ashamed of her blisters. She let the little page go without asking him any more questions about ai Ctesiphôn, as she had meant to do. In fact she said nothing at all, because she didn't trust her voice.

## XXX

TEMET AMBROSIUS, MAGISTER equitum, cousin of the king, wanted to turn and look south to Florence. But his men rode behind him, eyes on his back. Sweat trickled from his armpits down his sides. Each time a cicada ended its song, another took up the drowsy melody.

His heart sat at the bottom of his chest. He longed to see Florence one more time.

Sixteen riders followed him, not twelve. He'd chosen twelve of his own mounted Tagmata, as the king instructed. Then the mayor, with his bald head and unkempt mustaches, turned up and said, "Send two back to barracks; I'll give you six vigiles for the money." Tagmata were royal troops. Vigiles were city guard.

"What good are vigiles to me?"

"Tagmata are good for fighting. Vigiles sniff out criminals."

Temet Ambrosius liked that: this Crimson Knight as nothing but a criminal.

"I'll take them, Mayor, and thank you."

Now he rode north, rising and falling with the easy walk of his horse Boreas, a handsome gray beast, on the packed earth bed of Ligusticum Street. He listened to the pace of the Tagmata, familiar, heavy. The vigiles had narrower horses and sat lightly on them. The clank of their armor was almost musical to his ear.

He sniffed, then sneezed. Out in the fields, farmhands were baling hay, and the air was hazy with straw dust. He threw his head back and sneezed again, then made the blessing to Enantius, god of health. Eyes watering, he looked at the broad and empty bowl of the sky. Too much sky.

Lady Varo had come out to bid him farewell. They were as one regarding the virtues of Florence. Honor, probity, loyalty. Their virtues restrained them. But she touched the bare part of his arm and told him to take care.

He hated this assignment. He was a man of court and city. He hated leaving Florence, he hated the prospect of questioning the noblemen, his own people.

*And what will I do if I find the Crimson Knight?*

*I have ten Tagmata. We'll destroy him.*

*...what if we can't?*

He thought again about the light gait of the vigile horses. He raised his hand and drew his horse up. The men slowed and stopped, and the staffers, trudging behind, halted their pack animals.

Temet said to the vigiles, "You're fast-riders, aren't you?"

Their leader smiled wryly and said, "Aye, sir, the fastest."

Temet wagged a finger at him and said, "Your master is very tricky." The Tagmata looked at one another in confusion. Temet said, "I had thought to arrest the Crimson Knight, or fight him if we must. But our dear mayor was a step ahead of me. These vigiles are meant to flee, and carry word to Florence."

The decanus of the Tagmata said, "Flee?"

Temet said, "If the Crimson Knight defeats us."

The decanus made a rude gesture.

Temet said, "We will stop here to pray and eat."

He dismounted and fetched carrots from his saddle bag and fed them to Boreas himself. His horse snorted softly at him and he snorted softly back.

The cook and his assistant got to work; they had provisions for a couple days. After that, they'd be begging meals from the warrior nobles.

Before eating, the riders prayed. Temet faced his beloved Florence. The city was dark on the horizon, the sky dirty above it. There was ai Ctesiphôn, tall and narrow. He felt the serenity of choosing to let something go.

After they ate, they rode till the end of the day was upon them. They made camp at the mouth of a side road onto the farms. This was all king's land. The farmhands had gone home and the fields were thick with crickets.

The day had been hot, but the evening cooled quickly. A waxing moon rose. It looked shockingly close, as it does some evenings out in the country. Temet Ambrosius shivered.

## XXX

"AM I JUST one more Mathilda?"

Marcus put down the cold chicken leg he was eating and glared at her.

"Who have you been spying on, O Claire?"

He'd stolen a morning from working at the warehouse to see her. He could justify it to the king as discussing details of the expedition. But he didn't have to go see the barber first. And he certainly didn't have to take Claire to Desiderio's. He suspected she was feeling cooped up in the royal district, so he got her out – Desiderio's was on Primavera Circle, the wide road that ringed the district. At lunchtime you could get hot mulled wine there and a bite of chicken. There were outdoor tables and the day was warm enough, but he hid Claire in the dim interior.

The beautiful patricia wore a dull cloak, to hide her bare breast, and a woolen shawl, to hide her blonde hair, and thin buff leather gloves, to hide the jewels in her fingernails. To a casual eye, she looked just like a young bourgeoise, carrying on a hesitant midday affair of soft words and glances. She looked nearly boring.

"How do you reason I was spying?"

Marcus said, "Nobody's stupid enough to call you a Mathilda to your face." Claire admitted, "I was spying on the dormitory charwomen." He said, "They are old gossips with venom in their hearts. You are no Mathilda, Claire."

She continued, "You were very eager we should meet here." He was not yet used to her rude habit of changing the subject once she'd lost interest or found out what she wanted. She said, "What's special about Desiderio's?" She scanned the place: the small windows set in the thick walls, the glazed white tiles with their little scenes painted in blue, the door to the kitchen and the second door beyond it to the back alley.

Marcus said, "It was here Ambrosius first laid eyes on Antonella."

She tilted her head at him and said, "Oughtn't they have met at some fancy affair in the castle?" He said, "None of it, they met here, at the left-hand table in front. She was a girl drinking honeyed milk, and he was a handsome prince, riding around Primavera Circle." She waited for Marcus to tell her more, and he let her wait. She studied his face, a smile creeping up the corner of her mouth, but in the end refused to take the bait.

She said, "I have been thinking me upon the sermon of Reburrus." Marcus said, "Did you think anything especially interesting?" She sparkled at him from under her brow and said, "Everything I think is interesting. But listen, Marcus Irenaeus, his sermon confuses me." He said, "What is it confused you, Claire?" She said, "It was the sort of sermon one preaches on the eve of war, to firm up the bravery of men." The patricia had nearly teased this thread out. Marcus took a swallow of his wine and said, "Go on." She said, "The war is over. I cannot believe he is inapt in his preaching. So why does he pitch his moral so?"

He said, "O Claire, the war with Genova is over. But his concern is not the wars of men, it is the wars of gods. He prepares men for this alone." He watched the beautiful patricia worry out the last few tangles. She slowly said, "He thinks a war among the gods is in the offing. In this regard nothing has changed in Florence except – except..." She paused, and he munched his chicken at her, and she said, "...except for me. He looks at me, and sees invasion by a foreign god."

As if casually, around a mouthful of chicken, Marcus said, "Are you a god?"

She rolled her eyes, looking out the little window by the table, lost in thought. "This is why he takes me for an enemy. I am the alien inside the gate." His heart lurched in his breast; a world of murderers stood between her and Zanzibar. *Can I protect her in all directions?* But he said nothing.

She continued, "Why don't the Florentines think about ai Ctesiphôn?" She startled him again, dropping one thread, taking up another. He said, "How much have you learned about ai Ctesiphôn?" She said, "Only that it is a very big tower, right in the middle of Florence, and yet nobody thinks about it. It has a window in the top, and sometimes I think I see a tree in the window."

Her testimony shocked him. It told him that ai Ctesiphôn had taken an interest in the patricia, and shown itself to her not only once, but more than once.

She nearly succeeded in interpreting the look on his face and said, "Dear Marcus, are you going to tell me it is a ghost tower maybe, and substanceless?"

Marcus was very smart and used to winning every round of conversation. He would have followed the patricia for this alone: she was a woman, but sometimes beat him. He put down his chicken bone and wiped his mouth and his fingers on a scrap of cloth he carried. He said, "You are not far off the mark, O Claire. This troublesome tower is rarely seen, but when seen, it might be seen from anywhere. Even so, it can be reached from nowhere. Seek the foot of ai Ctesiphôn, and you will walk all day long, and come home dusty and dejected. It is called the tower of the king, but the king may take his finest men and horse and gallop the streets and never find it. The tower does not seem to care. It denies everyone, and then suffers whoever it pleases to reach it, a Tacamo so much as an Ambrosius. Few enough can find its foot, and those who find the door come down to us in gossip only; gossip and legends, and legends are nothing but the gossip of our ancestors."

Claire said, "I have heard the king's own brother, Ælius Pellucidus, made his way inside of it."

Marcus sighed and answered the credulous patricia thus: "So it is said, but only because they never found him. Did he go inside? He set out to, indeed he did, and the little prick took Sibyllam Cumis with him – the red sword, the sword of his fathers and his fathers' fathers. He was seeking the withered oak. That is the tree you saw in the window."

Claire said, "What is the withered oak, and why should Ælius Pellucidus have staked his life to find it?"

Marcus said, "That is two questions. The better answer to the second one is that Ælius Pellucidus was a hothead and a fool. Only the Ambrosii adored him – far better his little brother should wear the crown. For all that, he did have cause to seek the withered oak. Henceforth I speak again in legends and riddles and other ichneumonish nonsense. The withered oak is, in a way, the living power of the king. Until it blooms again, the hand of the king is weak, and his rule in doubt. Every king of Florence prays the oak to bloom, and yet the oak's been dying all these years, high up in ai Ctesiphôn. The inside of the tower is none but stairs, and every landing splits, so that even if a pilgrim finds the tower's foot, and walks around the foot and finds the door, and gets inside the door – even then he may not reach the oak, for there is a bewilderment of staircases in the way, and the tower may lure him into the stairs and never let him out. Ambrosius believes his older brother's bones lie at the foot of the tree, still clutching the red sword. Most likely they are scattered on the stairs. I say, 'most likely,' Claire, but this already grants the stairs exist, and who can say? All we can say is that there is one Ctesiphôn, and maybe two."

Claire said, "So the weakness of Ambrosius lies not in his character alone, nor in his brother's loss of the red sword, but also in the ill-health of this tree."

Marcus said, "It sounds fairly silly when you put it like that."

Claire absently remarked, "Not at all, my champion and savior. The world is very large, and full of strange things."

Marcus said, "Reason constrains even what is strange."

Claire raised one eyebrow at him and said, "Remind me what 'Diophantus' means."

He pursed his lips and said, "You know full well it means 'the one who saw god.'"

She said, "Just so," and turned back to the window. There was a little light on her face, and he could see her gaze was all intent and unselfconscious. Without turning back to him, she said, "Who built ai Ctesiphôn?" Studying her, he said, "O Claire, it must have been a king, but a king of what, we do not know. Perhaps he was a wanax or a gausileus, as they called the kings in the first days of Florence. But tell me – why are you asking all these questions about ai Ctesiphôn?"

The grave patricia said, "Well for one thing it is strange, and therefore interesting. And for another, it is right outside this window right this minute, and I am looking at it."

Marcus caused some small commotion lurching forward across the table, but covered it by brushing his lips against the cheek of the patricia. Her eye turned to him, bright and birdlike. He knew she had the king's order against romancing him, and she had clearly figured out he had it too.

She pressed her cheek against his lips.

The other diners, seeing the shaven dandy complete his move on the shy bourgeoise, went back to their lunch. Claire's eye flicked back toward the window. Eye by eye the two of them stared at ai Ctesiphôn. She whispered to him, "Would you like to go chase it right now?" He smelled the faintest smell of thunder and of honeysuckles on her skin. He said, "I might."

By the time they got to the street, ai Ctesiphôn was gone.

# 24

## THE WALLS OF FLORENCE

OH THIS FELT good. No more struggling in the morning to stand from his bed. Manfredi Ambrosius, king of Florence, ninth of his line, shook the dust off his legs on the Campus Iucundum. He trained for war.

He filled his lungs and opened his throat and shouted in his full battle voice – "Front rank fall in!"

Before him on the plain, the youngest Wardogs trotted toward position, armor clanking at the shoulders and the knees. A flock of legates and optios harangued their units – "All of you forward!" "Tighter on the left!" "Maintain spacing!" Ambrosius looked around at his elite Tagmata. They nodded to him, and he nodded to them. Bitsy Boots ran back and forth, waving his arms with excitement. He had all his armor on. Ambrosius ruffled his plume as he passed by. And all the time, he counted his breaths.

The front rank took shape: it wasn't one single line, but a forward line with gaps, and a rear line behind. The rear had gaps where the forward had men and men where the forward had gaps. Ambrosius had been reviewing old battles fought near Florence.

His second morax already knew the individual valor of street fighting and the massed force of phalanx clashes. Now he was training them to apply an army's might, but show a small unit's flexibility. Hill country warfare. There were rolling hills outside the city.

The clanking quieted. The men stood in position, shields up, spears up. Each tenman shouted "Hail Florence!" as it completed formation. The last tenman straightened its line and made its shout.

He paced back and forth along the front rank. He roared "*Ad victoria!*" and the Wardogs answered "*Ave Ambrosius! Ad victoria!*" Bitsy Boots added his voice to the cry.

Ambrosius returned to his Tagmata and looked at its tribune. He said, "Forty-three breaths?" The tribune said, "Forty-three." Ambrosius said, "Let's run it with the drummers and see if we can't speed it up."

## XXX

AFTERNOON FOUND HIM puffing his way alone up a tower in the tallest of the three concentric walls of Florence, the inner one. Training for war gave him back a flare of youth. Climbing stairs reminded him he was old. He didn't slow.

He gained the peak but hid in the stairwell till his breathing evened out. Then he emerged into the light, calm and commanding. He surveyed the splendid western view: sun and scudding clouds, hills and forests sharp in the distance. The Campus Iucundum ahead. At its far edge, he could see men building Diophantus's giant warehouse. The tent city of the Thousand lay just to the south. Nearer, the Wardogs still practiced formation under the eye of the Tagmata. The rhythm of their war drums punctuated the clamor of Florence at his back. Below him, the first wall and the second wall crawled with Redheads. His father's army, the third morax, wild men who'd never quite warmed to him.

He turned to Furius Nasica, the general of the third morax, and said, "Describe me what I'm looking at." Nasica was a hand taller than Ambrosius, with a furrow down each gaunt cheek that vanished in a beard gone bushy since the peace. They said he'd once marched six days without sleep.

With a cutting gesture of his cupped hand, Nasica said, "Yonder they are practicing response to massed attack." Ambrosius observed men collecting along a single span of the lowest wall.

Nasica gestured closer by and said, "Yonder they are practicing repulsion of siege engines." Ambrosius watched a team on the wide cobbled path behind the second wall wheeling a wooden petrary into place.

Nasica said, "They will practice with ladders, panels, rod-and-rollers, the bow, fire, anti-towers." He looked steadily at the king. "The Crimson Knight will never breach these walls."

Ambrosius gave the third morax the walls to defend, because he meant his beloved Wardogs to defeat the Crimson Knight long before he reached the city. It was a snub and the Redheads knew it. Nasica knew it. But he and his men worked with industry. Ambrosius said, "I'm impressed." Nasica nodded curtly. The two men watched the petrary rumble to a stop. Specialists rotated its arm. The shouted commands of Redhead legates echoed from the walls.

Finally Ambrosius said, "Have your tribunes uncovered anything of these rumors?" Nasica squinted into the distance. His mustache twitched once over his tight mouth. He said, "Barbarossa was up here again asking about it. We've interviewed all nineteen men now who heard rumors. There were four distinct rumors. Four rumors, four sources. We've found the sources and questioned each of them."

Ambrosius meaningfully repeated, "Questioned?"

Nasica said, "Let me describe what three of them told me."

Ambrosius said, "Speak."

Nasica's gaze came back from the horizon to his king. He said, "The Crimson Knight invited each of them to join his army. All three turned him down."

Ambrosius said, "Where was the approach made?"

Nasica let out a long breath and said, "The first was approached on Balearicum Street, two days' ride west of Florence city. A second met a man on the Vextal Road, coming down from the north. The third had it whispered to him in a public house on the shore of Syrtis Minor."

Ambrosius felt ice between his shoulder blades.

He said, "All of them named the Crimson Knight?" Nasica said, "Yes."

Rumors of one man, coming from everywhere.

He said, "All since the end of the war?" Nasica said, "All since the end. We've torn apart the public house, but found nothing." Ambrosius said, "Tell me about the fourth man."

Nasica said, "We had to question the fourth man with blades. He told the same story as the others: a soldier of the Crimson Knight approached him and invited him. But the fourth man accepted. The soldier gave him one medallion to wear, and another one to carry. The first medallion was an advance on his wages in employ of the Crimson Knight, and proof of his employment to his secret fellows."

Ambrosius said, "And the second medallion?"

Nasica said, "He was to choose a friend he could trust. When he chose the man, he would invite him. The new man would pledge his allegiance, and receive the second medallion. Thus he too would become a soldier of the Crimson Knight."

The general rummaged in his purse and brought out two gold medallions, blood-crusted. Ambrosius balanced one in his palm. It weighed about an aureus' worth – a month's pay to a common soldier. It might actually have been an aureus, broadened in an unlicensed coin press: it was quite thin and flat.

He set the two medallions beside each other in his hand and studied them.

Each had a little hole punched in the top, to allow it to be worn on a cord. One face was stamped as Barbarossa had described the banner: a knight on a horse. The reverse showed the

He set the two medallions beside each
other in his hand and studied them.

divided rectangle, emblem of Florence, with the inscription AT FLORENTUM HONORIADE – *To the honor of Florence.* It was the old city motto, from before the Ambrosii took the throne.

Ambrosius held a medallion up to Nasica and said, "What does this motto tell us?"

Nasica frowned at the motto, and finally gave a curt shrug.

Ambrosius said, "It tells us he thinks the ancient virtues sanction him. He acts on behalf of Florence. He's more the Florentine than I."

Nasica said, "Ordinary men cannot map the claims and slights of you warrior nobles."

Ambrosius said, "You'd have to be a noble." He handed the medallions back. "Deliver these to the vigiles. They'll investigate the goldsmiths."

Nasica said, "Any kind of smith could have made these."

Ambrosius said, "It's true, but we have to start somewhere."

Nasica stuffed the medallions back in his purse and said, "About this fourth man." Ambrosius looked at him. Nasica said, "You know the type of soldier who's got a craving to die in battle?" Ambrosius asked, "High honor or lunacy?" Nasica said, "Lunacy. This man had it. He didn't survive the questioning." Ambrosius frowned. Nasica said, "He'd make a fine decoration for Traitor's Gate." The Redheads, always needling their king's son. Ambrosius rebuked him: "We're done living in our filth like barbarians." Nasica had the sense to let it drop.

Ambrosius scanned the horizon, listening to the city and the land.

*Where are you, Crimson Knight? Have I guessed your plan correctly?*

He said, "The knight's recruitment scheme makes no sense, and he's recruiting madmen."

Nasica said, "Ask me where this madman was recruited." Ambrosius felt icy sweat on his back again. To ask it was to answer it. He said, "Florence city."

Nasica nodded his curt nod and said, "Serapetine Hill."

## XXX

Lady Varo said, "Stop worrying about the Crimson Knight for one minute and pay attention to your task." Her powdered cheeks were white in the light entering the door of the great hall. And beneath the paint – that furnace burn, faintly visible.

Claire said, "Aren't you worried?"

Lady Varo said, "I worry over what is mine to do. What isn't mine is none of mine."

Claire tilted her head at the fascinating noblewoman.

"I'll do what I can to follow your guidance."

Lady Varo said, "This is the start of wisdom. Think only about the Family Dinner. You will ornament the king –"

Claire gestured back into the gloom, "And if the Crimson Knight invades the hall, as the whispers have it?"

A cord stood out a moment on Lady Varo's long neck, poor as she was at concealing her emotions. She grated, "Then you will hide under a table and let the men do their work."

Claire said, "Aha. This is wise indeed. Good then, what was it you wanted to tell me about?"

Lady Varo took a breath to speak, then shot Claire a quizzical look. Claire looked at her, doe-eyed.

Lady Varo said, "You're not as guileless as you seem."

Claire said, "I am innocent, but not guileless."

Lady Varo said, "A fine asset. Share this only with those you trust –"

Claire watched her realize. Her cheeks flushed, underneath the powder. She murmured, "Oh."

Claire smiled and said, "Now. What is today's lesson?"

Lady Varo looked down at her palms, then turned her hands

over and looked at her fingernails. She looked up and said, "We will start upon the art of conversation: topics you may raise, topics a nobleman may raise before a lady. The implications of each topic. The structure of a discourse, from its introduction to its close. Quips, parries, transitions. Miscellaneous ploys."

## XXX

TEMET AMBROSIUS HEARD the distant voices of men. Happy shouts, excited; they must be playing football.

The farmhands hadn't mown the tall fescue out here yet, and Temet was nearly upon the field before he spotted it. Coming around a curve in Ligusticum Street, a clearing opened up before him, and football players, running, shouting, laughing as they chased the ball.

They protected their heads against the beating sun with red cloths. Redheads.

*What are Redheads doing here?*

Temet brought his party to a halt a little back from the field. The Redheads spotted him and waved, all good nature.

Temet called out, "What brings the third morax to Ligusticum Street?"

A barrel-chested fellow with a thick beard held up a finger and jogged to one side of the clearing. He grabbed a skin of water and took a pull from it and poured the rest over his bandana. The football hit him in the side of the head. He turned to the kicker and pointed and barked. Then he faced Temet and raised an arm, waving him over. Just like the Redheads: disorganized but somehow menacing. Temet warily dismounted. He could feel the Tagmata behind him, ready.

Temet said again, "What brings the third morax to Ligusticum Street?"

Beard dripping water, the barrel-chested fellow said, "Sir, it's a conspiracy."

Temet jerked straight and his hand went to his sword. The fellow laughed. The other Redheads, drifting over, laughed as well.

The man said, "Not to worry, magister. Magister? Yes, you're Ambrosius, aren't you?"

Temet nodded.

The Redhead said, "Constantine is paying us. We're guarding the roads into Florence."

Temet gawped.

The Redhead said, "Ambrosius has the second morax training to fight outside the city. He's got our boys guarding the walls. What's he missing?"

Temet shrugged, growing frustrated.

The Redhead said, "Early warning. We've got units on all the roads. Constantine gold is buying two days' warning of direction, size, and approach of the army of the Crimson Knight."

Temet frowned. The Constantines didn't hide their contempt for the Ambrosii. He said, "Why would Constantine want to help the king?"

The Redhead said, "Ambrosius has debts to pay. Crimson Knight can't have him, not till his account is settled anyway."

The Redhead spotted the unwilling little smile beneath Temet's dark mustache and pointed rudely at him, grinning. Temet confessed, "That makes sense."

The Redhead said, "Constantines."

Temet said, "Constantines."

The Redhead stuck his hand out, and Temet took it. The Redhead said, "Leander Rigellus." Temet said, "Temet Ambrosius," leaving out his middle name, so as not to wave his rank over the commoner.

Leander saw right through it, saying, "*My lord*, what brings you this way?"

Temet said, "We're on our way to question the warrior nobles."

"Looking for the Crimson Knight?"

"If he's there, we'll root him out."

"You need water? Feed? Stretch your legs with us a while, play a game."

Temet shook his head. "We're aiming for the estate of Lucius Vitus Pollius before sundown."

Leander turned and squinted north. He said, "Pollius is a ways up the road." He looked at the sun and said, "You're right, best go. You can still get there today." He gestured to his men.

The football players parted respectfully. Temet saluted Leander and climbed back on Boreas. He led his party between the Redheads. He listened after he had passed. Silence behind. The eyes of his men were on him and he didn't turn back.

When his cousin Manfredi had taken the throne, a lot of nobles had still supported the claim of his missing brother, Ælius Pellucidus. Likewise the old king's army, the third morax. They'd stood in a shadow ever since.

It wasn't till these unnerving pirates were far behind that Temet heard them resume their game.

## XXX

TEMET REMEMBERED POLLIUS as a grizzled lancer with a bronze rod for a spine. Now he was a feeble old man. He passed a hand demonstratively through his soft, wispy hair, and Temet turned away. Pollius said, "It's alright, lad, I know I've aged."

Temet said, "What happened?"

Pollius leaned toward the miserly fire and held his hands out to it and said, "Bad harvests. Lost sons. My youngest rode to his death just in time for the war to end."

Temet said, "May the god relieve your sorrow, *laudatus*."

Pollius made a joyless half-smile without turning. Then a thought occurred to him. He looked at Temet and said, "After all these years, your cousin has finally won me over. Nobody could figure out a way to defeat Genova without destroying it, and nobody wanted to destroy Genova, not really. Who could have imagined peace without victory? Brilliant, Temet. Brilliant."

He rocked back and forth, warming his hands by the fire. Temet looked at the *ultima cicatrice* on his right cheek, the scar an honorable warrior carved when facing death. Pollius had two. Temet had none.

Pollius said, "Peace. That's the relief for my sorrow."

Maybe it was the influence of the cider, or fatigue from two days' long ride, but Temet's whole body filled with tingling revelation, and his eyes brimmed with tears. Pollius said, "What's the matter, *carissimus*?"

Temet said, "I've considered myself a model of Florentine virtue, *patruus*. But sitting with you, I think I haven't understood honor at all."

Pollius said, "There is no honor without suffering. I'll pray to Deianira you remain ignorant of it."

Temet bowed his head.

Pollius said, "Now perhaps you'd like to check the stables."

Temet said, "What's in the stables?"

Pollius coldly answered, "Maybe I'm hiding the army there, with which I plan to overthrow my king."

## XXX

TEMET SAID, "THE Crimson Knight isn't here."

The Tagmata relaxed. The vigiles looked unsatisfied; they hadn't had their turn with Pollius.

The decanus of the Tagmata said, "The barn for the night?" Temet said, "The staff can take the barn. Pollius invites us to bed down in the great hall. Bring your blankets, it's cold."

The cook said, "Supplies?"

Temet said, "Oats and water for the horses. He's got food for us, only –"

The men waited.

He said, "Only eat lightly. An ancient name isn't the same as a full larder."

The men dispersed to their tasks.

Temet fished out the gold medallion that hung around his neck. He looked at it. On one side, the divided rectangle, with the city motto, AD GLORIA FLORENTIS.

On the other side, the emblem of the sun god, the circle inscribed in the square. Inside the circle, the king in profile.

He kissed his cousin's profile.

*May Pantokrator protect you, Manfredi Ambrosius.*

*May He protect Pollius, who has sacrificed so much for Florence.*

*May He protect us all.*

# 25

## WHAT REBURRUS GIVES

BITSY BOOTS KEPT asking Claire if she knew why he was so excited, and Claire would say, "Why are you so excited?" and he would say, "Because I get to go on my first hunt!" But his excitement dried right up when it came time for the benediction.

They did it after sundown the day before the hunt. They met in the porphyry chapel off the great hall, opposite the jade office. Where the office swam in green gloom, the purple stone of the chapel seemed to drink light entirely. Despite all the candles and rushlights, the chapel was sunk in eerie darkness. The pale faces of the supplicants looked blotchy and disembodied. Claire disliked the place immensely, even before Reburrus made his entrance. Beside her, she felt Bitsy Boots stiffen as the red priest swept in. *You and I agree on this, Domenico.* Reburrus scanned them with his locked rotating eyes. *False violet, like the chapel. Red and blue together. A false color for a false god.* Reburrus paused at the patricia, staring at her. She stared back. *Enemy.*

Ambrosius, in the middle of the line of kneeling supplicants, said, "Good my ichneumon, bless mine hunt." Antonella and

Marcus and the city dandies bowed their heads, so Claire did too. Bitsy Boots was trembling, and she reached over and took his stubby little boy hand. His palm was sweaty.

Reburrus spoke in his twanging voice, "Good my king, the god pours sweet waters on the head of the good hunter; he suffers his waters to splash the hunter's party, the wicked and the just alike. Ride with you I cannot, but Antivola rides for me. Fleet Vanadio rides with his worshippers. Him you will know from the star of the east. Pantokrator splashes his sweet waters on the good hunt."

He lifted a silver cup from the altar and walked along the line of supplicants. Each one took a sip of wine. Bitsy Boots squeezed Claire's hand painfully. She looked at him and saw he nearly swooned with terror. Reburrus approached. The king sipped. Antonella sipped. The cup was empty now. Reburrus went back to the altar and filled it again and moved along the row to Bitsy Boots. The boy pressed his lips shut and turned away. Antonella bent to her son and said, "What is it, Domenico?"

Bitsy Boots kept his lips shut and shook his head. Ambrosius craned around his wife and growled, "Domenico, drink."

Bitsy Boots wavered under his father's glare, but didn't yield. He hoarsely whispered, "Little boys mustn't drink what Reburrus gives."

The supplicants murmured. Claire saw a tremor pass through Reburrus. Reburrus looked to Ambrosius, and Ambrosius to Reburrus.

*What foul secret do the Florentines share?*

The patricia looked at her enemy and said, "Give it here." The eye of Reburrus shot to her, to her outstretched hand. His nostrils flared. Antonella said, "Good my ichneumon, *do as she says.*" Reburrus rubbed the bridge of his nose, and extended the cup with one hand. The back of his hand glistened in the candlelight. Sores. Claire took the silver cup.

She turned to Bitsy Boots and said, "Do I weigh twice as much as you?" He managed to say, "Maybe twice?" She said, "I will take two sips, and you take one. If he means to hurt you, he'll hurt me just as much." She tipped the cup and downed a good half of it. Reburrus hissed. She looked at him and bared her wine-stained teeth, the darkness of her mouth. Then she ostentatiously turned from him.

She sat on her haunches, so that she was the same height as kneeling Bitsy Boots. She said to him, "You are not yourself alone. You are not for yourself alone. A line of fathers stands behind you. A line of sons stands before you. You are one blood. You share one fate. Their gods are your gods. Your gods are their gods. There is no holier duty than worship, Domenico." She looked at Reburrus and said, "Wise my ichneumon, do I speak the truth?" Reburrus bristled, but said to Bitsy Boots, "My prince, the alien speaks the truth."

Claire held out the cup to Domenico and said, "Drink, Domenico. Join your family. Join your god."

Bitsy Boots said, "I will do as you say, Auntie Claire."

He held out his hands and solemnly took the cup from her. It shook, but he got it to his mouth and took a sip.

XXX

TEMET AMBROSIUS HAD his blade out before he was properly awake. The man who'd been shaking him backed off. He held his lamp up so that Temet could see his face: it was the decanus of the Tagmata.

"What is it?" Temet growled as he got his wits.

"We've lost a man."

"*Lost?*"

XXX

IT WASN'T MORNING yet and everyone milled miserably about. One of the night watch had vanished. The decanus mulishly repeated, "Fabius is no deserter."

Temet said, "Then where is he?"

The decanus turned to his men and said, "Three teams. Search the woods."

Temet held up a hand and said, "Let's say he didn't desert. What else could have happened?"

The decanus said, "Bandits? They say there's bandits everywhere, since the end of the war."

Temet said, "What kind of bandit abducts a single man?" He gestured at the horses and added, "Why would a bandit leave the horses?"

The decanus was about to answer, but a ruckus sounded among the staffers. The armorer jogged over and said, "The cook is gone."

Temet watched the fighting spirit dim a little in his Tagmata. They knew that life in camp without its cook is especially unpleasant. Temet had been pressing his dread down into his belly. Now it crawled up his throat. His men looked to him. He said, "The Crimson Knight is real."

Everyone went still.

"He's real, and he knows we're here."

# 26

## THE HART AT BAY

HER SEX TOOK an awful pounding. She swore herself a vivid oath she'd pad her saddle before riding faster than a trot again. The horse was a handsome auburn stallion with a white diamond on his forehead, and he ignored her and coursed down the alley as he pleased. They kept giving her horses such as one might give to a child or a stupid person.

The alley was a clear path through the trees, wide enough for a hunting party. Claire rode a little back from the king. Marcus rode a glossy black courser beside her, glancing over frequently to verify she hadn't fallen. Antivola kept up, gasping and clutching at his burly field hunter, nearly burying his face in its mane. The dandies rode behind them, and one of the king's Tagmata cavalry brought up the rear, one hand on the reins and the other tight round Bitsy Boots, sitting in front of him in the saddle.

Underneath Claire's legs, her horse's flanks bunched and flexed. With each beat he launched himself into the air, and Claire atop him rose and slammed back down into the saddle. Apart from the pain, there was a savage pleasure in it. Shouts and hoofbeats shook her top to bottom, and the sweat of men and horses perfumed the air she breathed. In her breast a crimson passion, very old and very solid, spread his giddy wings, and she thought, *I will find you, magnificent beast, and I will take your life.*

She felt her icy reason unclenching. Her loneliness departed from her, and she understood herself not as one single Claire, nor even as a citizen of Zanzibar. She lost herself, and became merely human, companion of horse and dog, pursuer of the hart. *I am here, and this is me.* She was alienated nothing from her estate. Everything was as it ought to be.

The forest spoke to her, as her huntress Aunt Moonlight had preached. She heard the thunder of the giant hart, approaching on the right. She heard behind him mounted foresters and dogs. By their sounds she knew they'd spread out in a furious arc that shoved the quarry toward the alley. She heard them coming. Her simple human reason traced out all the paths. She foresaw the hart bursting from the wood some several stadia beyond the king.

He would escape too, but on the left, she heard riders and their frenzied dogs, racing to meet the quarry. In the clarity of her foresight she saw them breaking out the wood just as the hart found himself in the alley. He would be encircled in that strip all cleared of trees, as the king closed the distance to him.

So it came to pass.

There was a burst of twigs and leaves and clods of dirt, and the fleeing hart left all his trees behind. He aimed to flash across the alley, but the force on the left appeared just then and startled him. He caught himself, his tremendous ankles taking the shock of his sudden halt, and rounded on the force behind him.

Pounding down the alley, Claire finally saw the majesty of her quarry. He was a great adult hart, taller than her at the shoulder, tawny-red of coat; thick and shaggy in the neck, antlers like fearsome bony wings. Cords stood out in his shoulder and his haunch as he turned, and turned a second time.

He was greater than each dog, each horse, each man that harried him. But he was not greater than all of them together. His inferiors combined to destroy him. Perceiving he was trapped, he stopped. He snorted steam.

The hart was now at bay.

Ambrosius closed the several stadia, and his party behind him, completing the circle round the hart. The hart paced, eye rolling, and the dogs assigned to this part of the hunt – barrel-chested slim-hipped hounds, brave and loyal – howled and edged toward him. The bravest of them, a sleek black beast with a sprinkle of white around the muzzle, darted in too close, and in an instant the hart gored him, flinging him away. One of the masters of the dogs flinched as if he had himself been struck. The hound fell on a broken hip, howling and bleeding, and the master dashed to him and knelt.

Ambrosius drew up his mount. Claire's horse halted of his own accord. The hunting party slowed and stopped. A staffer presented the king's bow and quiver to him. The king took them. He looked back to Claire, and she saw in his dark cheek, in his white teeth, the same crimson passion she felt. She was not to be the one who killed the hart. It didn't trouble her. Her sense of herself was at its ebb, spread out in brotherhood with those who rode with her. A kill by one was a kill by all.

The hart scanned his enemies. Terror bloomed in his vast dark eye. He raised his head and bellowed, a booming sound, melodious and pitiful, full of rage and grief. The dogs dropped back, and the birds of the forest fell silent.

Then he stamped and reared. He started forward, furious, head down, aiming for Ambrosius. By the time Claire's gaze scanned back to the king, he had a bow out and an arrow nocked. Chest swelling, arms spreading, he drew the bowstring and let fly. His arrow lodged in the hart's left shoulder. Two more times he shot the charging hart, striking his throat and his other shoulder. The hart fell forward, knees striking earth, then his chin. His surging weight skidded him toward Ambrosius, and he came to a stop twisted around to the side, just short of the king.

Ambrosius dismounted.

## XXX

HE'D SEEN HER eye turn black and wide, and this was what he wanted for her, needed for her.

Ambrosius worried for the sweet patricia. In the absence of her father, he held himself responsible for her upbringing. He estimated that her mighty goal must mix her up with homicide, and many times, before she hied herself to Zanzibar. Therefore he resolved to raise her as he would a son, and took her hunting. He wanted to awaken her blood-relish. He gladdened when he saw her set jaw and the black thirst for killing eclipse her pale gray eyes.

He said, "Claire, dismount."

The patricia climbed down.

He said, "The hart's mouth and eyes are closed. They die tongue lolling, eyes open. He nurses his wounds. He is still deadly to man and dog."

Claire studied the hart, saw his great flank rise and fall with his shallow breaths.

Ambrosius said, "You know how to shoot?"

Claire nodded and said, "I have a huntress in the family."

Ambrosius signaled to a staffer, and the staffer presented Claire with a lightweight woman's bow and a quiver. She accepted them, but didn't seem to understand what she was doing. She was hunt-drunk, dazed.

Ambrosius explained, "The kill is yours."

A little shock went through her. Her mouth opened. *Ah, there you are, finally with us here in Florence.* She looked at him. He gestured at the hart, then stood aside and watched.

Claire looked down, examined the bow. She drew the string and tested its give. She had the flat expression of the hunter. She wore a dark hunting jacket over her white gown. She spread her arms and frowned. She moved her quiver to her bow hand. With her free hand, she unbuttoned the jacket and shrugged it off her left arm. Then she shifted the bow and quiver to her other hand and shrugged it off her right.

Bare of collarbone and breast, she handed her jacket to the staffer. He shyly took it and stepped back. She slung the quiver over her shoulder and drew an arrow and nocked it and walked toward the hart.

The wounded giant heard her footsteps. His front legs shifted. He snorted and raised his head and looked at her.

She drew the bow and shot him through the eye.

His massive head crashed down. She never stopped walking. Without turning back, she called out, "Sword!" A staffer ran to her with a sword. She took it and rounded the hart, well within the compass of his hooves. She spayed him behind the shoulder, forward to the heart. He shivered once.

Claire turned and looked back, sword in one hand, bow in the other. A womanly pillar, glaring white, standing over the great red hart. She looked at each man in the hunting party. Ambrosius heard a wheezing grunt. Antivola.

Finally the patricia looked at Ambrosius. She said, "It is done."

## XXX

BERTHELOT DENYS VAZHIN, Claire's professor of metaphysics, forced himself up the path to her house. It was morning in Zanzibar, and the grasshoppers chittered and sawed, and the lantanas bloomed vivid under the swollen desert sun – red-and-orange and magenta-and-yellow, shedding their sharp scent either side of the path's big flat stones.

Claire's mother, Reason, opened the door just before Vazhin reached it. She always made Vazhin feel tiny: he was dry and stooped, and she was full and proud.

He said, "She's done it, hasn't she?"

Her crow's feet deepened with her smile and she said, "What has she done?"

He said, "She's chosen your path, not mine – she's learned good and evil."

Reason answered, "I saw many learn to kill, and yet they remained innocent."

Always rubbing his face in it, that she'd fought in the war, and he'd hidden from it.

He said, "But – then – what? I can see you're pleased – what has she accomplished?"

Reason said, "When the time came to kill, she killed. She hasn't learnt good and evil yet, *but now she can*."

He understood what she felt for him was worse than contempt. It was pity. As if he weren't a real Zanzibari. He straightened his back and looked her up and down. Without thinking about it, she touched her thick red-golden hair. This was the only facet of their cruel friendship that leveled things: he appreciated beautiful women, and she liked to be appreciated. All her other friends and lovers who might have dared to look at her that way, died long ago. It was him or nothing. She chose nothing, mainly, but she couldn't help who she was – she liked to be looked at.

She said, "Her gown is still white. If I saw her with the eyes of my body, I wouldn't know her. I would cast her out."

Thus she showed herself to him, and he saw her vast fear and grief had stained now her dearest treasure: her love for her youngest.

She held out her hand and said, "Come, let's report my daughter's progress to the Concordia Majeure."

## XXX

*MAYBE I SHOULD bed her myself.*

There she stood, sword hand bloody, her beauty at its fiercest. She said, "Jacket," and the shy staffer ran her jacket to her.

*If you could see her now, Livia Faustina Varo. You've never seen a woman more majestic.*

Claire gave the forester the bow and gory sword, and took her hunting jacket from him. She slipped into it and fastened the top button.

Bitsy Boots made a little sound. Just a little one, but Ambrosius heard it. The child was horrified. *Has he witnessed any killing before?*

The thought raised him from the maelstrom of Claire's beauty. *No, of course I won't bed her. I've got my son, I've just got my wife back. I'm so old since the war, it's time I stopped carrying on like a goat.* He felt a pang of regret. He consoled himself, *Besides, she's... she's...*

Claire gestured to Bitsy Boots and said, "Come." Now he was frightened of the deadly patricia, and he hung back, but Ambrosius put a hand on his back and said, "Go."

Bitsy Boots walked forward, down the open alley to the patricia and the hart.

## XXX

CLAIRE SQUATTED AS the boy approached. She looked at the hart. *My quarry. I killed you, I.* She saw faded scars on the legs of the mighty beast, earned from battles in the unwritten history of his kind.

Bitsy Boots stood before her, face downcast, frightened and ashamed of his fear. She said, "Do as I do, Domenico," and she set her head down on the neck of the hart. She pressed her cheek against him, still warm as he was. The boy knelt and did the same.

The hart smelled strongly in her nostril. She ran her fingers through his oily fur, smooth in the direction of the hairs, bristly against it. The black thirst for killing narrowed in her eyes and vanished, and their pale gray returned. She stared into Bitsy Boots's eyes, and he into hers. He patted the hart's fur with his stubby little hand. Tears ran down his cheeks. She touched his tears and left a smear of blood on the side of his nose.

XXX

AMBROSIUS GENTLY SAID, "Claire, we must undo the quarry." Claire looked up from the boy and said, "Of course." She took the king's extended hand and he roughly hauled her up, as if she were one of his own Wardogs. The half-coins of greeting clinked in the fold of her gown. The huntsmen clustered round the hart with their carving knives and peeled the skin back from his flank. Steam came off the pink muscles and white ribs. Bitsy Boots watched. Ambrosius put his hand on the boy's shoulders and said, "Soon you will be a man."

A huntsman halloo'd the king and offered him a chunk of dark offal. It was the prize of the hunt, the apex of the heart. Ambrosius took it and walked over to the masters of the dogs. They parted for him: the wounded dog lay whimpering on a blood-drizzled heap of yellow leaves. The other dogs paced near this dog and nuzzled him. His master, shoulders shaking, packed his wounds. The king offered the prize to the dog, who weakly gnawed it. The master said, "He'll live, but he won't hunt." Ambrosius said, "Bring him to me as soon as he can walk. I host the Family Dinner in five weeks, and my table needs a dog. He will eat and be loved, all the days of his life." The master's voice was thick as he said, "I will do it, my lord."

"What is his name?"

"Amicus, my king."

Ambrosius murmured, "Amicus," and touched the brow of the wounded dog, and the dog looked meekly at him, black lips wrapped around the bloody heart.

XXX

AT THE EDGE of the forest, they met an orderly group of men, with the senior members riding and the hangers-on on foot. One of the staffers held up a standard, showing a tree of crows and apples, embroidered on yellow cloth.

Claire recognized one of the lead riders: the queen's brother Cleon. Beside him rode a big man wearing leather armor with fresh gold shapes painted on it. He kept a thick beard dyed an absurd red color, maybe cochineal red. He didn't look like Cleon, but there was something similar about the shape of their faces. Another Constantine. He sat upon a handsome blood bay charger.

This big man said, "Ambrosius, New Forest is mine." The king spoke to the air between his party and theirs: "He will address the crown properly." Claire looked back at the redbeard and saw his cheek darken. He paused and said, "Your majesty, we meet as agreed, to transfer the forest and right of hunting in it."

The redbeard climbed down from his horse, followed by Cleon, and two more men who rode in the front rank and looked like family as well. Ambrosius said, "Have you men with you to record the payment properly?"

The condescension of it drew one of the Constantines forward in a rage. This one was solid and pale-eyed. Ambrosius coolly drew a gleaming handsbreadth of his sword.

The fourth Constantine said, "Cousin –" and came forward and put a hand on the third one's arm. This fourth man was beautiful, with silky blond hair and heavy-lidded eyes. He looked like the queen. He surveyed his fellows and said, "We come here honorable men, at the invitation of our king." And he turned and bowed at the waist to Ambrosius. His charisma calmed his kin. Their shoulders loosened. They inclined their heads to Ambrosius.

When they were done, the third man glanced at Claire. Claire had a shock, perceiving there was something wrong with him, as if he were a well that one might toss a stone into, and never hear it splash.

The redbeard scowled up at Ambrosius and said, "I've got my lawyers and witnesses." Still sitting high in his saddle, Ambrosius got a little scroll out from his horse's furniture. Two members of his party dismounted and staffers took their horses. The two approached the king: Salvatorio, chief judge of Florence, and his scribe. Ambrosius looked to Claire. She realized he'd brought her not only for the hunt, but to witness this as well.

Ambrosius said, "Claire, I present to you the frontmen of the Constantines," placing her above them in the order of introduction, "You met Cleon Tertius in Andropolis, for he has the honor of serving me in council. He" – gesturing at the redbeard – "was named Ineto Picolomini by his father, Ineto Tacitus, but he likes everyone to call him Barbarossa.

"This creature" – hooking a thumb at the pale-eyed one – "is Tarquin. And his cousin with good sense" – favoring the fourth one with a smile – "is Antonio." Antonio really was extraordinarily beautiful. He smiled slavishly at Ambrosius. Claire saw that underneath his charisma and polish, he was a good-natured dimwit.

Ambrosius continued, "With this high praise I introduce these men: they are kin of soft Antonella, queen of Florence, mother of Florence." Barbarossa made a look like he smelled something bad.

Ambrosius said to them, "Claire, Sower of Peace, a patricia of Zanzibar, the last daughter Reason bore." Tarquin sneered, "The king of Florence rides with women." The others tried unabashedly to look in the shadows of her jacket; she'd still only clasped the one button.

Claire spoke in her loud voice: "*I greet the blood of Antonella.*" When they were good and startled, she bowed sloppily in her saddle, so that her jacket bunched up and showed off her breast. An improvised bow; she had the hang of bows now that she'd put her etiquette lessons to practice. She noticed Marcus trying not to laugh at her performance. She was surprised how much that pleased her.

The king unrolled the scroll. It was a faded map of the forest. To Salvatorio he said, "The quill." Salvatorio handed up a quill, and the scribe opened an inkpot and raised it to the king. Ambrosius signed the map and said, "Thus the house of Ambrosius deeds New Forest to the house of Constantine."

# 27

## NOT LIT BY LIGHT, NOT MADE OF MATTER

THEY CROSSED THE babbling Narbonensis one horse at a time, mistrustful of the old wood bridge. Just west of the river lay Traian Fortunatus's estate. Its wall ran parallel with the Via Circumflorentia. The wall was stacked stone, as tall as a man's waist and covered with vines.

Temet was still shaken from the loss of his men, and feeling gloomy and put upon. He said, "If I have to, I can overrun yon wall." The guards at the gate looked at one another. Temet spoke harshly to their leader, "Come on, man, what's the matter here?"

The guard took a deep breath and slumped, defiance draining away. "Fortunatus is dead, my lord."

Temet said, "Dead – how?"

The guard said, "A gang of bandits approached the house. Fortunatus led us in the fight. He sustained a wound to the arm. The wound grew inflamed and produced matter. Four days he lay in a fever. On the fifth day he died."

Temet said, "You're protecting Marcella and the children?"

The guard said, "Until the inheritance is settled, nobody may go in. If you weren't magister, I should not even have confessed my lord's death."

Temet heard in his sullen tone the grief of a loyal servant, and his heart warmed for this guard. He said, "Open the gate, good man. I come by order of the king."

# XXX

Marcella Julia Fortunatus held his gloved hand and wouldn't let it go. Her eyelids were red and her wimple was crooked and her lustrous hair hung past it in strands.

Temet said, "Deianira will protect this house."

He was flirting: Deianira was a goddess of the low religion, and mention of her faintly indiscreet. Marcella was young enough that her grief demanded reassurance she still had her looks. She made a watery smile at Temet Ambrosius and let go his hand. The bones ached from her fervent grip.

She turned and walked down the hall, waving him in. "How are you so far from Florence city?"

Following her, he said, "The king sent me to visit all of us around the Via Circumflorentia. You've heard of the Crimson Knight?"

She turned and looked at him, head tilted, brow furrowed.

He said, "Somebody's raising an army against the throne. One of our people. He means to attack during the Family Dinner. He's hunting me right now, he or his men."

He saw something occur to her, rippling clearly over her face like a pond shivered by wind. He said, "Is he here, Marce?"

Her dark gaze shot to him and she said, "No – no, it cannot be."

Temet stared at her while he considered the possibilities. He listed her children. "Pintus, Iunetta, Felix, Nestor..." He paused. "How old is Nestor?"

She said, "It isn't him. It can't be."

Temet gave her a sober look and said, "Where is Nestor right now?"

Tears spilled from her eyes and she said, "He's seventeen. Please don't hurt him, Temet. Please."

He said nothing, but he put his hand on his breast. She nodded and crossed the hall and shouted up the stairs, "Nestor! Nestor, come greet the king's magister equitum!"

Two sets of footsteps: one excited, one reluctant. Temet waited, sword at his side, shoulders and hips ready to dance – to fight, to kill.

Felix, ten years old, entered first, excited to see the magister, resilient against grief like all children. Then Nestor, a wispy mustache unshaven on his lip, eyelids red-rimmed like his mother's. A farmer's son would have been a man by his age. He snarled, "What else would Ambrosius take from us?"

Marcella Julia Fortunatus strode to him and slapped him on the cheek. His mouth opened round in childish shock. She said, "You will respect your king." Her voice was nearly a shriek, and she didn't look young at all. Temet felt ashamed, inspiring such terror in a woman intimate to him in rank.

Nestor flushed and mumbled, eyes on the floor, "How may I assist my lord?"

Temet said, "The Crimson Knight."

Nestor looked sharply up at him. Temet waited.

Nestor said, "I heard a rumor."

Temet turned to Marcella and said, "I have with me vigiles from the city. They will speak to the boy."

Marcella sank to the floor weeping, and Felix ran to her and wrapped his arms around her, confused at what was going on, crying, "Mama? Mama?" A little girl appeared on the stair, sucking her thumb. A nurse stomped down after her with another little boy hanging on her hand. The steward came running from the kitchen, holding a bronze rod. The situation was fraying out of control. This was how accidents happened.

Keeping his eye on Nestor, Temet circled him till he could throw open the front door. He shouted, "Vigiles!" into the night.

Shortly the vigiles entered, slim, deadly. The room fell quiet. Temet gestured at Nestor, murmuring, "Gently," to them as they passed.

When the youth was safely out, and Temet's words could not furnish him with courage, he squatted by Marcella. His scabbard clacked on the floor, and she looked at him. He said, "There is a way of questioning that hurts the prisoner, if he be guilty or no. We will not question him that way. You understand?" She looked away, but reached out a hand and gripped his arm, steadying herself.

Temet said, "Your guards are led by a good man. Tell him to send me four he trusts. They will take Nestor to Florence. If he is the Crimson Knight, there is nothing any man can do for your son. If he is not, a stay in the castle will keep him out of trouble. You may collect him at the Family Dinner." He reached out his gloved finger and tipped up her chin. She stared at him through her tears, eyes frightened and direct, like an animal. "Five weeks. Only five weeks. You understand me?"

Little Felix crushed against her breast, she showed him her teeth.

## XXX

THE VIGILE SAID, "He's looking for mischief, but he's no Crimson Knight." Temet said, "Good. We can protect him from his bad passions. Arrange things with the Fortunatus guards – off to Florence with him." The vigile made to go, but Temet stopped him with a gesture. He said, "Tell the boy if he flees, he will be found, and when he is found, he will hang." The vigile nodded and left.

Temet looked around the orchard. Night had fallen now and a cold wind made everything clear and crisp under the swelling moon. Pear trees. Magnolias, bare of blossoms. With the excitement of the encounter fading, his heart found room to grieve for Traian Fortunatus, a brave warrior and good father. *How terrible it is, what a family suffers when their man falls.* He thought of Vestoria and his own three sons. Fear gripped him. *Protect me, Deianira! Not on my own behalf – for them! For them! Don't let them face life without my protection!*

He rubbed his cheeks. Stubble dragged against the leather of his gloves. He took off his gloves and touched his mustache. The points were a mess. With relief, he felt his fear transmute to anger. He stormed over to the tents his men were setting up, out in the pastures.

"Novacila! Novacila, where are you, you dumb ox?"

He found his groom on a stool outside his tent, head bare under the bright moon, sharpening his razor.

Temet said, "My cheek. My mustache." Novacila raised his eyebrows at the hour, but started setting up his tools.

The light was bad and the razor a little dull, and Novacila nicked Temet's right cheek. Temet felt the sting and slapped his groom. The big man stood there and took it. Temet slapped him a couple more times, until he felt better. He saw the question in Novacila's eyes, and he nodded: *I'm done now.* Novacila went on shaving him. When he finished, he trimmed and waxed Temet's mustache.

They lost a vigile in the night.

## XXX

CLAIRE SAID, "WHY did Ambrosius want me here for this?"

Marcus kept a straight face, so as not to betray his disappointment. He said, "Which part do you mean?"

They spoke softly in the stable of the hunting lodge. The hunting lodge was in the fields outside the forest. Therefore, though the king lost the forest, he kept the lodge. Claire had wanted private conference; Marcus, anticipating a romantic encounter, bade her wait a moment. When the men went in, he led her to the stable.

Claire said, "The loss of his forest."

Marcus found he didn't want to look at her. He looked out the stable door at the orange evening sun and said, "You depend on him for the success of your ambition. I think he wishes you to understand the weaknesses of the crown. He is a good general, and relies on the intelligence of his men."

Claire nodded and said, "The queen's folk, these Constantines – they're opposed to me. I've ruined their hopes for the war, haven't I?"

*Have you decided I'm nothing more than your informer?*

He said, "For sure. They mean to buy the crown."

He could feel her watching him, but he hadn't the heart to meet her gaze. She helpfully said, "Hungry war impoverishes the crown, and makes it cheap enough to buy. Peace enriches the crown, and steals it from the Constantines."

Marcus sighed. He glanced at her, but the sun made his eyes blind and she was a fog behind a floating circle of green. He turned back to the sky. He said, "O Claire, you've riddled it. But mark this: these Constantines have little sense of mystery. Most of them conceive the peace a thing between the kings, and you a little bit of gilded set-dressing. They oppose you, without quite seeing you. Do not disabuse them of this oversight."

She said, "I have met four Constantines today, but I understand they are many." He could tell she was annoyed at his sullenness, and aiming to fray his patience.

He closed his eyes against the brilliance of the sun. He said, "Just as you say, and everyone in Florence knows them: the cousins and their children and all the clever jobbers and pocketmen – the knee-breakers and other muscle – and most of the old men are still living, though not the queen's father. The four you met today are but the tip of the spear."

Claire considered this. He heard a sound of stiff cloth pulled a little. She softly said, her tone entirely different, "Should I fear main force from Tarquin?"

He opened his eyes. The image of the sun had cleared from them, and he saw she'd undone the button on her hunting jacket.

Marcus paled. He choked out, "Claire, how can you guess these things?"

She tugged the left cuff of the hunting jacket, pulling the left sleeve off her narrow shoulder, artless as a child. She got her arm free and let the jacket slip down her other arm.

She said, "It seems to me there is something the matter with him, as if he were missing his soul."

From the start till now, he'd taken her bare left breast for something innocent among her people. Now she made it naked to him with all the meaning a Florentine woman would give it.

Marcus stuttered, "Just – just so, missing, and run you from him, Claire. Not-among-the-lilies-Tarquin, Tarquin the bridge-walker… this man is their killer. He thinks himself a scholar and a philosopher. The Constantines tell him the victim's name, and he goes to the victim, he turns up on the doorstep of the victim. He says, 'Come, walk with me upon the bridge, and teach me what you know.' Then the victim and this Tarquin have a fascinating conversation, and compare many thoughts, and Tarquin learns the insights of the victim. Then he throws him off."

Claire said, "Throws him off?"

Marcus said, "He throws the victim off the bridge."

Claire nodded. The orange evening light went cold and sharp and gray.

She said, "I will beware Tarquin."

Marcus grasped her shoulders and harshly said, "Never you walk one step with him, O Claire, he is the strong right hand of death. When the Constantines send Tarquin for you, you may count them all for settled enemies."

He became aware of the sharp breath she'd taken. He dropped his hands. He looked her in the face. Her lips were swollen, parted. He looked down at her breast. Her nipple cast a long shadow on her flesh.

She looked down as well. He could see her blushing furiously. She pressed her lips together, and presently the shadow waned.

Face downcast, she said, "I love you above all Florentines. You are my savior and my champion, Marcus. But I am an exile in a foreign kingdom. I cannot give myself to you, because I do not belong to myself."

Marcus answered plainly. He told her, "You said follow me, and I had to go."

She looked up and faced him. Such an incredible grief in her gaze, a third part of the world from home. He touched her glowing cheek, and he was like a little boy to her beauty, touching her as if she were a seashell or a colored stone. He could see she understood his posture, his smooth brow, his undemanding touch.

He resented it, bitterly resented her beauty and her power unmanning him.

## XXX

Once they left, Ambrosius resumed brushing Fortis, his horse.

If Marcus had served more than a day with him, he would have known that Ambrosius always tended his own horses. He'd been in a stall cleaning Fortis when the two of them snuck in the stable. Now he continued, making short strokes with the hard brush, drawing sweat and dust from Fortis's flank. The horse snorted and tossed his head with the pleasure of it.

Like his wife, Ambrosius thought better if his hands were working. So he brushed his horse and reasoned on what he'd seen and heard.

The patricia was faithful to his command. As for Marcus – with his insight, he'd make as fine a counselor as the king had had. If only he could be trusted.

*Should I have him killed?*

Claire would never forgive him.

*If she knew.*

She'd find out. She was as smart as Marcus, maybe smarter.

*Is he the Crimson Knight?*

If he was, he clearly wasn't telling Claire.

Ambrosius brushed Fortis and hummed an old war-hymn to himself, anger and reason washing him by turns.

## XXX

THE CRIMSON KNIGHT had stolen away his other victims, but the dead vigile, he left for Temet to find. The man's upper arms had been slashed through the inward artery and there was a great deal of blood, black in the moonlight. He had no other wounds. His sword was clean in its scabbard.

The staffers were terrified. The vigiles wanted to storm off right away and hunt down the Crimson Knight. Most worrisome, the Tagmata leveled dark looks on Temet. When they decided as a group to act, he would be powerless to stop them.

Temet doubled the watch and ordered the vigiles to pull themselves together. He sent two Tagmata and four staffers and their donkeys to the woodshed at the Fortunatus house. They brought back logs and sticks and built a pyre. They burned the vigile properly. Temet invoked great Pantokrator and dread Syrinx. The ceremony calmed the staffers, and even soothed the wrath of the Tagmata. But there was no relief for Temet.

He watched the vigile burn. His temples pounded. As a warrior noble, he was a man of honor and he understood the warrior nobles in terms of honor. His kind were the world to him. Their honor made the world honorable. Dishonor in a warrior noble was offensive, but he dishonored only his name. Petty individual dishonor was nothing like this mad campaign of the Crimson Knight. It originated nowhere and permeated everywhere. It stained everything. It turned dishonor into an universal principle. It upended Temet's intuition of an orderly world.

He had entered an unmapped wilderness and now he was lost in it and might never get out.

# XXX

By cool of night, they built a big fire in the fireplace and the party gathered round and Ambrosius brooked no sorrow for the loss of the forest. They ate themselves into a stupor on venison, then revived themselves with draughts of disgustingly sweet liquor, flavored with lemon and anice. Antivola looked ill all evening and left early, claiming bellyache. Ambrosius spent dinner flashing angry looks at Marcus till Marcus noticed, then declined all the young tribune's advances till Marcus was well upset. Claire ate and drank portions fit for a man, and not a small man either.

When it came time to tell stories, Ambrosius said, "Claire, we've heard our own fables again and again – give us a tale of Zanzibar."

She was the only woman in the place, and they treated her like a trophy, or an elder sister. She looked around at the men and said, "Perhaps I will, for I thought of one only today – we have a tale of the red hart."

The dandies clapped, and she shushed them indulgently, and said, "There was a mighty city once, called Trebizond. If you do not know Zanzibar, you will not know Trebizond either. But in its day, vanished Trebizond was a great city of the world, and pilgrims crossed deserts to witness the wonders of Trebizond.

"Now there was one young prince of Trebizond who went out hunting the red hart. And he tracked his quarry in the wood, displaying great prowess. He confronted the mighty beast and made a fine kill, with one arrow in the flank, and a second in the gut, and the last one to the throat.

"At the end of day, he retired to his hunting lodge, just as we have done, and feasted with his companions. When everyone had gone to bed, he sat alone, staring in the fire, troubled someway, he knew not how. A soft knock came upon the door, and he found a beggar standing there, hairy and ragged. The prince said, 'I am uneasy; come and soothe me, friend.' So the beggar entered, and the prince served him by his own hand, meat and drink, and the beggar warmed himself by the fire and ate.

"The prince looked at the filthy beggar, and a creeping horror froze him, for he saw a wound in his neck, and through the holes in his ragged garments, another in his gut, and a third one in his flank.

"The hunter said, 'Are you that hart which I shot today in the wood? For I see you bear his wounds.'

"The beggar stood, and now the prince saw he was not a beggar at all, but rather a prince, like himself, wearing a fine white gown, that glowed like the desert beneath the full moon. The gown was black in three places with the blood from the wounds. The prince said, 'I am not that hart, but what the hart endures, I endure as well.' The hunter knelt and said, 'My prince, you are prince, and I beggar, because I beg your forgiveness.'

"The white prince said, 'I came from a great distance to bring you a gift.' He reached in his pouch and pulled out a bloody thing and offered it to the hunter.

"The hunter, as if compelled, took the thing, and saw it was a heart. He recognized it and murmured, 'This is my broken heart, that I had lost.' And the hunter put the heart back in his breast. It was as if he had been dead before, but was living now, and he wept and wept with the pain of it. The white prince knelt by him and embraced him.

"Finally the hunter said, 'What is your name, good prince?' And the white prince said, 'In the tongue of men I am called Étienne.' The hunter said, 'From this day I abandon me my name and principality. I will be your follower, and my name Sol Noir, for my soul was barren, but you have made it fertile.'

"He was as good as his word. He gave away his fields and herds, his gold and silver. He went and preached the doctrine of the broken heart. He drew many followers and they changed the world, as it was...

"But that is another story for another night."

Bitsy Boots said, "Did Sol Noir give up hunting the red hart?"

Ambrosius stared at Claire, so hard she glanced at him, as if his gaze burnt her skin. Facing Ambrosius, she answered Bitsy Boots.

"No, he went on hunting. Étienne gave him back his grief, but he was still a man, and men must eat."

Ambrosius sat back, satisfied that Claire had understood his meaning. Bitsy Boots, though, turned to his father, dismayed.

Ambrosius said, "Life cannot survive without that other life give way. The tragedy of men is that they recognize this necessary evil."

Claire gave him an appraising look, as if she were, in turn, well pleased with him. It warmed him. Her beauty, so fierce during the hunt, was at its most tender now. The room was quiet but for the crackling of the fire. Ambrosius looked around. He could see the dandies would repeat the tale. Marcus looked at her, ardor unconcealed but somehow generous, not grasping.

Ambrosius turned inward, chastising his anger toward his tribune.

*This youth brought peace to the valley of the world. He's a better man than I. Perhaps he's the Crimson Knight, but virtue is sweet water, and we are all cracked vessels. We carry virtue a while, then pass it along, and if a sip of it lasts till the end, we've justified our passage here.*

## XXX

ANTIVOLA'S ILL LOOK was real enough, but he didn't have a bellyache, the trouble was his mind. His mind could not escape the moment Claire stood over the fallen hart, looking at each man in the hunting party.

The icht sat alone in his cold room, wrapped in his great fur, the moon a blur on his blind eye, and his mind prowled that terrible moment. She'd turned and looked back from the hart, sword in one hand, bow in the other. A womanly pillar, glaring white.

Every fold of her gown crisp in the daylight, each point of gold in her filigree sparkling, the spattered blood bright red on her hand.

*He'd seen her clearly.*

He rocked back and forth with the horror of it, the bed creaking under his tremendous weight.

*What is this? What is this?*

The vision of her he'd had in his doze, as a shimmer of empty space, was true, but not in the way he'd thought. His eye could not clearly show him light falling on matter. So if he saw her clearly, she was not lit by light, not made of matter.

# 28

## KNIFE FIGHTS INDOORS

IN THEIR CAMP, Cleon sat beside a fire with Barbarossa and tried to make him understand. "Cousin," he said, "now you've met the patricia, you must see what I mean." Barbarossa was warm in his face from fire and mead, and very pleased about the forest. He didn't want to listen to Cleon, so he grunted. Cleon took it for an invitation to continue.

"We've been playing a game between ourselves and Ambrosius, and all the players named." He hissed quietly, because he wanted to persuade Barbarossa first. He needed them to stand together on this matter when they faced the others. "Barbarossa, listen. She is not the fig leaf of the peace. She is beautiful, she has a voice, she compels the will of men. It made a difference she sat in Pindar's car in Andropolis. The kings did not make peace alone. She has an agenda that we do not know."

Barbarossa turned from the fire and faced Cleon. His face was flushed with drunkenness.

"I'll grant you she is pretty, though she lacks meat," he said, "She is a woman. Why are you worried about a woman? Between the smartest woman and the stupidest, *this*" – and he held up his thumb and forefinger, spaced about the width of an olive from one another – "and neither one can stick to anything but making children and telling tales. Worry nothing, cuz. The king is on his back foot, and the girl is –" and he rudely clicked his tongue against his teeth.

In fact, he was lying quite well for a drunk and a brawler. It was not that he worried about Claire, but that he worried about Ambrosius, much more than he was telling Cleon. For the first time since they were boys, he kept his thoughts from his mild double.

## XXX

It was awkward, but the Constantines rode back with them. There was only the one road, and all parties had business in the city. Claire rode in the king's party, and the sullen Constantines rode a little ways ahead. The road crossed stubbled fields, dotted here and there with the green shoots of fresh winter crops.

Two riders came to meet them, clear on the curving road before the Constantine party hid them from view. Claire recognized the queen, dressed in mannish clothes of that same weak purple. The other rider was a bullish man in black, bald-headed, with thick arms and a thick blunt-ended mustache. They passed between the Constantines and pulled up their horses as they came to the king. The Constantines turned back and everybody crowded round.

Ambrosius asked, "What do they say on Serapetine Hill?" Claire could tell from his tone this was a common idiom.

The bullish man said, "The veterans and the city folk have boiled over." The king looked sharply to the queen, who showed him a solemn expression. The king said, "What happened?" Then, before they could answer, he held up a hand and said, "Claire, this is Neander Federicus – Nederick Frederick – the mayor of Florence. Nederick, the daughter of Zanzibar." Claire and the mayor, still on horseback, nodded to one another.

Nederick Frederick said, "The Sinici were putting up a gang of these brutes in the guest house, and one of them raped the oldest daughter, Doryla Sinica, overnight. There was outrage at it, your majesty, but also relief – everybody was waiting for *something.* Fighting started right away, and there are fires in the Ashpit and the north end of Via Di Speranza. I've got the bucket men working both spots, but the Via Di Speranza blaze spread to Via del Nono Giorno, and that place is all wood houses."

The queen took up the story now. She said, "There were knife fights indoors, my lord. Guest and host, butchering each other in the kitchen and the parlor. The veterans have mostly gone outside now, and they're sorting back into Wardogs and Redheads and what-have-you. They've barricaded the streets leading into the Piazza Campanula, the Piazza Ambrosius IV, and Raven's Alley.

"What do they say on Serapetine Hill? They say the veterans must leave the city."

Listening to soft Antonella, Claire realized she hadn't considered who ran Florence city. Now she comprehended it was not the mayor only, but this queen in partnership with him. *I have much to learn from her.* As if Claire's reasoning tickled the back of her mind, Antonella abruptly looked around to her, and broke her serious mood, smiling warmly. Then Cleon began to speak, and Antonella turned stern again. Cutting him off, she said, "Your precious houses are undamaged."

Behind the queen and mayor, a rumble had been rising. Now a force of mounted soldiers came around the curve. Nederick Frederick wiped his brow and said, "They'll accompany us into the city. We'll circle on the ring road to Circus Gate and go straight to the castle." Antonella added, "Constantines, you enter separately, or wait outside." The Constantines didn't grumble; they couldn't expect any better.

The soldiers surrounded the royal party, weapons bristling. Taranto and Brindisi emerged from their midst, white paint daubed across their breastplates at an angle, marking them for Thousand. They greeted Marcus and made their way to ride with him and Claire. The king addressed Claire's little army of three, saying, "Straight to the royal district with her, and this time keep her there. I won't hazard the patricia's life on the safety of the streets."

All rode quietly toward Florence. The sun already beat high overhead when a bend brought the city into view. The king hissed a curse. Above the ordinary haze of Florence, three columns of dark smoke drifted east on the autumn wind. Even from here they could smell it: the stink of the city was spiced with burning.

The Constantines split from them in silence at the ring road, and the king's party made their way around to Circus Gate. Partway there, Claire saw a man's naked leg in the dirt, still leaking blood. The road was empty, and nobody to tell what had happened.

# 29

## THE ELEPHANT'S HUSBAND

INSIDE THE CITY, the soldiers formed a porcupine, spears pointing outward in all directions. The porcupine processed from Circus Gate to the royal district. It was a short way on the Street of Kings, a side branch of Primavera Circle. There were shouts and clangs, but they were farther off. Claire glimpsed a confusion of bodies in an alley. Soon after, a gang of rowdies came around a corner, high-spirited, looking for a fight. The porcupine stamped once, weapons clanking. Between the heads of the soldiers, Claire saw the rowdies fall still, then flee back around their corner. *I chased war from Andropolis, and it followed me to Florence.*

At the district gate, the porcupine dissolved, so that Claire could see the wall and gate ahead, and a little body sitting crookedly beside the gate. She recognized this individual before the rest, and gave everyone a scare, crying "No!" and running forward to him. It was the boy page who had talked with her about ai Ctesiphôn.

She came up to him and saw his hand pressed on a gut wound of the very painful type, that there is nothing for it and you just hope to die quickly. It smelled foul, and blood and juices leaked between his fingers. The boy's face was pale as snow and he bled a little from the mouth. Beside him a basket was overturned, and quinces on the ground.

Claire cried, "No! Oh no, oh no," and he blinked dully at her; she could see he was in that land between life and death, without light and shadow, without passions, where the bulrushes grow. The men crowded round her, and somebody put a hand on her shoulder, but she twitched it off, like a horse twitches off a fly. Then she reached her arms around the boy and picked him up. This astonished those there with her, for she was not so much bigger than he. Nederick Frederick shouted to the district guard, and they swung the wicket open. Claire stood, with the boy's heavy head resting on her shoulder, and she carried him into the royal district, telling him all the while, "You're with me, you're alright now, you're with me."

This was very sad, but there was work to do, and once the men filed through the wicket, Nederick Frederick led most of them away. A smaller number came with Claire to the colonnaded courtyard, and she sat the page down against a wall and crouched and held his cold hand. Those who remained with her witnessed the miracle of Claire's gown: all her skin was smeared with blood, but the gown was spotless.

As for Claire, she saw only the boy page, and the light of life dimming in his eyes, as a puddle on a sunlit paving stone contracts, and the smaller it gets, the faster it diminishes, so that you can watch it speedily retreat across the last wet patch of stone, and then it is gone and the stone is dry; so too the light of life retreated from the page, and he went out from underneath the sun.

She turned blindly to those around and said in a ragged voice, "I didn't know his name." The queen said, "His name was Aeneas." Claire said, "Who will tell his mother?" and the queen said, "He hadn't a mother." Then Claire wept, and the sound of it was so wretched that the queen dismissed the distraught men, commanding even Marcus to depart.

When Claire's senses spoke to her again, she heard the tumult of the warring city, faintly, but mostly birdsong. There was a yellow glow to the air which made everything seem very crisp and clear. It was a lovely glow, and lit the cheek of the dead page like a breath of life. The patricia didn't recognize the glow; she hailed from the desert, and didn't know this light of an approaching storm.

The majordomo and his staff came to collect their boy. They brought a bucket of wet rags for Claire. They held up a half-fainting girl, Claire's maid Epida. When she saw dead Aeneas, she cried out and slipped from their grasp and fell on the ground. She howled an animal howl and crawled on hands and knees toward the dead boy, limbs clumsy and unwilling.

Claire looked from her to the queen, and the queen said softly, "They were betrothed." Claire bit her hand, as viciously as a dog, and squeezed her eyes shut. She listened to Epida's howls and scrapes, and heard when she reached her lover and her howls turned to sobs.

She made herself open her eyes and saw Epida curled up with Aeneas, touching his cheek, his chest, his soiled gut. She looked at Claire and said, "I – I – I – I did it – I didn't know how bad it was – I sent him out to get you quinces..."

Claire couldn't bear it and she flung herself on her maid and wrapped her arms around her, weeping and saying, "No, me, I killed him, I did it," so that it was the two crying girls and the dead boy, and it went on a long, long time. Finally the queen knelt with them and said, "He belongs to the god and the crown now. Let him go into our care."

She forced the exhausted friends to stand and give Aeneas over to the majordomo, who stood with his staff, helplessly witnessing this terrible scene. They lifted Aeneas gently, as if to keep his wound from hurting him, and carried him away. The queen sat Claire and Epida on the bench and washed them with the wet rags from the bucket, soothing them with her touch. When she was done, they were all shivering and hollowed out. Antonella stood and said, "Come," and took their hands and led them away from the courtyard, out onto the soft lawns of the royal district, under the stormy yellow light.

They came to a vast barn, with an uneven earthen floor and one wall missing to let in light and air. It turned out this was the winter home of Baldessaria, the she-elephant. The love of elephants is inborn in the breast of man, and so it was with Claire and Epida. The girls gazed upon the indistinct form of the giant animal. Soon their eyes adjusted to the dimness in the deep of the barn, and they saw that Baldessaria was picking objects off a high shelf. The delicate snout at the end of her trunk would feel about, touching first one object, then another, and select one. She would curl her trunk about it and fondle it, then put it back, trumpeting faintly, and feel around for another.

Claire looked at Epida, then back at the elephant. She walked into the gloom, through a forest of lights let by chinks in the barn. She heard Epida shuffling along behind her. Her pupils grew every moment, and she saw the objects Baldessaria was handling were gigantic bones. Claire spoke quietly, as if the elephant wouldn't hear. She said, "O Queen Antonella, what bones are these?" She had a good idea of the answer. Antonella said, "Dear Claire, they are the bones of her husband, Belisarius, the great albino elephant."

Claire stood at a respectful distance from mighty Baldessaria. She watched a while, then said, "She's mourning him." Epida covered her face in her hands and wept again, and the women embraced her, then left her alone with the elephant.

They came to the mouth of the barn and stared out at the lawns aglow in the yellow light. Antonella said, "The pair of them were given us by trading partners from the south. The wandering Ottolenghi tell us warmer lands are found beyond the southern mountains, and we trade sometimes with those who live there. Belisarius and Baldessaria were gifts, though she is barren; they wished us to have elephants, not to make them." Claire said, "She's an exile then, like me." Antonella said, "All women are exiles, for they marry and are exiled from the house of their father." She smiled sadly at Claire's startlement, and said, "O my Claire, you will grow up, and discover many things that are obvious to your elders."

They heard Epida's footsteps and turned to welcome her back to their company, and the three of them stood silently together, watching low clouds tumble past.

The storm broke. The thunder sounded very close and Claire's smell was lost in it. The three women stepped back from the mouth of the barn.

## XXX

TEMET AMBROSIUS LED his men through the woods. The Via Circumflorentia was just a track here, and sometimes faded entirely. This was wild land, equally the pauper's and the king's. The Fortunatus estate lay behind and the Ffidius estate ahead. The bandits who'd made a widow of Marcella Fortunatus probably passed this way. It had rained in the morning, and now heavy cloud turned afternoon dark as night. Wet leaves glinted in the dimness, and the horses picked their way carefully past branches and mudpits.

Temet found his thoughts drifting back to Vestoria and the boys. *Will I see you again? Have I performed my duty to you?* He twisted one mustache between his fingertips, shaping its point. He scanned the murk ahead. He waited for his horse to trip and throw him. He waited for bandits to fall upon him. He waited for the Crimson Knight to spear him. His jaw was so tight it ached. He could feel his men's fear, their eyes fixed on his back.

He squared his shoulders and belted out, *"I MET A BRUNETTE IN VINDOBONA!"*

Incredulous laughter erupted from his men. *What kind of a nobleman would sing that song?* Just as he'd intended, delight and relief rippled out amongst them. They gleefully disturbed the woods, joining in the scandalous lyrics.

The three of them stood silently together.

# XXX

- HAVE THEY ALL gone out?

- We went out, but the rain was so heavy, we came back in.

- What will the king do?

- There's nothing more to be done tonight. I expect he'll go have a talk with them in the morning.

- What does he intend?

- He'll ask them to leave the city. They'll make a camp outside, just like the Thousand, while the big men figure out food and work for them.

- I don't like him telling me to stay in the royal district like a prisoner.

- He's worried about you. If something happens to you, how will he face his nation? Or Genova? Or Zanzibar?

- Zanzibar has forgotten me.

- Don't be silly, nobody who knows you has forgotten you. ... Did I say something wrong?

- No, not wrong. I'm just sad. It's been a long day. All those dead. And Aeneas...

- I knew him. He was a little cuss.

- He was out fetching me quinces.

- I'm sorry.

- Everything he might have grown up to do –

- Listen to me. He's not your burden. Florence answers for his blood.

- Everybody has been fairly begging me to think of Florence as real, of myself as really here. Fine. I believe you. I'm here. A real boy died for me.

There was a long silence. She'd defeated him. Finally she looked back over and spoke again, softly.

- Tell me a story.

- A story?

- Tell me a Tacamo story. Aeneas told me the other one I heard, the one with Mathilda. I liked it. Are there any more Tacamo stories?

- Yes, there are plenty of them. Let me think... Oh, I know just the one. I'll tell you about the time Tacamo got drunk at his own funeral.

- That sounds like a good story. Tell me that one.

- Now it came to pass that my Lady Stone was buying her tomatoes from a gang of Cestans, and they got the idea in their heads to have fun with the poor girl, so they told her Tacamo had died...

Soon Claire was asleep. Marcus gently stroked her gleaming hair. She murmured something, it sounded like, "If I forget you." Her gaze shot place to place behind her eyelids, before settling and becoming still.

He looked at the strange symbols on the clasps of her gown. *Is it true a man who sees her naked will die?* The emerald in her fourth fingernail sparkled in the firelight. *Do her fingernails never grow?* Tiny golden hairs shimmered faintly on her white breast.

He felt a cold thrill of sin, and covered her with the wool blanket.

Marcus studied her a long time. There were dark circles under her eyes, and a line of worry creased her brow. The woes of Florence weighed heavily on her; her exile weighed heavily on her. She seemed too small to carry everything she carried.

# 30

## HOW TACAMO GOT DRUNK AT HIS OWN FUNERAL

NOW IT CAME to pass that my Lady Stone was buying her tomatoes from a gang of Cestans, and they got the idea in their heads to have fun with the poor girl, so they told her Tacamo had died, knowing she still carried a torch for him. Lady Stone broke down crying right away, and asked them how it happened. They told her he came out on the wrong end of a knife fight in Cesta, which is more or less how everyone always expected Tacamo to go, so Lady Stone believed them. Sobbing, she asked them where she could retrieve his body to give it a proper burial, and thinking fast, they told her they could bring him round next market day, in exchange for ten gold pennies.

My Lady Stone agreed without haggling, and next market day they came around with a smelly sack with blood all down the front. The sack was full of rocks, with a rotten ham thrown in to discourage opening it. The blood was from an ox. The Cestans put a stick and handkerchief-bindle, just like Tacamo's, on the sack for extra realism. Credulous little Stone began sobbing again when she saw the bindle, and took the sack for Tacamo's remains. She handed over the ten gold pennies she'd scraped together. Back then, you could buy a healthy male slave for eight gold pennies at the market in Palmyra, so the Cestan tomato-pickers got better than the price of a live slave for a false dead man. They kept from laughing till they were well out of hearing of the grieving lady.

My Lady Stone set about throwing a proper funeral for Tacamo, and sent word around to all the bums and prostitutes and scoundrels that he kept for friends. For her part, she spent another gold penny on a ribbon of fine black lace long enough to trim her dress and shawl, which was not a lot of ribbon, but it was very fine.

Soon enough, word of Tacamo's lamentable demise got back to Tacamo himself. He was very surprised to hear the story, and patted himself all over, but couldn't find any knife-holes. Still, he reasoned, he'd been wrong about all sorts of things before, so he shouldn't go leaping to conclusions. Therefore he hefted his stick and bindle over his shoulder, and walked into the west, till he came to the gate to Hell. There he met Quadronimo, an under-demon who worked the day shift, and was actually distantly related to Tacamo on his father's side. Tacamo hailed the smoky demon, and explained his confusion, and asked if he were expected in Hell. Quadronimo consulted the ledger and told Tacamo he was not listed for that day, nor any recent day, so he was not late for any appointment there. Tacamo scratched his head and said, "Well look, so long as I'm already here, could you check ahead a bit, and save me going all the way away, and having to come back again if I'm due tomorrow, say, or the day after?"

Quadronimo frowned at Tacamo; both knew full well that Tacamo was trying to get away a little bit with something here. The demons are not supposed to tell mortals their fate in advance. Tacamo innocently stood there, buffing his nails on the ragged hem of his coat, and finally Quadronimo sighed and said, "Seeing as how we're cousins," and he flipped ahead in the ledger. He shook his head, saying, "No, no," and ran his claw down the columns, and finally he said, "I don't see you listed here before the full moon,

Tacamo, and really, that's as far ahead as I dare to go." So Tacamo thanked him, and sent his best regards to his mother, and hefted up his stick and bindle. He made his way back east, very much confused, but along the way he chewed his blade of grass until he figured out that somebody was funning with gullible Lady Stone.

He got back just in time to attend his funeral, and being very curious, he went to see. There was a pleasingly large crowd, and some of the mourners greeted him. He walked around, marking those who demonstrated a vivid and heartfelt grief, and those who just cracked jokes and ate the snacks. He picked the pockets of these latter ones, accounting them no true friends of his, and filled the pockets of the former ones, as the fancy took him.

When he came to my Lady Stone, he found her fairly blind with tears, and hoarse with wails, and altogether devastated. It was touching, but also embarrassing. Tacamo found it easy to slip a considerable amount into her purse, since she was oblivious to all the world. By chance it was ten gold pennies. Then he tapped her on the shoulder, but this did not rouse her from her miseries, and he shook her, and finally he slapped her on the cheek. Then she recognized him, because he'd always treated her badly back when he was alive. But he had a time of it convincing her it was really him, showing her his true stick and bindle, and the patch on his bum, and recounting certain of their love-secrets, and dancing his little jig. Then she opened up the smelly sack in the grave, and everybody saw the trick the Cestans had played on poor Lady Stone. They all laughed and drank like fish and celebrated, and Lady Stone dissolved in fresh rounds of tears.

This was how Tacamo managed to get drunk at his own funeral.

When his hangover cleared, the unpunished perfidy of the Cestans gnawed at Tacamo. Even though he'd got Lady Stone's ten gold pennies back, there was still the matter of the penny she'd spent on the black lace trim. He begged the trim of her, and she was glad to give it to him, unstitching all the mourning-ribbons from her dress and shawl. Tacamo waited on the new moon in the planting season, and dug up the tomato seeds of the Cestans. In their place he planted the black lace trim, so that when the Cestans went to pick their tomatoes, they found they'd grown mean black serpents instead.

# PART IV

# Florence: Serapetine Hill

# 31

## THE ESCAPEMENT

THE TOOTHED ESCAPEMENT replenishes the motion of the swinging pendulum. In turn, it uses the swing of the pendulum to regulate the timekeeping gears. The teeth of the escapement keep the gears turning at a constant rate, and the clock keeps time properly.

The escapement uses only basic mechanics, but it is not an obvious device. If the water-lifting screw is the simplest invention that is dazzling in its ingenuity, the escapement is probably the simplest invention that is profoundly strange.

Claire puzzled out the escapement when she was a little girl. All analytic mortals prize the first puzzles they master. Claire prized the escapement.

Alone in her emptied-out apartment in the women's dormitory, high up in the younger castle, she made all the parts of an anchor-style escapement: pendulum and bob – anchor escapement – saw-toothed escape wheel. She used her silver stylus to mark a strip of wood, and a knife to carve it.

Her thirst for learning quickened, and she sank into joy in

knowledge. She filled the morning with the project. Her hands stopped shaking, till she finished.

Cold air came in the window. The storm had quenched the fires in Florence and rinsed the foul air. The city was quiet.

At lunchtime, there was a knock at the door and Claire hid the escapement. Two servants came in bearing food, a big girl with dull features and a tiny birdlike thing with round eyes. Claire said, "What news of Epida?" and the big one said, "We gave her enough syrup-wine to knock over a bull and now we've put her to bed." She set her tray down and started arranging it. The tiny one put her fingers on Claire's forearm, carefully, as if Claire's arm might burn or sting. Claire looked at her, and she looked back with her round eyes. Finally she said, "We heard how you took care of Aeneas." Then the big one got done with the food, and the two of them left.

Early in the afternoon Claire heard riders entering the royal district, and went out seeking news. She stopped by the kitchen first and, when nobody was looking, pitched the escapement in the cooking fire. Lips tight, she watched the wooden pieces burn. The law of Zanzibar was clear: she must not donate technology to barbarians of the outer nations.

On her way out, she withstood an evil eye from the pantler. This was so startling that her reason slid off it without solving it. Apart from the surprise, it was not difficult to solve. He was the one who failed to stock any quinces, forcing Epida to send Aeneas out to fetch them. Being a little man, the pantler's miserable guilt over Aeneas's death had swiftly curdled into hate for the patricia.

## XXX

THEY'D SHUFFLED THE storm-bedraggled veterans out the city, herding them through Shepherd's Gate and onto the Campus Iucundum. This is how it happened:

The king took his guard and addressed the Wardogs barricaded in the Piazza Campanula. He cited the example of Claire, Sower of Peace, who had broken the deadly wheel of war. Was this how

Florence wished to spend her gift? Was this how they wanted to begin the peace – in blood, in bitterness, in civil strife?

The men declared for peace. They smashed up their barricades and made their way toward Shepherd's Gate.

Barbarossa wrapped his old red kerchief around his head and addressed the Redheads, barricaded in the Piazza Ambrosius IV. He framed a different argument. He called on their sense of honor, on their fighting spirit that never ceased defending Florence, on the victories they'd won together in field and forest. He promised better times ahead.

Grumbling, these soldiers did as he asked. They remembered that he'd always shared the brutal work, and rich man though he was, called each man "comrade" and "brother."

The force camped out in Raven's Alley was a mix of elements from the first morax and the seventh – it was His Majesty's Own Ichneumon, Flavius Papellus Reburrus, who addressed them, and he went alone. In his twanging high voice, he invoked furious Pantokrator, slinging suns like pebbles; and the awful pan of Syrinx, that judges souls and worlds. He firmed up in their spines the ancient virtues of the Florentines, and set their hearts trembling at the long reach of the gods. Reburrus got done with his dark recital and shut his mouth and eyes. The soldiers poured out from the shadows of Raven's Alley, flowing round the ichneumon, gently touching his robe. When they had gone, he opened his eyes and brushed the itch on his nose. The rashes on his hands flared pain.

The three bodies of veterans met on the plain, each with its own motive for leaving the city: ardor for Claire's peace, or pride in their army, or fear of Florence's gods. They met and mixed and found their moods distinct from one another. It was as if the day of fury and the drenching rain were a dream, and they'd washed up on this plain with no true memory of what came before. It was like a second Andropolis that way. In quiet bafflement, they set about making camp.

Nederick Frederick coordinated with the castle and the second morax's quartermaster, and carts rolled up with tents and necessities. Surveyors marked off new roads with pegs and twine. The regular camp-city of a Florentine army rose up, as if from the soil of the plain.

Not far to the north, the Thousand watched, and behind them, the expedition warehouse loomed.

## XXX

CLAIRE WAS BORN after the end of Guerra Domestique, the civil war in Zanzibar. Florence was her first experience of civil strife. It seemed hideous to her, much worse than war. In war, the sons of a nation come together to repel a foreign threat. She'd seen that at Andropolis. During civil strife, hate and madness boil the skin off civilization, and all men wade gleefully into a river of blood. War can be won. Civil strife must simply burn all its fuel. There was plenty of fuel left in Florence.

Wounded and heartsick, she retreated to the gold palanquin, where no Florentine could follow her. She sat glowering at the thirty-two clock she had built.

*What am I? What will I become?*

She thought of her mother's critique of Professor Berthelot Denys Vazhin. She despised him. They'd always known each other. During Guerra Domestique, while Reason was leading the defense of the republic, Vazhin hid among the bookshops of Ixanahade Street. While his friends were fighting and dying, he was hunched over a book of philosophy, pretending it was peacetime. Claire's mother had suffered terribly in the war, and could not forgive those who didn't.

Claire felt torn between two ethics now, her mother's iron commitment to her people and her city at whatever cost, and Vazhin's majestic flight of the mind toward knowledge. She couldn't reconcile it. She laced her fingers and pressed her thumbs against her brow.

*Do something, Claire. Choose something.*

She arranged in her mind the powers in Florence city: the king – his ichneumon – the Constantines – the veterans – the Thousand – the burghers – and the poor.

*Some of them are enemies.*

A crazed bark of a laugh escaped her lips.

*How did* I *become the kind of person who has enemies?*

She covered her mouth with her fingertips.

The king was her ally. The poor were devoted to her, after she'd served them three begging days.

*I don't care. I don't care! Come springtime, I'll leave and never see any of you again.*

*Lies. I'm lying to myself. I do care.*

She had pledged herself to Florence. She had a sense, bone-deep, that if she didn't keep her faith with Florence, she should never get to Zanzibar.

*I love you, and you love me. Without love, I don't deserve to be saved. You will save me, Florence, and I will save you.*

The thirty-two clock ticked and ticked and ticked, measuring sidereal time before her eye.

She suddenly had an idea what to do.

*Let Reburrus croak his sermons of death, perched like a vulture on the Epicondyle. I'll go up Serapetine Hill and preach love.*

Action, certainly, but so thin-blooded. If she told her mother, her mother would scorn her Vazhin-style strategy.

*It's the best I know how to do.*

There was one more power in Florence than the ones she listed. It had not announced itself to her yet.

# 32

## SURPLUS MATERIEL

TEMET AMBROSIUS SLUMPED in his chair, tight shoulders softening. Rufus Quintus Ffidius slouched in his own chair, watching him and smiling. Temet drank; Ffidius had cracked an amphora of last year's wine. Temet groaned with pleasure and said, "Your wine could soothe angry Pantokrator." He set his cup down and stared into the honey-colored wine and said, "It's been a parade of widows and orphans and ruined men. I can scarcely bear to witness the suffering of the warrior nobles."

Ffidius said, "No ruin here. I'm just back from Lutetia. We had such good fighting there, Temet! Whipped them like dogs. Word of the peace came just in time to ruin a really fine sally. Old Decius Mus rode in with the news. I had to go out with him and tell the boys it was off, I swear you they were on the edge of tears." He emptied his cup. "Here I am, *senex*, drinking sweet Ffidius wine in my own house. Looking to live many years and die in bed." He raised his eyebrows comically, but the look in his eyes was wistful. He flung the lees of his wine in the fire and got up and refilled his cup. Then he sat and sipped. His bleary gaze wandered back to Temet.

He said, "Which of us do you think he is?"

Temet shrugged. He said, "At first I was sure he must be an Ambrosius. Who else could be so angry at the king? But now I'm not so sure. I don't know what I'm doing, *frater*. I've got a unit of Tagmata thugs with me, and a squad of Florentine police. The Crimson Knight knows where we are, he or his men. They're picking us off in our sleep. When we're few enough, I suppose he'll destroy the survivors. And what do we buy with our deaths? All I'm doing is bruising feelings, up and down the Via Circumflorentia. I see one of our kind, I say, 'Could this be him?' But I've got an idea in my head, you see, what kind of man the Crimson Knight must be. And none of us is him. None, or I'm a fool. I may be a city boy, Rufus Quintus, but I'm not a fool."

Temet glared into his cup, then looked up at Ffidius.

"Is it you? Are you hiding an army in your little vintner town?"

Ffidius smirked. He said, "I'm happy enough to find my people still at their jobs. Don't know I could make an army of them, only a week home from the north myself."

Temet pointed unsteadily at him and said, "You see? Everyone has a reason it's not him. They're all good reasons. But the best reason is – they haven't got the rage. Have you got that kind of rage? You could have brought your northerners back with you if you'd wanted a war in Florence district. Did you do that?"

Ffidius shook his head. He leaned forward meaningfully, so Temet leaned forward. They were the same age. They didn't know each other well. Temet found himself fond of this handsome warrior, and felt the sentiment was mutual.

Ffidius said, "Temet *carissime*, consider this. You know the Crimson Knight. You just don't recognize him. When you find him, you will find, in a sense, you've known it was him from the start. Your job is not to march the Via Circumflorentia with your ridiculous little army, letting him murder you one by one. Your job is to sit in your tent and think. *Think*, man. Think of what you already know."

Temet closed his eyes and shuddered. Then he opened them and looked at his peer. He said, "Will you forgive me for having the vigiles in for a word?"

Ffidius said, "Nothing to forgive. You have your duty and I have mine. Your men have a hungry, ragged look. Everybody knows Ambrosius hasn't the money to pamper his soldiers. Eat and rest. You'll be safe inside my walls. Take what you need for the days ahead."

Temet shut his eyes again, brow wrinkling.

Ffidius said, "It can't be so bad, Temet."

Temet opened his eyes and said, "This nation has a generous bosom, but not for me. I'm riding a cursed road."

## XXX

LADY VARO SAID, "Your legs."

Claire said, "What about my legs?"

"Is your maid shaving them?"

Claire said, "I am fortunate to grow fine blonde hair on my legs, so that it takes a blast of sun to see it at all." So saying, she stretched her leg into a patch of sunlight by the window and showed off what she meant. They were in a game room in the younger castle, ordinarily used for sparring with blunted swords.

Lady Varo eyed Claire's leg. She picked at her sticky bun and said, "Your armpits?"

Claire said, "What have you got in Florence for taking care of women's hair?"

Lady Varo chewed her morsel, swallowed it, then said, "The razor, which I do not recommend; pumice, which is very painful; and a cream, which is rumored to be poisonous."

Claire frowned and said, "You don't present the choices in a way as to persuade me."

Lady Varo said, "Yet choose you must. Consult with your girl – Epida? Find out which method she excels in."

Claire was surprised that Lady Varo knew the name of her maid. Lady Varo tore a larger chunk from her sticky bun and popped it in her mouth. She waved her hand vaguely at her nethers and said, around her mouthful of food, "And below?"

Claire blushed and said, "Nobody will see that but me."

Lady Varo swallowed and said, "Good answer, princess. " Then she sucked the honey off her fingers.

## XXX

CORNELIUS SAID, "MARCUS, I think there's something crooked at the warehouse."

Marcus looked regretfully at the remains of his lunch. Cornelius had timed his entrance just so; Marcus could not use his meal to beg off attending the problem. He still shone with sweat, like the several tenmen of the Thousand he was eating with. They'd all been practising rapid palisade construction.

Cornelius eyed the fresh walls enviously. Aged as he was by the unnatural storm, he couldn't hope to sling lumber that way any longer. He couldn't march west to Zanzibar with his friends.

Marcus wiped his mouth and stood and said, "Thank you, Cornelius, I'll come with you right away." Cornelius said, "Give us a moment," and took a plate and collected food from the serving dishes.

Marcus turned to his men. He gestured at the wooden wall and said, "After lunch, build another one. You can use the same posts, but take them down the hill. Figure how to get them standing steady in the wetter earth." They nodded. He gave them a wicked grin and said, "I'd wager you need to dig the holes deeper." They all groaned, and he waved his fingertips and said, "I'll see you after," and loped away, Cornelius hobbling behind.

They came up on the warehouse, mostly finished now. Marcus thought he knew what Cornelius was talking about. He pointed at the curved shapes leaning against one inside wall and said, "You mean the boats."

Cornelius said, "It would be fair to ask if you're meant to haul a navy to Zanzibar."

Marcus said, "Perhaps Constantine figures it's mostly ocean between here and there."

Cornelius said, "Absurd enough. But the boats aren't what I mean."

He led Marcus into the warehouse. Philo sat at Marcus's old table. He had the dead man's skull in his hands and rubbed his thumb over and over the notch in the cut across the skull's brow. Marcus looked uncomfortably at him and said, loudly, "Afternoon, Philo!" Philo looked up at him, eyes vacant – but suddenly the warmest, kindest smile filled his face, like sunrise, and Marcus regretted missing out on his Stonebreaker's long life. Cornelius gently set the dish of food in front of Philo. He bent to his friend's ear and said, "I'll be back in a little bit and we'll eat." Philo didn't respond. Cornelius straightened and gestured Marcus deeper into the warehouse.

After he'd finished his supply lists, Marcus had left Cornelius in charge of all this. They'd put together a little place for Philo to be comfortable out of the rain, and Cornelius kept up with the deliveries, making marks in the ledger as Marcus showed him. Marcus was neglecting the ledger and Cornelius both. Training for the expedition was more fun.

Now Cornelius led him around and between heaps, half-lit by daylight passing through oil-paper on high windows. He stopped in front of one orderly set of heaps and said, "Consider this rope."

Marcus evaluated it. He said, "That's quite a lot of rope."

Cornelius said, "You smell it?"

Marcus took a deep breath and smelled it – damp and mold. He said, "It's old."

Cornelius kicked the rope and said, "Useless useless useless." He led Marcus along. They came to piles of tent-canvas. Marcus breathed again, but it smelled firm and clean. He bent and felt it: fresh canvas. He said, "But this is new."

Cornelius said, "It is. How many tents could be made from this?"

Marcus backed up from the piles, taking in how far they extended into the half-light. He said, "We'll never need this much. How would we even carry it?"

Cornelius said, "A good question. Come this way."

He led Marcus to shelves where tools were arranged – hatchets, saws, adzes, hammers, flints, whetstones. Far too many of each. There was no order to the new ones and the ones so old as to be worthless. Marcus frowned and started to speak, but Cornelius cut him off and said, "One more, and I'll stop."

He led him to a back wall, where a web of sparkles resolved itself into an impossible wealth of helmets, breastplates, shields, spears, swords, and other arms and armor. All glitteringly, brilliantly new. Marcus folded his arms and said, "Would have been nice to have had these in Andropolis."

Cornelius scratched his pate and said, "All that's so long ago for me." Marcus looked at the old man and said, "My youngest Stonebreaker. You were a little brother to me." Cornelius smiled. Marcus looked back to the weapons and said, "Do they expect me to fight every step of my way to Zanzibar?"

Cornelius said nothing. Marcus turned to him.

"You said 'crooked.' Something crooked at the warehouse. What's going on here?"

Cornelius said, "I spend a lifetime away from men, and I come back and find nothing's changed. Men, corrupt as ever."

Marcus said, "What is this?"

Cornelius said, "This expedition is very expensive. It's a joint venture of Florence and Genova. With a little supplemental investment from the Constantines. Correct?"

Marcus nodded.

Cornelius said, "Who's the main supplier?"

Marcus said, "Constantine."

Cornelius said, "Constantine. And what sorts of supplies are these, mainly?"

Marcus said, "War supplies."

Cornelius said, "Exactly. It's surplus materiel. The Constantines are making good their losses on war contracts. They're shuffling their own warehouses out to the Campus Iucundum and charging the treasury."

Marcus was awed at the audacity. He said, "That accounts for the old stuff. We had plenty of rubbish like that at the front. What about the new?"

Cornelius said, "I've thought about that as well. The Constantines must have paid out their own contracts – armorers, smiths, weavers, what-have-you. Shipwrights. The product is still coming in. It had nowhere to go till we turned up."

Marcus threw up his arms and said, "But what am I supposed to *do* with all this?"

Cornelius shrugged and said, "The requisition orders have your name on them."

Marcus's cheeks grew inflamed with anger and he turned to leave. Cornelius stepped into his path and said, "Decanus, wait. They're not out to ruin you. Most likely, you'll take what you need in the springtime and they'll make sure the rest gets quietly re-sold outside the city. They've only set you up in case the king finds out. Imagine how they reason it: better the king should think his pet soldier is a profligate fool, than that his treasurer Cleon Constantine's a crook. And if the king finds out, you'll be well gone and unable to defend against the charge. Thus they reason it. But you have friends in the city too."

Marcus paused, still shaking with rage.

Cornelius smiled a wry smile, a smile the young man Marcus had known would never have been able to summon.

His friend said, "Men, corrupt as ever."

Marcus said, "I'm going to go find Cleon."

# XXX

"WHAT KIND OF a game is this?"

The couple tenmen of Redheads turned and looked at Marcus, distinctly hostile. Barbarossa said to them, "Behold Marcus Irenaeus Diophantus, ancient of name and august of blood."

Marcus hadn't found Cleon Constantine at the Counting House and the factotum didn't want to tell him where he'd gone. Marcus gave the factotum such a hard time that he coughed it up. So Marcus made his way to Cardester Bend, in the dense wedge of tenements between the Epicondyle and the Royal District. The Cardester wives were all put out, because the third morax was blocking their street, training under the eyes of wan Cleon and ruddy Barbarossa.

Cleon said, "We're practicing defense of city streets." He wasn't contemptuous like Barbarossa, but he wasn't friendly either.

Marcus said, "Preparing for the Crimson Knight?"

Barbarossa swelled his chest and said, "General Nasica and I came up together in the third, *decanus*."

Cleon said, "What do you want, Marcus Irenaeus?"

With a nod at Cleon and a sneer at Marcus, Barbarossa jogged back over to his men and resumed arranging them and the various wood impediments they'd brought.

Marcus was still hot with rage himself and went straight for the heart of it – "I'm here about these trash heaps you've been sending to the warehouse with my name on the requisition orders."

Cleon's eyes lit up. Marcus, being young, didn't recognize anticipation of causing misery, which does not look as ugly on the face as it should.

Cleon warmly said, "I'm glad you've noticed! Now we can agree to a firm policy on the matter... You will accept what Constantine deems necessary for the expedition."

Marcus spat and said, "I'll go straight to Ambrosius and tell him everything."

Cleon tilted his head a little and said, "Then I'll go to Ambrosius and tell him a very interesting story I heard from a friend in lawless Rhegium."

Marcus froze.

Cleon said, "Constantine has got its fingers in all kinds of businesses, young man. The kinds that name themselves in daylight, and the other kinds. My friend in Rhegium was meant to smuggle to their liberty a unit of the Wardogs. A tenmen, name of Stonebreakers."

Cleon paused. Marcus said nothing.

Cleon said, "Isn't that the silly name your boys gave themselves?"

Marcus felt as if he would fall straight through the paving stones. He looked past Cleon at the impressive barricade the Redheads had built across Cardester Bend. He closed his eyes.

Cleon said, "You'll accept what House Constantine deems necessary for the expedition, and we can all protect the king from ugly little stories."

Marcus opened his eyes, pale and sick, and whispered hoarsely, "There were three Stonebreakers I never found. Do you know if they caught up with our friend in Rhegium?"

Cleon smiled at him and said, "You poor boy, swimming in a sea of honor. It's a good thing he's sending you to Zanzibar, you wouldn't last a year in the royal district."

Marcus mulishly said, "They were my men. My responsibility, Constantine. Now. Forever."

Cleon said, "Information isn't free. But I'm always ready to buy and sell."

Marcus scowled at his feet, feeling like exactly what he'd always been, an orphan with nothing in his pockets.

## XXX

ANTIVOLA TENDED THE scarlet cherry tree. It grew in a corner of his private garden, the same garden Claire had tried to spy into.

It was a difficult tree, always sprouting white rot or black rot, or flies. But Antivola, who loved all the poisons he grew in his garden, was especially devoted to this tree, and performed whatever work it took to sustain it. He and Reburrus had harvested its gentle poison in the final turn of the Correction of the Weights and Measures.

Half its leaves had gone ashy around the edges. Blind eyes right up against the leaves, Antivola picked tiny aphids from them, one by one, carefully smashing them between his wide blunt fingers. He was so absorbed in his task he didn't realize his fearful double was in the garden till he was right beside him, helping with the aphids.

Antivola squinted over and said, "Your hands look terrible."

Reburrus said, "They'll heal when she's gone."

They worked in silence a while, deftly picking aphids and smashing them.

Antivola said, "Springtime. The expedition leaves in springtime."

Reburrus said, "It won't."

Antivola stopped and looked at Reburrus. The fleshless man viciously smashed a couple aphids, refusing to look back.

Antivola said, "I pray you'll explain."

"Her god has his claw in Florence. If we do not eject her, she will never go. The cult of the Maker of Hands already worships her as a god."

Antivola sighed. He said, "We haven't spoken since you sent me on the hunt."

Now Reburrus did stop and look at Antivola.

Antivola said, "I saw her."

Antivola felt those great rotating eyes bore into him.

He said, "I saw her clearly, as I have seen no mortal thing since I was young."

Reburrus breathed out loudly and scratched the phantom hair on the bridge of his nose.

Antivola said, "She is not flesh nor matter. Light does not light her. What she speaks is not speech; what she breathes is not breath. You were right, Flavius. She is not from the world."

Reburrus spoke simply and urgently.

"Can we kill her?"

Antivola said, "The king ha' forbad it."

"*Can we kill her?*"

"I beg you will wait upon the spring."

Antivola bent to his leaves and aphids, waiting on his friend's response. It shocked him when it came. The ichneumon whined like a bitch in heat.

"I want her hands. I want her hands."

# 33

## LIBRA

THE ROYAL GRANARY was nestled in a crook of the royal district wall. One of the maids recommended it, so Claire sent her request to Marcus that he meet her there. Her message found Marcus dull and quaky with fear of Cleon. Like every man condemned by an oversight, he had trouble believing his woe was real. He welcomed diversion from it.

He hurried to the granary and found the place all warm and pleasant-smelling: there was a bank of ovens with low flames in them, where the grainers warmed a different fraction of the grain each day, to chase off moisture and drive out the mice. The grainers worked the grain with big wood paddles, pushing it around on tin pans in the ovens. They ignored Marcus and the beautiful patricia as the pair passed by. Step by step, Marcus's mood lifted: his troubles weren't upon him yet, and Claire and the scene gave him means to forget, and soon he pretended to himself that things would sort themselves out in the end.

Claire led the way to a line of great clay silos in the back, where everything was cold and quiet. When they arrived, she calmed down, and Marcus realized she'd been fidgeting around like a naughty child. He said, "O Claire, what can I do for you today?"

Instead of answering, Claire made a great show of stretching, raising her arms high above her head. Marcus found it baffling, and when Claire got done stretching, she studied him. Marcus was utterly mystified. She slumped dejectedly. He said nothing. She squared her shoulders and said, "O champion and savior, I was hoping you could help me sneak past the king."

This gave Marcus a jolt. "What do you mean to do?"

She said, "I've been told the priestess of that religion I met in the woods works as a butcher, and she'll be in Florence city today for the full moon market. I should like to meet her again, but the king has restricted me to the royal district. Therefore, I beg you'll spirit me away to Serapetine Hill."

Marcus considered this, but before he was done considering, he caught Claire giving him a troublemaking half-smile. He paused only a moment more, then embraced this new trouble, innocent trouble. He said, "Of course I'll do it."

The patricia hopped up and down and clapped her hands lightly and said, "Oh! Oh! How can we do it? How will we get past the guards at the gate?"

He said, "We'll use Lovers' Gate."

She frowned, and he said, "The other gate, around the south end of the district."

She said, "I hadn't found it yet."

Marcus said, "Fortune smiles on me, giving me another quirk of Florence to show you."

Her half-smile flared up, and Marcus realized she knew all about Lovers' Gate.

## XXX

WHILE THEY WERE walking across the soft grass of the bailey, Marcus casually said, "Regarding the king's prohibition on our intercourse."

Claire looked to him, eye dark and intense. He said, "There is a codicil. Come the spring, we venture west to Zanzibar. Once we leave the valley of the world, he cares nothing what I do with you."

She stopped walking. He stopped as well.

He said, "Therefore I thought I should warn you, the minute we are past the mountains, I will –"

And he leaned in and whispered in her ear.

He stepped back and looked at her. Her ears flamed red.

She said, "And what –" she swallowed "– what else do you plan to do to me?"

XXX

THE GATE OF the Wedding of Coelestin and Iolanthe, generally called Lovers' Gate, was really more a large hole in the wall. Marcus had never seen it closed. It had gate doors, but they were swung wide open and covered in morning glories, and the hinges all green and mossy.

Claire surveyed the thing and said, "What's the use of a wall if you never close the door?"

Marcus said, "The royal district used to be all of Florence city. So the wall separated us from our enemies. Now it would separate the king from the people. Therefore the gate lies open."

They passed through, and nobody gave Claire any trouble; but it was a long trudge around Primavera Circle back up to the Via Floribus. From there they headed west, toward Serapetine Hill. Claire kept finding reasons to raise her arms above her head, though what she wanted from Marcus for it, he couldn't figure out. She tripped on the crooked paving stone at Via Strocchia, but he caught her and she didn't fall.

XXX

THE PATRICIA ONCE visited a smithy and saw men sweating there, shirts off, not one thing extra to their bodies. They had muscles stern as stones and tendons like wires. She'd admired their beauty, but felt foolish in her admiration: they weren't there to be beautiful. Their beauty served their work.

The priestess from Rusadir was like that. Old and brown and wrinkled as a walnut; capable and hard. She halved the hanging carcass of a cow, then cleaved it along the cuts, handing them down to her assistants. It was a kind of performance for the crowd. Claire watched till she'd reduced the carcass. She wiped her frightful curved knife on a rag and ran its edge back and forth over her left thumbnail, sharpening it. Then she turned and smiled at the crowd. They cheered her prowess. The ichts at the edges of the market observed without expression. The crowd shuffled along to the assistants at their long table. The assistants began to slice the cuts. Claire and Marcus remained where they were.

The butcher priestess approached and said, "Sower of Peace," and took Claire's cheeks in her bloody hands. Claire saw Marcus aghast at the gore smeared on her face. It had a good thick stench. The woman still had her faint old woman smell. She kissed Claire lightly on the lips, as she had before.

Claire took the old woman's hands and looked her in her lucid eyes and said, "I am Claire."

The priestess said, "I am Libra."

Claire said, "Hello Libra."

Libra said, "Hello Claire."

Libra spoke quietly and simply, as if to a god. Pleasure shimmered over Claire. She had a flicker of a memory of herself, gown red, not white. But then Libra dropped her hands, and the memory was gone.

Libra fetched a fresh rag and a bucket of water and offered them to Claire. Claire washed her cheeks. Then she stretched, raising both arms. Libra took the hint and said, "Alone in a strange land, but you manage smooth armpits." Claire turned to Marcus and gave him a sharp look. His eyes widened as he finally understood.

She turned back to Libra and curtsied and brightly said, "Pumice!" Libra said, "A suffering only noblewomen have the constitution for," and pulled back her chiton, baring white hairs in her own armpit. She raised an eyebrow at Marcus, who colored.

Then she said, "What do you want to tell me, Sower of Peace?"

Claire said, "From the start, I wished to join you and your followers again, in…" She paused, unsure how to phrase it.

The old woman gently said, "The rites?"

Claire said, "Yes, the rites."

Libra made a little bow with her shoulders and said, "Tonight, in the woods nearest to the city. A short walk across the Campus Iucundum, but unsafe for a young lady –"

Marcus cut in, "I'll take her."

Libra turned a birdlike eye on him and said, "Oh? You practice the people's religion?"

Marcus took a moment, and then spoke carefully. He said, "I follow Pantokrator, but I am a friend to those who follow the Maker of Hands."

Libra said to Claire, "He'll take you." She addressed Marcus: "In the ravine behind the tomb of John the Pilgrim, after dark." Marcus nodded.

Claire said, "I wanted to tell you one more thing…" But again, she found she had trouble speaking. She looked down. She noticed a divot in Libra's left thumbnail, with a little ridge to each side. The knife's path. It looked like a fixed thing, a habit of the flesh, like the jewels in Claire's fingernails and toenails.

Libra said, "Speak freely, Claire."

Claire said, "I lost one I cared about during the late unrest. Florence saved me, Libra. Without Florence, I should certainly have been lost. Therefore I reasoned how I could come to her aid in her terrible days. I had an idea, but now it comes time to say it, I worry you'll think it foolish."

She felt Marcus's attention centered entirely upon her. Libra murmured, "Say everything."

Claire said, "I saw Reburrus preaching war and death up on the Epicondyle. I thought to climb Serapetine Hill and preach love."

Libra and Marcus were still a long time. Marcus said, "Hers was the word that ended long-lived war. It was like a lamp in a dark wood. I was there."

Libra said to Marcus, "I wasn't." She said to Claire, "Mortals see before they hear. Do not preach love; show it."

Claire whispered, "How?"

Libra said, "If you favor Serapetine Hill, go to the king of the costermongers and beg a job serving the customers. Let them have from you their pears and plums and all things sweet upon the tongue."

XXX

THERSITES SAID, "ABSOLUTELY not."

Marcus glared at him, but the ugly little man glared right back. The side of his mouth twitched. Claire watched them glare at one another, just exactly like a father and his eldest. Finally Marcus turned to Claire and said, "Why don't you explain to Tiresias why I had to accompany you here today."

Claire turned this over for a moment in her reason, and puzzled it out. She said, "King Ambrosius has restricted me to the royal district. I needed Marcus to smuggle me out."

Thersites looked at her and said, "You're defying the king?"

Claire innocently said, "I am."

The old king-hater mulishly lowered his brow at Marcus and said, "You know me too well, you rascal. Everything but my name."

Marcus said, "So you'll do it, *Thersites*?"

Thersites sighed. He said to Claire, "Foreigner, I'll let you try it out, working the counter as you say. We'll see how it goes for you and for me."

XXX

LIBRA SAID, "Is this how she works on begging day?"

Marcus said, "I haven't been by, but they say she's tireless."

Libra folded her arms and watched. A little ways away, Claire stood behind the counter of Thersites's stall. Word had gotten around the market that the girl from Zanzibar was selling fruit, and the usual line had lengthened, snaking down the lane between other kiosks. Claire had found her rhythm, turning, lifting fruit, presenting it, accepting coins, making change. She had a smile for each customer, and frequently touched hands with them. They wished to touch her and be touched by her.

Libra said, "Not tireless. She's pushing her weariness away. You can tell she's got noble blood, but she's not like one of their spoiled daughters."

Marcus said, "She's *good*."

Libra heard his fervor and looked at him. He had the impression he'd just now gained her approval. But she said, "She means well enough."

Marcus said, "That's all you'd credit her?"

Libra spoke slowly, as if she were forming her thoughts by speaking them. She said, "You're crediting her more because you've lost your head for her. She's only a little younger than you, but you are a man and she is a girl. She may turn out good. She may turn out evil. She might even become nothing much. Right now, she is not good or evil. She doesn't understand good and evil yet."

Marcus said, "Don't your people worship her as a god?"

Libra nodded solemnly and said, "We worship the Sower of Peace. The god is not the same as the girl she inhabits."

# 34

## DAWN

THE GUARD CAME back to the gate and said, "I'm sorry, sir, but my master won't receive you."

Temet Ambrosius said, "Will he come to the gate and speak with me?"

The guard said, "No. He told me to tell you if you asked. He won't."

Temet brooded on that a little while. He said, "May we enter and provide for our needs and rest the night?"

The guard said, "I have been instructed to deny you everything."

Temet said, "We are on the king's business! We have a right to provide for ourselves from the bounty of your master's estate."

The guard grimaced and turned to his fellow. His fellow took up the argument. He said, "That may be, but the king's in Florence and you're here." He cast a skeptical eye over Temet's diminished party. He said, "If you think you can defeat the gate, and all the men-at-arms of Petrus Secundus Iustinius, then try it. But that is what you'll have to do, if you want anything from us."

The decanus of the Tagmata nudged his horse forward, right

alongside Temet's calm gray Boreas, and said, "If we do it, you'll die first."

The second guard eyed him and said, "If."

Temet was forced to put an arm across the chest of his man to keep him from drawing. He said, "Iustinius is not the Crimson Knight."

The frustrated decanus wheeled on him and shouted, "Then what are we doing here?"

Temet slapped the decanus hard across the cheek. Now the decanus did half-draw his sword. Temet waited. The decanus collected himself and slid his sword back down its scabbard. Temet slapped him again, across the right cheek, then the left. The decanus stared fire at Temet. The man's charger snorted and clopped its hoof uncertainly on the paving stones. Temet spoke in a quiet, deadly voice.

"We will leave this good man's estate and make our camp, and I will speak to you there."

The decanus nodded and turned his horse. Temet sensed the second guard preparing a rude comment, and aimed a warning finger at him. The man held his tongue.

Temet led his men silently back along the branch road to the place it split from the Via Circumflorentia. He said, "We'll make camp right here. Pull paving stones from the estate road to bare the earth, then dig the latrine in it."

The afternoon was cooling down and the trees were turning black. The western sky shaded from blue to a peachy glow. Temet saw what he had to do. He dismounted and approached his Tagmata, twisting his mustache till it was straight again and well-pointed.

He looked up at his remaining men, where they still sat their horses. *How few is the Crimson Knight aiming for, before the final attack?*

He said, "The king gave me an order. I have executed it faithfully. But I have also executed it thoughtlessly. Like an ox yoked to his task, I have gone from house to house among the warrior nobles. I have dragged you with me on this hopeless road.

"I was wrong."

The vigiles were listening too, and the staffers were edging over as they went about setting up camp.

His crisis finally at hand, Temet discovered in himself that natural leadership which served his cousin Manfredi, king of Florence, so well. Temet knew his stiff posture, his clicking speech, and his ostentatious mustache seemed funny to commoners. Now he exaggerated all these traits. He made himself helpless before his men, nothing more than himself. He spoke so that all could hear.

"I have been weak. I have been indecisive. I have shown myself unfit to lead you. I beg you will forgive me, and lend me patience but a little longer.

"I will go into my tent this evening and consider what comes next. We will complete the king's mission, but we will not throw away our lives like dumb beasts shuffling to the slaughter. We will do what we must and we will fight and we will *live*."

The Tagmata did not turn to their decanus to read how to respond. *Good.* Each man nodded for himself. They grunted their assent. A great tension eased in the camp.

The staffers set the tents, and Temet ordered patrols all night, not excluding himself from the roster. Then he withdrew into his tent to think, as he had promised.

## XXX

THE TURQUOISE FIELD of evening was ripening dark blue, and the full moon was rising, clear and pure. Marcus held Claire's hand, her palm and fingers alive with pleasure, and led her through the vague gloaming of the Campus Iucundum. They came to a bower and Claire glimpsed a small white building, oddly shaped, inside it. But Marcus steered them around the place, and they picked their way down a flight of sodden, splintery steps set into the slope of a forested ravine. As they descended, the canopy sliced up the giant moon, until they were submerged in a confusion of dim silver edges. They didn't speak; the chorus of crickets was overwhelmingly loud, a melodious rhythm that filled the woods. They followed the winding floor of the ravine, their feet soft on a bed of damp leaves. The crickets' roar diminished till they could hear the drip of water among the trees, and then crackling. The floor rose slowly and dried out. They rounded a bend, and a fire on a stone altar came into view. Several dozen men and women sat on blankets spread around the altar, talking and eating. This convivial scene was entirely different in aspect from the gathering Claire had stumbled on in Rusadir.

Libra waved Claire and Marcus over, saying, "Children! Come sit with me!"

Claire hesitated and Marcus guided her forward. He settled himself familiarly on Libra's blanket and Claire sat down beside him. Libra turned to a knot of people near the altar. She called, "Wanesa! Drinks for the Sower of Peace and the man with the sword!"

She looked to Claire and Marcus and said, "You're hungry?"

They nodded vigorously and Libra called, "Bring them what to eat as well!"

A moment later Wanesa approached. Claire saw it was the maiden who'd assisted Libra by the pyre.

Claire said to Libra, "Your daughter?"

A shade of sorrow darkened Libra's face and she said, "Niece."

Marcus took the cups from Wanesa and said, "Claire, these are the followers of the people's religion, that survives in the hills and fields, forests and gullies."

Wanesa scurried off to get the food, and Claire drank: sweet wine, with something acrid at the bottom of its taste. She held the cup away and looked at it. Libra laughed and said, "It's just a little something mixed in for a pleasant evening," and took a deep draught from her own cup.

Claire drank.

# XXX

THE DRUG GAVE Claire a happy dizzy feeling. She ate seconds and thirds of chickpeas and mutton till her belly felt tight. She leaned her head on Marcus's shoulder, steadying her dizziness against his strength. She felt goodwill toward all the world, though she wasn't sure she could have stood without help.

The other congregants came by in groups of two or three to touch Claire's arms and cheeks, or stroke her hair. She looked up at them, face open, as if she were the child of everybody.

Some stayed a while to talk and drink. They told their stories of bitter war, of the suffering of the Florentines. The stories were sad, but they were not told sadly. Drink and good company made it easier to tell them. Telling them helped to heal the wounds.

Finally somebody said, "Sower of Peace, now you've come to us in Florence, can't you stay?"

Claire smiled a sad smile and said, "My heart keeps time, and one day it will run out of time, and I will die. Every Zanzibari must come home again, or die."

Libra said, "Tell us what to think of, when we think of Zanzibar."

Claire straightened herself back up. She drew up her legs and wrapped her arms around her calves and rested her chin on her knees. She tried to think what it was permitted to tell them, just as she had with King Ambrosius, by that other campfire on the long road to Florence. Speaking then had hurt her terribly. Now she found her grief less jagged.

The eye of her imagination abruptly slipped from Marcus, from Libra, from Florence altogether. She saw Zanzibar.

It was daytime, and there was nothing doing at Café Null. She drank the last of her tse and licked her finger and dabbed up the crumbs of her handcake. She shut her book and left the patio and went out into dusty, sun-baked Ixanahade Street. You'd never know they'd fought a war there. Keeping to the shadows, she walked west, past the rug merchants and the booksellers, and the sun got brighter, and the salt smell of the sea got stronger, and she heard the waves.

She came to the bear, Volucteur, the civic bear of Zanzibar. Volucteur sat on a low pink granite plinth, a great bronze bear, twice so tall as a man, his toes rubbed shiny by the hands of children. There was a commemoration chiseled in the plinth to those who gave their lives there, restoring the happy republic. The road forked at the bear, a south fork toward Port Zanzibar, and a north fork to Angoulème.

Claire took the north fork, past the gaudy shops, until the road became a boardwalk, with sand and tall grasses on each side of it, and she was at Angoulème, Angoulème of the hundred boardwalks. She was back among the boy youths and the girl youths, with their wheeled shoes and the sails along their outstretched arms, laughing and racing down the boardwalks on the wind, a nearly avian species.

Claire squinted in the light and shaded her eyes with her book. She watched a wave roll in, the white foam on its flank so bright until the sparkling sunlight, brighter still, reflected off the curling water. Now another wave, and the sun showed through behind, so that the dark seawater lit bluish-green. Three boy youths competed in excellence at ocean sports, and seven girl youths showed off themselves, each more beautiful than the last. A little girl ran screaming from the waves, and laughing hugged herself to her mother's leg. A boy and girl, ankles in the foam, embraced, convinced their love the first and best since time began. Here were people living as they should, in their own skins, happy at the moment they were living, hard by the sea.

Claire's eye scanned up from these tranquil scenes, to the sea that loomed above them, that goes out to the end of things, to the very sky, and she recognized its call, that says man comes from the sea, and must return to it, but for all that, he shall end among the stars.

This was Angoulème, land's end, the beach of Zanzibar, where the desert meets the sea.

Now here she was landlocked, night forest dripping, face warmed by firelight. Libra touched her arm at the level of the bicep. Claire said, "Forgive me, friend, I was reflecting on fond scenes of Zanzibar."

Libra said, "If it pains you, do not speak of it."

Claire shook her head and said, "Let me tell you about my mother. She is called Reason. When the Creator first thought of the world, He thought her. The world is a thought called Reason in the mind of the Creator."

She stared at Libra, as if daring her to argue it. But Libra only listened, eyes soft.

Claire said, "Reason is a god of war. There was a war in Zanzibar, and my mother fought it and won it. But the price of victory was terrible, and she will never be the same."

Claire looked down at her empty cup, at the dark worms of the lees in it, arranged just the same as the crumbs of her handcake. She stuck her finger in and swiped it around and sucked the lees from her finger.

Claire said, "I am the last daughter Reason bore. If she loses me, then she will die."

Libra said, "And you?"

Claire said, "It is just the same for me. If I cannot drink the sunshine of her beauty – if I cannot salve her wounds - if I cannot hear again the evening wind, sighing in the leaves of olive trees, planted by my ancestors on the land they tamed – if I cannot do these things, then I will die."

Claire heard a low murmur. She turned her head unsteadily and saw the congregants were all gathered around the blanket where she and Marcus and Libra sat.

She said to all of them, "You think I'm a god, this is true?"

And she gestured to herself. Her gown was red, in the edges of her vision.

Wanesa said, "We do believe it."

Claire said, "If I met a god, I would be utterly undone. How comes it you are so comfortable with me?"

Wanesa looked at Libra, and Libra inclined her head to her.

Wanesa said, "We don't know how things go in Zanzibar, but the valley of the world is rich with gods. We have many tales of one or other of them taking mortal form to visit with his followers."

Claire pushed, saying, "Did you worship any Sower of Peace before I came here?"

Wanesa shook her head and said, "Your miracles in Andropolis and afterward taught us your worship."

Claire said, "And Claire is a mortal form of the Sower of Peace?"

Libra said, "The god has a finger, and the finger is a girl."

She waited expectantly, and suddenly Claire understood. They were all looking hopefully at her. She unfolded herself and put her hand on Marcus's shoulder. Refusing his help, she tottered to her feet. The woods spun around her. She smelled her own smell, her honeysuckles and the new perfume, the thunder.

*A demonstration of my power.*

She considered unfolding time, but she remembered again the storm which carried her off from Zanzibar; the storm which appeared again when she unfolded time in the face of Reburrus. She didn't understand the storm, and she didn't dare invoke it. So she could not unfold time for them.

She rummaged around herself, and realized that godlike feeling Libra seemed to settle on her, was giving her back more of what she'd forgotten.

*Mother, I can show them one of your old tricks.*

In the wild fields of her vast inland, she called to the forest, this forest right here, in the world, in Florence. Her song shook the inland grasses, and it rustled the leaves of the real forest.

Presently they answered her call: footfalls approached, some agile, some very heavy. The congregants turned at the movement.

All around them shapes emerged from among the trees. As the shapes approached the firelight, some of the women congregants gave little shrieks. Wolves and bears came out of the forest.

Claire's Aunt Moonlight understood the creatures of the forest as hunters or quarry. But her mother saw everyone in the world as enemy or ally. She had made allies in the forest as well. Claire was calling on their alliance.

The congregants crowded together, awed and terrified. Claire said, "Be nothing afraid, these creatures are my friends." The leader of the wolves padded to Claire. He was a great old wolf with brown fur and honey eyes and one white paw. He stretched and whined and bowed, and she scratched him on the head, between his ears.

The ring of wolves and bears watched silently. One bear stood on his hind legs; the others on all fours. The wolves sniffed the breeze. The alliance was tattered and, if asked, these animals might not fight. But they were glad to attend when their ally's daughter called.

Libra had not shrunk back. She gazed at Claire and the old brown wolf, and her lined, hard face showed a very satisfied expression, as if old hopes had been rewarded.

Claire said to Wanesa, "Is it possible to feed them from our meal? They don't ask for much, just a bite or two."

Wanesa got busy, and all the congregants helped to feed the monstrous beasts the Sower of Peace had summoned.

## XXX

THE PARTICIPANTS IN the religion of the poor bedded down in the ravine behind the tomb of John the Pilgrim. The wolves and bears had retreated into the woods. It was the middle of the night, and anyway Claire and Marcus were very drunk. Libra commandeered them a blanket and they shared it, a little ways away from her.

Eyes glittering in the dark, Claire whispered to him, "Tell me some more of what you plan to do to me, once we cross the mountains."

He thought, *Cleon's blackmail – the Crimson Knight – mayhem in the city – let it all hang, she's right here and this is living.*

He smiled at her and whispered, "No."

She reared back a little bit and said, "*No?*"

He whispered, "If I told you any more, you wouldn't be able to keep your hands off me, and then the king would lop off my head, and I am very fond of my head, on account of it is pretty."

"*Your* head."

"Very, very pretty."

"You're going to make me work for this, aren't you?"

"Oh yes."

He shushed her before her laughter woke Libra. She struck him lightly on the chest.

## XXX

TEMET AMBROSIUS SAT in his tent in the dark of the night, staring into the flame on the wick of his oil lamp.

*How does the wick burn, and it is not consumed?*

The flame danced each time a breeze slipped in the tent. If the breeze was strong enough, he would hear the flame dance. He stared and stared, thinking about the warrior nobles, about the Crimson Knight, about his journey along the wretched Via Circumflorentia.

*What do I know?*

*Rufus Ffidius told me that I already know who the Crimson Knight is.*

Rufus Quintus Ffidius, who plied him with drink and showed Temet his friendly face. This same warrior noble must have been the one who sent word ahead to Petrus Secundus Iustinius, so that Iustinius had time to consider his options, and turn Temet away at the gate.

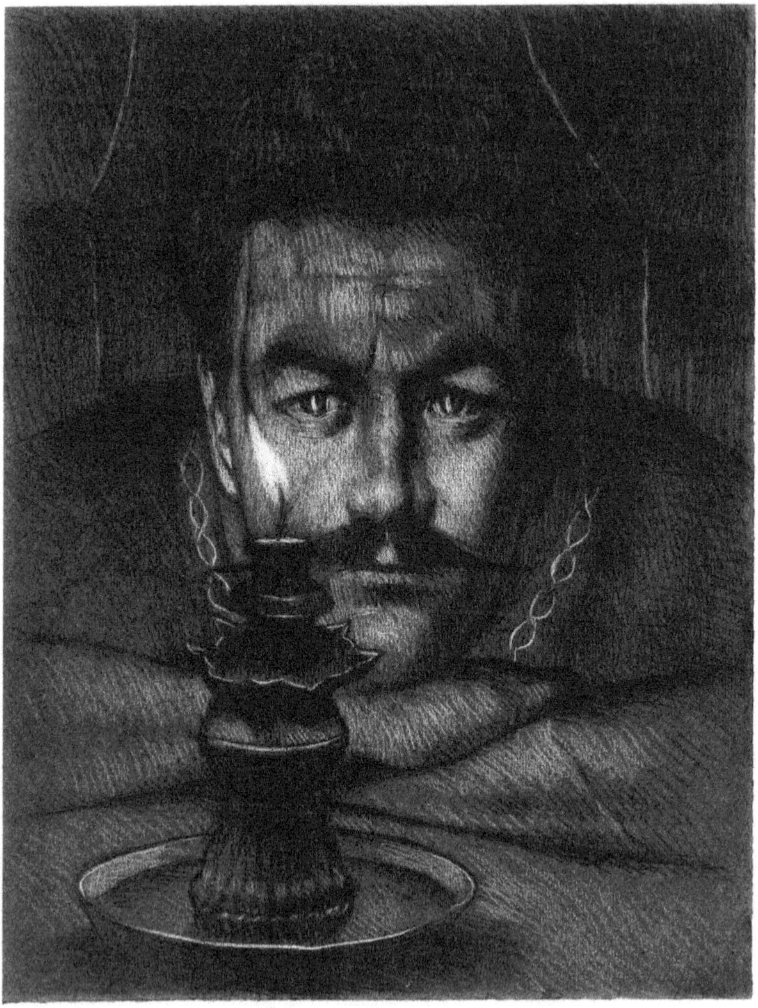

Temet Ambrosius stared into the flame.

*What do I know?*

*I know Ffidius is not my friend. But he* should *have been my friend. We are alike in rank, in temperament, in honor...*

And suddenly, Temet Nosce Ambrosius knew something about the Crimson Knight. The skin contracted across his chest.

Temet's canvass of the warrior nobles was an obvious idea for an investigation. Therefore the Crimson Knight had anticipated it. And it was turning the warrior nobles against Temet. It was turning them against the king.

*What do I know?*

*I know the Crimson Knight has made me a blade, to sever my king from his allies.*

Now that he saw it, a series of realizations tumbled into place.

*I know I have to put a stop to this investigation right away.*

*I know the Crimson Knight knows where I am, because he is sending men to ruin me night by night.*

*I know that if he's doing that, if he's whittling me away, then I have nearly served my purpose, and soon he can dispose of me.*

*I do not know who the Crimson Knight is. But by Pantokrator's wrath, I can tell who he is* not.

He unrolled his map of the estates along the Via Circumflorentia. He looked at the great houses ahead, judging each one:

Maecius – *no.*

Vanescens – *no.*

Cosconia – *no.*

Priscus – *no.*

Varo –

Varo...

Sandor Pilvax Varo.

Cousin of the chaste lady of the castle, his own Livia Faustina Varo.

Son of the failed usurper Lucius Catiline Varo.

Sandor Pilvax Varo, the shaggy-bearded eccentric, openly defying the order of extinction by siring those children of his, the Pilvax children, born naked of their ancient name.

Temet stared into the flame on the wick of his oil lamp.

After a long moment, he bent back to the map. Underneath the dancing light, he traced his finger along the Via Circumflorentia. A day's ride ahead, there was a spur road angled back toward Florence city. The map showed it stopping after a short morning's ride, in the middle of the king's fields. Temet happened to know it didn't end there. It turned, cutting straight across the fields. It met up again with the Via Circumflorentia not far from Varo's estate.

If he led his men down the spur and along the straightaway, he could save two days and avoid insulting innocent nobles.

He could baffle the Crimson Knight as to his location.

He could surprise the Varo estate, appearing as if from nowhere.

He rubbed his silty eyes. This was good. He should have been pleased. Instead, a terrible ache burned his heart.

*Are you involved in this, Livia?*

## XXX

Marcus Irenaeus Diophantus woke before dawn. A voluptuous feeling filled him: anticipation of departure.

He lay with his eyes closed, gradually becoming confused about where he was. He heard rustles and drips, snores and intermittent birdsong. The wind on his face was cold, but his bare arms and legs were warm. With a tiny movement, he recognized the feel of wool on his skin. His tongue was thick and furry. He smelled wet leaves and burnt wood and meat. Then he smelled another smell, honeysuckles and thunder. *Her.* He spread his arm a little ways from his side, until he touched the curve of her belly. She shifted in her sleep.

He opened his eyes. He lifted his head a little and it throbbed. The other congregants lay sleeping all around him in their woolen blankets, on the floor of the ravine. Libra was snoring. The forest slumbered. He remembered the first night of the peace, in Andropolis.

He leaned his head on his hand and looked at the patricia.

Her face was pale in the faint pre-dawn light. The worry had smoothed out of her brow. The corners of her lips curled up, just a little bit, so that she faintly smiled.

He sank into the sight of her. Gray light slowly painted color on her. Dawn was coming.

Her eyes opened. Her pale gray irises were nearly luminous. She didn't move. She looked up at him.

He thought about dawn, about the anticipation of departure. He was on the verge of forming an important thought.

He spoke quietly to her, "You've accepted what they offer, creation of you as a god."

He saw some flippant answer gather on her lips. Then he saw her reconsider. He watched her choose to be where she was. Something unclenched in his breast.

She whispered, "I accepted it from you first."

*How shall a man love a god? How can a god love a man?*

He said, "I remember what you said before the hunt. You told Bitsy Boots about the holy duty of worshipping old gods, the gods of his fathers and his fathers' fathers."

She licked her dry lips and said, "That is his religion. It is not my job to steal his religion from him. But his religion is not mine. I am a daughter of Zanzibar."

"What is Zanzibar?"

He watched her thinking what to say. Finally she said, "Zanzibar is the start of things."

His thought crashed together in his head, and he saw all of it at once. He saw his favorite time of day, the time of departures, the hour of beginnings. He saw a fresh goddess, from the land of new things.

*I will name you, beloved.*

He said, "I know your god-name Claire. They've got it wrong, it isn't Sower of Peace." She pressed her lips together and scanned his face.

"It's Dawn."

She closed her eyes. The corners of her mouth turned down and her chin pocked, like a little child's chin. He brushed his hand over her eyes; her lashes were wet, her cheeks were wet. At his touch, her shoulders shook and she rolled over, turning away from him.

The melodious roar of morning birds filled the forest. Soon everyone was awake.

# 35

## THE GOD OF SLEEP

MARCUS AND CORNELIUS stood, arms folded, and looked across the haze at the nearby army camp. Men were busy over there. One team was digging a ditch in one direction, and another team was building a palisade in the other direction. They were walling in their little city on the Campus Iucundum.

Marcus said, "I don't like it."

Cornelius scratched his wizened brow. "Maybe they're finding ways to keep the men busy. An idle army –" he *tsk*'d the thought.

Marcus mulled it over. He said, "Pretend for me they actually need a palisade. Why?"

"Ward off bandit raids?"

"You think bandits would attack thousands of soldiers?"

"Hum. Defense against the Crimson Knight?"

Marcus said, "I can almost believe it. But how many men could the Crimson Knight have? Enough to take on the Wardogs and the Redheads both?"

They kept on watching. The two teams, the ditch-diggers and

the wall-builders, met up. Shouts and laughter drifted across the plain.

Cornelius said, "What do you figure that's all about?"

Marcus squinted, then laughed. He said, "They've measured it wrong and got the ditch inside the wall."

Cornelius said, "Must be Redhead engineers in charge."

"Must be."

They watched a while longer. The commotion quieted, across the plain, and the ditch-diggers went right on digging, and the wall-builders went on building their wall on the outside of the ditch.

Cornelius said, "Decanus..."

Marcus said, "I agree. We'd best build our own palisade. I'll go tell the Thousand."

## XXX

At the Académie some years before, Claire heard a whining from an empty room. It was a blinding day outside, and when she went into the room, its marble walls glowed with a cold pure light. In that bright room, she found a great black dog, so dark against the white all round as to seem featureless. She'd never seen this dog before. He whined again and padded to her, chest as high as hers, claws tapping on the marble floor. She suffered only an instant of fear, then held out her hand to him, and he licked it. It emerged later that a visiting philosopher, a specialist in the theory of mind, had lost track of his beast companion.

There was a new thing in Claire's bedroom and it reminded her of the dog. Against the pale walls and fair light in the room, this thing was black and featureless and nearly out of nature in its lack of explanation. It was quite large, taller than she was, and shaped somewhat like the gold palanquin. Without the palanquin's rails, it took on an aspect of a ship, with a bow higher than its stern. It had four corners, and a horn atop each corner. She got a rushlight off the wall, and walked toward this thing, then began to circle it. Openings came into view, and she realized it was like the small family room inside the great hall of the other castle. This was a little room of oiled walnut inside her stony room, and inside of it space enough for her bed.

Coming up to it, she saw its bow had, as it were, its own figurehead, that was a carven face of a man. He had a strong square jaw and a wide, expressive mouth; a mighty nose, manfully crooked; pronounced and comely cheekbones; and lids closed softly over enormous eyes, beneath a glowering brow full of deep thoughts. The blond wood of the face seemed much older than the oiled walnut of the rest. Claire thought, *It is Trypsomayne, their god of sleep.* She thought, *The carving must derive from some real model, it is too like life.*

There were receptacles at each side of the head of Trypsomayne, with great antlers in them. She recognized the size and points of these antlers. They came from the great red hart she'd shot in New Forest. Immediately she called the whole wood bedroom Trypsomayne.

Continuing around it, she found it covered all about in blank wood panels, framed by stately wooden ridges. Toward the back she found two panels that were not blank, but carved. In a top one was a fanciful rendition of clashing clouds, with rain and lightning indicated. In the middle of it all there was an image of her own palanquin, heaved aloft upon the mighty shoulder of the storm. Letters at the bottom read CLAIRE LEAVES ZANZIBAR.

It took her a little longer to decipher the panel underneath. It was very complicated, and when she placed it, she realized the carver hadn't seen with his own eyes the scene he carved. A little image of her stood between two kings, and around them were The Thousand, and they all stood on the bridge, the Pontus Sextus Trassinope, with the swollen Sinope rushing underneath. The shape of the bridge, and the arrangement of her thousand soldiers were all incorrect, but they had the sense of rightness of an artist's eye. At last she confirmed her understanding of this, reading at the bottom CLAIRE MAKES THE PEACE.

She concluded the blank panels, fourteen in all, were meant to be filled in with legendary scenes from her life to come. *Fourteen more wonders in my lifetime.* The thought was like worrying a sore tooth, a delicious kind of pain. *Someday I will complete my work, whatever it is to be. Someday I will die.*

She trod the stair of Trypsomayne and climbed into the little bedroom. This did not resemble the interior of the gold palanquin, but that was natural enough. She assumed they'd tried to open it and found what happened for everyone but her: not so much that it couldn't be opened, as that there was no inside.

The little space inside of Trypsomayne was a soft bed strewed with covers. She lay herself down in it, as snug as a mouse in his mouse-hole. She took the two half-coins of greeting from their separate folds in her gown, and tucked them underneath a pillow. Looking up, she perceived that stars of silver and of gold were set into the walnut panel right above her head. They glimmered in the flicker of the rushlights, showing real constellations.

This was one of the finest gifts anyone had ever made the young patricia.

She climbed back down from it and knelt before it on the floor. She rested her elbows on the floor as well. The mistress of bows now made a complete bow: she pressed her brow to her clasped hands. She thought *O let me be worthy of your kindness to a stranger. Let me bring you peace.* And her hands shook.

## XXX

Claire started at a sound. She was still white-knuckled and nervy; she didn't know how long she'd been kneeling. She turned and said, "Epida! O Epida, you've come back to me." She stood but then buckled; her legs had gone to sleep. Epida caught her and held her, and as Claire's legs tingled back to life, she came to hold the little maid as well. Epida said, "I heard you're turning fruit on Serapetine Hill," and started crying. Claire whispered, "Epida, Epida," and stroked her hair and kissed her crown. Epida grat her teeth and said, "I thought I'd got all done with crying." Claire said, "Shh, shh," and held the grieving girl for as long as it took.

## XXX

TEMET AMBROSIUS WAS on his shift patrolling the camp's boundary. It was near the end of the night. The moon had set and he could see a little ways into the trees by starlight. These were untended public lands between estates, and the road was just a track again. He heard a branch snap, out beyond the limit of his sight. Squirrel? Deer? Then an urgent whisper. Temet drew his sword, shouting "*Parati! Pugna!*" – *Ready! Fight!*

The men in the woods gave up hiding and sprinted toward the camp.

Temet kept shouting. The Tagmata were on their feet in moments. They slept in their armor, swords by their sides.

The attackers burst from the trees, their surrounding maneuver cut short. Temet roared, "*Impetus!*" and his Tagmata attacked. The vigiles were up now too, and the staffers. The attackers had no tidy camp to fall on, and crossed swords in a melee.

Temet spotted a knot of attackers and charged into it. The attackers rained blows upon him. Their bronze clanged against his breastplate. He swung and struck and men cried out and ran; some fell. He heard the Tagmata barking. He barked as well, barked and howled into the starlit woods. His breath burned in his lungs and his sight pulsed red.

After so many days of building dread and anger, he found release now in terror and rage. He blocked, parried, thrust. He struck the standing, smote the wounded, trampled the fallen. He roared "*Ave Ambrosius! Ave Florence! Ad Victoria!*" One of his men shouted "*Ave Temet!*" and the others took up the cry. In the dark of his mind he used their cries to map the attackers they fought.

He made his way from one clash to the next. Once, nearly blind, he bumped into a man. He smelled unfamiliar spices on the man's hot breath and wrapped him in a bear hug. Drawing his little knife from his arm guard, he stuck it in the stranger's neck. Another time he bumped into a man and the man hissed, "Temet, it's me!" Temet spun away, not knowing who it was. He fought one fight, then another, and finally –

Finally, the fighting was done.

He put his hands on his knees and wheezed one last order, "*Numerabit*."

His men counted off. He'd kept them all. Finally a fair fight, and he'd kept them all.

He stood and said, "Our horses?"

A groom called, "Safe!"

He searched around for a living attacker and found a shape gasping on the ground. He called, "Light!" and a staffer brought a lamp. Its flicker lit a man in filthy seventh morax armor. He'd taken a stab in the gap at the side, and his hands were pressed on the wound. He was sweating and pale and his eyes were squeezed shut.

Temet kicked him. The man whimpered, and Temet kicked him again. He opened his eyes and breathed, "Mercy."

Temet said, "You're the Crimson Knight's men?"

The man said, "Who?"

Temet knelt by the man. He hissed, "The Crimson Knight. He sent you to hunt us."

In agony though he was, the man's brow furrowed and he said, "I don't know any Crimson Knight. We spotted you at sundown and followed you."

Temet's nostrils flared and he drew his sword. The man's eyes widened in terror. He started to struggle as Temet carefully fit his blade between dented segments of the man's armor. His struggle availed him nothing; Temet got the sword positioned as he wanted it, and thrust, and the man went out from underneath the sun.

He stood wearily and spoke loudly.

He fought one fight, then another.

"Bandits. They were just a gang of veteran bandits."

Groans of disappointment. The woods were lightening now. Morning was coming.

"Novacila! Where are you, you great brute? I need a wash and a shave."

The big man made his way out from the tight cluster of scutlers and shoulder boys and donkey drivers. He had an open razor in one hand and a heavy staff in the other. Tremors still shook his arms. He'd been ready to fight.

## XXX

CLAIRE TURNED UP in the jade office as she'd been instructed, clearly mystified to find him there, with Judge Salvatorio at his side. He felt a dull pain at the thought of what he had to do to her, to *her*, but he walled it over with clay. He was the king before he was a man.

The beautiful patricia said, "My lord, how can I serve you or Florence today?"

Ambrosius said, "It is a little past a month now since you first came to the valley of the world."

She blinked and softly exclaimed, "A month! A month already," and smiled at him all innocent.

He said, "When I required chastity of you, why didn't you tell me it was already too late?"

She said, "Too late?"

He said, "A little past a month, and you haven't had your menses."

She blushed. The red of her cheek was very dark in the green light of the jade office.

She said, "How could you –"

He stood and shouted, "The sovereign knows everything!"

She looked at her feet. In a tiny voice she said, "I have ever been a chaste patricia. There is another explanation for it, my lord."

He gave in to his rage, his voice blistering in its fury. "You aren't too young to bleed! Are you ill? Are you with child? Whose – *his*?"

Claire cowered and stammered, "Hear my explanation, I b-beg you."

Salvatorio put a hand on Ambrosius's wrist. He shook it away, but he made himself sit before he spoke again.

He said, "In one month, the warrior nobles meet in the great hall to celebrate the peace. You are to be my ornament. The trophy of my victory. By then, your naked breast will swell, or it will not. Your womb will swell, or it will not. The queen herself will touch your belly."

He watched her firm up her will. She wiped one eye with the back of her wrist. She looked up at him. So pale her gaze, the gray eyes that saw all.

He softened his voice and said, "See none of Marcus Irenaeus Diophantus. Tempt not his lust. See none of me. Tempt not my wrath. Comport yourself with dignity. I will not have a color-braided pulsivar in my house. You boast yourself a noblewoman; show it."

He stood and left. It tore the clay off his dull pain, but he didn't look back. He was the king before he was a man.

The question Claire had asked him on the bank of the Euxis rang in his ears: *Do you have the heart to go on being king?*

## XXX

IN THE PEACH light of late afternoon, Epida let herself in Claire's apartment to dust. She found Claire sitting in the alcove of the window, looking out into the day. She called, "Hallo, Claire."

Claire turned and Epida felt a thrill of horror; the patricia's face was cold and full of hate.

Epida said, "What –"

"You've been going through my rubbish."

"Your –"

"He set you looking for my rags, and you *told* him."

"I –"

"Get out. *Get out!*"

Epida fled, confused and weeping.

## XXX

CORNELIUS CRUNCHED AN apple, eyes closed under the warmth of the low autumn sun. Marcus waited a while, then cleared his throat.

Cornelius blinked at him, then looked down at the paper in his lap. He said, "Fire in the southwestern district."

Marcus raised the dented city horn to his lips and blew notes on it.

Three short: *Florence city*

Two long: *southwest*

Four short: *fire*

Cornelius ran his finger over the symbols on the page and said, "You've got it now. Alright, try this: runners to the royal district."

Marcus breathed and raised the horn, but then stopped, confused. The royal district was one long note, but what was *runners*? And how did one summon them?

Feeble-minded old Philo, bundled in a blanket and sunning on his low bed, blatted through his lips, mimicking the horn.

Long-short: *the royal district calls*

Short-long-short: *runners*

Then he laughed, wheezing, and three soldiers of the Thousand, climbing the hillside toward them, laughed as well. Marcus ringed his fingers at the Thousand and jabbed the mouth of the horn back and forth through the ring, but they just kept laughing at him.

Cornelius said, "Why do you insist on learning the horn code?"

Marcus said, "If I'm to be a tribune, I should know how to do the job."

The men had arrived and nodded solemnly now. One said, "You're right to do it, sir."

Marcus scanned them and saw they carried a small pot. He said, "What's that?"

One offered him a ladle and said, "Try it."

Marcus filled the ladle and took a sip of the thick gray liquid. Right away he spat it on the ground, wiping his lips and blurting, "What *is* it?"

The men grimaced and said, "Mostly ox hooves probably. They call it portable soup. A fellow from the cooks' guild brought some by. We think we might order up a great load of it for the expedition."

Marcus said, "Why would we do that?"

Beside him Cornelius had taken a sip. He spat it on the ground as well, then took a big bite from his apple and chewed vigorously.

One of the men extracted a little gray cube from a cloth bag. He handed it over to Marcus. Marcus turned it over in his hand. It was heavy and dry and had bits of stuff in it.

He said, "Is this –?"

The man who'd given it to him said, "Yes. You mix it with water and heat it up. As long as it's dry, they say it keeps for years."

Now a runner approached from the direction of the city. His grave look quieted the men immediately.

Marcus said, "What have you, friend?"

The runner said, "Orders from the king."

Marcus said, "Let's have them."

The runner said, "Perhaps I could tell you in private."

## XXX

CLAIRE FLUNG HERSELF down in Trypsomayne. She stared at the inlaid constellations and suffered waves of anxiety and anger and self-pity.

The royal family did not make themselves known to her that day, nor in the days that followed. She remained furious with

Epida, but without her, grew lonely. Marcus was nowhere to be found.

In the mornings, she retreated to her gold palanquin. She practiced her austerities, which she'd been neglecting. When her passions were calmed and her mind was clear, she rewarded herself with her stack of puzzles:

She pondered why the storm appeared when she unfolded time. She revolved the problem before her reason. She approached it from angle after angle, but she did not solve it.

She studied the symbol on the bottom of Reburrus's abandoned sandals, the circle inscribed in the square. She finally remembered where she'd seen it in Zanzibar: it was just like the parable of the red astronaut and the blue astronaut. But that wasn't what it meant in Florence. Here, she'd seen it on religious medals and standards, on the back faces of coins. She knew that Pantokrator was a sun god. So the circle must be the sun. And the square?

She studied the strange symbol of Florence city, the rectangle with the awkward shading-lines. It was on the front faces of coins, on flags and tapestries, everywhere. On this, she made some progress: following a hunch, she found a cloth with the symbol sewn on it and counted stitches between shading-lines. The first line appeared exactly halfway across the rectangle. The second, three-quarters. The third, seven-eighths. And the fourth, fifteen-sixteenths. They weren't shading lines at all. They were a geometric series with a ratio of 1/2. What this meant, she had no idea.

Hidden from sight and sound in the palanquin, she worked on all these puzzles till her mind was weary. Her delight in reasoning was tempered by a growing dread. She did not reason for reason's sake only, but also for her own, to save her. She panicked faintly as she failed to solve her puzzles, under the stern gaze of the thirty-two clock.

In the afternoons, she practiced horsemanship and archery. She recognized she was a girl of the city, with a city girl's skills.

She envied Lady Varo's rough hands. She violently embraced the chance to make herself into her own woman, strong of limb, at home on street and field alike. She practiced till she ached, and the exhaustion of her organism, simple and innocent, buoyed her sour mood. The company of horsemen, armorers, and kitchen staff was all she had of human intercourse.

She worked the next begging day, showing up with a downcast look. Cecilia Cluvia and the other women tried to be kind to her, but understood she didn't want company, and gave her room. Epida steered clear of her entirely.

Most of the beggars were veterans now, coming in from their walled camp on the Campus Iucundum. They seemed aimless and angry. Often they could not meet her eye.

Claire had any number of ideas for public projects for the betterment of Florence, that could absorb the labor of these surplus men. She had certainly read enough about infrastructure and civil engineering. But this nation was a quilt of private taxmen, and the royal treasury in a bad way, and she was at a loss how anything could get funded.

## XXX

In the evenings, lying in Trypsomayne, she touched her belly and her thighs and worried at one last puzzle: once they crossed the mountains, how could she bare herself to Marcus? She had told King Ambrosius the truth, whosoever saw her naked – not from a distance, but at an intimate range – that one must die.

Like all her other puzzles, she couldn't solve it. Her failure made her feel she couldn't breathe.

When she finally lay drifting off to sleep, Aeneas sometimes hung before her eye, hand pressed to his side, eyes gone nearly flat. His ghastly palor reminded her of something she wished to leave forgotten. Something about Angoulême. Her recollection would skitter over the boardwalks and the youths, and the glassy sunlit sea. But as the memory came near, she would thrust some other image before the eye of her imagination. She didn't want to face the memory.

Day by day, her mood darkened. She would lie in bed and think, *I will grow into myself in this wretched place.* She thought, *I'm far from those I love, and the streets and gardens where I lived.* She thought, *I will come home a new person, forged in a place that means nothing to me. I will have no place, no people. My face will be a stranger's face, and I will be nothing.* She thought these sad thoughts and stared at the metal constellations, gleaming right above her in the twilight of the valley of the world.

# 36

## A VISIT FROM THE BRIDGE-WALKER

ON THE SIXTH day of her isolation from the king, after lunchtime, Claire went into the stables to dress her stallion, Polpetto. She was setting her padded saddle on his back when Tarquin entered the stableyard, dressed all in gray and fawn. As he approached her, she heard a sound from the stalls, like a man making the call of a bird. She kept her eye on Tarquin. He settled his pale depthless eyes on her, and smiled his thin smile in his broad handsome face, and opened his mouth as if to say something. But then he looked at his knuckles, and back up at her, as if apologetically. Claire stroked Polpetto's withers, flattening the hairs near to the saddle, and said nothing.

Tarquin said, "O Claire, I am not Tarquin among the lilies. No, I am not that Tarquin." Claire furrowed her brow; she had no idea what he was talking about. He said, "Someday, if there's leisure for it, I should like to walk with you the scene of your triumph, and hear from you your thoughts about it." Claire said, "My triumph?" Tarquin said, "Yes, upon the Pontus Sextus Trassinope, where you made the peace."

Claire recalled Marcus's words: *Then the victim and this Tarquin have a fascinating conversation and Tarquin learns the insights of the victim. Then he throws him off the bridge.*

There was a long silence.

Claire said, "Do the Constantines invite me, or you only?"

Tarquin laughed lightly, almost convincingly, and said, "Oh, it is just a whimsy of my own. For now."

Claire leveled a very serious look on him and said, "When our day of leisure comes, O Tarquin Constantine, I will be glad to walk the bridge with you, and tell you what I know."

Behind Tarquin, Brindisi and Taranto darkened the stableyard, white daub of the Thousand angled on their breastplates, right hands on the pommels of their swords. Tarquin raised his hands, showing Claire the tattooed palms.

He turned slowly round to face Brindisi and Taranto and said, "Thousandmen, I visit Claire in peace, all unarmed." And he let himself out. Brindisi and Taranto made bows to Claire, a little bit more deeply than they had to, and let themselves out as well.

All this helped Claire to comprehend where she stood. She was in the bad register of the king, but remained inside of his protection. It appeared the Thousand had permission to observe her and keep her safe. This knowledge exerted a revitalizing influence upon her mood. She set down her lassitude and found herself – angry.

Not long after, the coarser page delivered a basket of quinces to her. They were spotty, and brown around the stem, so that Claire understood the delivery had been delayed by several days. This told her where they came from, and how things were changing in the stance Ambrosius took toward her.

## XXX

Taranto and Brindisi explained it all to Marcus, watching his eyes bulge and his cheeks go white, then red. When they finished, he breathed in and out five or six times. They looked at each other.

The decanus had never been so frightened, not on the eve of battle, not ever, nor so angry, not even when they drew that wretched stonebreaking job.

He said, "Is the king speaking to you yet?"

Taranto said, "He extends to us his ban on you. He permits us to guard her, nothing more."

Marcus paced around his table at the warehouse, idly touching the jagged cut on the skull as he passed.

"I'll go by the third morax and tell General Nasica. He's on the council and he's not a Constantine. He can tell Ambrosius."

He stopped pacing and noticed his men again.

"Back to the royal district with you! Go!"

They wished they could mollify his fear. But the best they could do was guard his patricia. They went.

## XXX

AFTER THE COMMOTION, Claire returned to her apartment a little earlier than usual. As she was opening the door, a door scraped open down the hall. She looked up sharply. A woman emerged. She spotted the patricia and made to step back in the door, but realized she'd been seen and gave up the effort.

Claire said, "Lady Varo."

Lady Varo said, "Claire."

Claire said, "I didn't realize you lived here."

Lady Varo looked at the walls and ceilings and doors and remarked, "This is the women's dormitory."

Claire said, "It was you, wasn't it?"

Lady Varo said nothing.

Claire said, "You've been going through my rubbish, Livia."

She slowly walked down the hall, back stiff and straight, approaching the silent noblewoman.

"Holding my rags up to your eye, looking for a spot of blood. Pressing them to your nose, sniffing them. You *filthy spy.*"

Now Claire was right up to her, nostrils flaring like a bull, the smell of thunder mixing with her sweat. Lady Varo stepped back one step.

Face placid, voice icy, the noblewoman said, "Before I serve my dignity, I serve Florence. Morning to night, birth to death, I serve Florence in all things. My king told me to guard against foreign usurpation, and I did."

Claire said, "And you let me blame Epida. Epida! Is that part of your famous honor, letting innocent girls suffer for your crimes?"

Shame rippled across Lady Varo's face.

*There's your weakness, Livia, you can't conceal your emotions.*

Claire lowered her voice and said, "Redeem your sin, Livia Faustina Varo. Find Epida and explain what you did to her. Prepare her to receive me when I beg her forgiveness."

Lady Varo said, "You're going to humble yourself before a serving girl."

She said it like a statement, but Claire heard the anguished question.

She answered, "I don't repeat my honor, I live it."

## XXX

THREE REDHEADS WERE pissing on a corner of a broad fresh mound outside the palisade and laughing about something. They worked up straight faces when Marcus approached.

"Anything we can do for you, Thousandman?"

Marcus said, "Where's your general?"

A pockmarked little punk with flyaway hair got done pissing and dropped his tunic and said, "In his tent I think." He looked at his fellows and said, "Is he training in the city today?" One of the others said, "Not today."

The punk looked back at Marcus and said, "His tent most likely."

Marcus traded *ave*'s with them and continued toward the open gate of the palisade. When he'd passed, the Redheads went on laughing. *Such assholes.* He bounced over the planks they'd thrown across their misplaced ditch. *Such incredible assholes.*

He saw Wardogs, Redheads, and elements of the seventh inside the palisade. Their numbers dwarfed his Thousand. It was like a city in here. Camp followers had set up streets of shops. Redhead tents clustered on the north side. He made his way toward the place a general keeps his tent, turning down wide aisles and narrow lanes. Some Redheads jeered the angled daub of paint on his breast. One called him a Genovan-lover and Marcus planted his foot and made ready to fight. The man quailed at the last minute. Marcus continued on his way.

Nasica wasn't at his tent. Marcus bullied the staff, but they were vague about when they'd seen him. Marcus spent an hour wandering the camp, chasing rumors. Each led nowhere.

Finally he came to a stop by a mess table and cajoled a chunk of bread and a lump of cheese from them. He stood aside, watching the crowds and chewing over the bread until he moistened it enough to swallow.

*Ten or fifteen thousand soldiers here, and Nasica in charge of all of them.*

He went back to the table and got a cup of water. It tasted of red clay.

*Nobody can find this man? Something isn't right.*

He headed for the palisade gate, devouring his lump of cheese on the way. He still had the matter of Tarquin to deal with. Back at his camp he sent one of his own to the castle. Let Ambrosius banish him over this foolishness regarding late menses. If harm came to the Zanzibari, Marcus wouldn't suffer alone. King Pindar might well invade Florence.

# 37

## I CARRY HONOR STILL IN MY BREAST

TEMET AMBROSIUS BURST onto the broad Via Circumflorentia. The sun shone bright, the sky was clear, and his heart soared. Days' slow march, sneezing, endlessly sneezing from the straw dust, his men threaded single file along the narrow straightaway, and he'd slipped the cruel grasp of the Crimson Knight. The night raids had ceased. He hadn't lost a single man.

He turned in the saddle, face glowing, and shouted, "The road! The road!" His men echoed his cry, all the way back along the line, until those at the rear knew their exile in the fields was over and started cheering. They were back on the road, in the world, almost at the end of this frightening, absurd journey.

Camp tonight. Sandor Pilvax Varo tomorrow. If Varo wasn't the Crimson Knight, he had a single prospect left upon the Via Circumflorentia. One day or three, Temet was headed home to Florence city.

XXX

Here they were, of course, a gang of Redheads, right where the western spoke road, Balearicum Street, branched off the Via Circumflorentia and made its way back to Florence.

Weeks ago, he'd found the Redheads posted on Ligusticum Street in high spirits, playing football in the fields. These Redheads were listless, hunched over their cards and dice. They perked up when they saw Temet and his party. Their optio stood and stretched, then approached. Scratching underneath his stubble, he said, "Have you caught the Crimson Knight?"

Temet paused and said, "You know me?"

The man said, "You're going the long way around, but news takes the short route, straight through the city."

Temet said, "I gather you've had no sign of the Crimson Knight?"

The Redhead said, "It's like the southern front out here." Temet laughed with him; the southern front had been notoriously dull during the war.

Temet said, "As much as I'm hunting him, he's hunting me. I gave him the slip a few days back. I'm sending a vigile up your road to report to the crown and bring reinforcements. I'm aiming to meet him on equal terms."

The Redhead said, "Will you wait with us till your vigile returns?"

Temet hated to disappoint the man. He shook his head and gestured along the Via Circumflorentia. "We need to keep moving. We're off to see Varo. The reinforcements will come up the next spoke road."

"Ibericum Street or the Cartenna Trail?"

"Ibericum. Cartenna's too narrow." At his straight-backed clicking finest, Temet added, "I won't have my reinforcements till I'm past Varo's place. Can you lend me a few men in case Varo's who we're looking for?"

The Redhead looked away.

Temet said, "What's the matter?"

The Redhead squinted up at him and said, "I wish I could. We're Redheads, sure, but we're not the third morax. We're hired men at arms. We can't go back. We can't go forward. As long as Constantine's gold holds out, we stay where we are. Any chance you could provoke the Crimson Knight to show himself right here? My men are bored silly and spoiling to throw some fists."

Temet clasped hands with this Redhead and took regretful leave of him. He led his men along the Via Circumflorentia, curving south now, so that the setting sun was on their right. It was a warm evening and the waning moon rose before sunset. Spirits still high, Temet led his men a couple hours after dark.

He lost a donkey driver and two horses and one of the Tagmata in the night. The camp threw an uproar about it, a dismayed uproar that the Crimson Knight resumed his torments.

Seeking to calm them, Temet tripped on a heavy brush in the dirt. He shouted, "Novacila!" till the big man showed himself. Then he flung it savagely at him. Novacila flinched, and the brush struck him a clout in the soft flank, and he cried out in pain. The general uproar went silent.

Temet growled, "Clean that before you use it on me. Keep track of your tools."

He looked around at his men and said, "We are not women and children. Pull yourselves together."

Then he stormed off, and left silence behind him.

## XXX

THE DISTRICT GUARD hauled open Golden Gate, the main gate of the royal district, as it did every morning, under the benevolent eye of Laurentius, the round old captain of the guard. A line of petitioners was already waiting to enter, and they shuffled in. A second line of staffers and overnight guests made their way out. Among them was a war-widow, in her undyed wool himation and white linen veil.

She kept with the little flock that angled up the street toward the Via Floribus. At first she nearly stepped on the heels of those in front of her. She walked much faster than other widows, and without deference to men. But soon she matched her pace and manners to the women she was walking with.

When the flock merged with morning foot traffic on the Via Floribus, she headed west, with the servants and wives intent on first pick of the wares on Serapetine Hill. The sun was still below the city wall in the east, and mist was thinning in the streets. The war-widow could be seen to inhale deeply as she walked. It could not have been the fine smell of Florence that inspired her, and therefore she must have been feeling happy, or free. She tripped on the crooked paving stone at the corner of Via Strocchia.

The traffic spread and thinned, like a river delta, as it approached Serapetine Hill. Nothing about the hill is well-planned: just as it is a stupid place to put a market, so there is no especial path from the Via Floribus to its summit. There is a maze of little streets and alleys, and everybody chooses a favorite route. The war-widow took the sloped alley in back of Tender, making her way between the beer-soaked heaps of garbage. She came to the turn in the alley, and climbed the worn staircase, and came out on the east side of the market.

She described the southern periphery of the market, coming at last to the stall of the king of the costermongers. He sat up front himself; he'd been there long before daylight, receiving deliveries and provisioning his costermonger army. The war-widow approached him, and he looked up as she came near. She scanned the market, then leaned in and pulled aside her veil.

"I came to thank you for your basket," she said. Thersites goggled. She slipped around the counter. The old man said, "I sent that days ago." She took her work smock down from its hook and said, "Here, help me tie this on in back." While the befuddled costermonger helped her with the smock, she said, "I've only just received your basket; the king is out of sorts with me." Thersites laughed and said, "Then you're doing something right, O Claire." An inveterate king-hater, Thersites.

XXX

MARCUS SHOUTED "AGAIN!" and six soldiers of the Thousand raised fresh-hammered horns to their lips and blew. They managed to make more or less the same sound. Marcus grimaced.

He turned to a little knot of officers and said, "Who can tell me what they signaled?"

They hesitated. One said, "Scenario four, sir?"

Marcus said, "Good! What is scenario four?"

Silence. Marcus looked over at the threatening camp of the main army. There were the Redheads outside the wall, pissing on that corner of their little mound.

Marcus said, "In scenario four, the Crimson Knight sends columns through Traitor's Gate and Jubilee Gate at the same time. What do we do then?"

Laughter. Most of the scenarios had the same outcome. One officer said, "Fall back to the royal district and defend the king."

Marcus saluted him, smiling. Then he turned to Cornelius and said, "I have a job for you, my friend."

XXX

SANDOR PILVAX VARO hadn't aged a day. The same shaggy auburn hair, gold highlights shining in the sun. The same messy beard with breadcrumbs in it, like a northerner. The same broad smile, showing off the gap where he'd lost an eyetooth in a fight. It would have been difficult to imagine him a cousin of fine Lady Varo, except for his daughter. Flaminia was a woman now and looked just like Livia when she was that age. Temet remembered.

Pilvax swung the left gate door open himself. Flaminia and her little brother Gaius swung the right gate door open. Pilvax said, "Magister equitum, come. Your men as well. You look like Death licked your neck in the night. What brings the likes of you so far out from the city?"

## XXX

TEMET FINISHED, AND Pilvax clapped his hands and said, "Should I be honored you thought it might be me? Perhaps. I'll take it for an honor, how about that, Temet?"

Temet found himself embarrassed. Pilvax suddenly looked regretful. He had big emotions and, like Lady Varo, couldn't hide them. He said, "I don't blame you. My father would have been the Crimson Knight, if he'd had the chance. He would have loved the idea."

Temet said, "Why aren't you angry at Ambrosius? He hanged your father. He sentenced all of you to extinction."

Pilvax gestured at the door to the garden, that his children had left through, and said, "Do I look extinct? And why shouldn't the king hang Da? He tried to take the throne. He failed."

Temet said, "Catiline was your *father*." He surprised himself with his vehemence. His losses in the night had him off-balance. He'd felt Florence almost within reach yesterday. Today he felt like he hadn't slept in years.

The good cheer dropped off Pilvax's face and suddenly he blazed anger. He said, "Lucius Catiline Varo made his choices. I do not praise them or condemn them. He took our honor from us and left us alone to raise ourselves, hated by our nation. What have I learned from my fate? You want to know, Temet?"

Temet nodded, fascinated.

The anger fled Pilvax's face, replaced by serenity. He leaned back against the pillows on his chair and said, "We lose all the good things of the past, and all the bad ones too. Life is not lived backward, Temet. He who seeks to live backward doesn't live at all. Life is lived forward."

He leaned in, accusingly.

"Are you living forward, Temet?"

Temet said, "I – I –"

Pilvax waved a hand, dismissing the question. He said, "None of my concern. I have only ever wanted good things for you, Temet. If Da hadn't ruined everything, you'd have been my cousin and a happy man."

Temet looked down to hide his flush. He said, "I love Vestoria and my sons."

Pilvax sneered, "Good for you." Then he was serious again. "Temet Nosce Ambrosius, listen to me. Love them with all your might. Love is more important than honor."

Temet found an argument he wanted to make, in the face of Pilvax's disconcerting flood of thought and feeling.

"You don't believe in honor?"

"I'm not a puppet of honor."

"You're writing your own code of honor out here, aren't you? Of you, for you, to you."

Pilvax pointed at him, eyes bright. "You're sharper than you used to be. Tell me this: what makes the nobles better than anybody else?"

Immediately, Temet said, "We hold to the Florentine virtues."

Pilvax pulled a disgusted face. He said, "Don't make a fool of me, complimenting your intelligence. The virtues are a relic of the will of the founders. And we ourselves have founded nothing. What makes us different is merely that we are one another's people. We have been bred for power. We are no better or worse than anybody else. Just different."

He stopped and gently looked Temet in the face. Temet had nothing to say.

Pilvax said, "Why should I care my childrens' name? My own? We are living well and doing what is good and just. No man has the authority to condemn us."

Temet ruefully smiled and said, "So you're not the Crimson Knight?"

"It would be beneath my dignity."

Temet made as if to rise. There were a few hours of daylight left.

Pilvax suddenly looked anxious and said, "No – what? I have strong walls. Stay with me till your reinforcements come."

Temet stood and said, "How could I shelter with a man outside the honor of Florence?" Sorrow stunned him as he said it, but he felt the sorrow would instantly give way to something else; what, he didn't know.

Face riven by anguish, Pilvax said, "You could *survive*."

The sorrow gave way, and Temet saw what was behind it: certainty.

"I must be what I am."

## XXX

CORNELIUS FOUND HE couldn't meet the eye of his king. Ambrosius stood on the soft lawn and looked him up and down.

Finally the king said, "You're saying you're a Stonebreaker?"

Cornelius said, "My lord, I am one of Tribune Diophantus's Stonebreakers."

Ambrosius said, "I don't remember sending old men to fight the war."

Cornelius said, "That's a long story, strange strange strange, and I will tell it to you sometime if you'd like to hear."

Ambrosius thought it over, then set it aside and said, "Very well. What is your business here today?"

Cornelius said, "The decanus – Marcus – the tribune, sir –" He caught Ambrosius nodding impatiently and became tongue-tied. Ambrosius helpfully remarked, "Marcus Irenaeus Diophantus."

Cornelius blurted, "My lord, everybody knows you've banished him from your presence, but you must understand, he's never the Crimson Knight –"

"I know that! What business, old man?"

Cornelius blinked, surprised. Finally he said, "Well, alright then. The decanus sent me to tell you what he's planning with the Thousand."

Ambrosius said, "And what would that be?"

Cornelius set his jaw and said, "He's planning to save your life."

## XXX

ON HIS WAY back to the gate, Temet came across Flaminia and Gaius in the sunlit garden. He looked at Gaius with the same tenderness he looked at his own boys. He marveled again how much Flaminia resembled a young Livia Faustina. She was happy like Livia had been, hair untied, free. He turned to Pilvax and said, "May the gods bless you for preserving your line."

He returned to his men with a shake of his head: the man they sought wasn't here.

He said, "We have one more noble house to visit. Ambrosius. The king's uncle and mine, Geometer Modi Ambrosius, is there. None other on our road could be the Crimson Knight. We ride. We will meet our support at Ibericum Street. We will fight as we must. If we must shed our blood for the throne, then shed it we will. We will shed it to the last man, to the last drop, firm of faith in our gods, our nation, and our mission."

*Even if the Crimson Knight has poisoned everything – even if he's turned the world inside-out and honor means nothing – I carry honor still in my breast, and that is all great Pantokrator wishes from the Florentines.*

His men followed him without complaint.

# 38

## THE SHOPGIRL AND THE DEMOCRAT

CLAIRE'S FIRST DAY back working for Thersites set the template for the rest.

Each morning she snuck out the royal district, disguised as a war-widow, shuffling like a meek Florentine woman. Sometimes she tripped on the paving stone at Via Strocchia, and sometimes she remembered and avoided it. Each morning she saw ai Ctesiphôn, in different places and sizes, though it was always a round tower with a window in its top, and in the window, the withered oak. She liked to picture the bones of Ælius Pellucidus at the foot of the oak, still clutching the red sword, Sibyllam Cumis. It was too good a story not to be true. At least she hoped the headstrong boy had found what he was looking for, in the end.

Every morning, she split from foot traffic at the alley back of Temper. There were much nicer routes up Serapetine Hill, so she had the alley to herself. She dodged the sopping trash, and climbed the steps up to the market.

Each day she worked among the smells of fruits, good smells out front and sour smells from the rubbish in back. She found the mood of the city had changed. The Florentines were shocked at their divorce from the veterans. The knife fights indoors had left them shaky. Everybody felt there was violence ahead. They hungered for comfort while they waited, for beauty and sweetness. With Claire at his counter, the king of the costermongers prospered. Children squealed to have a plum from her. Servants pressed extra coins on her like votives. The burgher women held Claire's hand between theirs. As Libra had told her, it is better to act than to talk. Demonstrating love, she spread it. Only once, a lady from a noble house spit on her, outraged she demeaned herself in a fruit stall. The patricia bowed her head and completed the woman's business in silence. Those who saw it repeated the story, and it burnished the good name Claire was earning. Thus virtue bends even vice to its ends.

She worked each afternoon until the crowds thinned, and then she sat a while with Thersites and he rubbed his lame foot while they talked. He had the moribund, cringing aspect of a man who sells things that he doesn't make. But life had not quite choked the hope from him. As much contempt as he held for all men, from the king down to the pauper, he also harbored hope for men. He found it difficult to express the idea that possessed him, but Claire puzzled it out – he had conceived a concept of the People, as distinct from the individuals all around. It was in this People that Thersites placed his faith, and yearned for the day they should cast off the yoke of kings and priests and rich men, and make their own way, free in the world.

At that late hour of the quiet afternoon, the setting sun upon him, this ugly old man with scarred cheeks and yellowish hairs sprouting from his nostrils and his ears – this shrill wretch, this outcast – impressed Claire as the finest man in Florence. He saw that she understood his idea, and in those hours, he didn't feel alone.

One afternoon he asked her what happened inside King Pindar's car, that first day in Andropolis – how exactly she had brought the enemy kings from war to peace. It was a famous mystery among the Florentines. Claire hadn't realized that anyone was wondering. She wasn't hiding the story on purpose, so she told it to him, and it was from Thersites the Florentines eventually learned the tale.

## XXX

THE THOUSAND STOOD on the bridge, their metal tinking uneasily. The sky over Andropolis was such an aching, brilliant blue. The pale king of Genova leaned forward from the open door of his sedan chair. He looked past her at Ambrosius, then back to her.

"Come in my royal car now, both of you. We will talk."

Ambrosius looked askance to Pindar. Pindar smirked and said, "If we meet on the field tomorrow, trust me to stick a blade in your breast. Today we are brothers." Ambrosius nodded and approached. He held out a hand to Claire. His skin was hard and rough, and though he clasped her fingers gently, there was a hunger to his touch. *How lonely war makes men.* He led her to the sedan chair.

Claire entered first, stooping at the door. Now she could see into the gloom, she beheld the fabulous clothes of good King Pindar: layers and layers of robes, dazzling with color, sparkling with gold, thick with brocade. His diadem was crusted with jewels, his fingers were heavy with rings, his slippers were gilded and curled at the toe. He wore a black pectoral cloth with a golden emblem of a tangled tree or bush. It was no less strange than his opposite's divided rectangle. His sedan chair smelled of old leather and oiled brass, sweat and sandalwood. Ambrosius climbed in behind her. A footman shut the door.

Pindar said to Claire, "Quite a lot of trouble, aren't you?" Claire said, "We've all got our talents." Pindar, pleased, bared his sharp teeth at her. Then he looked to Ambrosius and his face turned to stone. He said, "King Ambrosius."

King Ambrosius looked him up and down, and answered, in a tone as if to say, *You dress like a woman,* "King Pindar." Clearly they had never met. Pindar gestured, and Claire and Ambrosius sat. Pindar was facing west, so Ambrosius faced east. A chair sat to the north and Claire sat in it, facing south. The chairs were arranged around a little table with a golden top engraved with scenes from ancient tales. A fine table of greeting.

Pindar gestured at the dish in the center of the table, saying, "Guests, eat, drink" and he went first to show good faith: little rolls of date paste, squares of crispy pastry with meat and honey in it, peeled almond halves, dried currants. Pindar poured them tiny silver cups of black tea, thick and sweet. Claire hadn't eaten in days and severely restrained herself to sip her tea, to pick at the snacks in a ladylike way.

Once they'd eaten very demonstratively at each other, and set aside their empty cups, good King Pindar and wise King Ambrosius drew daggers. Each raised up his dagger, and settled a solemn stare on the patricia. She brushed the crumbs from her fingers and stared at them unblinking, turning her head from one to the other. Finally they bent forward, laying weapons on the table, each with his point aimed at himself. Ambrosius said, "O Claire, do you have your own weapon to lay on the table of greeting?" Claire said, "I am a woman, and therefore my weapons are inseparable from me." Ambrosius might have smiled a little. Pindar certainly did.

She guessed what came next. Nodding at the table, she said, "My purse waits." King Pindar fetched out a gold king's coin, with his seal upon it. He scored it with his dagger. Then he demonstrated his strength of hand and snapped the coin along the score. One half he gave to Claire, and the other half he placed on the table. Ambrosius scored his larger king's coin, that was silver. But the coin was firmer, or the hand was weaker, and Ambrosius had to set the coin down and strike it two or three times with the pommel of his dagger. He dented the table nicely. When his coin split, Claire accepted his half as well. She made a show of holding the halves with one hand, so they touched, and then slipping them into a fold of her gown, so they clinked. Then good King Pindar and wise King Ambrosius retrieved their daggers and sheathed them.

Ambrosius said, "Now, O Claire, Florence and Genova have greeted you properly. Until you declare your allegiance, keep both tokens of our hospitality. After you declare, return you one half-coin, and call its king your enemy. For now, we crave you give full scope to your speech. Tell us further who you are, and whence you come, and how we may earn esteem in the eyes of this so-called mighty Zanzibar."

Claire wished these fine barbarians to get her home to Zanzibar. This expensive project placed her in competition with costly war. Therefore she had first to defeat the war.

When she'd figured this out, her heart had swelled with joy. She loved peace fiercely, and chased it as she could. When Marcus Irenaeus asked her how to get what she wished, she'd said she needed peace. That was what made the runner Egidio weep.

She had an idea now of how and where to lead them. There was a certain tired aspect to their enmity. It was a habit in them. She craved their passion. It is from passion that habits brake. She spoke carefully:

"In the time that I was in the sky, I looked down upon Andropolis and saw the fighting here. I saw each man in this maze-city, where he was and where he went and what he did. May I tell you the story of the last two – the very last two who died by force of arms, on the last day before the storm?"

Thus she spoke, ignoring the questions Ambrosius asked her. When she was done, she put her hands upon her arm-rests and leaned back. She slouched a little bit, so that the tokens clinked in the fold of her gown. She flicked her clear gray eyes from one king to the other.

They traded glances. They had two real choices what to do with Claire – they could stab her apart, or they could do everything she asked. They considered that universal human tongue she spoke, and the fearful perfume that still rolled off of her in waves. By agreement through glance, they chose to do as she asked. She had somehow half-coined them.

Pindar meekly said, "Tell us the story."

## XXX

WE HAD LOST our commander the day before, to an unlucky blow in battle.

Now we were retreating toward the bulk of our army, waiting outside the city. Quietly, our unit made its way among the circling streets, hugging up against walls, stepping over ugly things. I traded glances with my protector – *Claire interjected, "I couldn't make out the name in your languages; in the human tongue it is pronounced Gaganam."* – traded glances with my protector Gaganam, and Gaganam saw my unease and nodded gravely. He felt it too. There was a dreamy quality to the day. There was a smell of thunder from some unseen corner of the bright flat sky. There was a faint scent of honeysuckle on the air. It was as if we were stepping out of the world.

Rounding a corner, we faced suddenly a mixed group of enemy foot and horse. He heeled his horse around toward us, and his scattered men formed up in ranks and files, chanting the battle cry we all shared: *Andropolis! Andropolis! Andropolis!*

Dread choked us like an evil air. It blurred our sight, and muffled the sound in our ears, and made us slow and heavy. Our eyes caressed the far-off pastures of our tribes, and we felt ourselves already gray and dead. The enemy had a hundred men for sure, a hundred men and a dozen on armored mounts, snorting steam and panting for war. What had we? Thirty. Thirty men in a wide street.

We never even made formation. Some scattered back, and others right, and others left, pounding for cover in the ruined buildings. They smote us face and heart. I saw with my own eyes one of our own, lying in the road with his shiny guts spread out around him. I saw another with his head stove in. I saw old veterans and sweet recruits alike, sacrificed on sword and spear, hoof and fist, falling and wailing, moaning as they shed their precious living blood.

Stumbling in the whirl, I came upon a soldier of the enemy, raising his spear against my protector. "Gaganam!" I cried. Leaping in, I took the blow, at the level of the bowel. That masked soldier saw me trade my life for Gaganam's. Cruel man, he waited till I had a good view from the ground, then turned his sword against my friend. Gaganam raised his arm in pitiful defense. The soldier slashed his bicep just below the shoulder guard. Falling to his knees, he faced me, so that his last sight should be my face, and mine his. The soldier, dark and solid as a demon, stuck his sword in the old man's breast. Gaganam fell on his face, and the soldier moved on.

## XXX

IT IS NIGHT and we alone survive, Gaganam and I. Gaganam has got a weeping arm and a foaming hole in his chest. My bowel wound is flaming hot and smells terrible. If I wish to move, I must drag myself by my hands. Lying among the dead, we blinked at one another, waiting for silence. Then we hauled each other into a house off the corner, and through it to the courtyard garden. Now we lie here looking at the great unploughed field, that is a billion stars growing untended on a million acres.

"Come, son," he says, "let us abandon the names we had when we struggled and lived. Let us imagine that the war is over."

I say, "Father, the war still holds us in its grip. But if we two are the last two, then we must take the names given the last two soldiers to die in a war. Therefore am I named Nemo, because I am younger, and you Omen, because you are older."

He smiles with his dry lips in the darkness, and his chest foams in the darkness, and he whispers, "Yes, Nemo, call me Omen, and let us be the last two, and our suffering the last suffering."

What scarce joy is this? I say, "Omen, I will gladly go beneath the Earth with you, and we two raise the curse from the valley of the world." And he nods in the darkness, and we look deep into the great unploughed field. I say, "Omen, I am tired. Tell me a story so I can go to sleep."

He says, "Late in the summer, when I was eight years old, I went out in the evening, when the sky was a deep and dreamlike blue, just as it was this evening. The fireflies were flashing lazily in the lantanas and honeysuckles, just as they did this evening. They flew slowly, and I caught one, but though it crawled along my hand, it would not light up for me. In my anger, I crushed it, smearing its juice over my palm. The juice lit up with the beautiful yellow light I craved, so that the shape of the smear was made of light. But soon it faded, and I considered that it would never light again, because I'd killed the firefly. By the time my mother called me in, I had been weeping for an hour."

I can hear him weeping now. In his time he has been a fearsome warrior.

He says, "This I have remembered all my life, and never ceased regretting it."

He holds up his hand to me, the scarred old hand of Omen, and I hold it, with the strong young hand of Nemo.

A cloud slowly spreads its broad palm across the great unploughed field, its fingers hiding vast precincts of stars, a cloud in the sky, or in me, I cannot tell. It carries a smell of thunder on it, so strong my teeth tingle. The wind kicks up, snapping leaves across the courtyard, and a terrible stink of honeysuckles rolls over me. I say, "Omen? Omen?" But he does not answer.

I sleep a while, and dream of my own mother. I see again the red knuckles of her hand, holding the heavy basket of linen. I hear the loud cicadas and see the sunlight on her freckles. When I wake, the crickets have gone silent. The walls of the ruin glow: a swollen moon is up. I can't see the moon. I can't see my protector. My neck won't turn at all. My hand holds Omen's, but of the two hands, only mine sheds warmth.

I whisper my secret. I say, "Omen, it was me. I was the fool. Our commander moved somehow. I saw from the corner of my eye. I turned without thinking and struck him. I was still hot-blooded from battle." I am sobbing in the silent night of Andropolis. "I killed him, Omen." My sobs raise the hot taste of metal in my throat. My teeth chatter. *Pantokrator all-powerful, watch over me. Reialia, gather me within your sparkling hem. Have mercy, dreadful Syrinx, on my soul!* I feel the wound pulling. *Let me be Nemo. Let it end with me. Save my nation.*

*Save my nation.*

## XXX

CLAIRE FELL SILENT, and the kings stared at her, tears brimming in their eyes. She leaned forward –

> Thersites said, "Hold now Claire – Nemo and Omen – you saw all that from the sky?"
>
> Claire said, "Does it matter what I saw?"
>
> He stared at her strangely a long time, then said, "I don't suppose it does."

– she leaned forward and reached out her hands, her left hand to Pindar in the east, and her right hand to Ambrosius in the west. Like children, each one clutched the woman's hand that was offered him. She looked to Pindar, and then to Ambrosius, and then to the south end of the table: where they were to link hands with each other.

They looked from her to the spot, and to each other, and withdrew their hands from hers.

*Very well. If it will not be love, then let it be hate. Only give me your passion.*

The beautiful patricia said, "My Nemo and Omen, do you figure they were Florentines, or Genovans?"

Ambrosius said, "With such fortitude and bravery, they could only have been Florentines."

Pindar said, "With such loving-kindness and good faith, they must have been Genovans."

The two kings turned to each other.

Ambrosius said, "They were my sons of Florence."

Pindar said, "They were mine of Genova."

Their cheeks darkened.

Ambrosius said, "Florence!" and Pindar said, "Genova!"

*Here is the hot breath of War. Show me your face, War, I will cut off your head.*

"Florence!"

"Genova!"

They shouted at one another like men possessed, they barked like madmen. Claire let them go a few more backs-and-forth. They put their hands on their swords. She stood abruptly, startling them. Eyes flashing, she thundered, "Enough!" Even though she was a small woman, they had to look up to her, as boys look up to their mother. She said, again, "Enough!"

They blinked at her bewildered. She said, "You have forgotten who your children are. Come with me and I will show you your son."

Claire thrust open the door of the sedan chair. The crowd looked in. Exposed to their subjects, the kings started. Ambrosius stood jerkily. He stared at the crowd, then gravely climbed out from the car. Claire looked back at Pindar, alone by his golden table. *If you will leave this sedan chair, Pindar, then you are ready. And if you are ready, it can be done, if only I do not fail.* Pindar looked from the crowd to her, his thinking all disrupted and confused. *You are never seen by common men. Your majesty is your invisibility.* Claire ceased moving utterly, gazing to him with that purity of love which exists only in memory. She was like a carven marble Sorrow on a great man's tomb. *Come, King Pindar. Let me do for you what you cannot do for yourself.* He looked back from her to the sea of eyes outside and shuddered. Claire held out her hand. Pindar stood from his seat, stooping only a little inside the royal car. A second time, he took her hand. Now his palm was freezing cold. She guided him from the car. The Genovans gasped, seeing their king direct, so close you could touch him. He squinted before the army in the orange light of afternoon, and joined Ambrosius.

XXX

THERSITES SAID, "AND then you preached that sermon on a headbone."

Claire said, "Marcus has it with him even now, the headbone. He keeps it on his table at the warehouse, and looks at it sometimes."

Thersites said, "Marcus killed him, Claire. In a way, he died too. You said so in your sermon, but I think you only know it in that brilliant head of yours, and not in the gut. I know in the gut, because I've killed men in my time. I worry awfully for you, Claire. Before you get home again - in order to get home again – you will learn in the gut."

It was getting late, and she took her leave, heading back to the royal district with coppers in her purse and a quince in her hand. She reflected on Thersites's foreboding.

*What sort of patricia will I be, by the time I get home?*

XXX

EVERY ONE OF those charmed afternoons, she went back to the royal district with coppers in her purse and a quince in her hand.

Reburrus was up on his Epicondyle, hounded by his fiery visions of the infinite. Cleon and Barbarossa were hatching their schemes in the Counting House. Ambrosius was sizing up his enemies. The Crimson Knight, wherever he hid, was surely spinning visions of war. Outside the impenetrable walls, the warrior nobles were slowly converging on Florence city.

A third part of the world away, those who loved her wept. A third part of the world away, the swollen desert sun quenched itself each evening in the boundless sea. Her heart lay a third part of the world away.

But none of that mattered to her. She went about her tiny life, and Florence just as much as Zanzibar fell outside her circle. The six hands of her thirty-two clock might as well have fallen still.

One afternoon, while she was counting figs into sacks, Claire burst into laughter. Thersites said, "What's this?" She couldn't stop herself a while, and when she calmed down, she saw he feared her mockery. She said, "I can't explain it, but I'm not laughing at you, Pater." He stared into her face, and she met his gaze openly, and he went away satisfied.

She was laughing because she'd suddenly remembered a proverb of the Zoni people, her other ancestors:

*The life of Man has these three parts – the age of study, and the age of action, and the age of contemplation.*

It had never meant anything to her before, but now she recognized herself in it.

*I'm at the end of the age of study. My work here is preparing me for action. My last professor is no dusty scholar, but a sweaty vendor. When I graduate at last, it won't be with a medallion from the Académie, but calluses from the market on Serapetine Hill.*

And she was so delighted she'd burst into laughter.

It was an extraordinarily happy time in the life of the young patricia. It lasted seven days.

# 39

## ULTIMA CICATRICE

THE AWFUL YELLOW light of the sky fell through the ruined dome.

He stood and walked to the temple's door. He looked toward the sea. The oily surf pounded the shore, thick, dull, like the heartbeat of a dying man. The glow of the sky rippled on the slow waves.

He stepped down from the doorway. The black sand hissed under his bare feet. He'd never stood on a sandy beach, so it was vague in his dream, a field of black soil. It burned his soles and the pain felt like stinging ants.

The hideous yellow dripped down the flaming sky. Squinting into the glare, he saw black marks on the bowl of heaven: crude pictures of the moon, the sun, the planets and stars. *This is the universe now, scribbles of a careless god.*

He looked down at the skull in his hands. Its top was hacked off, a messy cut with a little notch in the front. He grieved for the dead man and for himself, condemned by his sin. He sobbed into the skull and its bowl filled with tears. They were a thin clear pink, like wine too heavily mixed.

He felt a gentle hand on his shoulder. He knew who was there, all mortal woe smoothed from his brow. He found he was ready to look. He looked –

The gentle hand shook him.

"Wake up, Marcus."

He struggled up from the bonds of his dream. It was still night.

"Wake up, decanus."

He woke.

"Cornelius?"

"Come, decanus, it's Philo."

"Philo?"

"Your Stonebreaker is dying now."

Marcus shook himself awake and stood. He wrapped his blanket around his shoulders and left his tent with Cornelius. They crossed the empty camp. There were only enough Thousand staying here to keep an army's worth of dust and smoke rising from inside the palisade. Cornelius softly hailed the guards at the gate, and he and Marcus crossed the short distance to the hulking warehouse, dark against the sky.

A low campfire flickered in the sleeping area, casting gleams and shadows around the giant room. Dread chilled Marcus. Cornelius came to a low bed, where the giant forms of Taranto and Brindisi crouched. They heard the movement and turned, murmuring, "Marcus," murmuring, "Decanus," gently setting their hands on his shoulders when he squatted too. Ancient Philo lay in the bed, shallow breath rasping in his throat.

Philo's flighty, birdlike eye traveled over Cornelius and Marcus. He raised his hand to his mouth, mimicking drinking. Taranto raised a cup of wine to him, and his hand scrabbled to it. He dipped a finger in the wine and reached for Marcus. Marcus leaned toward him, and the finger rose to his forehead and traced a mark across it.

The eye turned to Cornelius, and that generous smile spread across the dying man's face. Philo glanced at Marcus, then back at

Cornelius, and Cornelius looked at Marcus's brow and said, "Yes, Philo."

Philo blinked and, still smiling his luminous smile, made a brushing gesture at Marcus: *Go now.*

Marcus stood. Taranto kissed Philo's brow. Brindisi squeezed Cornelius's hand. Then the two tremendous Stonebreakers left their aged friends and made their way to the door.

Marcus went the other direction, deeper into the warehouse. Behind him he heard low talk and the crackle of the fire.

He came to the dimness in the back of the warehouse and took one of the shiny new helmets from the armory. His pupils were wide. Dawn was breaking through tiny gaps in the wall. Holding up the helmet, he could just make out his reflection. He squinted at the mark on his brow.

It took a little while, but he deciphered the shape Philo had drawn with wine: a messy cut, with a little notch in the front. He found his grief had followed him from sleep to wakefulness. It filled him now and he bit his hand so that Cornelius and Philo wouldn't hear his sobs.

## XXX

THERE WERE REDHEADS posted at the mouth of the Cartenna Trail as well. The trail wasn't much more than a cowpath. Did the Constantines really think the Crimson Knight might try to send an army down it? They'd be tripping over each other's heels all the way to Florence.

Something about it bothered Temet, and he worried at it like a bit of stuck gristle as they forded the shallow Cartenna Creek, and then he went on worrying at it as they made their way along the Via Circumflorentia toward Ibericum Street, toward the great house of old Geometer Ambrosius.

Finally he worked the gristle loose. He raised his arm and turned in the saddle and faced all those men with their eyes forever on his back.

"Halt! Halt!"

They drew up and waited.

"I need to go back to the Cartenna Trail. Vigile fast-riders with me – the rest of you wait here."

His men straightened. They could see he'd solved it.

Ffidius was right. He did know the Crimson Knight. He'd always known him. And this dark campaign had nothing to do with honor, nothing at all.

## XXX

THE VIGILES RODE out of the tall grass, swiping at a cloud of little white flies. Their leader scanned the scene and turned, confused, to Temet.

"What is this?"

The litter remained but the Redheads were gone. All five tenmen of them had abandoned the head of the Cartenna Trail. Temet looked around, satisfied with himself and relieved that the world, in the end, made sense. He said, "They've finished their job here."

"Isn't their job to protect the city?"

Temet shook his head. The vigile hunched forward, impatient to hear the answer to the riddle.

"What was their job?"

Temet said, "They were watching for us. On behalf of the Crimson Knight."

"You know who he is."

Temet twisted his right-hand mustache, sharpening the point. He said, "Yes –"

And he named the Crimson Knight.

The vigiles took a moment to absorb this news. Then their leader said, "What are your orders, my lord?"

Temet said, "Earn the mayor's regard for your speed. Ride hard to Florence city and tell them what I've told you. Do not rest. Worry nothing to live. If even one of you survives, let him spend his last breath telling the first burgher he sees, and die knowing he did his duty."

The vigiles saluted him, properly his men at last. In unison, they crisply shouted, "*Ave Temet Ambrosius!*" and turned their tall narrow horses east on the trail. They came to a gallop before they were lost to Temet's sight in the grass.

XXX

WHEN THEY WERE gone, Temet took a moment to savor his revelation. He climbed down from Boreas and patted his soft nose. Boreas ducked his head and Temet fed him chunks of apple and touched brows with him and breathed his warm living smell. He breathed the smell of clean air and dry grass. He smelled traces of meat and firewood and surveyed the trash the Redheads had left. *How expensive this effort is.* He thought what Florence could have done with all that wasted gold. What the king could have done with it.

He expected to be angry, but he felt contempt instead, and it comforted him, because he felt despair as well.

Across the trail, on the edge of the grass, two sparrows and a bluejay hopped and took to the air and came down again. A squirrel joined them, leaping toward one bird and then another. *They're playing.*

The white flies caught up with Temet and swarmed his nostrils. He swatted at them and climbed on the horse and made his way back through the grass. He splashed across the creek again. He was light in his saddle, riding at ease as he skirted whatever forces trailed his men along the Via Circumflorentia.

XXX

KILLING A HORSE IS a noisy business and Temet Ambrosius had made it as difficult for his enemy as possible, roping all the horses together and hiding them apart from his camp and sending a guard with the grooms. He woke with a start to the sound of horses screaming. He led the remaining Tagmata to the place, and found what he feared from the noise: dying men and horses. Boreas lay kicking weakly, blood pouring from a great wound in his neck, black against his gray coat, visible even in the dark of night.

He hissed, "Break camp. We move now."

They returned and roused the staffers. They abandoned most of what they had, and walked. When Temet had returned from the Cartenna Trail, he'd told them who the Crimson Knight was and where things stood with the Redheads. He'd commanded them to leave the Via Circumflorentia, travelling concealed in the west end of New Forest. They would reach Ibericum Street before lunch the next day and wait in hiding on reinforcements.

Instead, they'd been found, even here in the woods.

Now they trod leaves and chestnuts, listening to the whisper of New Forest, the chitter of crickets, the padding of bears and large cats. Their ears strained against the noise, seeking the approach of the Crimson Knight.

Temet walked in the lead, chin tucked, fists raised.

*Why didn't you attack me?*

He thought over what he knew of the man. And the more he thought, the more he liked what he learned.

*You'll wound me unseen in the night, but you want to finish me in daylight. At the end, you want to face me man to man. You confuse your vanity for honor. Vanity is a fool's guide.*

He worked his jaw, easing out the cramps. He dropped his aching arms. He spoke quietly to his men. "March at ease. He won't attack before sunrise." A soft chorus of weary sighs, and their footfalls relaxed.

They walked all night, and dawn found them unmolested, not far from Ibericum Street. Temet called a halt and said, "Novacila, you giant oaf, are you still living? Where have you wandered off to?"

The enormous groom made his way forward, stubble on his cheek, dark circles under his eyes. His coat hung a little looser from his breast. It was tragic to behold.

Chin high, voice demonstrative, Temet said, "Make me presentable. It ends today." As Novacila set up his stool and razors, Temet addressed his diminished party: "Eat well, but do not indulge. We will work before noon."

The men ate their bread and salted meat and drank their water and cider. They silently watched Novacila at his labor. He shaved Temet Ambrosius, then trimmed his mustache and waxed the tips, and twisted them to fine points.

## XXX

TEMET HAD SIX Tagmata left, twelve staffers, and four donkeys. They walked south and he felt that his soul approached that inward cliff named Death and soon would simply jump from it. *Will I swoon? Will my eye stay wide and clear? Will I see whither I go?*

He thought of Vestoria and his boys, and of Livia Faustina, and felt equally apart from them all. If anything troubled him, it was this weightless sense of universal solitude. He would have liked to have regretted leaving someone.

On he marched, and ahead the light seemed brighter, and he realized he was approaching the great break in the wood where Ibericum Street passed. He held up his hand and his little party slowed. He gestured to the decanus of the Tagmata, and the two of them crept forward.

They came to the bluff that overlooked the street, and surveyed what presented itself.

Two centuries of Redheads, spread along the road. Mounted optios riding back and forth along the line. The Crimson Knight, exactly as Temet had identified him, waiting.

*Money, planning, numbers. You'll have a hard time, cousin – but at least my swift vigiles have stolen his advantage of surprise.*

The decanus whispered, voice trembling, "Can we go around them?"

Temet shook his head and whispered, "They found us before. They'll do it again."

The decanus whispered, "Shall we try to punch through them?"

Temet said, "Let us simply attack."

The decanus thought it over and nodded. He stuck out his hand and whispered, "My lord, it's been a blessing."

Temet found tears blurring his eyes. He took the man's hand, and they clasped hands a moment. Then a mocking voice disturbed them.

"Magister equitum! I can't see you, but I know you're up there somewhere!"

Temet turned. There he was, the raging man, strutting back and forth, clenching and unclenching his hands. Contemptible.

"I rode hard all the way from Florence! Come out and take what you've been looking for!"

He reached a mounted optio and received a heavy sack from him. He raised it, then upended it.

Well – there it was.

The heads of the vigiles tumbled on the ground.

"Their lips are sealed, magister equitum!"

Temet felt a pounding in his forehead. He willed his reason to master his passions.

*Show off, worm. You may defeat me, but you are a slave to wrath and vanity. Your vices will undo you.*

He put his hand on the arm of his decanus and whispered, "Come." They made their way back to the men. Temet said, "Staffers, remain in the woods. Do nothing brave. Flee if you can. You are good men and I'm sorry I could not preserve you.

"Tagmata with me. We're going to give them a bloody nose."

The Tagmata mustered, grim and determined. They returned to the bluff. Temet waited while they surveyed the endless line of armored Redheads. In his heart, he performed his final duty to those he had loved.

*Goodbye Vestoria. Goodbye my Arrius, my Justin, my naughty little Bucculus.*

*Goodbye Livia Faustina Varo.*

*Goodbye cousin king. Goodbye Florence.*

*May Pantokrator smile upon you all.*

The Tagmata grunted softly. They understood what they faced. Temet stepped out from the cover of the woods, and his men followed.

The Crimson Knight tracked the movement and spotted them. He said, "Magister equitum. Worthless cousin of a worthless king."

Temet touched his smooth cheek. He drew his little knife from his sleeve. The Crimson Knight cocked his head.

Temet opened his jaws, keeping his mouth shut. He raised the knife to his stretched cheek and carefully stabbed deep. He dragged the knife down a short ways. He felt its point touch his tongue. He pulled the blade out.

The pain of the *ultima cicatrice* was astonishing. The Tagmata looked at him with deep respect. Early in the history of Florence, the noblemen had argued whether the fateful wound depressed the fighting spirit of the men or raised it. Experience had shown it raised it. The tradition was handed down, warrior to son. Temet finally took his place in the line of his ancestors.

The Crimson Knight barked and said, "Playing dress-up, magister equitum?"

Cheek bleeding furiously, speech slurred and whistling, Temet said, "You wouldn't understand."

He saw something he did not expect: he'd shamed the Crimson Knight.

*He wishes only to be thought a man of honor. How can I exploit his weakness?*

He said, "Know this. Florence was a little place when we founded it. A little house, and a small number of families. We all knew each other then. We all know each other now."

The Crimson Knight said, "What are you getting at?"

Temet felt hot blood between his neck and his bronze collar. He said, "Your Redheads may defeat the Wardogs, but if you want the warrior nobles to welcome your rule, you must defeat Ambrosius yourself, man to man."

He saw his words impressed the Crimson Knight.

*I hope it makes a difference for you, cousin. You can't beat his army, but you might beat him.*

He prepared his soul to jump from that dread inward cliff. But then, in his weightless solitude, he found one human bond still tugging at him. He held up a hand and addressed the Crimson Knight by his name. The man said, "Going to beg?" Temet ignored him.

"An observation. Your hair is repulsive to a man of my station. We will never accept a king so slovenly."

The Crimson Knight's hand shot to his cheek and he glared at Temet. Temet went on.

"I assume you're going to hunt my staffers without mercy. There is a big fat bear among them. He is my groom Novacila, and there is none finer. Spare him. Let him clean you up before you try to take the city."

There was a long silence. The Redheads looked from Temet to the Crimson Knight. The Crimson Knight stood there. He looked around and nodded to his men. Then he turned back to Temet and said, "It will be done. Have you anything else to say, condemnèd stickman?"

Temet said, "I am magister equitum Temet Nosce, of the house of Manfredi Ambrosius, ninth of his line, the true king of Florence."

The pain was gone from his cheek. No – not gone; transmuted.

It filled his entire body with vital force. *The ultima cicatrice has more than one purpose.*

He looked left and right to his few remaining men. They understood and started up the war-bark of the Tagmata.

He drew his sword.

## XXX

IT DIDN'T TAKE long. When it was done, the Crimson Knight waved over Leander Rigellus, the football player who first spotted Temet coming up Ligusticum Street. Leander gestured at the bodies and said, "Why now?"

The Crimson Knight said, "He had work to do, turning the warrior nobles against Ambrosius. Once he figured out to pick and choose, his work was done."

"Why not let him go?"

The Crimson Knight hissed, showing his bloody teeth to Leander. His eyes were tiny and livid underneath his crumpled brow. Leander had never seen a more terrible mask of hate. Strapping centurion though he was, he shrank back.

The Crimson Knight saw his fear. He collected himself and spoke in a soothing voice.

"Brother soldier, I need you to reason with me on dates."

"Certainly, sir."

"He sent for reinforcements three days ago, correct? We let that vigile through on Balearicum Street."

"That's right."

"So the vigile got to Florence yesterday, right before the rider who summoned me. Therefore when I left, the king was already arguing money with Cleon... What?"

"Does Cleon know how Constantine's gold is being spent?" Leander indicated the army filling the road.

"No. He thinks the third morax is protecting Florence from the Crimson Knight."

Leander nodded with a crooked smile. The Crimson Knight, so fierce in his anger, proved generous in mirth, and smiled with him. Then he continued:

"Today Ambrosius is mustering and supplying the reinforcements. They'll set out on Ibericum Street tomorrow morning. Or would you guess different?"

"No, I think tomorrow morning at the earliest."

"Good. The day after, in the evening, they'll reach the Via Circumflorentia. Right where we're standing. 'Where is Temet?' We'll leave evidence he's been here. All very confusing. They'll camp overnight. That takes us to morning, three days from now."

"Correct."

"They wake up. Still no Temet. Around lunchtime they divine something is wrong. Search parties, one in either direction on the Via Circumflorentia. Will they leave before evening?"

Leander thought about it. He hadn't spent much time in the presence of the Crimson Knight. He was beginning to comprehend the great man's genius. This was one tiny set of moves in a giant model of the war he carried in his head.

The Crimson Knight cut short his reasoning, "No, they won't leave. The mystery will frighten them. They'll prepare, but preserve the safety of their numbers overnight. The search parties will leave on the morning of the fourth day."

Leander realized the Crimson Knight didn't need his reasoning at all. He just needed an ear.

"Will the parties ride a half-day or a full day? No, wrong question. They'll have to visit the noble estates along their routes. A full day's ride, but three days there and back. They both return by evening on the sixth day."

Leander was losing track, but nodded helpfully.

"In the morning their commander sends riders east on Ibericum Street. Two days' ride. On the evening of the eighth day, Ambrosius knows Temet is missing. Correct?"

Leander said, "I think so, sir."

The Crimson Knight squinted east on Ibericum Street, as if he could see all the way to Florence. He absently lifted the medallion on his neck and brushed his lips over its motto, AT FLORENTUM HONORIADE. The old motto, from before the time of the Ambrosii. Leander wore the same medallion.

The Crimson Knight turned his medallion over and eyed the little figure of himself, riding his horse. Then he tucked it away against his breast.

"The war begins before the evening of the eighth day."

Leander was stunned. He said, "I thought it was to be at the Family Dinner."

The Crimson Knight said, "I let everyone think that, so that the king would never hear otherwise. He assumes he has time left to prepare. It was always to be before then."

"So when will it be?"

The Crimson Knight scratched at his beard; his fingers came away red. He scowled east.

"Market day in Florence is in six days."

Leander said, "What difference does that make?"

"The city gates are open on market day."

Leander felt like a fool.

A passing knot of Redheads crossed the Crimson Knight's eastward gaze. He waved them over and pointed to the bodies and said, "Move these to the woods and take their heads. There's mess enough already to clean up in the street."

Then he did a strange thing: he squatted by the body of the king's cousin, the magister equitum. He clumsily shaped the mussed tips of the dead man's mustache back into points. He briefly touched the awful wound in his cheek.

He stood and squared his shoulders. The Redheads got to work. The Crimson Knight turned to Leander Rigellus, eyes piercing, will overwhelming.

"In six days we take Florence."

# 40

## MURDERERS' BLIND

THE LIGHT IN the alley back of Tender was an interesting story. The alley lay on an axis south of east, so that the rising autumn sun aligned with it. At the time of morning Claire walked it, the sunlight bounced around the whitewash and the red paint of the walls, and the alley was suffused with pinkish light. Beery as it smelled, it was a delight to the eyes, and Claire's heart rose each time she entered this luminous gallery.

The lane inclined upward to the bend that hid the stairs. As the sun climbed between two steeples in the east, its light painted a downward-pointing sword of flame on the back wall. Claire came to time her morning walk so that she reached the end of the alley just as the sword descended to the level of her head. Before she turned the corner and climbed the stairs, she would look back for a moment, and the sun would pierce her veil and flood her pale gray eyes. Then she'd turn away, and scamper up the steps, sword-tips of red and green dancing in her vision.

One morning, in the very moment that she stared into the sun, she heard a burst of motion from the alley. It had seemed empty to her, as it always did, and the light in her eyes kept her from seeing anything now. By instinct, she flung herself sideways across the wall. Metal bit plaster where she'd been, and a shadow grunted and blocked the light. Claire unfolded time.

Everything stopped.

The alley was a confusion of brilliance and shadow in her dazzled eyes. As soon as she was safe, terror of the storm consumed her – *not here! not now! not in precious, fragile Florence!* – she let go time and hazarded the present.

Still blind, she crouched and rolled, and instantly she was behind the heavy shadow. A shout came from farther down the alley, back toward the Via Floribus. She blinked against the swimming spots and made out a second figure running toward her; sweeping her eyes to the side, she saw his broad chest at the edge of her vision. *My savior and champion.*

Marcus leapt past her, thudding into the man at the back wall. Something metal clattered to the ground. Claire reversed herself and scuttled back. Looking away, she saw a knife in the clear corners of her eyes and snatched it. She dared not swing the knife, Marcus and the knifeman making a single jumbled form. So she crept away, keeping low. She heard growls from each man, then a crash. Claire's spots were clearing and she saw the knifeman on the ground and Marcus above with his knee in the knifeman's chest. The knifeman flailed up, and Marcus struck his face.

More shouts from the mouth of the alley. Soldiers running. Claire saw the diagonal white daubs of paint on their breastplates. *How many Thousand have been watching over me?*

Marcus kept on striking the knifeman, his eyes, his nose, his jaw, his ears. The knifeman howled and tried to cover his head with his hands.

The Thousand reached Marcus and grabbed him, shouting, "Hey! Hey!" and "Stop – you'll kill him!" Arms restrained by his men, Marcus kicked the knifeman in the belly, then the balls. The knifeman's limbs went slack.

The Thousand dragged Marcus back. Marcus raised a hand in surrender, breathing hard. His men waited a moment. Marcus didn't struggle. They let him go.

Claire's sunspots had faded but she found her vision blurred, and jarring rhythmically. The blurring was tears, but it took her a little while to place the jarring. It was her heart, knocking blood against the backs of her eyes.

She tore off her veil. Surprised at her anger, she shouted, "Why did you abandon me?"

Marcus's eyes bulged and he shouted right back, "In Florence! If the king – notices you! You have – to do – what he says! And there's nobody, Claire, *nobody* – better than you at making the king notice!"

Claire started crying. The Thousand sought someplace to look.

Marcus put his hands on his knees. His knuckles oozed blood. "Every morning, Claire. Seeing you safe to Thersites. My favorite thing all day."

The assassin stirred. His face was a mass of bruises. His eyelids were swelling and he moaned little moans and stared at the sky. Then he collected himself and looked around. Spotting Claire he whispered, "How did you get here?"

Suddenly unsteady, she said, "I was always here; 'twas I you meant to kill."

His face crumpled up and he hoarsely lamented, "I didn't know, I didn't know."

She said, "How didns't know? Doesn't everybody know the foreign woman sells apples on Serapetine Hill?"

He whispered past his broken teeth, "I was only told to wait upon a war widow, that I could depend on her, a war widow would stick her head in the morning light at the end of Tender's alley. And didn't you do it? Didn't you? Did your husband die in the war?"

She said, "Who bade you do it?"

He wept bitter tears and said, "Not bade – paid."

All the fight was gone from him.

Claire said, "Who paid you?"

He blubbered, "*I don't know.*"

Marcus spoke now.

"Murderers' Blind?"

The weeping assassin nodded.

## XXX

AH, MURDERERS' BLIND.

Marcus and the Thousand dragged Claire back to the royal district. She wanted to explain to Thersites what she was doing, but who knew how many others were hunting her.

In the district, Marcus convened the men he needed. Claire refused to go away, so the bossy little patricia joined in with the gang he summoned: Taranto and Brindisi, the mayor Nederick Frederick, and Laurentius, the round old captain of the district guard. Laurentius brought word the king still held himself aloof. Marcus, temper hot, shouted at Laurentius, "Then *you* tell him to stop mucking around and arrest Nasica!"

Laurentius, shocked at the outburst, said, "Who?"

Marcus glared at him and controlled his breath.

"General Furius Nasica, supreme commander of the third morax."

Nederick Frederick said, "Why should the king arrest Nasica?"

Marcus said, "Because he's the Crimson Knight."

Nederick Frederick jolted back. "You're sure?"

Marcus glared at him, then studied the ground. "No."

"But you have reason to suspect?"

"All of this has something to do with the Redheads. Of that I am certain."

Claire said, "Did Nasica order me killed?"

Marcus said, "The Crimson Knight must certainly oppose you, but hired murder seems unsoldierlike. I don't know."

Nederick Frederick turned to Laurentius and said, "Go tell

the king. Nasica's been out of sight for days. Hiding somewhere in their tent city on the Campus Iucundum. We'll need Tagmata."

Laurentius bundled himself out. Nederick Frederick watched him go and said, "I wish we had Temet Ambrosius here. Nasica is a job for the magister equitum." He sighed and turned to Marcus. "Now how did Claire run afoul of assassins?"

Marcus said, "Murderers' Blind."

Nederick Frederick's lip curled under his thick mustache and he said, "I should level the place."

Marcus said, "Better to know where they do their business."

Nederick Frederick said, "Spoken like a true Serapetine alley rat. *My lord*."

Marcus smiled a little. The mayor said, "Show me the man fool enough to take that particular gold."

Marcus led the little party back to the cell where they'd left the assassin. He sat all wrapped in rope, a miserable man with eyelids shiny black and swollen shut. Marcus told the mayor, "He didn't know, the client sent him after the war-widow." The assassin tilted his head, trying to discern who studied him.

Nederick Frederick barked, "What trophy was demanded?"

The assassin sniveled his answer, and Claire gasped and stepped away. Marcus saw her fear, and rage climbed back up his throat. He kicked the assassin in the thigh. The assassin's chair tipped and he fell over on his side and the landing banged the breath from him.

The party left him like that, coughing blood in his cell.

## XXX

Murderers' Blind.

Before the war, Florence was nearly as elegant and mannered as Genova remains today. In that time, the influence of the ichneumonoi and their stern morality was less, and the penury of war had not made everything so coarse.

In that distant age, the city fathers abandoned a public project, a section of misrouted aqueduct bridge. It was located in the flat waste at the rear foot of Linthicum Heights, between the hill and the city wall. It was the usual construction of a wall of arches, very charming to behold. For a while it stood abandoned, with grass and thistles springing up around it. In the daytime, it retained this useless aspect, and the children of rich men chased one another round its stony feet. But at night, especially in summertime, it found its use: it became a vast open-air brothel.

After dark, the polite and well-dressed crowd would gather. The fishmonger paid musicians, and they played their slow, bewitching music. At a certain note, as one, the women would step out from behind the columns of the aqueduct, one woman to a column. Naked and white under the icy moon, eyes wide and unreadable, they seemed the same woman repeated many times. There was something out of nature to the sight, and the crowd would shiver, a delightful thrill of fear and awe. Then the music ended and most of them went home. The punters stayed and bid on the girls. The winners handed their coins to the fishmonger, and the evening concluded with a hundred writhings in the bushes.

In fact, Claire would have recognized this ritual, or at least its spirit: at the zenith of a nation, there is a little span when it has the grace to fuse the high and low. The savage and divine meet each other in this interval, and recognize themselves in one another. Great poems and sculptures come from it. The Florentines accomplished it at the abandoned aqueduct bridge. Zanzibar had this quality in the time of Claire. Perhaps it has it still. Ordinarily, it lasts its hour, then it is gone. Old Florence, at any rate, soon passed its zenith.

The war began and the best Florentines left to fight and the ones who stayed were a shameful lot. Crime was so common women didn't leave the house. Therefore whoring became a private, drawing room activity, and the aqueduct bridge was abandoned again.

The slothful, cowardly burghers wouldn't take care of their own villainy. They employed a rabble of professional criminals to handle their murders and rapes and arsons. The criminals had little honor, and hiring them was messy. Arranging crime gave rise to as many crimes as crime itself. King Ambrosius IV considered emptying the city.

After a period of upheaval, the ichneumonoi impressed upon the people the importance of lawfulness, and failing that, of taking responsibility for one's own mayhem. They installed ichts to supervise public morals, the mayor hired a squad of reformed thugs to hassle miscreants, and eventually the city righted itself.

The one relic of this squalid time is Murderers' Blind, located in that same useless section of aqueduct bridge. It's where they hired their criminals back then. Some crimes still demand professional assistance; perhaps the crime is tricky, or the criminal incapable. In Florence, crime for pay is brokered on the north end, at Murderers' Blind.

## XXX

THE THISTLES AND grass still grow at the base of the aqueduct, but fishing nets and portable wooden walls divide the place and it's no fun for children any longer. The whole field is strewn with greasy rubbish: slips of paper, fragments of meat and bone, bloody bandages and blade-tips.

The action still takes place at night. This is how it works: the client enters Murderers' Blind from the left entrance, and the supplier enters on the right. Wherever two men meet to make a deal, a third man wants to get between them and skim a little gold. The man at Murderers' Blind is a small tough bastard named Caeso Barbutus, though everybody calls him Jackdaw. Jackdaw assigns the client and the supplier a number, and the two men meet at the corresponding column. The walls and nets ensure that Jackdaw has seen neither party, and neither party sees the other. Words and gold and trophies are exchanged, but never faces. That's how we contract crime in Florence.

Marcus and his several Thousand, and Nederick Frederick and a squad of well-armed vigiles, went to see Jackdaw now. Marcus had had a decent time of it keeping Claire from tagging along.

"I don't know who hired him. Go stick a hot rod up your ass."

Nederick Frederick eyed the ancient bridge and said, "Perhaps it's time the city tore this eyesore down."

Jackdaw said, "You wouldn't."

Nederick Frederick said, "I might. Who hired him?"

Jackdaw glowered at the vigiles and Thousand. His archers on the bridge were better suited to a gang of two or three. He said, "You know how this works, Nederick. What's the point of a blind if we all get a good look at each other?"

Nederick Frederick said nothing.

Jackdaw pleaded, "I'm finished if I spill a name."

The mayor coldly answered him, "You're finished either way."

Jackdaw stared miserably at his feet. Nederick Frederick folded his burly arms. There was a long pause, and they heard a cart in the street, and a very late cicada in the grass. Jackdaw looked at Marcus, as if appealing for support. Marcus offered him nothing.

Choking, Jackdaw said, "I dare not."

He was shrunken now and sweating. Marcus looked to Nederick Frederick and said, "What could they hold over him –?"

Nederick Frederick studied Jackdaw, saying, "Caeso, has he taken your mother? Your daughters?"

The whites showed all around Jackdaw's eyes. He swallowed and his dry mouth clicked. Even to affirm it or deny it revealed too much. Marcus thought about the texture of his fear. It was beyond family and fortune; he had a sudden insight who the client was.

Gently, he said, "Jackdaw, do not tell us anything, but only this – what night does the client return to claim his trophy?"

Jackdaw looked in Marcus's eye and Marcus let him see he understood. He coaxed him, "Tell us the night. The rest we take upon ourselves. It is not yours."

Tears squeezed from Jackdaw's eyes. He forced the answer out between his clenched teeth, in a whisper that was almost silence.

"*Tonight.*"

## XXX

CLAIRE, FINALLY A true prisoner of the royal district, had begged Marcus to explain her absence to Thersites. It was a few hours till dark, so Marcus crossed town and climbed the hill to see the man who raised him. He told him about the assassin in the alley behind Temper. Thersites turned white and wobbly. Marcus soothed the old man's fear with his report of Claire locked safe behind the royal district walls.

Nicking a pear, Marcus said, "Pater, you were all frowns when I first brought her to you – what changed?"

Thersites said, "I don't like a foreigner within the city gate. What is she, my boy? What does she crave for us and from us? What gods claim her blood?"

Marcus shrugged; it was all a lot of ichneumonish talk, as far as he was concerned.

Thersites shook a finger at him and said, "You godless prat, you'll learn faith."

Marcus returned to his question: "Tiresias, what changed?"

Thersites looked at his favorite orphan from under his brow. He sat on his stool and rubbed the pointy top of his head.

He said, "She's very beautiful, and works without complaint, and is kind to high and low. This predisposes one to like her. But prudence never leans on outward things. We sat and talked, and she understood. This, Marcus Irenaeus – surely reason is the same nearby and abroad? Surely so? That one and one makes two in Florence and the antipode? We traded reason, and she understood."

Marcus saw Thersites's eyes were glistening.

The king of the costermongers said, "I knew I couldn't keep her. But I'm grateful to the god he gave me my season with her."

Marcus walked back munching on his pear, so lost in thought he tripped on the crooked paving stone at the corner of Via Strocchia.

## XXX

Now here he stood in the shadow of the aqueduct, beneath the silver moon, waiting on Claire's murderer. The blind was emptied out tonight. It was just his gang on each side of the nets, hidden, waiting. He stood behind column seven, sheltered by Jackdaw's mildewed wooden wall. The crescent of the moon cast light by his shadowed foot, and a cold wind nudged the grass. Crickets creaked. He thought of the legendary beauties who stood on this spot, of a warm evening, an age ago. *Who is like in beauty to Claire?* Under the arch, the great unploughed field of stars spun slowly, and Marcus waited.

Finally he heard the client. He imagined the footprints he was pressing in the dirt. Surely he had new sandals by now, carved with a circle inscribed in a square. Marcus hadn't told the others who was coming, because he feared they'd lose their nerve. The client approached column seven and took his place behind the mildewed wall. Marcus waited on the fearful twang of his high voice, but he already knew it wasn't who he'd thought. The footsteps were too heavy. This man wheezed with his exertions, and the height of his wheezing told Marcus he was very tall.

He said, "I've got the gold. Have you the trophy?" Marcus reached through the net, and handed him two fat pig's feet. He heard the client turn them over, again and again, confused: these weren't the trophy he'd demanded, the patricia's hands.

While he was distracted, Marcus's strong men quietly converged. One of them hooted like an owl, and Marcus stepped into the moon's icy light. The client squinted at Marcus and his hands clenched the pig's feet. A spasm shook his giant frame, then a sigh, as peaceful as the wind.

Marcus said, "Iacomo Antivola."

Antivola said, "Reburrus knows nothing of this."

# 41

## THE CORRECTION OF THE WEIGHTS AND MEASURES

WHEN THEY WERE riotous youths, sixteen years of age, Reburrus and Antivola executed the Correction of the Weights and Measures. They plotted it three years. It was an ambitious plan and full of risk. Each step offered them two outcomes: success or death. The knowledge Reburrus shared with Antivola made them desperate. Their youth made them foolhardy. Fear could not hold back their imaginations, and mercy had no grip on their hands.

Antivola took the first move, the springtime before. He ventured down from Massafra, the enormous temple complex on the Epicondyle, and made his way to the backside of Serapetine Hill. Reburrus couldn't do it; everybody knew him in the alleys of his childhood. So it was Antivola who carried their little hoard to a very questionable armorer, and came back with an osculum.

The fascinated boys played with it, cocking and releasing the scolex, until it took off the tip of the little finger on Antivola's left hand. They were so drunk with excitement they laughed at the spurting wound, but they stopped playing with the lethal thing.

Later on, when a pulsing pain set in, Antivola whimpered and swiped away his tears and raided the medicine garden for poultice fixings. They hid away the osculum and waited.

The next step went to Reburrus. It came toward the end of autumn, when the summer campaign was done and young King Ambrosius the Ninth was back in Florence, touring the city and getting his Constantine wife heavy with child.

Reburrus sent out a messenger late in the afternoon. The timing was important, and he nearly ruined everything. The messenger hit his schedule, but Reburrus was late. After evening prayers, when the priests were asleep, he stole into the cell of his mentor, Ius Iunt, the Songbird of Pantokrator. The sturdy old ichneumon was asleep, snoring his rumbling snore. Reburrus placed the osculum, and struck the ball. But he placed it wrong, and the teeth of the scolex caught on one of the man's ribs. His eyes sprang open and, like a mindless puppet, his body tried to sit up. Reburrus didn't weigh much, but he had the osculum and he leaned his whole body into it. It pinned Ius Iunt, and the dying ichneumon began to gasp and thrash.

Reburrus had meant his master to die instantly. But perhaps he hadn't meant it entirely, and he was satisfied that Ius Iunt lived to know who killed him. Iunt stared into the pale eyes of his favorite student. He was horrified a moment, then he understood. His tongue curled back in his mouth and he made an awful rattle, and Reburrus pressed with all his hate on the osculum until it bit through Iunt's rib. This method defeated the discreet intention of the wicked device, and blood gouted everywhere. Reburrus was covered in it. It stung in his right eye, and it was salty on his tongue. Ius Iunt died beneath him.

A moment later Antivola rushed in to find out why Reburrus was late. Antivola was already near-sighted, and in the blue dimness, he had a hard time deciphering the mess his friend was making. Reburrus had pulled the osculum free and used it to open up the ichneumon, and he was digging around inside him. Antivola couldn't see it, but he riddled it immediately: Reburrus was working over the dead man's liver.

Antivola hissed, "The king and the haruspex are in the room of common prayer."

Reburrus turned. He was black with blood from top to bottom. Antivola cracked a grin and tutted at him. There was stirring in other cells; the commotion was disturbing Massafra's left wing.

Reburrus said, "I'll get the wrists, you get the ankles." He spoke indifferently, as if they were taking in the wash.

They dragged Ius Iunt down the hall, leaving a wide gleaming trail.

As for the osculum, this was the same one with which Reburrus would, decades later, fail to kill Claire on the first night of the peace. He never did become proficient with the tricky thing.

## XXX

THE YOUNG KING said, "What is this? What is this?"

The haruspex sat down as if he might fall, and the king's Tagmata drew their swords.

The ichneumon and his fat friend dumped famous Ius Iunt on the floor, and the ichneumon looked like he'd come through battle in the front rank. He stared into the face of the king, eyes blazing through his mask of red. The king recognized that look. It was joy-in-bloodshed, the madness that breeds victory. Pantokrator was at this boy's back.

Ambrosius repeated, "What is this?"

Antivola shut the heavy door to the left wing and barred it.

Flavius Papellus Reburrus said, "Good my king, god hates this man. Therefore have I sent him back to god, to take his punishment."

The haruspex said, "What have you done, Reburrus?"

Reburrus said, "I asked you be here to confirm the justice of it."

The haruspex said, "What wild evil are you talking, lad?"

And Reburrus said, "Liver reader, read this god-hated man's liver."

The mouth of the haruspex went wide and he stuttered in his horror – "A haruspex r-reads the livers of *birds*."

Reburrus skinned his lips back from his teeth, and his teeth looked very white against his mask of blood. He said, "Then read the liver of the Songbird of Pantokrator." The haruspex put his face in his hands and rocked back and forth.

Reburrus barked, "*Do it*."

The haruspex did what the ichneumon said. All this Ambrosius observed. He knew what all kings know: it is fatal to wish things otherwise – one must play the pieces on the board. He looked at Reburrus, and Reburrus looked at him, and he saw Reburrus knew it too. Therefore Reburrus thought as a king thinks. He thought as a man above the law thinks.

The haruspex had the liver out and pawed it over, humming and blinking. He said, "The lobe which houses lust is swollen. It has been fed. The texture of it is rough, indicating his lust attaches to the male. But it is speckled, indicating it inclines to youth. It is very speckled." He realized what he was saying, and his head snapped to Reburrus.

*Interesting*, thought Antivola. *He didn't know*.

Reburrus kept his pale gaze on the king. His nostril flared once, but he spoke evenly. He said, "This man is a corruptor of youth. He brings shame on the religion of the Florentines. He turns Pantokrator away from Florence. He is no true ichneumon, but a heartless icht."

These things he said evenly, but then he turned and looked down at the livid face of Ius Iunt.

He spoke again, thickly, as if his throat swelled shut. He said, "The white blossom of Florence lies trampled in the mud beneath the sandal of this man." He kicked his cheek once, savagely, and cracked the bone.

Then he turned to the king again and said, "This man and his friends."

Ambrosius saw what Reburrus wanted: leave to purge Massafra. The king raised a hand, and the Tagmata sheathed their swords. Reburrus comprehended. He said, "Good my king, this man was called the Songbird of Pantokrator. But I will be called His Majesty's Own Ichneumon. Where you go, there I will go. You will be the hand of god, and I will be his eye. Pantokrator will never leave your side, so long as I am with you."

That was his offer. Ambrosius considered it. He was a new king. Though his brother Ælius Pellucidus was gone – though he must be dead – yet still he had his followers, in the city and among the warrior nobles. The Epicondyle had never declared for or against the kings of Florence. It held itself apart. Therefore none weighed it in the pans of mortal power. But it was formidable, and Pantokrator and Reialia commanded the hearts of the Florentines.

Ambrosius said, "My own ichneumon, go and clean the house of god."

## XXX

CONFRONTING THE KING was the second greatest risk they took. After that, it was easier a while. Underneath the kitchen was a cellar. It was a damp room dug into the earth of the Epicondyle, with a great stone floor that was always cold. The temple kept stores of cheese and dried pork in it, and potatoes and almonds and pecans and apples, and casks of wine. Reburrus and Antivola had it emptied, except for some of the casks.

At Reburrus's invitation, the throne invaded Massafra. Under the young ichneumon's instructions, the Tagmata rounded up the twenty-three defiler priests and pitched them in the cellar. Twenty-two actually, one of them was nowhere to be found. Reburrus and Antivola had the cellar sealed but for a little gap, to let some air. A terrified silence fell over the Epicondyle, except the priests in the cellar, hooting and hollering their outrage, all muffled by the thick earth between them and daylight.

Reburrus was no crueler than he had to be. The priests in the cellar were to him like a bucket of centipedes: once the lid was on, he had no further interest in the disgusting things.

Not so Antivola.

Antivola sat around the kitchen eating, listening to the defiler priests beneath the ground. They had never hurt him, but he relished following their fates. It was apparent to all why Reburrus was frightening. Nobody feared Antivola until they beheld his peculiar fascination. Then they feared him more. The bloody ichneumon seemed innocent in comparison.

On the sixth day the vigiles discovered the twenty-third priest, hiding out in a cheap room off Via Lacrimosa. He had clearly heard the fate of his fellows, because he was busy stuffing himself sick when they found him. He meekly submitted to the vigiles, and they turned him over to the Tagmata. The Tagmata hauled him up the Epicondyle and opened the cellar and threw him in.

While they were in the kitchen, the soldiers wore cloths soaked in turpentine over their mouths and noses. Even so, as soon as the cellar was closed back up, a good half of them fled out back and vomited in the garden. The sight of Antivola, sitting in the kitchen munching his cheese and apples, astonished and dismayed them.

There was a terrible argument in the cellar on the night of the sixth day, and on the seventh day the priests beat their new fellow to death, and on the eighth day they drank a great quantity of wine then ate him. From there, the cellar was a carnival of drunkenness and wantonness, murder and unholy feasts.

As dawn woke the world with her loving light and warmth on the seventeenth day, Antivola grew certain there was but a single priest left, an icht. The ichneumonoi had not outlived the ichts. Sturdy people, ichts. No visions, lots of sense. Antivola drew a fine pride from this. He wiped his greasy hands and opened up the cellar and descended into it.

Even in the dim light from the open skylight, even with his failing eyesight, he could see the humble earthen storage room had become like a grotto in the worst precinct of Hell. His guess was correct: only one mortal survived. The icht was not a man any longer, but a naked, hairy, filthy animal, teeth bared, eyes darting.

Antivola strode to him and came quite close to him so he could see him clearly. An acrid perfume of terror rolled off the man. His bloodshot eyes fixed on Antivola without comprehension, tears streaming in the sudden brightness of his prison.

Antivola placed his enormous hands around the man's neck, humming like the haruspex, scrabbling his fingertips around and thinking it over. But then he decided he didn't like it, and he turned his back on the ruined man and searched around among the carcasses and shattered wood till he found a good stone. He picked it up, and came back over, and smashed the icht's head with it.

Then he went up into the world and found Reburrus and told him it was done. Reburrus told him to go take a bath. It was about this time the high mad twang first entered Reburrus's voice. Antivola remarked it, but said nothing.

## XXX

NOW THEY CAME to the riskiest part of the plan they had nursed, like a black serpent, in the poison garden of their hearts these several years. They announced the overthrow complete. The house of god was cleansed.

With the shadow driven from the sky, the rest of the victims of the defiler priests came forward, accusing the fangless dead. Few on the Epicondyle cared to consider the imprisonment in the cellar. None knew for sure what happened there. None but Antivola, and Antivola, in his new authority as Icht Most Capable, hired city laborers to fill in the cellar and dig a new one. The remains of the defiler priests were left where they fell.

The chief ichneumon of Florence, Flavius Papellus Reburrus, His Majesty's Own Ichneumon, threw a feast for all the boys, and them alone, who had been victims of the priests. The oldest was nearly a man, so that there was some question who was the corruptor and who the corrupted. The youngest was six.

They gathered in the room of common prayer, and slaughtered a fatted calf. They trimmed the finest cuts and burnt them with incense on the altar of the great gold Pantokrator. Then they ate and drank and gave praise and thanks for their deliverance. They ate and drank deep into the night, until they all grew drowsy, and went to sleep right there in the common room.

Thirty-four and one hundred boys and Reburrus went to sleep, and only Reburrus rose in the morning.

The rest had drunk scarlet cherry in their wine. The dose was small, but there were many ritual libations, so they drank a lot of wine. They grew drowsy and went to sleep and never woke. There was no terror; no tears; no pain. Reburrus was no crueler than he had to be.

In the morning he opened up the room of common prayer. All those living in the temple complex of Massafra saw what he'd done. Into the stunned silence, he ordered a pyre prepared. That unleashed the screams and curses; a general uproar. The Tagmata who were still on the Epicondyle had to keep the crowd from tearing the young ichneumon in pieces. The soldiers turned to him for answers. They were appalled. Reburrus demanded the king.

When Ambrosius beheld the massacre, he said, "What fresh monstrosity is this, Reburrus?"

Reburrus answered him, so that all the guards and children and initiates and priests could hear as well – "Shall the orcharder preserve the blighted pear tree, from his love of pears? No, all the more shall he uproot the tree and burn it. Save he his orchard from the blight. The priests corrupted the youth, and the youth were corrupted. I have done as you bade me. The house of god is clean."

The king considered it. He leaned in to Reburrus and said,

"We both know this is not what I permitted you." But he said it quietly, so that nobody else could hear.

From that day, Massafra lived in terror of Reburrus. In the night, they burnt the bodies in the yard. All Florence saw the pillar of flame, and the oily smoke, rising from the Epicondyle. The entire city smelt of a burnt sacrifice. From that night, Florence lived in terror of Reburrus.

Reburrus asked Antivola, "What do they say on Serapetine Hill?" and Antivola said, "They say Florence has a demon for an ichneumon."

Reburrus smiled one single smile and said, "The god of Florence is a furious god, and his chosen intercessor carries his fury to a fallen people."

Even Antivola shuddered at that smile.

The riskiest risk was not past. Massafra was a law apart, and its people under the justice of the ichneumonoi. But bronze was bronze; Ambrosius had an army, and Reburrus did not. The king could not abide a murderous enigma. Reburrus had to demonstrate his loyalty, or die.

This too the boys had planned, sitting on the roof, aged fourteen years. Even on the hill, they kept track of politics in Florence. They knew the young king was in a weak position, and many still waited on his brother's return. They wove this knowledge into their plan. Now Reburrus asked the king if, as His Majesty's Own Ichneumon, he might come to the royal district and lead prayer in the great hall, for the great men. He promised peaceful and decorous behavior. The king looked in the rotating locked irises of the ichneumon, and chanced it. They set the day for the holiday of Heseveth. She was older than Florence, an orphan goddess inherited from an otherwise forgotten religion. Her holiday was very soon.

Reburrus came down from the Epicondyle, and processed to the royal district. At the back of the great hall, he saw a half-built little room of wood. The rest of the hall was dim and drafty and enormous. The big men of Florence convened. Nobody was sure exactly what had happened in Massafra; the most lurid rumors raced around the city. The big men were fascinated to witness for themselves the king's blood-drenched new ally.

He appeared to them behind the altar, in the dimness, through the smoke. He was difficult to make out. So difficult, and his voice so high and strange, that the crowd came under a strange impression they faced Heseveth herself. She was the goddess of whispers and sighs, with a black robe, and eyelids that looked like lips, and lips that looked like eyelids, so that her face had three black holes in it, each one rimmed with long, beautiful, dark eyelashes.

The apparition of Heseveth appeared to the great men of Florence, speaking in her high voice, that sometimes sounded like three voices, and she admonished them for their dissolute behavior, and their wicked thoughts, and their whining cowardice in the face of Genova.

Then she told them the saddest story they ever heard, of a generation of priests who left the path of goodness, and walked in a dark and forlorn valley. They abandoned their people and their gods, and the people and the gods became strangers to one another. These priests had the beguiling voices of the lost, and they called their followers down into the grievous valley, and celebrated there a celebration of midnight, far from god and hope.

But this sad story had a happy ending: a priest came out of Florence, and he shut the gate of the valley of the damned, and he listened to the cries of the damned with a cold heart, for his heart was only warm for the good, and not the evil. And this priest was himself a true ichneumon, an intercessor standing in that fearful place between worlds, linking Pantokrator and Florence.

She whispered and sighed these terrible things to the great men, and they trembled and their flesh crawled.

Then Reburrus stepped through the curtain of smoke and darkness, so that they saw he was no Heseveth, but a young man in a red robe, deathly thin, pale eyes wide and furious. He spoke to them in a lower, stronger voice.

"Dear my friends, citizens, free men, Florentines, I walk my feet, and the god puts them. I am the rind of a man. Behind my eye is flame. The Pantokrator fills me. My voice speaks? He speaks. Listen, dear my friends. I was taught, and I will teach you in turn."

The crowd listened to this strange man. Ius Iunt was a comfortable ichneumon. He softened the harshness of his religion; he spoke the word of god in the language of men. Young Reburrus made no effort to shield them from the brilliance of Pantokrator. They'd still pictured the dancing sun-slinger of myth, but Reburrus gave them an inkling of the sun itself, that was the truth. The religion of Reburrus came from the epoch when men shivered in caves.

Reburrus said, "The god put my foot inside ai Ctesiphôn."

A murmur. Few mortals reached ai Ctesiphôn. The crowd included partisans of the last man who had done it.

Reburrus said, "I stood inside the tower, Reburrus. I walked inside ai Ctesiphôn. The god put my foot, and I climbed the branching stairs. I walked my feet, and the god put me at the top of ai Ctesiphôn. I understood the death of Ælius Pellucidus – yes! yes, my friends! – I saw the grim remains of beautiful Pellucidus, lying huddled at the foot of the oak of kings. He it was, for I saw the red sword at his side. It lies there, good my Florentines! Sibyllam Cumis lies there by the sweet prince's side."

One partisan said, "Why didn't you bring the sword back?"

Reburrus said, "The god showed me the error of Ælius Pellucidus. He tried to bring a sprig back from the dying oak. But it is impossible. No thing in ai Ctesiphôn can be taken from it. The oak is the oak of the tower. The sword is the sword of the tower. The prince – alas, the prince – is the prince of the tower. Nevermore they come into the world. Pantokrator showed me this, and now I show it you."

Murmurs. Everyone understood: the Florentine religion certified the death of the man who should have been king. Thus

Reburrus, in his way, affixed the crown to King Ambrosius the Ninth, called the Wise by his friends, and the Weak by his enemies.

Doing it, he saved himself. The king spared him.

XXX

THEREAFTER, HE RODE with the king, and firmed up the heart of the army. It was many years before he realized the king was keeping him away from Florence, and protecting Florence from his wrath. This he had not planned. His promise to the king chained him to the king. He was a prisoner.

He found his scouring mission underneath the sun endlessly delayed. Defeated by life, he retreated from the world, roaming the fiery realm of the spirit. Ever onward, he rode beside the king. The king protested that he loved him, and this was true. But he also snatched the heart out of him, and ruined him.

Antivola grew to moderate his ambitions by the same means he once used to fire them: making plans. The foolhardy youths became timid old men. Reburrus felt himself turning into somebody who had done something interesting when he was young. To the soldiers, he suspected he was a joke. Reburrus – silent, fearsome, broken.

The peace brought him home to Florence, to the Serapetine Hill where he was a boy, to the Epicondyle where he became a man. But his project remained delayed – the war in heaven was beginning, and dear Antivola ever counseled against action.

His account of ai Ctesiphôn was the only big lie he ever told. Like other mortals, he never found the tower. But Pantokrator blessed him in the lie. The child Antonella got heavy with that year was not Domenico, called Bitsy Boots; all this happened many years before. She lost two sons to the war, and several boys and girls to infancy and childhood. Domenico was her last, and she loved him fiercely, from the other side of despair.

XXX

THE RUSHLIGHTS HAD all gone out by the time Marcus finished telling the story. In the gloom he couldn't read what Claire was thinking. She thought a long, long time.

Finally he heard her let her breath out. She said, "Why is it called the Correction of the Weights and Measures?" Marcus nearly laughed – he'd forgotten.

He said, "Oh, at that time there was a spat brewing on Serapetine Hill. Some of the vendors were chiseling the weights and measures. They started slow, and the buyers didn't notice for a long time. Later they got pretty brazen about it, and even bribed a treasurer to chisel the reference weights and measures so they wouldn't get caught. After the massacre, Reburrus heard about it, and sent Antivola to tell the vendors that Massafra had a second set of reference weights and measures. The vendors corrected their false weights and measures right away."

Even in the dimness, he could see Claire's eyebrows rise sharply at this ridiculous addendum. Then they drew together: "Was Thersites cheating the customers?"

"No," he said, "Never."

# 42

## O MY BROTHER, WHAT HAVE YOU DONE?

THE KING SAID, "How about I march the second morax up the Epicondyle and execute them all?"

Nederick Frederick squinted at him. The king let it hang a long moment before he cracked a grin.

Nederick Frederick said, "I'm afraid not."

The king rode a horse and led men against the enemy. The mayor negotiated garbage fees and water deliveries. They both knew how to get their hands dirty. Ambrosius felt they respected one another as men good at their jobs.

He said, "What will the city tolerate?"

Nederick Frederick said, "I am reasoning on it. It's not only old women who follow the ichneumonoi. Massafra commands the Florentine religion. What is Florence without her gods? Where else is the virtue of her people? We must tread carefully here."

Ambrosius said, "Do they love Reburrus?"

The mayor craftily answered, "No more or less than you do, my lord."

Ambrosius bared his teeth in a frustrated smile. He said, "Have I leave to kill Antivola?"

Nederick Frederick hesitated, then said, "Your foreign girl has been making herself very popular, selling apples for Thersites on Serapetine Hill. Therefore the public mood is in her favor, and against those who would destroy her... Let us say there is leave for Antivola to be dead. But this is not so much as to say there is leave for you to kill him."

Queen Antonella said, "We will reason on it."

Nederick Frederick took it for his dismissal, and made his farewells and retired. The king and queen remained alone in the jade office, off the great hall.

Ambrosius stewed a while. When he glared at the queen, it was nearly in shame. He said, "I ordered Reburrus away from the patricia. Antivola is his other him."

Antonella said, "My lord, answer the important question, then let the answer make your path."

Ambrosius said, "My lady, what is the important question?"

Antonella said, "Is Reburrus good or evil?"

Ambrosius looked at her in silence, overcome with love for the queen. Her question wasn't the most important question for her, but she understood it was the most important question for him. She was the heart of his virtue. He meditated on it a long time, in the strangely colored gloom of the jade office.

Finally he said, "He conceives himself a good man. He is persuaded everything he does aims only toward the good. There is not a splinter of corruption or self-seeking in him."

Antonella waited.

He said, "All my reign, he's been a demon on my back. I tethered him to me, and carried him, who had little knives for teeth and fire for breath. Can man blame the demon for his nature? Is the demon evil?"

He looked at her, and his breath whistled in his nostril, and she waited.

He said, "I have loved him as I loved my god and nation. I invited him for my own ichneumon, and he has been faithful to me every hour, even though it cost him the map he made of his own life. He knows that I betrayed his hopes, and yet he followed me down to perdition. To the verge of atheism, has Reburrus followed me, and he has guided me and been gentle with me each cruel day of his interment in this disappointing world."

The queen looked mutely at him.

Anguished, Ambrosius said, "I took a great man, and made of him a mediocrity. My god, Antonella, what have I done to Reburrus?"

Antonella said, "Is Reburrus good or evil?"

Ambrosius struck his brow and said, "I don't know! I don't know!"

She said, "Is Claire of Zanzibar good or evil?"

Ambrosius said, "Why good of course." Then his jaw dropped.

From there, devising the fate of Antivola was fairly simple.

XXX

THE TAGMATA FOUND reason to bust several heads on the Campus Iucundum, but search as they might, they could not turn up General Furius Nasica.

When they reported back to King Ambrosius, they noted a reckless aspect to the Redheads they questioned. They found the Redheads' giddy indifference disconcerting. People right in their reason did not grin at the Tagmata like this.

Ambrosius pondered it. Marcus seemed to have read the third morax correctly. It was still two weeks before the Family Dinner. Therefore Nasica must be farther out from Florence, assembling resources for the attack.

The king took great reassurance from this turn of events. The plot was discovered in plenty of time to unspool its climax.

XXX

THE THIRD TIME Marcus noticed Redheads laughing as they pissed on the corner of that mound outside their palisade, his reason took account of the mound. He went back in his empty camp. There were just a few tenmen of the Thousand here, Genovans all, tending false cook-fires and stomping around on the dusty paths and loudly talking nonsense to one another. They cheerfully waved to him. He gathered them together and gave them orders. Then he went to his tent and lay down and arranged his humors to wake him before first light.

## XXX

*This was the place*, Reburrus thought. *I have been happy, bounded by time and company, the way that mortals are happy, and this was the place.* He marveled at it. He'd never thought of it that way before, but then, one doesn't, until it's gone, or going. The moon and stars, the wind and crickets, atop Massafra, atop the Epicondyle, above Florence and the world. With Iacomo Antivola. *I was happy here.*

That morning, a tenmen of Tagmata had come out from the royal district. They drove a cart, and in the cart, sheepish Antivola. Their decanus read the charge against the Icht Most Capable.

Reburrus, affrighted, said, "Antivola, is this true?"

Antivola said, "It's all true."

The decanus said, "We turn him over to the justice of Pantokrator. Teach Florence what is just, Ichneumon, as you have always done." The soldier's voice was tight and his eyes were sharp with hate. Looking at him, Reburrus realized he knew him: he'd been a fresh recruit in the Tagmata stationed on the hill during the Correction of the Weights and Measures.

Now it was night and Reburrus looked over at his giant double, sitting in the other chair, wrapped in wool and fur against the winter cold, wheezing lightly, staring into the dark. *If this is the last time we sit here together, then I will never be happy again.*

"O my brother, what have you done?" he murmured.

Antivola turned and squinted at him and smiled sadly. He said, "I threw away my life protecting yours."

Reburrus shrieked, "It wasn't yours to throw away!" then clapped a hand over his mouth, as if it had acted against his will. He dropped his hand, but raised it again, to scratch the phantom hair on the bridge of his nose. The rash on his hand was cracked and oozing.

## XXX

THAT SHRIEK WAS the most human sound Antivola had heard from Reburrus since the first night they'd met, when the ichneumon was weeping. It was almost unbearable to him, that he'd provided the second anguish in his friend's life.

Reburrus said, "We could imprison you, for years – forever if need be."

Antivola shook his head: "It wouldn't be enough, and besides, I don't think I'd like it."

Reburrus, desperate, said, "Exile. We could send you to the Genovans. To Kharkhadia. You could preach the doctrine of Pantokrator to the barbarians."

Again Antivola shook his head: "It wouldn't be enough, and besides, I don't think I could convince anyone."

He knew Reburrus would shortly accept he was right, it wouldn't be enough, none of it would be enough.

The giant icht gently said, "For the sake of Florence, you must condemn me."

With his weak sight he couldn't make it out, but he knew Reburrus shut his eyes. He saw him bow his head. Antivola loudly called down to the attendants, and presently a young icht popped his head up from the kitchen. Antivola gave him the message to convey to the castle. The attendant let out a cry, and Antivola calmly chastised him and sent him on his way. Reburrus never raised his head.

When the attendant was gone, Antivola ruefully remarked, "It would have worked, if only it had worked."

Reburrus couldn't help a grin. "You would have gotten away with it, if you hadn't been caught."

Antivola sighed, "I failed at every step. Who knew she was so fast? Who knew the king kept allies watching her every minute? Most of all: who knew I'd get such an idiot for an assassin?"

Reburrus chided him, "Dear my friend, this is what happens when we plan our plans apart. Your foolish plan – *that* was why you kept on counseling we wait?"

Antivola said, "You were under the king's orders. You could have narrowly survived her murder if the order came from me alone."

Reburrus said, "How should a good man die, Antivola? Apart and quietly? Before the mob? The summit of the hill, its foot? Stone or blade? Water or fire? How, Antivola?"

Thus they planned their last plan.

When they had worked out every detail of it, they fell silent. The great unploughed field wheeled above them and the wind dropped into the fearsome cold of deep night.

Antivola hunched forward and said, "I'm afraid."

Reburrus put the hand of comfort on Antivola's back, as Antivola did the first night they met. A long time passed. The warmth of Reburrus's hand, old now and diseased, passed into Antivola.

Finally the giant icht said, "I don't believe any of it, you know."

Reburrus waited a long time, until he felt he had to speak. Haltingly, he said, "Speak – speak this to me, brother."

Antivola said, "Pantokrator the big man with his sling – Pantokrator the circle in the square – none of it. I have never believed these things."

Reburrus said, "Did you set your will against the god?"

Antivola laughed quietly and said, "You know me better than this. There was no will to set, no god against whom to set it. Perhaps there is a muscle of faith and it is weak in me, like every other muscle."

He grat his teeth in self-recrimination, then turned his great head, his innocent blind gaze on Reburrus.

He said, "When I have meditated, and left the world, and gone inside myself, seeking the golden field of heaven, what did I see, Flavius Papellus? I saw nothing. I met a vast inner silence. So long as I had more life in front of me, I could hide this silence from you and from myself. But now it presses me – gods, it presses me – I am afraid."

A little sob came out of him, like a gasp. The hand of his friend, his brother, his double, never moved from his back.

A very long time later they realized they had one more plan to plan – the career and works of Reburrus alone. They found some of the old delight in spinning ideas, but it faded, for each one came to a bad result.

In the end, they simply took contentment from sharing one another's company. They were still sitting together on the roof and speaking quietly when the sun came up.

## XXX

THE BURNING SAND stung his feet and the crack of thunder echoed from the oily sea. Marcus looked down into the bowl of the skull, filled with saltwater, a thin clear pink like wine too heavily mixed.

He felt a gentle hand on his shoulder and turned. His eyes teared, but it was just the glare of the dripping yellow sky. There was his Genovan enemy, his dead man. All mortal woe was smoothed from his brow. Look at that generous smile, just like feeble-minded Philo's smile, a smile that withheld nothing. Now Marcus's tears were real. The dead man squeezed his shoulder and said, "Don't cry, my friend. All those meant to live will live. All those meant to die have started dying."

But the dead man misunderstood, he always misunderstood. Marcus found he was able to speak what he normally could only think.

"I'm not weeping from grief, my friend, but from guilt. I've a craving in my gut for murder. How can it be? After everything I've seen, how can it be that I miss death?"

The dead man's smile faltered and he stepped back.

Marcus continued, voice full of bitter wonder, "How strange life is, that in the end, having thirsted for everything else, we thirst even for death."

The dead man said, uncertainly, "We must be what we are."

Marcus looked at him. *Dare I walk away from so profound a love?* He swiped at his tears and his hand came away bloody.

He said, "Must we?"

His humors woke him. It was time.

## XXX

MARCUS DRESSED IN full armor. He put on his old helmet, the one with the missing piece in its plume. He strapped on a shiny new sword, just the right length and weight, that he'd selected from the heap of fresh inventory the Constantines were dumping in his warehouse.

He returned to the gate and found his Genovan Thousand waiting solemnly, armed and armored, carrying the shovels he'd told them to fetch from the warehouse.

The crescent moon had set and the big army camp across the plain was dark and silent.

They exited the gate and quietly walked the distance between the camps. The Redheads had built guard towers on their palisade, but if guards manned them, they could not be seen against the stars. The Thousand came to the broad fresh mound and sniffed around until they found the corner the Redheads liked to piss on. They dug there quickly and quietly.

They extracted the long dirty sack Marcus had told them to look for. Then they built the corner back up, as nearly the same shape as they could.

They carried the sack back to their camp. It stank of corruption.

Behind closed gates, Marcus pulled his ankle blade and slit the sack. By the dying light of one of the false cook-fires, the men all looked at the body inside the sack. Between the wounds and the vermin it was in a wretched state, but the furrows in the gaunt cheeks still vanished in a dark beard, grown bushy since the peace.

Marcus said, "That's Nasica."

# 43

## I AM NOT ENTIRELY A MORTAL

CLAIRE USED LOVERS' Gate to escape the royal district.

She was still restricted to the district, but she heard them gossiping in the kitchen: her would-be murderer was to be burnt alive this morning, a public spectacle on the Epicondyle. The staff were annoyed about the date, because today was market day. They figured Reburrus wanted to keep the crowd as small as possible.

The patricia conceived a desire to face this man who had decreed she die. She didn't know what good could come of it. But she wanted to glimpse a mind that craved her extinction. It fascinated her to stand at the lip of so terrible a void.

Therefore she packed a little bag and went out to visit Massafra. It was still early in the morning and she walked around the empty Primavera Circle and headed east on the Via Floribus, the other way from Serapetine Hill. She cut northeast toward the dark prominence of the Epicondyle. She didn't know this area so well. It looked like mostly smithies, but they weren't open yet.

Still shaken by her meeting with the assassin, she scanned more closely where she walked. Therefore she became aware a man followed her. He was difficult to see, keeping to shadows and confusions of shop implements. She was still somewhat angry with him, so she increased her pace. He sped up to overtake her, abandoning his careful movement and clanking noisily. Glancing back, she saw he was wearing full armor. There was that helmet of his, with the plume so fetchingly damaged. She sped her pace again, so that she nearly ran, and Marcus called "Claire!"

She spotted an alley between a farrier's and a cooper's, and shot down it, past buildings ringing with clangs. She came out into a little yard with a couple chickens strutting around. The yard lay in the blue shadow of a wall at its far side, made of enormous old well-fitted stones, worn now and growing weeds and lichens. Stumbling forward, she came to the wall. Hand on its cold flank as though it were her horse Polpetto, she looked up and saw it curved, and was so tall its dark shape seemed to bend over her. A broken line of sun glared out a single window just below its peak. She yanked her hand away as if it burned.

She stood at the foot of ai Ctesiphôn.

Just then, Marcus popped out the alley, shouting "Claire! Claire!" His voice dropped off and he stumbled to a halt. He stood dazed, looking up. He took off his helmet and ran his hand through his sweaty hair.

He looked at her and said, "We found it."

Claire said, "So it would seem."

He walked up to stand beside her at the wall. He hesitated, then touched the tower with the tips of his fingers. Then he pressed his palm entirely against the cold stone, and murmured, "Ai Ctesiphôn," and grinned his breathless grin at Claire. She did not smile back.

He said, "O Claire, can we please not waste time being sullen?"

She glared at him a minute longer, till she couldn't help it and she smiled. She looked him up and down. Beneath his face, he was all leather and bronze: breastplate, arm guards, pteruges, greaves. She said, "You're looking very handsome today."

He shifted the helmet under his arm and said, "I came to warn the king. We thought we discovered the Crimson Knight - the general of the third morax. But he's been lying all this time outside his army's camp, beneath a mound of dirt."

"How did you find him?"

"I noticed the Redheads liked to piss on the mound, so I dug it up."

Claire grimaced.

"What do you want to tell the king?"

Marcus frowned and squinted up at the summit of ai Ctesiphôn. He looked back at her.

"Whoever the Crimson Knight is, we've found his army. The Redheads must be put down right away."

Claire looked regretfully up at the tower. She said, "We should go then."

Marcus shook his head. Claire tilted hers.

"The tower has shown itself to us. We dare not ignore it."

"But the Crimson Knight –"

"The tower of Florence will not betray Florence. Whoever is meant to live will live. Whoever is meant to die is already dying."

Claire looked at her hand on the cold weathered stone.

She said, "I want to get inside it, Marcus."

He said, "Walk with me, and we will see if we can find the door into ai Ctesiphôn."

## XXX

MARCUS TURNED LEFT with her. The two of them began to walk along the wall, passing out the little yard, and crossing other yards, and alleys, and streets. No one but a stray dog took any notice of them or of the wall. The dog yelped once, then turned and ran away, tail between his legs.

Claire slung her little bag over one shoulder, and they walked side by side and hand in hand. They traded turns being closest to the wall and running fingers over it as they walked. Holding hands was not uncommon among friends in Florence at that time, neither men and men, nor women and women, nor men and women, and Marcus didn't take it for more than it was. He noticed that her palms were rougher than they'd been.

With fair solitude and no immediate demands on their attention, he found himself abruptly shy with her. He recalled his dream, in which he could say everything he'd only thought.

He said, "That butchered skull you picked up in Andropolis."

She eyed him but said nothing. They kept walking.

"I killed that man. You knew that right away."

She nodded briefly, as if she were ashamed of what she'd seen.

"He died slowly. He lived long enough to forgive me. I could bear the burden of my sin, but I couldn't bear his forgiveness." Claire pressed her lips together.

"I dream about him. In my dream, he's there beside me, even though I'm holding his ruined skull. He goes on forgiving me."

He looked at the beautiful patricia, walking resolutely round the great curve of ai Ctesiphôn, her white fingers trailing over its ancient face.

"Understand me, Claire. In confessing to you, I give myself to you."

Claire shut her eyes. He couldn't read her expression. He held one of her hands and her other touched the tower. They went on walking. He looked at her till she opened her eyes. Then he looked at the streets of Florence, unfamiliar streets, passing by as if beyond a sheet of water.

She said, "How comes it we still face the shadow side of the tower?"

Marcus stopped in the blue shade of ai Ctesiphôn and looked up at it. Its dark shape rose so high it seemed to bend over him, and the same window still glared below its peak.

He said, "Before we met I had never any luck with ai Ctesiphôn, and I don't know what it does."

Claire put her fingertips back on it and the two of them went on walking, speeding slightly now their pace. The only sound between them was their footfalls on the stones and grass and gravel.

The day abruptly dimmed and cooled. Thick cloud had come from somewhere. Claire stopped, so suddenly Marcus tripped against her, and he felt through his armor the substance of her curves, her hard thigh and soft breast. She seemed not to notice. She was squinting up at the heavy cloud and the blue shadow of ai Ctesiphôn. There was a look on her face so frightening he shrank from her. Finally she dropped her gaze to him, and the gray of her eyes seemed brighter than the day.

Marcus said, "O Claire, what did you see?"

Her gaze was strangely vacant. "The flow of time did something unusual just now."

A shiver galloped up his spine, and his whole scalp stood up from his head.

Her brilliant gaze focused on him. He felt pinned, like something very tiny. She said, "I'm not a god. But I am not entirely a mortal."

Marcus understood.

*In confessing to you, I give myself to you.*

She blinked, and her irises darkened to the darkness of the cold shade they stood in. Her mouth opened; she leaned hungrily toward him. Dizzy, he leaned toward her as well. He smelled her smell of thunder and of honeysuckles. When his lips touched hers, he had a shock, like touching metal on a dry day in winter. But after the shock, her lips were soft. Loud Florence was, for once, entirely silent. Marcus kissed her, and she kissed him, in the blue shadow of ai Ctesiphôn.

Afterward they sped along the round foot of the tower. Finally she said, "In the springtime we will travel west, and cross the mountains." She smiled uncertainly at him. She said, "Be kind to me, Marcus. I answer to a host of powers."

*Mercy, Marcus. Even the gods need mercy.*

He said, "Once we cross the mountains, I am going to –"

And he leaned in to her and whispered something that made her ears burn. Then he stood back and looked at her. But instantly his gaze rose above her and he exclaimed, "The tower!"

## XXX

CLAIRE TURNED AND looked at the wall her fingers rested on. She saw the character of the wall had changed, and was now small rounded stones all stuck together with cracked mortar. This wall was straight, and scarcely taller than she. Looking back along the path, she saw the straight wall crossed a yard and terminated not far away at a private house. Turning further, Claire observed the yard was full of sunflowers, most of them shabby and brown and past the brightness of their blooms. A profusion of bees wandered lazily amongst them. Therefore the yard was all buzzes and dry rustlings. She let go the wall and Marcus stared at her and said, dismayed, "Ai Ctesiphôn ha' shook us off." His face swam in a gloom beneath that heavy cloud.

The householder came out to rebuke them, but when he saw it was the Sower of Peace and her man, he drew up short and made a bow. He offered them a snack of sunflower seeds and honey, and they ate with him, and he asked how they'd got in his yard without his seeing them. Claire told him she was on the way to climb the Epicondyle, and he said, "For sure the execution's done by now." Marcus was astounded, but Claire wasn't. She moved to go, and the householder insisted they take sheets of waxed paper in case of rain.

When they reached the street, Marcus exclaimed, "But this is the Aventine Way!"

Claire said, "Is that very strange?"

He said, "We're in the southwest quarter, up Clodian Hill. Nowhere near where we started."

They crossed the wealthy residential district. They made their way northeast, passing through the ruins where Via Di Speranza burned. As they crossed the stinking Liliana, Claire said, "Would you utterly abandon me at the word of Ambrosius?"

Marcus said, "I would try, but I think I could not."

Claire said, "Why not?"

Marcus answered, "When you said follow me, I had to go." He made a strange motion with his fingers, like playing scales on the clavichord. He saw Claire looking and said, "It's the pickpocket's warmup. My hand runs it when I'm nervous."

Claire said, "I think you are the bravest man I ever met."

She saw him swell with pride. The clouds were clearing now, and a pale sky was shining through. Oil on the river caught the light in slowly curling patches. They threw their sheets of waxed paper in the water as they passed.

Without having to consult about it, they stopped by the alley where they started. But when they got there, they found no evidence of it. The cooper and the farrier had no gap between them. Rather, they shared a large common workshop, though not peacefully, for the farrier's horses were always kicking over the cooper's barrels.

Near the hill, they started passing many burghers walking the other way. They smelled of burnt meat and smoke. Claire stopped, breathing deeply, all hurry forgot. She said, "The city, Marcus. Like a single beast. Hectic, giddy." Marcus stopped with her, and she saw him savor the hour and the mood of the city, just like her.

When they'd got over their intoxication, they heard what the passing burghers said: they were chattering about the execution of Antivola. Marcus had trouble crediting the gap in time, but the hour now was clearly afternoon. For her part, Claire considered the yard that had butted up against ai Ctesiphôn, and wondered what became of the chickens.

## XXX

THAT MORNING, THE morning ai Ctesiphôn stole from Claire and Marcus, Reburrus and Antivola paced soberly through the steps of their plan. They went into the part of the garden walled with hedges, where the poison grew. They'd agreed on scarlet cherry, from the tree Antivola had cared for all these years. Reburrus collected a handful of berries, then turned to the minor ingredients of the recipe.

While he took care of business, Antivola shuffled round the garden, softly touching each plant in turn with his thick fingers. He'd spent many peaceful afternoons alone with them and his thoughts. In the religious literature of Florence, the letters of Reburrus are distinguished for their bloodshot quality, for a reckless passion that elevates the reader to the madness of the author. Antivola's treatises, in contrast, appeal to the phlegmatic soul. He reasons patiently on complex topics, turning puzzles over and over until he and the reader, at the same moment, discover the hidden seam. There is no trace of his forlorn atheism to his writing. He perfectly pretends to faith. He wrote all those essays after long sessions in the poison garden, when his mind roamed and he imagined god. Thus he ran his fingertips gently over his plants, one last time. Reburrus completed the list, and they left.

Antivola went to the baths. One novice icht attended, and Antivola dismissed him. Gross man that he was, he was dainty about privacy. Once he was alone he undressed and sat into the water, on a marble step. Then he leaned back and floated out to the center. Windows let a little light, and coals heated the room. Eyes closed and ears submerged, Antivola separated his senses from the world. With time so short, his reason stumbled only briefly before trotting to its goal: that inner silence which had always answered his call for meaning. Floating in the water in a dim and soundless world, weightless, facing the great silence, he felt himself the thinnest membrane between two voids that thirsted for each other, the void of the cosmos at large, and the void inside himself.

*Why should it disturb me so, to puncture finally this thin membrane?*

There was nothing for it though, it did. His teeth were chattering when he got out. He dressed with shaking hands, and went to find Reburrus.

Reburrus met him dressed in his full priestly raiment, the red robe, the red miter, the pectoral hanging from its bronze chain round his neck. The pectoral was a bronze square on his breast. In the square there was a silver square, and inscribed in it, Pantokrator's circle all in gold.

Reburrus offered his own bronze bowl to his friend Antivola, and Antivola took it and shut his eyes and drank from it. Reburrus had flavored the tea with a large portion of good Sophia honey, expensive Genovan contraband. It was kind of him. The shaking in Antivola's hands stilled. There was no saving him now; let the king ride up the hill and order clemency, the world itself should disobey. Antivola was leaving.

Antivola took a last look at the great gold Pantokrator in the prayer hall. Gaudy thing. The ichts pushed wide the doors, and he and his double marched down to the pyre. His ichts bound the Icht Most Capable. The crowd maintained respect, though Antivola could tell they panted with excitement. In his fearful twanging voice, Reburrus made his speech behind Antivola. Then he circled round the pyre to the north and faced his friend. Antivola understood; the winter sun shone on the pectoral, so that his last sight in the world should be the bright sign of the one true god.

The poison was spreading through his giant frame. His fingers were numb and his legs were weak and he supposed he'd have sunk without the ropes. He felt a coolness in each vein, just as they said this recipe provided: a calm fine death. In one part of his passions his teeth still chattered and his hands still shook, but the rest of him was quiet as a hill under a new moon. It came as a surprise to him the flames were lit, he hadn't noticed when they did it. He saw the metal sign of Pantokrator through the smoke and sparks. Being nearly blind, Antivola perceived it as a squarish blur of light.

He felt his organism fraying. Even with the numbing poison, there was some discomfort. His scalp stung and tugged, and he realized his hair was burning. His brains must be near boiling now. He suddenly regretted his miserable eyesight, he would have liked to see sharply the last part of his life. As if Benevolence was listening, and answered, he found abruptly he saw clearly. But the thing he saw was not the same as what there was to see –

*For behold, three suns rose up in the northern sky, a high one and a lower on each side. He recognized them for dim old suns, with great flares coming from their spotty skins, in violet and in green. Underneath the suns rose five red moons of equal size, also in an arc, so that a crown of suns hung above a crown of moons, and even so, the sky was dark as night, and full of unfamiliar stars. The Earth beneath the moons was broad and scarred with craters and dry river valleys. It was a lonely Earth, and a man could lose himself in it, especially a lonely man –*

It was overwhelming in its beauty. *I am seeing what he sees,* thought the dying icht. If he'd understood before, and the girl from Zanzibar had come to see him, then he could have told her: he'd been wrong about it all. Now he saw the one right plan for Reburrus, a plan with a happy outcome. He wished he could tell it to him. *Too late, too late.* Casting his tremendous reason forward through misty time, Antivola saw that Reburrus would hit on this plan as well, but only after he had destroyed everything, even himself. *Ah well,* he thought, *you'll get there, my brother.* Then he died.

The crowd did not know of the poison, and took it as a mark of the steadfast faith of Antivola that he suffered the pyre with serenity, in utter peace. As is the way of men, he didn't start burning in good sincerity till he had passed from underneath the sun. But then, owing to his great size, he burned ferociously. The crowd stood back from the scalding heat and the spattering grease. His jaw fell open and burning fat rolled down his black tongue and dripped from his black teeth, as if he spoke words of flame. There were a lot of ropes and they held him a long time. They were threaded with bronze for strength. Finally the ropes burned, and the bronze melted in the awful heat, and the remains of Antivola collapsed in a gust of raw white flame. The flame was famished for its fuel, and not long afterward the fire died down. When it went out the ash had barely a shape.

## XXX

A LITTLE LATER Marcus came up the hill, young and full of life, swaggering his broad chest. The crowd had dispersed, leaving only those who lived atop the Epicondyle. They all wore sooty white except Reburrus. Marcus spotted him sitting in his red clothes on the temple steps, left behind like the husk of an insect. A company of pigeons had started pecking on the marble yard between the steps and the pyre. Reburrus lurched up and scattered them, and Marcus thought perhaps he'd never seen a man more miserable. When he looked up from the pigeons he saw Marcus.

Both locked pupils rotating, he fixed his terrible gaze on Marcus. His eyes were steady, but his organism betrayed him. He made the same nervous gesture Marcus had, the pickpocket's warmup. All at once Marcus understood the ichneumon's beginning. He was a Serapetine boy, a grubby child of the alleys, beaten, starved and thieving, just like Marcus. *How different the two of us have grown, coming from the same cradle! Was it the gulf between my Beno Tiresias and whoever raised this monster? Was it life's parade? Were we always spun from different stuff?*

The gaze of the grieving ichneumon skittered from him like a beetle, landing on Claire, and his dextrous fingers leapt to the bridge of his nose. Raised into the light, Marcus saw the backs of his hands had awful sores on them, like wet-wounds.

Claire kept on approaching, passing Marcus, and the incandescent hate on the face of Reburrus took on character and texture. It was fear-hate, the fear-hate of a lioness with threatened cubs. He glanced back toward the doors of Massafra, open wide upon the public hall of prayer. Looming at its rear, gleaming in the dimness, stood the golden Pantokrator. It was this he feared for and protected. Claire had kilt his friend and come to steal his god.

He raised his hands and his followers obeyed as if they were his limbs. They formed a curve to either side of him, ready to clamp shut round Marcus and the patricia.

*Why did I let her bring me here, today of all days? We should be off telling the king about Nasica.*

He caught up to her and put a hand on her arm, but she rolled her shoulder and her winter cloak unwrapped from her, so that he was compelled to catch it. Straight-backed, white-gowned, bare-breasted, she kept walking. She stalked up to the furious ichneumon.

He hissed, "Alien bitch, you've murdered a great man."

She looked him in his face, matching his gaze with her own, and said, "Your pet ape cut his own fat throat."

Reburrus goggled and Marcus did too.

She raised that little bag that she'd been carrying all day, and shook something out of it. She flung the thing at Reburrus and it clanged off his metal pectoral.

*Is this you Claire? What happened to the gentle patricia who soothed kings, who won the heart of Florence in her costermonger's smock?*

She shook another item from the bag and bounced it off the ichneumon as well. Marcus looked at them on the ground. Sandals. Even from here, he could see the circles inscribed in squares in their soles.

The sandals Reburrus had left beside her in Andropolis.

*She's always known.*

The tiny foreign woman said, "You're a murderer, Reburrus, and you are a fraud."

In a vague way, Marcus deciphered it: she'd graduated from the age of study to the age of action.

## XXX

HIS WHITE LIPS trembled.

*Am I a fraud? Have I been mistaken in it all?*

The witch turned and walked the short distance to the pyre. She stooped into its hot coals and dragged her fingers through the shapeless ash heap at the center. She turned back.

*I am magnetized to you, and you to me.*

She drew her fingers over her lips, so that the ash of his friend made her lips white like his. Then her pink tongue darted out, lizard-like, and she licked her lips.

*An eater of the living, and an eater of the dead.*

She held his bright locked gaze and whispered again, so softly it was not clear she spoke at all. But the ichneumon heard her.

*Enemy, I will destroy you.*

An outraged cry escaped him, and his men converged toward her. The handsome young tribune drew a shiny new sword. But the alien with her straight back and her naked breast seemed not to care at all. In another second his men would have fallen on both of the intruders –

But then there was a new sound in Florence. Strange notes, very loud.

*low-High*		*low-High*		*low-High*

City horns, but not the city code. Icy dread spread from Reburrus's heart.

*low-High*		*low-High*		*low-High*

The tribune turned, lowering his raised sword, the ichneumonoi forgotten.

*low-High*		*low-High*		*low-High*

It sounded like there were hornblowers all along the mighty walls of Florence.

Reburrus said, "What – what is it?"

The tribune spoke, as if to himself.

"Scenario three. He sent his column through Shepherd's Gate."

The tribune jogged to the lip of the Epicondyle. His sheer indifference to Reburrus and his men persuaded everybody. They crowded to the edge to see.

The height of the hill above the city gave a vantage on its streets, and even the plains beyond the walls.

There was a tumult in the big tent city on the Campus Iucundum. The little tent city was on fire.

Shrouded in dust, a column of men flowed through Shepherd's Gate, open for market day.

With his fearful rotating eyes, Reburrus looked. Through gaps in the dust he made out details.

The men in the column wore fresh armor, just like the tribune.

Their breastplates were painted red. The plumes of their helmets were dyed red.

They carried banners, a red horse on a white field.

Voice quiet, Reburrus said, "What is going on?"

Marcus Irenaeus Diophantus said, "The Crimson Knight has entered Florence."

# PART V

# Ai Ctesiphôn

# 44

## THE ARMY OF THE CRIMSON KNIGHT

MARCUS SAID TO the astonished priests, "Bring me the prayer-horn," and one of them did. It was silver and a strange curved shape and he knew it made a mighty sound – Massafra used it to announce prayer to the city. Reburrus gestured to seize his holy thing from Marcus, but if it came to main force, he was no match for the tribune's youth and vigor. Marcus rudely turned his armored back on him, squinting down the hill to Florence. He put the horn to his lips and blew –

Five short: *Claire*

One short: *with*

Long-short-long-short: *Diophantus*

He saw heads turn in the royal district.

Long-short-short-short: *The Thousand*

Short-long-short: *close the district – defend the castle*

With his hawk-like eyes, he scanned west up the Via Floribus. There, at the foot of Serapetine Hill. From out the maze of alleys, out the nest of speakeasies and boltholes and flophouses and smugglers' closets. You might be able to hide a thousand men in there, if you knew the place well enough and had a few local friends. If you were raised a pickpocket on Serapetine Hill.

Where there had been only afternoon foot traffic, an army formed. It mustered and sprinted east down the Via Floribus toward the royal district.

His eye left his men and returned to the army of the Crimson Knight.

It was gigantic.

*Did every Redhead pledge loyalty to him?*

It was so big it had split up. His view interrupted by the forest of steeples, he saw columns marching down Via Miseri, down Via Ambrosius III, down Locksmith's Lane. He watched them pour over the three bridges of the Liliana on the north side. He watched them mass at Destry.

At their head, there rode a man. The Crimson Knight himself. Marcus recognized him – his great size, his animal posture, the commanding way he sat a horse. But he couldn't quite place him.

*Who are you?*

The Crimson Knight led his men toward the royal district in an imposing, orderly march. He didn't realize he was in a race.

*He doesn't know the city horn codes.*

Marcus looked away from the terrible army, back along the Via Floribus. His sprinting Thousand were drawing ahead of the Crimson Knight. He'd trained them for this. From Serapetine Hill, they could beat an invading army to most places in the city.

Finally he turned back to the royal district. There was round old Laurentius, the captain of the district guard. He did know the city codes, and Marcus's strange new notes. He had teams forming at the gates of the royal district. Ready to accept the Thousand as they arrived, and shut right after.

Primavera Circle was emptying out. The burghers who understood the horns were spreading word to those who didn't.

He turned back to the scene at hand: Reburrus stood staring down at Florence, stunned. Around Reburrus stood his gang of priests, all uncertain what to do. Marcus addressed them: "Fighters, prepare – if the Crimson Knight is smart, he'll have men up here soon. The rest of you inside of Massafra and barricade the doors."

Suddenly he remembered something. He spun and looked.

*How could I have missed that?*

Lovers' Gate, the Gate of Coelestin and Iolanthe, which no one ever closed. A team was struggling with the mossy little thing. It was stuck.

He looked over at the patricia. She faced the city now. Her pupils were enormous and her teeth were bare. She'd looked at the hart in New Forest like that, but then, all warriors look like that, going into battle.

He said, "Come," and wrapped her cloak back round about her. Then he pounded down the winding Epicondyle road, and the patricia followed.

## XXX

PRIMAVERA CIRCLE IS wide by design, a defensive circle outside the district walls. If men stood with their arms out and touched their fingertips to one another, it would take a score to bridge the street. Marcus sprinted across it and beat his own army to Lovers' Gate. Laurentius's district guard were tugging at the heavy door, but underneath the vines, the hinges were fused with corrosion.

Claire stood breathing heavily from her run. Marcus took her hand, near crushing it, so that she winced; but she looked where he pointed with his other hand, through Lovers' Gate. "In there, take refuge, the street will be a battle in a minute." He let her go and she rubbed her hand.

He'd forgotten her already; a detachment of the Thousand were coming round the bend. He shouted to them – "Front four tenmen, door – the others hold the street!" The door team joined the district guard, straining at ropes. Castle staff ran back and forth across the ward, passing arms out the gate. Marcus tightened the straps on his armor, checked his sword. Ran a hand through his damaged plume. He accepted shield and spear and hefted them, good new Constantine stock. It felt like he wore his true clothes, held his true tools.

*I missed death and I missed its home – I've missed you, War.*

He led his men into formation, a phalanx clad in leather and bronze, a brotherhood sharing a single soul, spears vibrating in their fists, ready to hold the street – ready to fight. Shouts and cries and steady footsteps approached. He heard the outraged army of the Crimson Knight, striking at the shut gates round the curve of Primavera Circle. He glanced up: late afternoon – gathering cloud – white-daubed Thousand patrolling the battlements of the royal district wall. He heard the scratch of leaves on stone, driven by the wind.

Then the wind fell, and the day seemed darker, and the scratch of leaves ceased. The shouts and cries and footsteps ceased. A vast silence muffled everything. His soul flew from his men and returned to him. He looked at the sky and saw a dark blur in the depth of it. Just a tiny blur, far distant still, but his organism seized with terror. The storm.

He caught a smell: thunder and honeysuckles. Heart thundering, he tilted his head and chinned his spear. Thus he freed a hand to take his helmet from his head. He lifted it from his hair, already soaked with sweat. Unblinded by the helm, he turned and saw.

Claire had never left the street. She stood behind him now, pupils shrunk and ringed by liquid gray, so terribly sad, hair gleaming under a cold sky.

The phalanx was frozen around him. He turned his shield and slipped between his motionless men, their postures tense, eyes fierce. When he jostled them, he found them hard as bronze. Finally he was free of the three ranks he'd mustered. He squatted and set his arms down in the silent street.

*Time itself obeys your command. You are not entirely a mortal.*

He felt the chill and chaos of the approaching storm, but he didn't look back. He looked only at her, shining in the fading light. Above her stood ai Ctesiphôn.

It was some thirty paces back, its curved wall blocking Primavera Circle, its door plain to see, a wood door black with age, a small door, but large enough for the patricia. Now he understood. He'd seen the tower several times with her, but it was not there for him, nor him-and-her, but her alone, and it came for her now, ai Ctesiphôn.

He approached her, pulling his Florentine medallion from his breast. When he reached her he made a wide circle of its lanyard and set it on her shoulders, so that his tarnished coin was dark against her flesh. She raised her hand and touched it with her fingertips. He said, "Dawn." She looked speedily to him, the way one does when one hears one's name.

Then Reason's daughter leaned her brow toward him, and he toward her, and they touched brows to one another, his fever-hot and bathed in sweat, hers cool and smooth. He pulled back and kissed her brow, that held thoughts enough to remake the world.

He remembered what Thersites said – *I knew I couldn't keep her. But I'm grateful to the god he gave me my season with her.*

He said, "Go."

She pressed her lips as if she wished to cry, but turned and went, toward ai Ctesiphôn.

Marcus turned back toward the phalanx. The maw of the storm was a wide uneven circle in the sky. He looked nothing further at it. He bent and hefted his arms. He slipped between his frozen Thousand, taking his place at the center of the front rank, where the enemy would concentrate his force.

When he was in place, the day abruptly brightened, and the wind rose, and the scratching of the leaves was lost in a din of shouting men, clanging metal, horses' hooves on stone. Half-blinded by his helm, Marcus couldn't see the sky, but he was sure the storm had gone. Packed tight among his men, he couldn't turn. But he was sure ai Ctesiphôn was gone, and she with it.

Here he came around the curve, the enemy. A red horse on his white banner, face grim and furious behind his many helms. Seeing Marcus's men before the open gate, he paused and considered. Twelve hundred feet set themselves on the paving stones of Primavera Circle. The spears of the front rank swung down and leveled on the Thousand. The army of the Crimson Knight prepared to charge.

XXX

TIME FLOWS DIFFERENTLY in Zanzibar. They were still descending the wide marble steps of the Concordia Majeure when Reason sank to her haunches. Denys Berthelot Vazhin had to hold her to keep her from falling. She cried out, "My baby! My baby is gone!" Her voice was raw and harsh and she clawed at her womb as if something had been stolen from it. The blood-drenched savior of Zanzibar, helpless. Eyes blind, she wailed, "She's gone inside the *thing*! I can't see her anymore!" Vazhin understood how a mother couldn't bear to name where her daughter was.

*Claire has gone inside the hypertrochaic device.*

*If she dies, she fails. If she lives, she fails.*

*What will it be, Claire – Florence, Zanzibar? Or the way of the tree?*

XXX

THERE NEVER WAS a Crimson Knight. Or, rather, most everything in the rumors was a lie. They were seeded to keep the king and his magisters and his Tagmata and his vigiles chasing ghosts, and they worked very well. This was characteristic of the Crimson Knight: he solved some problems, like raising a secret army in plain sight, to the smallest detail. Other problems, big obvious ones, he overlooked entirely. Because he didn't think to take the high ground first, Marcus and the Thousand cost him the element of surprise. His one-hour war turned into a siege. He'd understood he might face a siege, but an indolence had seized him every time he considered it, and he never formed solid plans.

The mad zealots he sent to Nasica for interrogation told carefully crafted fables. There were no nighttime recruitments, no system of gold medallions, no carefully selected friends. Rather, the entire third morax had gone over to the Crimson Knight. He was no mystery to them. Some years before, he'd served with them, a dashing knight upon a blood bay charger. A man of means, he'd been generous with them, seeing to their bread and boots. He was hotheaded like they were, and like old King Ambrosius the Eighth, and like Ælius Pellucidus. When the veterans came home to Florence, he sought out his old friends of the third, and they took him in as one of their own. They all shared a disdain for the peace, for it was a dishonorable peace. Mediated by a woman, it was a woman's kind of peace: the enemy Genovans went undefeated.

The Crimson Knight took the measure of his old morax's mood, and when he sensed they might go where he wished to lead, he recited his ambition. He craved to overthrow the weak king, and march for Genova, and restore the honor of the nation. Revealing treason to them, he bared his throat. Any one man could have undone him. This bound his army to him fervently. They began to carry out his plan.

He hid from Nasica alone, because Nasica was loyal to Ambrosius. When Nasica found out, he appealed to any Redheads who had doubts. A small number rallied to his side. They should have fled their camp and gone straight to the royal district. But they were still Redheads, hotheaded and not quite fond of the king. Nasica couldn't bear to admit so thorough a loss of command. He confronted his army, and his army slaughtered him and his loyalists and buried them outside the palisade. Now the Redheads belonged entirely to the Crimson Knight. He brought with him a partner who would wear the crown, but his men knew who held the power.

This was the sense in which there was no Crimson Knight. Those who knew him simply called him by his name, and those who knew him as the Crimson Knight had never met him.

## XXX

Wise King Ambrosius the Ninth circled the flat roof of the north tower of the older castle. Walking round and round, he passed from one embrasure to the next, peeking through each slit. He watched the progress of the army of the Crimson Knight and cursed himself for a fool, not having anticipated this. Well, now he'd pay. He calmed himself and carefully took measure of the scene.

The tenements outside the royal district were safely distant, but the mighty wall of Florence loomed nearly overhead. Younger than the castle, it rose above the royal district in the east. An army in the streets? Three tenmen of skilled archers on that wall could have won the royal district, Thousand or no, Lovers' Gate stuck or no. But there were no archers there. This told Ambrosius everything about the Crimson Knight: the man had no patience for reading terrain.

Consider Ambrosius. At broad Fluctus, his men had roared for vengeance on the Genovans. "Wait," he'd told them. He had knelt and taken a handful of soil. It was soft and damp in his hands, and it had the faint foul smell of nearby standing water. "Let them come to us," he'd told them. It was dawn and the Florentines held the high ground. There was still time to run his men down gentle Fluctus, crashing into the Genovans before they formed ranks. But if the soil was damp up here... "Let them come to us," he'd said, and so they had – charging across the undulating field, where high grass hid what the soil confided to him: marshy land, flooded with snowmelt. Fluctus couldn't hold up the Genovans. Their feet sank in the muck. Clouds of mosquitos tormented them. They arrived for battle all disordered, bootless and miserable. Only then did

Ambrosius unleash his men, and they surged into this Genovan rabble and smote them cruelly.

Some men said wars were won by their supply trains. Ambrosius had always left that to one Constantine or another. He made his home closer to the snout of war. Above all things, he read the land.

The Crimson Knight neglected the Epicondyle. He neglected the impenetrable walls. No doubt he neglected Serapetine Hill. He couldn't read terrain. As far as Ambrosius was concerned, the Crimson Knight didn't know how to make war.

Ambrosius sent a precious third part of his royal district Tagmata up on the city wall. His district folk he set to laying ramps between the district wall and city wall. The ramps were for provisions. The men at arms could stay up there all winter if need be. There would be no overtopping the castle. Thus Ambrosius closed the high ground to the Crimson Knight.

Scanning again the approaching army, Ambrosius considered his provisions. The royal district had the granary – livestock and the pantry – wood for cook fires – and access to the second river, the clean one, dark Tristana running hidden under Florence. Siege was premised on starvation, but starvation was a tricky beast, biting his master as often as his master's foe. Winter was at hand, and Ambrosius could feed his people till spring. Could the Crimson Knight? He doubted it.

Ambrosius stopped at an embrasure, stopped and stared into the clouds of dust that cradled this terrible army. He felt safe exposing his outline to the eyes of the army: they were out of bowshot, but range didn't matter – they had no archers. Where were their archers? What kind of an army has no archers? His eye roamed the city, searching for them. Finally his gaze jogged over the city wall, passing Shepherd's Gate and flying to the Campus Iucundum. He couldn't make out men at that far distance, but he could see pale clouds rising from the main camp, and black smoke from the abandoned camp of the Thousand. His grizzled reason showed him what his cloudy eye could not. The Crimson Knight was conducting two sieges, not one. He'd left his archers on the towers of the palisade around the veteran's city. The third morax built the towers and the palisade. They dug the ditch inside the palisade's tall walls. They'd claimed it was an accident, placing the ditch where it was only good for holding men in, not keeping them out. Ambrosius saw it in his reason: their archers high up the towers, sighting inward, penning his Wardogs inside the veteran's city.

The third morax. Those sons of whores, his father's men, come now to unthrone him.

*Is this you, Nasica?*

The clarity of crisis flared his intuition.

*No, we couldn't find you because you're dead.*

What did the Crimson Knight want? To place the crown on Ælius Pellucidus? Impossible. His brother was dust and bones in ai Ctesiphôn.

*Who did Temet miss? Who is so angry at my rule?*

Abruptly it came clear. Ambrosius's fists clenched, white-knuckled. He'd always known him. The Crimson Knight vanished from the mind of the king, replaced by the figure of his adversary.

Ambrosius reined his far gaze close again, sweeping it over the approaching army. Light infantry all. The enemy gambled on surprise to take the castle. He brought no towers, no rams, no sows, no miners, no slings or catapults. He gambled on surprise; gambled and lost.

*Not because of me. Because of my tribune, Marcus Irenaeus Diophantus. The most surprising man in Florence.*

The warrior king smiled at the thought, but he sighed through his teeth. Every element of war favored him but one: he lacked men. His Tagmata and the Thousand were fine to have, but the Redheads were near fifteen thousand. He could hold the district till he starved, but he could not break out of it and retake Florence. If only he had men! But he didn't. Therefore he must lose.

His adversary, this hothead mumming as a Crimson Knight, this brute, this all unworthy man – must climb the throne, must end the dynasty of house Ambrosius, must rule Florence.

## XXX

Marcus stood in the center of the front rank, braced against collision with the enemy. He had a moment left to wander alone among his passions.

*Have I atoned enough for my sins?*

He thought of the Genovan with the ruined skull, and all his other dead, and felt a pang of regret.

Marcus was young, but he was wise beyond his age. It is said that wisdom comes from suffering. Marcus had suffered, but not more than other Florentines. Rather, the handsome orphan found more joy in life than others had: the taste of good food, the light-headedness of drink – running in a cool wind underneath a clear blue sky – the laughter of friends, the beauty of women. He'd had little enough of these pleasures, but he'd taken unreluctant joy in all of them. Wisdom comes from suffering, but it comes from the opposite of suffering as well. Marcus's extraordinary joys informed his ordinary suffering, and made him prematurely wise.

Therefore, in the face of death, he answered his question with the imagination wisdom provides.

*Of course I haven't atoned enough. I never will. But this is not the entire question – the entire question is: have I lived all the life I could?*

His passions thundered in time with his pounding heart:

*Yes*

*Yes*

*Yes*

His solitary soul returned to the world. He faced death without fear.

The army of the Crimson Knight cried their awful battle cry and charged. The protectors of the open gate stiffened their arms behind their shields. The two sides struck one another, a clatter of shield against shield, helm against helm, spears bending and snapping. Each line held, men shoving and jostling, grunting their fury.

The defenders couldn't defeat the army of the Crimson Knight. Once both lines held, it came down to mass. The Crimson Knight had more men, more ranks to press from behind against the backs of those in front. The defenders grat their teeth and leaned in at the shoulder. They could keep their places, but each minute they would slip backward, feet dragging over stone, tripping, falling, trampled, stabbed. It wouldn't take long.

But they weren't there to defeat the Crimson Knight. Even now, even over the din of battle, they heard a deep ugly creak behind them, then a grinding crash. The Gate of Coelestin and Iolanthe came unstuck. Marcus felt a heavy hand on his shoulder, heard a voice roar in his ear.

"Go! Go!"

He could hear it over the clamor of battle.

"Take the Thousand and go!"

He felt himself lifted like a kitten and shoved back into the dense-knit ranks.

He recognized the great round man stealing his place at the front. It was Laurentius, captain of the royal district guard, who neglected to maintain the gate.

In the press of men, Marcus snaked his arm down his side and retrieved Semaion's city horn. He got it to his lips and loudly blew:

Three short: *Retreat*

Amid the jostling, his Thousand heard him. He'd made them all learn a few horn calls, and now they followed his order. They ceded their places to Laurentius's small squad of royal district guard. Laurentius and his men held the line while the Thousand retreated through the gate.

Marcus saw the last of them in. He shouted, "Laurentius, come!" In the scrum of battle, the old captain heard and shook his head, like a great cat who loosens his shoulders.

Marcus stepped inside and swung shut Lovers' Gate.

XXX

BARRING AND REINFORCING a gate takes time, and the district guard held out surprisingly long. Finally the army of the Crimson Knight managed to get around the side of them. Attacking from the flank as well as the front, they broke their line, mingling with them, pushing them, stabbing and slashing with their swords. Stab, slash – it's too late, the royal district is shut.

When it was done, the army of the Crimson Knight milled in Primavera Circle, sizing up the hard walls of the royal district, facing the grim prospect of siege. Indifferent feet walked past the dead. There lay Laurentius, the rock of the first rank. His strength made strong his men around him. His foot would not be moved from where he planted it. Because he held, the line held. Because the line held, the castle was saved. No thrusting spear or sword could penetrate his mighty shield. He held until the end, and all his wounds were on the sides.

XXX

KING AMBROSIUS THE Ninth of Florence descended the steps of the castle wall, a twinge in his knee with each step. The thunder of the invading army receded to a low roar as he crossed the lawn and faced the Thousand. He breathed five times, cooling his lungs as he surveyed the shining, bloodied ranks of men, arrayed on his well-kept grass beneath the cloudy sky. This inscrutable army – Florentines, Genovans, rebels, defenders.

*What am I to make of you?*

If his crown was to be saved, it was up to them. They could unmake him. Were they his? No, but perhaps his to win over.

*How shall I speak to them?*

They stood there waiting, and he felt like a father of moody sons. He thought of his own sons. He thought of Bitsy Boots, even now sitting terrified in the castle with Antonella.

*I am the father of all of you. I will tell you a story.*

He spoke clearly and loudly. He said, "Hear a tale of my ancestor Ambrosius the Sixth, the first Ambrosius who was called Wise. He led the fifth morax, the Eagles. It came to pass that one of the Eagles deserted his post and fled the war."

The Thousand murmured, and Ambrosius held up a hand for quiet.

"The Tagmata caught this deserter and hauled him before the king. The king sentenced him to death. The condemned man said, 'When we marched in the spring, my wife was heavy with our first child. Give me a month to go home to Victumulae and meet my child, and set affairs in order with my wife, and perform my obeisances to my parents and my gods. Then I will come back and die the death.'

"King Ambrosius said, 'How can I trust a deserter to go? Why would you come back and die the death?'"

"Then the decanus of the man's unit stepped forward and said, 'Take me for hostage. If he does not return, then I will die the death in his place. For though he is a deserter, yet he is my friend, and I trust him utterly.'

"My ancestor King Ambrosius let the deserter go. And he did not come back."

The Thousand gasped. Bitsy Boots was always breathless too, when Ambrosius got to this part.

"On the last day, at the very hour of the execution, King Ambrosius said, 'Decanus, do you regret your folly?' But the decanus only said, 'I trust my friend.'"

Some among the Thousand cheered.

"The King took the decanus for a fool, but behold – the deserter came running and said, 'Forgive me, I was delayed, but I have returned, take me, take me.' And he pushed his friend aside and stuck his head on the executioner's block."

More of the Thousand cheered. Ambrosius waited for them.

"When he witnessed this, my ancestor King Ambrosius called to the executioner, 'Stay your hand! No Eagle will die the death today!' He went down into the dust and raised up the decanus and the deserter and said, 'From you I have learned the truth of friendship. I beg you will ride by my side and provide me with your counsels, and allow me to join you in your holy friendship.' And from this day, the three of them were friends, and my ancestor was acclaimed the Wise, because he learned friendship from the friends."

He paused. The Thousand leaned forward, anxious to hear the moral of the story.

"Like my ancestor, I have learned the truth of friendship from my deserters and their leaders. You have served Florence better than your king. I beg you will allow me to be your friend."

Now the whole Thousand cheered. Ambrosius bowed his head. The men broke ranks and came to him. He grasped the hands of all who reached toward him. His hands were hard, and so were theirs, but his face was soft with feeling and he did nothing to conceal it.

Finally, he sat on his soft lawn, crossing his legs and putting his hands on his aching knees. The Thousand sat as well.

He said, "I have heard of the doctrine of the new world, which you proclaim among yourselves. They say only those who survived Andropolis know the new world. I crave somehow to learn it."

His tribune Marcus said, "It may be true, but the man who made peace with Genova made the world new."

Ambrosius said, "I made peace because Claire showed me how."

A tremor shook Marcus. That weirdly ancient Stonebreaker put a hand on the tribune's shoulder. One of the two big Stonebreakers addressed the king.

"You are nothing different from us, my lord. We Thousand entered the new world because she showed us the way."

Ambrosius studied Marcus's distress. He remembered the message Marcus had blown on the temple horn: *Claire with Diophantus.*

"Marcus, where is Claire?"

# 45

## HOUSE OF STAIRS

WITH A START, she realized the gold palanquin couldn't reach her here. There was an obscure channel between the patricia and her car. Even in the castle, with one stone wall after another between her and the carriage house, she was not apart from her palanquin, but connected to it still. Not now. As she passed through the little door into ai Ctesiphôn, her gold palanquin vanished from her flesh. Her skin crawled. Her gut clenched. *What Art made this thing?*

Claire's reason had trouble seeing what her eye showed it. Ai Ctesiphôn was round on the outside, but it was square on the inside, and larger. The tall square hollow was everywhere crisscrossed by stairs. She craned her neck: above was an abyss of stairs. The staircases were stone. There was no order to their profusion. Some of them grew from the walls, and some were held by mighty buttresses, and others seemed to fly.

Beyond a certain height, Claire saw nothing. It was afternoon in Primavera Circle, but night was falling inside ai Ctesiphôn. How did she know it was not simply windowless and dark? She didn't know. She found she knew the answers to some questions as one knows them in a dream, without first having learned them. She knew the tower had indeed admitted her on purpose, and only once – the ancient little door would never open to her again. Night was falling inside ai Ctesiphôn. Crickets chirped and water dripped, and breezes sighed on stone and moss. The tower was disjunct from time outside it.

Claire couldn't say how she saw anything at all, in that unlit wilderness of stairs. A thick fatigue befell her, as if she'd inhaled it like spores. Her long day had started with chasing this very tower, and continued with the ghastly pyre in front of Massafra, and ended in civil war. As night fell inside ai Ctesiphôn, so night fell now on her spirits.

She yawned and laid herself down at the landing by the little door, with stone for a mattress and stone for a pillow. Sleepily she thought, *Why don't I fear hyenas and wildcats? Aren't there any night-hunters in ai Ctesiphôn?* But she knew there weren't. She understood the tower willed to test her, and death the price of failure. But not like this, like a thief in the night. Stripped of her gold palanquin, alone in the house of stairs, she was as safe as she was in her mother's house. Her fatigue filled her and she slept.

## XXX

*WHERE AM I?* she thought. *Am I here?*

Her eye saw only stone. Her cheek was pressed on clean white limestone, but it was slightly warm and not uncomfortable. She'd rolled over in her sleep, and thrown an arm above her head, so that she made a little tent around her face. She saw before her eye a crack in the stone, and in the dimness of the crack, a pebble, and a twig, and a tiny beetle caught in a drop of water. The twig in the crack reminded her of the withered oak in the window of this tower, and of the king's older brother Ælius Pellucidus, who should have been king, except he went searching for the oak. He was in here somewhere with her, whatever was left of him. She blinked and rolled over.

It was daytime in ai Ctesiphôn and the little door was gone. She saw no exit any longer, but she was not afraid. The daylight was a wondrous thing, painting lemon light over the broad faces of the giant limestone blocks of the wall opposite. Mosses grew between the stones, and there were streaks where water had been dripping for a long, long time. The refreshed patricia couldn't see where the sunlight came from; stairs blocked her view. She couldn't spot a window anywhere.

Her eye descended to the bottom of the tower, and the scattered skeletons of men. *Let me reason on this.* She stayed where she sat, leaning on one arm, breathing the cool damp air, eye flickering from one skeleton to another. The bones were broken but not shattered. *Flesh padded their landing.* She glanced into the daylit staircases above, so many tons on tons of wicked stone. Then she looked back to the skeletons. They were whole, and wore their tattered clothing still. *Men admitted by the tower. Why did they fall?* She did not think ai Ctesiphôn would stoop to pitching men from its stairs. *They jumped. Why did they jump?* She looked up at those tangled heights. *They got lost on the stairs.* There were plants here, and little beetles, but she saw no evidence of animals, or even birds. *It was miserable hunger for them, or a quick end.* Was Ælius Pellucidus down here?

She stood, meaning to visit with the skeletons, but found there was no path from her landing to the broad square plain of the floor. The landing was a platform with sheer sides, the floor too far below to leap. Even if she did, and didn't snap an ankle, there would be no way to climb back up.

No guest of the tower could reach its bottom sensibly. There was some kind of madness to the place, to cutting these enormous stones and fitting them together, all to make a thing no man could reach. Had human masons shaped this stone and set it? She couldn't riddle it. *Why do I feel comfortable here?* She smiled in the clear fine daylight of ai Ctesiphôn, though tears ran down her smooth cheek. *Why am I crying?* She wiped at her tears, and laid foot on the stair ahead, and climbed.

The staircase was long. There was no railing, but the stairs were wide and set against the wall, and the dextrous Zanzibari did not fear a fall. The stairs went on rising, and Claire kept on climbing. She recalled circling the tower with Marcus. Once again ai Ctesiphôn showed one dimension in excess of its others: the stairs crossed a far greater width than the edge of its square base. Abruptly she recognized the nature of her comfort in monstrous ai Ctesiphôn: the Art that made it was not so different from the technology of Zanzibar. Its makers had lived in the valley of the world, and passed from it. Civilizations had risen and fallen before, and would rise and fall again. Each created the trap of its own failure, according to the shape of its achievement. *Will Zanzibar fall one day?* This was why she'd cried. *Yes, Zanzibar will fall.*

She climbed.

## XXX

DISTANT LIGHTNING LIT the king. He looked up and saw clouds whirling, but then they scattered, leaving only stars. One more prodigy in a day of surprises. Ambrosius went back to work. He threaded the rope through the hole in the gravicula, then carefully knotted it. When he got done, he rolled the heavy stone into place, and ran the rope back over the simple pulley-bar. It was midnight and menial work, but the effort pleased him. He put his hands in his mouth and blew on them till his fingers warmed.

That one dog somewhere up on Linthicum Heights started howling again, and soon he had every dog in the city howling. The Florentines were uneasy tonight, and so their dogs were anxious. Ambrosius listened a while, then returned to the heap and chose a fresh stone. As he and his companions worked, lines of waiting graviculae grew along the wall-walk. In battle, they'd be dropped, and once they'd struck, jerked right back up. A castle under siege has only so many stones to spare for dropping on the enemy. In this case, the entire gesture was likely useless. It took one strong man to drop a gravicula, and two to raise it. How many men could he spare for that? Not enough for effective gravicula defense. Well, let them lie where they fell. It was better than nothing.

He'd led Marcus and some of his commanders to the armory and they'd stood and scanned the siege machines: graviculae, hives, three-tails, sand – oh, he liked sand – and sand pots, pincers, jabs, piercing machines, the rod-and-roller, a crushing panel, petraries, caltrops, bows.

He said, "Diophantus, who commands the Thousand?"

Diophantus understood the question and said, "If we live to springtime, I will lead them west to Zanzibar."

Ambrosius said, "How will we live to springtime?"

Marcus drew his fresh sword and offered it to the king, glancing round at his commanders.

He said, "Your wisdom will lead us to springtime."

The king gravely received the sword. Then he examined it. Well-cast, with a distinctive double fuller – Antigonus's workshop. The Constantines had spared no expense. He handed it back and said, "The crushing panel would be fun to use, but it requires specialists, and we have none. The rod-and-roller demands virtually its own army. We will leave it. Set up petraries on the platforms. Prepare the sand and sand-pots along the walls, the caltrops and the bows. Place pincers in the corner towers where they'll be easiest to move as needed."

He'd led them out along the walls, pointing to locations and describing defenses. The Redheads had hurled abuse at them. The Crimson Knight elected not to show himself.

*You know how badly you've stumbled here.*

Now it was cold midnight, not a bad night really, and he was knotting ropes into the ancient, pitted stones. The work was pleasing, and it was good to let the Thousand see him doing soldier's labor. But mainly he was fighting nerves. Like his cousin Temet, his emotions heightened as he approached a crisis. The longer he had to wait, the deeper subject he would fall to tides of sensitivity, especially at night. He knew this about himself and fought it.

Finally, though, the work was done. His organism was exhausted and demanded rest. He couldn't put off thinking any longer. He stood in an embrasure craning out, staring down into the street. Primavera Circle was clotted with an odd mix of elements. A lot of the Crimson Knight's men were concealed beneath what looked like upturned boats. The rest hid under hides draped over posts. There was the night crew, wetting the boats and hides. Protecting the army from eyes and fire. Good for them, showing a little sense.

His eye rose and scanned the city. The dogs had gone quiet for now. Almost every building was dark. Flames still flickered out on the Campus Iucundum. The waning quarter moon swelled as it sank. An icy wind brushed past him.

*What is Claire doing right now?*

He chided himself bitterly, not patching things up with her when he'd had the chance. His anger had passed. Why had he waited? Now he'd never see her again. Unlike Marcus, he wasn't especially worried for her. If anyone could navigate ai Ctesiphôn, it was the girl from Zanzibar. But he couldn't see how he'd survive this siege. Nerves jumping, he thought of all the things he still had to say to her. No chance any longer. He whispered his heart to the night:

"When the god forgave us, he sent you to us for a messenger of peace. Girl, woman, puppet, goddess – it doesn't matter what men call you. O Claire, I've seen how you doubt yourself, how each time we call you god, you name yourself impostor. Let me tell you the truth. When you sat with fools, you were wise. When you met cruelty, you were kind. When you faced doubt, you showed faith. That is what you are. I pray hands more capable than mine will carry you to Zanzibar."

The last word choked him up. Tears swam in the eyes of the king, so that the forest of steeples twinked and winkled in his gaze. He closed his eyes and wiped them, and turned from the city.

Even at that hour, Claire was watching him. He couldn't see her, but she could hear him.

## XXX

HER THIGHS BURNED and each time she raised a knee it felt like blades cut in it. Her head throbbed. She formed an impression that she couldn't quite glimpse most of what there was around her. There was no whispering or music underneath the trickling of water and the soughing of the breeze, but she sometimes thought she heard it. There was an intent fullness to the empty tower. She climbed through the stone and daylight. The yellow light of morning turned to white midday, and ripened into golden afternoon, and rich orange evening. Still she never saw a window; never saw the sun behind the stairs; never saw beast or bird. She passed other staircases, though she had no idea how one reached them, for her staircase never branched or ceased. Human bones lay on other stairs and other landings, as if men had forever flung themselves against ai Ctesiphôn, as if mortals had been losing a war with ai Ctesiphôn for centuries. Claire was not afraid.

As the light inside the tower faded into dusk, Claire saw her staircase coming to its end. It terminated in a wide landing, and she reached the landing and stood. There were six routes from the landing: three long staircases up, one level bridge, and two short staircases down, descending to landings that offered their own further paths. Suddenly dizzy, the youngest daughter of Reason pressed her hands to her weeping knees and panted.

As she panted, she thought, and an intuition wakened Terror in the garden of her passions. As if against her will she turned, she turned and looked, and saw – there were no stairs leading to the lofty spot she stood. Whatever she had climbed had gone. Terror beat his wings against her ribs. She rubbed the heels of

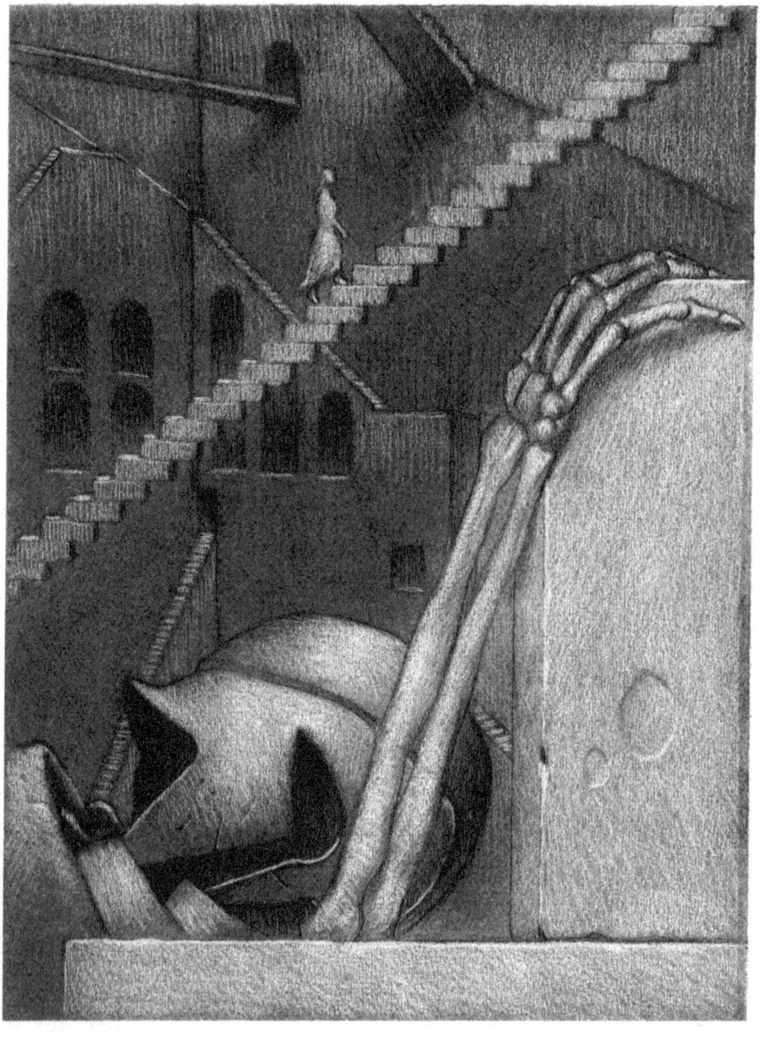

She passed other staircases.
Her staircase never branched or ceased.

her hands against her gritty eyes. She looked again, but it was still gone. Her breathing galloped, and she remembered the missing door she entered in. The silent tower offered only forward, never back.

Unsteadily, she sat, away from the fresh edge. She leaned her head against the wall, and the last of the light faded, and soon she was beneath the dim night of the house of stairs. A cricket chirruped somewhere, and water trickled. Her terror calmed and she discovered herself hungry. Leaning against the wall, she shuffled along till she came to the water, and licked it from the wall. It was sweet and cold and fresh. Favored with a sip of it now and then, she would never starve.

She lay herself down on the landing, so far above the Earth, and far below the summit of ai Ctesiphôn. She lay on her side, and her hip and her shoulder made hills in the night. Other mortals had made like hills, sleeping in the tower, and they were bones now. They were none of her concern. The tower was not built for murder only. It did what all mazes do: protect against those who did not belong. Therefore it had a path.

Weary, sore-legged, Claire grew drowsy. She thought about that article "ai" – one of two – there were two Ctesiphôns, Aeneas had told her. Aeneas! The poor boy, pale as dawn, dying in the street, flat eyes and a basketful of quinces. She felt a pang of grief, felt pressed beneath the weight of guilt. Then she slipped one step closer to sleep, and she forgot the child.

She imagined the other tower. Pictures filled her head: perhaps it stood in some remote place in the north of Florence, or lost in a Genovan waste. Perhaps it was buried underground, so that its summit was a low flat circle men trod over without noticing. Perhaps it lay tumbled somewhere, a fallen column of a thing, cracked in several places, and perhaps the soil had collected on it, so that it seemed no more than an odd long hill covered in grass and hollyhocks. Perhaps it stood watch over fishes, at the bottom of a sea. Reason drifting into sleep, she feared it had, most likely, not survived, and whatever both Ctesiphôns did together could be done no more.

She slept.

## XXX

SUNLIGHT WOKE HER in the morning, and she opened her eyes. She saw six choices where to go. It seemed clear whichever path she chose, the others should fade away and trap her with her choice. This was how men grew lost, how they met lingering deaths on the stairs or fast ones at the base. She dared not advance without solving the stairs. *You'd have loved this place, Professor.* She wished Vazhin could see ai Ctesiphôn. It was not sidereal, like the garden Aurillac, but it was magnificent.

She wasn't ready to wake up yet. She shut her eyes and let her mind drift.

Reflecting on Vazhin, she found her opinion of him had changed. When she'd studied under him, she'd worshiped him. Later she'd wrestled with her mother's contempt for him. Now, here in the vast stone wilderness of ai Ctesiphôn, she discovered she understood him as an adult, loved him for all his terrible flaws, as an adult.

She recognized some assumptions she'd inherited from him: that knowledge is its own reward, that study is the highest virtue, that ignorance carries no price. She saw these now for the beckoning song of scholarship, not false perhaps, but not the only truth.

Examining her fresh understanding, she tried out a harsh formulation: she told herself she saw an impotence to him, a perverse delight in chasing knowledge without getting anywhere. This too was neither true nor false, but both. What was good for a Vazhin was not good for a Claire.

She had tasks to complete – she always had: find her father, salve her mother's wounds, make her way home. Knowledge had a purpose for her that it did not have for him.

Looking back, she saw the contrast in their methods now. Vazhin extended knowledge through reason. And she? She'd tinkered the cosmos itself.

That last morning in Zanzibar, at the back of the crowd, she'd glimpsed her mother and Vazhin sitting together on the bench. Reconciled and speaking quietly. She summoned the strange scene again and studied their faces. They were anxious, but also – grieving.

What did it mean? She hadn't noticed it then. She couldn't comprehend it now.

She opened her eyes.

Here she faced another deadly maze. She scanned again the six choices. She wished she could share it with that man who treasured knowledge and ignorance alike, the man who did so much to raise her. *Oh Professor, it's true we both love reason. Just look at this spectacular place. A world scoured of pettiness. I think perhaps I'd like to live here, in the home of final things.*

She sat up on the landing. She was young and her organism resilient; she crossed her legs without aches and set her hands upon her recovered knees. She relaxed herself and breathed, and her eyes half-closed. Her lashes caught the sunlight and cast false rainbows on the calm gray of her irises, on her pupils, expanding and expanding.

The false rainbows twinkled before her gaze, lulled her. After some unnumbered time she came round with a start and shook her head to clear it.

Panting, she scanned the scene. It was midday in ai Ctesiphôn, and she still had a sense it was full somehow, of active life and the ruined works of men. But she saw nothing more than sunlight on the stairs and the far stone wall. A world scoured of pettiness. *Is this what you were seeking, Papa, under the cold light of the galaxies?* She fingered the Florentine medallion Marcus had given her. They were cheap and common enough, but it touched her that he'd give her his. She half-smiled.

Her fingertips brushed the divided rectangle on one side, and the circle inscribed in the square on the other...

Something felt different about the circle.

She took off the medallion and looked at it. Her fingertips were right: the large raised outline of the circle had contracted to a tiny round dot, pressed against the raised outline of the square.

She lifted the medallion toward her eye, and as she moved it, the dot slid slightly. She tried rotating the medallion, and as she rotated it, the dot slid. Always touching the square, it moved against the rotation, remaining in the same place while the square turned around it.

Her heart knocked against her breast and she sat and considered the medallion. She turned it round and round. She turned it over. She searched the divided rectangle for changes. She tossed it gently hand to hand, till she spooked herself, thinking it might slip and go flying over the edge of the landing. She put it back on. When it touched her flesh again, she felt a thrill of pleasure. Because it was his.

She settled her heart, and then her mind, and traveled inland. The garden of her passions was quiet and empty and she passed easily through it. She went around the temple of her soul. She came to the thousand blazing windows of the palace of her reason. She unlocked the door and entered it. She sat down at the clavichord and ran her scales, her long fingers tumbling over the keys. They moved exactly as Marcus's did when he was anxious. The sound of music filled her ear, and the sight of gears filled her eye, and she contemplated the staircases of ai Ctesiphôn. There was nothing more to her than this. She sat and played music and considered.

Her eye caught on the thirty-two clock on the wall. She had an intuition of an awful thing it hid from her. All she had to do to check was take it down and open up the back. But she couldn't bear to do it. She didn't think she'd ever riddle out ai Ctesiphôn, if she looked inside that clock right now. She stood and pushed the clavichord bench in and took leave of the palace of her reason, locking up behind her. The thousand blazing windows warmed her back, and she crossed the vast inland, passing between the bulrushes, returning to the world.

When she opened up her eyes, it was night again inside ai Ctesiphôn. One day, one night. How long before she solved it?

## XXX

IN HER DREAM that night, she smelled home: salmon sizzling in olive oil, coriander, fennel, dill. Her mother was cooking their catch, and Claire sat in the corner of the kitchen where she did her tinkering. She looked around the kitchen as if she were a stranger – as if she were an exile. Her eye roamed the tiles, the hanging utensils, the dried herbs, the scorched stone of the hearth. She saw now how humble it was. All needful things were in it, and nothing more. *Like Antonella's wooden house.*

Claire's mother was a weaver and an olive farmer, and she worked hard. She could have done anything she wanted, but that was what she chose. She came from a wealthy family; even her wild half-sister, the huntress Moonlight, was rich. Claire had an impression her mother renounced her wealth after the war, though she never talked about it. Whatever happened, she lived modestly by the time her youngest was born.

Claire sat in the corner of the kitchen where she did her tinkering. She had ai Ctesiphôn on the table in front of her. In her dream she understood it. It was a technology, but not a technology of doing, like a railroad train. It was a technology of being. The math was simple; it was merely astounding somebody had managed to build the math into matter. This maze would have been easy to solve for those raised with its technology. For an alien – nearly impossible.

The dreaming patricia took ai Ctesiphôn apart and checked her understanding, and found she understood the truth of it. She wanted to show it to her mother, so she called to her. Her mother ignored her. Dread seized Claire and she stood and shouted at

Reason's back. She found herself as angry as she'd been when her mother first told her about Vaẓhin in the war, as angry as ever a daughter got at her mother.

Finally her mother turned, and Claire saw her red eyes, swollen from weeping and fear. Her mother didn't look at her. She wiped her mighty hands on a dishcloth and eyed the dissected Ctesiphôn on the table. Then she addressed the whole room.

"Baby, I can't see you. I know where you are, but I can't see you in there. You're a clever girl and I can see you've solved the first puzzle. Watch out for yourself, the tower isn't what you think."

She stopped and blinked and got her voice back. When she spoke again, she spoke quietly.

"I wish I could touch you. I love you and I will be proud of you no matter what happens."

Claire grasped how very much danger she was in: her mother never bent her pride for any failure.

## XYX

THE QUEEN WAS waiting for him in the castle. Midnight stretched, as it does in war. There was going to be a lot more midnight before morning. Antonella was waiting for him in the castle.

She could tell from how he walked that something was not right between them. He didn't wish to slow, but she planted herself in his path, so he did. The look she caught by firelight scared her – not the anger in it, but the grief. "Good my lord..." she started, but she stopped. She waited, and his nostrils flared with his breathing. A cold wind gusted around him, as if he stood by an open door. But the wind was colder than the night, and there was no door. She spoke his name. He closed his eyes, then opened them.

He said, "Do you know who is the Crimson Knight?"

She thought over the question and his agitation. She turned white. She said, "He didn't tell me."

Ambrosius glared at her. His passions told him she was innocent, but his reason told him that her guilt was not impossible.

She glared at him as well. Her reason told her it was just for him to doubt her, but her passions burned with pain that he should even think it. Finally he made to speak, but before he could, she said, "All your wars and lovers, all my years alone, burying our children. Better you and Domenico and I had been three pairs of hungry frightened eyes, staring from a hedge. We'd have spent our lives together, as a family, instead of... this." As she spoke, the matronly tone of her voice rose into a hysterical register, but she gulped it down on the last word. The grief eclipsed the anger in Ambrosius's look; his queen turned and walked into the darkness of the castle. Midnight stretched and stretched. Claire was watching, and saw everything.

## XXX

BUT TIME INSIDE the tower was disjunct from time outside of it. What happened in the castle had not happened yet for Claire. When she woke it was morning. She remembered the smell of home, but not her mother in the kitchen. She took off the medallion and looked at it. She understood it now.

Both the symbols of Florence were pictures of ai Ctesiphôn.

The divided rectangle was a simple diagram of the tower itself. The only whole part of ai Ctesiphôn was the height of the entire tower. The staircases were fractions. They were an infinite sequence with a finite sum, equal to the height of the tower. The single correct path lay up rising staircases; each would be shorter than the one before, until the pilgrim reached the summit.

The circle inscribed in the square was a cross section of the tower. But now that she was inside the tower, it had become a compass. The large circle of their sun-god Pantokrator had contracted to a tiny symbol of the sun. The dot always lined up with the source of the sunlight. How to choose which rising staircase? *Go toward the sun.*

If a pilgrim took a wrong turn, he would never sum the height properly. He might reach a smaller height, or a larger height, or an infinite height. But he would be trapped in the tower forever, unable to reach its top.

## XYX

Claire's day of rest had restored her vigor. She lined herself up with the dot and found herself facing a long upward staircase. She started climbing right away, irretrievably abandoning the other five paths. She climbed without complaint.

By afternoon, her knees were crying again, and she pressed her knuckles in the aching base of her back. All thoughts left her head and she became nothing more than a thing that climbed. She completed the second staircase and began a third. She reached a colder region; the light dimmed and rain began to fall. Stairs blocked her view of the clouds. She ducked her head and went on climbing, careful of her footing. Darkness gathered and a wind kicked up and the rain turned to snow. But the snow didn't stick, melting on the faint warmth of the limestone.

Shivering, Claire lay down along a stair, a chasm at her head, a chasm at her foot, the embrace of stone to comfort her. She pressed the medallion to her breast with the palm of her hand and bared her teeth at heaven. Squinting, her gaze lost itself in the depth of the snow. The flakes spun slowly as they fell, white damp triangles and hexagons, and there were great hexagons and lesser ones, and smaller ones very tiny indeed. The daughter of the desert had never seen snow before, but this snow was much as she imagined snow must be. It landed in her eyelashes and she blinked and it melted. She wiped her cheeks. Ai Ctesiphôn was its own narrow world, alive but scarcely, like a patient who breathes shallowly and may never awaken.

The snow cleared, and she got up and climbed. She saw a long-shelled species of snail for a while, then it gave way to a smaller, rounder species. She wondered where the living things went when the stairs faded behind her. There were fewer mosses now, and what there were were denser and blacker. Most of the lichens up here were a dusty orange. She began to see a livid yellow fungus here and there, its broad thick shelves stacked one atop another, rippled and folding like hyperbolic time.

By evening she could scarcely bend her legs. She stopped for the night on the landing at the end of the third staircase. She sat down unsteadily. One leg at a time, she gripped herself around the thigh, massaging the cramps, satisfied at the feel of muscle. With a burst of laughter, loud in the empty tower, she deciphered how she saw at night inside ai Ctesiphôn: it was moonlight. She craned her neck, but the stairs above blocked her view of the moon. She licked trickling water from the walls and slept.

## XXX

THE KING OF Florence lay abed from midnight until morning, alternating sweats and shivers, his sheets coiled around him, his attendants waiting in the hallway terrified. Ambrosius lay first on his back, then on his front; now with one arm underneath his head, and now the other. Visions of the siege chased each other across the stage of his imagination, but no matter how the players danced, the castle could not win. As black night turned dull gray in the east, Ambrosius met sleep at last.

Some few hours later he woke. He swung his legs down from the bed. His rest had broadened his view of the field. Now he noted forces that he'd missed before: the people of the city, and the warrior nobles, due in another week. Was this hope? He shivered as a freezing wind passed over him, then stood.

An attendant heard him stirring and came in, saying, "My lord, the army of the Crimson Knight has been demanding to see you since sunup."

Ambrosius had meant to go out right away, but now he paused and said, "Bring me what to eat." And he ate slowly.

When he was good and full, he summoned the attendant back and said, "Find Lady Varo, send her to the west stair of the wall-walk."

He dressed and crossed the district, attendants trailing him. He sent one for the city horn. He sent another on ahead to order three pots of sand moved to the western wall. Lady Varo arrived at the wall-walk just as he did, making long strides in her blue gown, cheeks unpainted and red, one strand of hair escaping her wimple. She said, "My lord."

Ambrosius, hearty with daylight, said, "Livia!" and hugged her as he would a man. She recoiled, and he said softly, so that only she would hear, "Likely we will not survive this. But I have a fine thing to show you this morning."

She tilted her head at him, those sharp eyes penetrating.

He said, "The Crimson Knight isn't yours. He isn't mine. He is none of ours. Honor doesn't enter into this."

Her stiff shoulders softened, and her face lit. She said, "Show the scoundrel to me, Manfredi."

He explained to her what he intended on the wall. She was pleased no end at his plan. The attendant he'd sent for the horn came back. Knees protesting, Ambrosius led his party up the stair. It was a miserable gray day today, and cold wind ran its fingers over his skull beneath his thinning hair.

On the wall-walk, he looked down at the army of the Crimson Knight. They'd come out from underneath their boats and hides and milled about, waiting on orders. Then he looked farther over Florence: the city was quiet, and there were few pedestrians about. He told himself he scented apprehension. Above the murmur of the army, he heard a clop of hooves and rattling of heavy wheels on stone. A cart was moving up the empty Via Floribus. He knew the type; they delivered produce from the farms outside the city. This cart was headed for the army camped below in Primavera Circle. The king looked back down at the soldiers. They hadn't seen him yet. He roared:

"Barbarossa!"

Lady Varo gasped. She was delighted as a child. The men below looked up. Some of them were overawed, and others jeered and pointed. Each faction impressed the other as the one that had it right, and they dissolved back into an uncertain rabble.

"Barbarossa, show yourself!"

Ambrosius spotted motion a little down the way. Barbarossa emerged from the crowd, holding a sack. His livid red beard was neatly trimmed now, and his cheeks were smooth. Ambrosius had to hand it to him – at least he was trying to look the part. The third morax parted for their leader as he sauntered up Primavera Circle. He drew up opposite Ambrosius, but kept a little out of the way of insults such as stones and arrows.

He bellowed, "You have kept me waiting, Ambrosius! But I will have to wait only a little longer."

He reached in the sack and pulled out the head of a man. He held it up for them to see.

Lady Varo stiffened.

Ambrosius put a hand on her clenched fist. He breathed twice.

Barbarossa dropped the head in the street. It rolled once and was still.

Lady Varo was silent a moment, lips a thin hard line. Then she said, "He died with honor."

Ambrosius said, "He did." He'd seen it too – the dark slash of the ultima cicatrice marked Temet's gray cheek.

Barbarossa shouted up the wall, "I'll have the crown of you!"

Ambroius shouted back, "By what right?"

"Your debt to Constantine –"

Ambrosius sneered, "A debt-collector king!"

Barbarossa said, "– and your woman's peace with Genova."

The Redheads cheered. Ambrosius comprehended what Barbarossa was saying. Ice shot through his heart.

*I dare not let him defeat me. If he prevails, it's war again, war forever.*

He tried a different approach. "You think you can put on a crown and Florence will follow you to war?"

Barbarossa said, "The crown's not for my head. Antonio will

wear it. The brother of your so-wise queen; surely he's not less than she. They are one blood, Manfredi Ambrosius! If she's fit to rule mighty Florence, he's fit just the same."

That was troublingly workable. Cleon made all the plans, but this didn't feel like Cleon. When had Barbarossa turned into a clever schemer? Ambrosius scanned up the street and saw Antonio, pale and sheepish, working up the good face of defiance. No, Cleon wouldn't do such a thing to him. Simple, pretty Antonio. How had Barbarossa tangled him up in this?

Barbarossa spoke again.

"What do you say, Ambrosius? Will you stand aside?"

Ambrosius turned to Lady Varo and said, "Livia, would you like to give the order?"

She nodded.

He said, "My dear, go right ahead."

She curled forward like a bird of prey and loudly hawked up a mouth of phlegm.

## XXX

BARBAROSSA ROARED A roar preceding language. With wit and daring he was going to defeat this awful man, but still he'd never get respect from him. He couldn't even be bothered to spit on him, he was having a woman do it. Barbarossa's cheeks flamed, and he hated himself. His vision went crimson and a din filled his head, like a thousand shouting men, so that he missed the giant hissing sound above. But he felt his army turn and duck, and looking up, he saw –

Three glowing masses gusting down, thinning on the wind to dim red curtains, flaring wide as they fell from the royal district onto Primavera Circle.

The woman wasn't only spitting on them. The rude sound was an order. They had sand. Barbarossa knew sand. Pots of sand were kept heated in forges fed by bellows, like the forges smiths use, till the sand glowed red. Ambrosius had three teams working metal rods to tip three pots.

The blazing sand streamed down toward him and his men. He flinched away, as they had –

Grains struck his bare head, sizzling in his hair, needling his scalp. Grains stuck between his breastplate and his skin, digging themselves into his flesh. Grains burned his forearms and his hands.

– but he flinched after his men did, flinched too late –

One grain struck him in the eye, and he swiped at it in a panic. He shut his eye against the shrieking pain, then opened it again; his vision blurred, and tears flowed down his cheek.

Truth be told, this attack aimed mainly at humiliation. The sand was not dumped from a short height on a windless day, a deadly load for men grouped at the wall; it was scattered on the wind from high above, to harrass whoso it touched. The grains stung and burned and refused to brush away, but they were tiny and cooled quickly. The men stamped and brayed like angry beasts, swatting at their burning clothes. The eye of Barbarossa wept, and his heart turned black with fury.

When the third morax had settled, they heard Ambrosius shouting down at them. He said, "For shame, third morax! Who is your king? What is your nation? Where is your god? For shame, betrayer men! You should know better than to follow this dog, this wretched, wounded dog that no like dog would make his company with. What do your fathers say? What does Florence say? For shame!"

Then he turned and vanished from the wall-walk. The specter-woman of the castle went with him. Weeping Barbarossa bristled that the king spoke to his men around him, tried to turn them from him. He jabbed his aide in the arm and said – "Mine eye is wounded. Get me ribbons, get me cloths, fetch me a physician."

The man went. Barbarossa found Antonio and laid a hand on the pretender's arm. It trembled. Barbarossa made to speak, but a series of notes cut him short, blasting from the city horn. The cousins looked up at the wall-walk, frowning. Stout-hearted Barbarossa wished that he'd sat longer, studying the city codes. It wouldn't have mattered if he had; the king was using parts of the code known only to a tiny circle.

## XXX

ONE MAN OF bronze and blood, another one of paper and committees, and a third one of baskets and carts. Here were King Ambrosius and Mayor Nederick Frederick and Beno Thersites. The king's horn summoned the mayor and instructed him to bring the king of the costermongers. It was daytime, but so dark their faces swam in a sea of dimness, and they could scarcely read one another. They huddled together outside the postern. The little gate was concealed by vines and brickwork and obscured in perpetual gloom. It was halfway down the mucky narrow lane between the royal district wall and the taller, thicker wall of Florence city. All castles have other ways out, and the postern was one of the hidden exits of this castle. Usually the racket at Traitor's Gate, just up the way, echoed down the nameless lane. But today the gate was shut, and quiet like the city. The men conferred in low voices, underneath the nose of Barbarossa. It was cold in the lane, but a wind colder still kept troubling them, so that they looked around for it, as if the wind were a man.

Nederick Frederick had to try: "You won't use this very lane to escape?"

King Ambrosius said, "I might as well surrender. A king without honor is no king."

He turned to Thersites. "Deliveries for the city: fruits and vegetables, grain and meat, beer. What should Florence expect?"

Thersites hesitated, and the king said, "Speak, man."

Thersites said, "The last of the carts rolled in this morning, and the Crimson Knight seized them for his pirates. He didn't pay. Between that and forest brigands, word will go out that Florence city is a risky market. The farmers and the great estates will redirect their goods to peaceful cities north and west. We're top of their lists, but we can be replaced."

In the dim lane, Ambrosius turned to Nederick Frederick.

"If Thersites is correct, how long before the city's belly starts to rumble?"

Nederick Frederick considered it. He said, "There's no way to move grain from the royal granary?"

Ambrosius said, "If you can riddle how to sneak it past the siege, it's yours. How much have they got at the Epicondyle granary?"

Nederick Frederick said, "You should have worried about that before you made Reburrus cook Antivola."

Even in the dimness, they could see Ambrosius wince. He muttered, "A pricey meal."

Nederick Frederick snorted. The king repeated, "How long?"

The mayor sighed. "Four days, maybe five."

Ambrosius sucked air sharply in between his teeth. "And if Barbarossa manages to steal what-all he can, how long can he feed his men?"

The mayor hung his head. Ambrosius said, "Out with it."

Nederick Frederick said, "Perhaps a month."

Ambrosius let out a breath like a death-rattle. "Ah, then we are lost."

Thersites said, "How lost? The royal district has food to last a season."

Ambrosius said, "What matter I? I measure my resistance by the hunger of the Florentines. Either way is ruin – if he prevails, he chases war; and if I hold out, the city starves. Could I bear to rule an empty city, king of none but smoke and crows?"

He turned sharply to Thersites and said, "I couldn't bear it."

Thersites recoiled as if accused. He said, "I didn't say –"

Ambrosius said, "I know you fought beside my father. I know my brother cruelly wronged you, before the disaster at Ēnu Šarr-im. You were right, and he was wrong. Three thousand Florentines threw their lives away, storming that cursed fort, instead of listening to you."

Thersites didn't answer. After a moment, Ambrosius saw the costermonger's shoulders were shaking.

He gently said, "Was Barbarossa there?"

Thersites collected himself and stood straight. He cleared his throat and said, "No, that was before his time. I don't think he ever knew your brother." His voice was terribly sad. He turned away to face the vines and bricks.

Ambrosius spoke to his back. He said, "I am not my brother. I am not my father. The mayor brought you here today because I wrote your name in the secret horn-codes of the city, as among the first rank of Florence's protectors. I know you, Tiresias. I have known you from the start. Let any man love Florence and that man shall be my brother."

He held out his hand. He made sure his sleeve rustled. The ugly costermonger heard it and turned.

Thersites said, "My name is Thersites."

Ambrosius said, "Thersites."

Thersites doubtfully held out his hand. They clasped hands, and a long time passed, there in the sea of gloom, until Nederick Frederick indelicately remarked, "So what's the plan, King?"

Ambrosius dropped his hand and said, "Wait and do nothing."

Nederick Frederick skeptically repeated, "Wait and do nothing."

Ambrosius said, "Barbarossa isn't ready to make his assault, because the fool didn't plan for a siege. While he's scrambling, the warrior nobles might relieve me. Claire and the tower might do something fancy. The city might cast him out. All sorts of things could happen. As long as I'm in here and he's out there and the

Florentines have a loaf in the cupboard, there's hope. We wait and do nothing."

## XXX

ON THE MORNING of the fourth day, she reached the region of cloud. A cold damp swathed her and the stairs alike. The only thing she saw was a little stretch of the staircase she climbed, emerging from a murky gloom below and vanishing in a bright vagueness above. Every sound was hushed. Beads of water formed on her hair. She went on climbing, head down. It was a little while before she realized her footfalls splashed a little – the vapor wet the stairs. She looked up and met a black stare.

She yelped and even as she slipped, she realized it was a skull she'd seen. She fell and her ribs thumped the sharp edge of a stair. Slick with damp, she slid down it, and found herself bumping down one step then another. A stair edge struck her jaw and stars sparked in her eyes. Terror emptied her. She was bumping down and skidding right, toward an edge.

She felt her feet clear nothingness, and then her ankles. Reason screaming, she clenched her entire body. Rigid as a board, her body turned and ceased to slide. Now she rolled down one step, legs edging out over the drop. Her motion slowed but she kept rolling. She fell another step. When she faced down again she flung her arms above her and grasped, grasped anything – one hand on a stair-edge, another on a scaly patch of lichen. Each one damp, but dry enough to catch on her palms, so much rougher since she'd come to Florence. The tendons rose from her long white hands.

She held. She stopped.

She stayed motionless where she was. The merest mistake would murder her. The muscles swelled and warmed in her arms. Her legs up to the thigh hung over the abyss. Her momentum was gone and just over half her weight rested on the stair. She had a margin to calm herself and think this through.

As her heart slowed, she became aware of a tingling on the fronts of her legs. She could hold herself in place but she couldn't pull herself forward. She carefully began to swing her left leg left, so as to get it to a stair. The tingling ran up and down her legs, thigh to knee, knee to shin, shin to ankle to toe. It was as if the abyss tugged her legs, and the tugging were a delicious heaviness. She slowly swung her leg around and felt her gown was up around her hips. She spread her bare sex over the abyss and the tingling filled it. She felt deranged with the intensity of the pleasure, braced as she was against the verge of death.

Slowly, slowly, she bent her left leg. The bottom of her sandal brushed onto a stair. She rested there, cheek on limestone, biceps jumping, naked over the deep. The madness of her pleasure ebbed. She felt her bladder full, whatever she hadn't sweated out from three days' fresh drinking water. Laughing in the muffled silence of ai Ctesiphôn, she pissed into the fearful drop.

When she was done she calmed herself again. By foot and hands she dragged herself forward, and finally restored herself to steady stone. She tore the lichen loose and wiped herself. She tugged her gown back into place and straightened it. A fit of trembling came over her, and she hid in the center of the stair, eyes shut, clenching and unclenching her fists.

Finally she turned herself over and began to climb again. She climbed like an animal, using hands and feet alike. She spared a thought for the skeleton as she reached it again, grunting as she passed, and kicked the skull. Its rolling made a hollow sound until it fell.

Presently she broke through the cloud into a cold bright region of the tower. She saw no more bones. Shivering, she stood and wrapped her arms around herself and went on climbing. She walked through puffs of her freezing breath. The staircases were rapidly declining in length, and she knew she was near the end. Soon she was climbing small numbers of steps between each landing, and then she could see each landing from the one below, and finally the staircases began to fold into strange flat shapes. It was as if she witnessed the Drunkard's Excuse:

*A drunkard fails to come home one night. He turns up in the morning, unshaven and hungover, and his wife berates him. "But dearheart," he exclaims, "This is how it was – I meant to come home last night, I did. First I walked half the distance from the pub to the house. Then I walked half the remaining distance. Then I walked half the remaining distance. And another half again. By then I was on the doorstep, the doorstep of our own house!" His wife says, "So why didn't you come in?" He says, "I kept walking half the remaining distance, see, but I never quite got all the way there, because there was still half the remaining distance to go. Finally I got tired and went to sleep, snoring right here on the doorstep. Didn't you hear me?"*

The story doesn't say whether this excuse mollified the drunkard's wife. At any rate, Claire came to a frost-rimed zone where the stairs collapsed into weird folds that made her dizzy to look at. So she stepped over the entire mess, into the summit of ai Ctesiphôn.

The first thing she saw was Ælius Pellucidus. She had been numbed by her journey, but the sight of him awakened her. She blurted, in a mix of sorrow and awe, "O you marvelous man!"

# 46

## THE CASTLE AT MIDNIGHT

THE ARMY OF the Crimson Knight had lost the advantage of surprise, and they didn't bother to conceal their business from the castle. They started building siege towers in Primavera Circle. The king's archers set them on fire, and the tower builders put out the fires and kept up their work. They built faster than the archers could destroy.

In high spirits, the Redheads caroused and sang war songs after sunset. Keeping the burghers awake combined nicely with the spiking prices on Serapetine Hill to turn the city against the Crimson Knight. Barbarossa was obliged to empty out the neighborhood around the royal district and block up all the streets with planks and stones.

On the fourth day, the warrior nobles began entering the city. Ambrosius got word from the watchers on the wall, and climbed up to see for himself. There were their banners, there were their handsome horses and guards. Ambrosius watched messengers of the Crimson Knight hurry up the Via Floribus to meet the visitors. The processions stopped. They made conference. While they spoke, Ambrosius sought out the banners of Valerius Corvus and the venerable Decius Mus. He found them – his old friends had come. The conference ended and the messengers returned. Ambrosius felt his bowel turn heavy and his fingers grow numb.

The warrior nobles took up stations on the far sides of Barbarossa's barricades. They weren't declaring for Ambrosius. They weren't declaring for Barbarossa. They would wait and see.

*Can you despise me so much?*

*Can you crave the war's return?*

He wished he had that ridiculous red sword to wave in their faces. With a heavy heart, he turned and descended from the wall-walk. The troubles of the last few days crashed down upon him now, and his nervy sensitivity seized him. He felt very persecuted and alone.

The nobles he'd put such work into corralling for the Family Dinner scattered now upon an open field. Where was his own morax? Letting themselves be held in a yard, like a feckless brood of chickens. Where were the Florentines? Hiding in their houses, thinking evil thoughts.

Where was Reburrus? Sulking in his temple, all because he and his double couldn't take an order. Where was Claire? Adventuring around that evil tower. Where was Antonella? In her own tower, pouting. *Have I done her wrong?* Of course he had, but he was the one alone. *Have I done them all wrong?*

Afternoon was drawing on toward evening as the lowly king crossed the northwest ward, between the granary and Golden Gate. Bitsy Boots was out playing. When he saw his father, he stood and ran toward him. The king squatted and swept up the boy in his arms and spun him around. How heavy he was getting! Ambrosius held him and felt his warmth and smelled his little boy smell. Bitsy Boots whispered in his ear, "King Papa, are we to die?" Ambrosius squeezed him and whispered back, "I've gotten out of worse." It was a lie, but it isn't right to let a child be frightened, and he felt the boy's fear relax. He set him down and Bitsy Boots ran off to his toys.

As soon as he was gone, his warmth fled the king as well. Ambrosius steadied his limbs against the twitches of his nerves. He entered the castle, heading for the kitchen to grab a handful of nuts, a handful of raisins, some cold meat, anything. He heard a high, muffled sound, and as he walked, it grew clearer. It was a heartbreaking forsaken sound. Somewhere in the castle, Lady Varo was wailing a dirge.

Ambrosius hurried down a hall, casting long shadows. His eye fell on a bright spot in the hall. Up ahead, on the left, there was an open doorway down into a cellar. The stairs curved, and a rushlight burned just past the curve, so that it was unseen, but its glow lit up the stairs and wall.

The king felt this light summoning him. He slowed and approached the door and looked through it. The stone walls inside were slick with damp, and little trickles ran down them. The hidden rushlight glowed yellow on the suppurating stone. In the eye of the king, there was something hideous to this especial shade of yellow. It seemed to him the color of death itself.

He stood transfixed in the hall and watched trickles gather, swell, and roll down the damp staircase wall. His ear was full of a song of unbearable grief. He nearly turned himself inside-out with horror, but the longer he stared and listened, the less the horror, and the more the terror. He felt death scraping out his guts. He remembered the superstitions of the country people, of the birds that peck away a dead man's memories. These monstrous yellow trickles were dissolving the wall, and they were dissolving him. His eyes bulged in his head and his breath stopped in his throat.

He stood, and stood, and could not move from where he stood.

## XXX

THE REDHEADS KEPT up their shouting and singing till late in the night, laughing at the howling dogs and bitterly complaining

Florentines. There was an element of performance to it, and Marcus found it wearisome, like theater. Finally they got tired of their japes and went to sleep.

Marcus was on watch, but he found his gaze returning, again and again, to the unlit hulk of Serapetine Hill. Home, if he'd ever had one. Finally he heard soft footsteps: his replacement come to relieve him on this part of the chilly wall-walk. He was surprised to find it was Cornelius.

"How did you drag yourself up here, old man?"

Cornelius made a comic scowl at him in the moonlight.

"I was your youngest Stonebreaker, you rascal. I'm not so old even now."

"But Philo was ancient."

"He started older than I was, and time seemed to flow faster for him than for me."

"What was it like, Cornelius? A lifetime on the riverbank?"

Cornelius looked out over the city. He craned forward and looked down at the boats and hides concealing the Redheads. He said, "Those hides were in the warehouse too. Clever clever clever."

Marcus waited. Finally Cornelius said, "It wasn't the life I expected. I remember, I was so sure I would die in the war. And if I didn't? I suppose I expected I'd find a woman, raise crops, get me sons. The things men do.

"All men crave love, decanus. The amount and species of it varies, but if a man will not find love, then I think that he will die. I wanted the love of a man for a woman, but I couldn't have it. So I had the love of two men who are friends. We made a life together on the riverbank, Philo and I. You know we had a while in the middle there – it must have been years – where we got so angry at each other we didn't speak? Never more than a hundred paces apart, and we didn't speak for years. Philo got over it, but I wouldn't. So he learned to speak without words. Finally I couldn't help laughing any longer, and we patched things up."

Cornelius paused, and Marcus looked over and saw tears running down his grizzled cheeks into his beard.

"It was a strange life, but a good one."

## XXX

MIDNIGHT CAME AROUND again. The king lay in his bed alone, thinking disordered thoughts. They seemed like shadowed figures, all confused together, capering across the dark stage of his reason. His room as well was all confused to him. Its size and shape kept changing, and the darkened furniture wouldn't keep its place. Sometimes his eye was open, and he looked at the fluctuating room. Sometimes his eye was closed, and he looked at the shadowed figures of his thoughts. Sometimes he forgot if his eye were open, or closed, and couldn't tell if the jumble he beheld was inside or outside him. The bits of it began to move like foam upon a wave. It pulsed in time with the blood in his ears, that pounded like an army on the march.

He must have slept, because he suddenly awakened. Still midnight. His head was clear and he had before his reason one single question, Claire's question, *Do you have the heart to go on being king?* And finally he had his answer: *No.* No starving city, no factions with their swords and spears, no last assault upon the castle. Let the killing end, finally. Let this miserable tale end.

His solitude weighed lightly on him now. To lose the crown dwarfed all the rest; queen, prince, priest, patricia, nobles, army, people... now he set down the nation entire. He was light as a breeze in the spring, gusting over the hill, tousling the grass, carrying the smells of growing things and the laughter of children. Nothing bound him any longer but regret, and the regret had a dull edge.

*What good can I do for the Florentines?*

His calmed reason offered him one answer, and he left his bed and dressed. He fetched the city horn for himself and crossed the ward, disturbing some dozing sheep to mild baa's. Refreshed in spirit, he climbed the rampart. He had only one more call to climb it after this. When he gained the wall-walk, a watchman turned from his post. It was the impossibly old Stonebreaker. He called, "Ave Ambrosius," and Ambrosius answered, "Ad gloria Florentis." Ambrosius joined him at the rampart and they stood together, watching the dark city. In his wondrous clear mood, Ambrosius said, "Let me ask you something. Assume this Crimson Knight prevails. Assume he wishes to resume the war. Do you think the Florentines would follow him?"

The old man sniffed. He said, "I think they'd butcher him first."

Ambrosius said, "The Florentines are a great people. He'll figure it out or pay the price."

The Stonebreaker said nothing.

Ambrosius said, "I'm of a mind to surrender."

The man turned sharply. He blurted, "My king!"

Ambrosius stared levelly at him. He said, "Hear my reasoning. The warrior nobles have abandoned me. My army lies captive on the Campus Iucundum. I have you Thousand, but I do not wish to throw your lives away."

The Stonebreaker said, "You have your honor!"

Ambrosius grimaced. "I do have that. But I am the master of my honor. Let history spit on my name, if Florence be spared starvation."

The Stonebreaker said, "And your son?"

Ambrosius said, "He will survive. The tyrant will fall. One day Ambrosius will resume the throne."

The old man looked back out over the city. He whispered, "And the war with Genova..."

Ambrosius said, "We agree. Barbarossa may lead, but only his Redheads will follow."

Both of them were silent a while. Ambrosius said, "Old man, I think you understand me."

The Stonebreaker nodded.

The winter wind brushed Ambrosius's beard. He raised the city horn. Its cold metal scalded his cracked lips. He blew –

Three short: *Florence city*

Long-short: *the royal district calls*

Short-short-long: *the mayor*

The city seemed to him to murmur restlessly. He could almost see the third morax, waking in confusion where they camped below. A short time later, he saw what he was looking for: a candle in a pan turned a window opposite into a dim square of bronze. A familiar voice cried out to him, "My king! –" but he cut it off before it could go further. Barbarossa was listening.

Ambrosius croaked into the night - "O my mayor, Nederick Frederick, what is your job?"

The man in the window had heard the public horn-code for the mayor, not the secret one. Therefore he'd hurried to Primavera Circle, not the hidden postern. He'd chosen the evacuated tenement opposite and scrambled up it. Now he paused a long moment, parsing the king's question. When he understood, he spoke. He cried, "I am the mayor of Florence, and I look after the city of the Florentines." The king heard the sadness in his voice. Nederick Frederick understood Ambrosius's intentions.

The third morax listened. Barbarossa listened. The king nodded, satisfied with his mayor. The man came from poor people, but he was smart. Ambrosius croaked, "Is your first allegiance to me?"

The mayor quickly answered, "No, yours is my second." The king said, "To whom then is your first?" The mayor cried, "The Florentines! The Florentines!"

The city murmured. The heads of the soldiers rustled as they turned back and forth. Barbarossa could have taken Nederick Frederick by now. But still he listened.

The king croaked, "How do you care for the Florentines?" and Nederick Frederick answered with a list, starting with the city guard, continuing with the council, the courts – the budget, the granaries, the fire brigades, the hospitals, the street sweeps...

Thus they conversed, voices floating over the city like two unquiet ghosts, through the winter's night. This was Ambrosius's only chance to teach Barbarossa how to govern.

At the window of her tower, the queen understood what he was doing, and wept.

## XXX

PRUDENCE DICTATED NEDERICK Frederick absent himself from capture before full day. Perhaps not prudence so much as diplomacy: they weren't aiming to embarrass Barbarossa into rash behavior. Therefore the king conversed with the mayor till the sky was rosy in the east, then let him go. He climbed down from the wall-walk and aimed for the older castle. He brushed past those who wished to speak with him, because he did not wish to speak with them. He entered the great hall and trod over the ancient paving stones, past the cracked third buttress pier on the right, past the absent seventh piers, past the giant dusty tapestries. He made for the back, for the little wooden room that Antonella built, his only real home on Earth. Firelight glowed drowsily past the door where it was ajar. He pulled it open. The light from the crackling fire dazzled him, accustomed as his eyes had grown to dimness.

He entered into that dark shape of polished wood, with its low ceiling and its fireplace and rugs and portraits and chairs. His queen was waiting for him there, lying in a bed pressed up against the left wall. He went to her, and there was a youthful spark to their attraction. By means of dark glares and forceful advances, he pretended he still doubted where her loyalties lay, and by means of coquettish glances and suggestive smiles, she pretended she was part of the coup. In their fever of fatigue and loss, neither one was entirely pretending. He lay with her, and before they were done, he was bathed in sweat, and she was blushing like a girl. Then they slept, and never a word passed between them.

# XXX

THE DREARY LAYER of cloud cleared on an almost absurdly beautiful day. The sun lit up the sky, painting the dome of heaven a gemlike blue, gilding the edges of the scattering low clouds. The fine clear light coaxed color even from the drabbest heaps of leaves and rubbish in Florence. The air was cold but the city seemed suffused with hope, hope for everybody but the king.

When he and Antonella woke it was well on toward noon, and they washed and dressed and ate without hurry, knowing as they did they were halfway through the last day of their lives together. They didn't speak of Florence or of war or peace. They traded memories of the children they'd lost. No one but the two of them would remark again on the soft touch of this one's cheek, or that one's dimples when she smiled, or the beautiful gold hair of this one, who whimpered in his sleep. Therefore they celebrated their children, and laughed quietly, and wept silently, and hoped their little souls were watching over their parents, condemned for now to go on living.

When they got done, they flung the lees of their wine in the dying fire for a sacrifice, uttering a prayer to Pantokrator and another to Reialia. The cold breeze that haunted the king touched the room, but swiftly departed.

They went out to the colonnaded courtyard between the castles, where Claire had spoken with Aeneas. They sent for Prince Domenico, and while they waited, they enjoyed the sunlight on their skin, and played knucklebones and looked at the clouds. When the boy arrived, hanging on his nurse's hand, he found his parents in a garden glowing with life and color. He ran to them and they drew their last son into the circle of their love. The king said, "Domenico, I have a job for you and Queen Mama, and you must keep it secret, and be very brave." And he explained his plan to them. Antonella objected, but Ambrosius fell back on the power of the crown, and the queen relented, and showed the wisdom not to let it ruin their remaining hours. They spent a very happy afternoon together.

When it was almost sunset, Ambrosius sent them off with detailed instructions for how to prepare. For his part, he made his way among the Thousand till he found Marcus. When he found him, he led him to a place apart and had a profound conversation with him.

## XXX

EVENING, AND ANTONELLA had a problem. Bitsy Boots was refusing to walk.

She and the prince were far beneath the castle, at the west end of Exile's Tunnel. She had touched her king's cheek one last time, kissed him one last time. After so few years shared together, she'd looked one last time on his face in this world. Then he'd shut the hidden door behind them.

Exile's Tunnel ran east out of the city, to a place men and carriage waited during unrest. The waiting men didn't know what they were doing there. Nobody but the king and his family knew about the tunnel. They could walk the tunnel into exile and no man would know how or where they'd gone. In the hundred years since Ambrosius III had dug the tunnel, Antonella and Domenico were the first to use it.

Exile's Tunnel was square and the air in it was damp and still and Antonella's lamp lit the stone walls a grisly yellow. Beyond the light of her lamp, the tunnel shaded off to an impenetrable black. In fact, it was quite terrifying, and Bitsy Boots refused to walk down it.

Antonella set down her – well, her vagabond's bindle, like something Tacamo would carry – and said, "Sit with me." Back freezing against the wall, she cuddled Bitsy Boots and calmed him down, and reasoned with him, and they stood to go. He looked off into that hideous distance and went stiff again and wouldn't take a step.

Antonella said, "Are you thirsty?" and Bitsy Boots said, "I could have a sip," and she got out the little skin Ambrosius, who knew his son, had insisted she carry. She said, "I've got only wine. Are you prepared to drink a man's drink?" Glamorized, he nodded, and she let him drink the sweet honeyed wine as if it were water.

Not long after, he was asleep.

She slung the bindle over one shoulder. She lifted Domenico and settled him upright, with his head on her shoulder. She awkwardly squatted and picked up the lamp, holding it in a hand crooked away from her son. It hurt her wrist, but she could manage it.

She started down the tunnel. She and the boy cast shadows over the spill of light, and her lamp lit mostly the floor. She proceeded into the thick darkness nearly blind. It felt like the tunnel wanted to steal her breath away from her. *How far have I gone? Am I still beneath the royal district?*

Her arms ached and she had to stop and rest. She sat, away from the freezing wall, and settled Domenico in her lap. She looked at his face and ran her hand through his hair. He mumbled in his sleep and shifted. Abruptly he smiled, without opening his eyes. He looked like he had as a baby, when he'd first smiled.

*I can do this.*

She got up, settling everything in place. She walked. The fearful black consumed her, and she had no impression she was making progress. She had to stop again after a briefer effort than before. She was strong for a woman, but Domenico was a strapping eight years old, and she felt her arms going numb and jumpy.

A short rest and she went on. But she tired more swiftly, and her arms took longer to recover.

*I must do this.*

Twice more, and her thighs were burning and her back ached. Her arms felt like wet cloth and her grasp slipped and Bitsy Boots nearly fell. Antonella sank to her knees, then sat, and the floor was painfully cold beneath her. She looked back into the darkness behind, and ahead into the darkness ahead. She had no idea how much farther she had to go. She wept over her sleeping son.

She thought she heard a sound. She quenched her tears instantly and listened.

Yes, a sound, from ahead. Becoming more distinct as it approached. Footfalls clacking against the stone. Something walking.

Not two legs.

Not human.

Heart pounding, eyes straining against the blackness, she set her son down on the stone. She set the bindle down. She stood between Bitsy Boots and whatever lay ahead. She drew her short sword and raised it in her right hand and the lamp in her left.

The clacking advanced steadily.

She shouted, "Hallo! Who's there?"

It neither sped nor slowed.

She gasped with terror, sweeping the lamp back and forth, and there – *there* –

A point of light in the darkness. It bobbed and she couldn't place its nature or size or distance. It clacked patiently toward her.

It increased in brightness and took on a golden cast. But it was no longer a point. Rather, it was two.

Eyes.

Her lamp wavered. Her sword wavered. She shouted, "Name yourself!"

Gradually, a dark form resolved out of the nearer dimness. She gasped and gasped.

*Control yourself, Antonella. You'll faint dead away if you don't control yourself.*

Her entire body felt like thin ice, ready to shatter.

It padded out of the darkness: a great old wolf, over half her height and surely all her weight. He had brown fur and honey eyes and one white paw. He did not speed up as he approached. He did not slow. A cold wind accompanied him. A thrill of terror rooted the queen in place.

The wolf came near to her, but not so near that she could reach him with her sword. He looked steadily at her, then stretched and whined and bowed.

Antonella let her breath out with a cry. She squatted and set her sword down. The wolf watched her do it. Lamp held high, she approached the wolf. He waited for her in his bow. She bent and scratched him on the head, between his ears. He growled softly, then swiftly raised his head and licked her hand. The cold wind persisted by him. It didn't come from ahead or behind. It was simply present, like a man.

The wolf stood. Keeping his gaze on hers, he walked to sleeping Domenico and ducked his head and nosed him. Antonella suddenly understood. She lifted the boy and settled him on the back of the wolf. She draped his arms and legs around the wolf. The wolf waited patiently while she fetched a length of thin rope from her bindle and tied Domenico in place. The wolf's fur was thick and rough, and his belly soft and warm. When Antonella was done, she stood, and the wolf began to walk, back the way he'd come.

They walked a long time, the queen and her son, and the wolf and the cold wind. Possessed of an intuition, Antonella said, "It was not by chance I met Manfredi at Desiderio's."

The wolf turned at the sound of her speech, but comprehending she wasn't speaking to him, he returned his gaze to the black tunnel ahead.

"My father always took us there when we were young – me and my brother Antonio. He bought us milk and cakes and pointed out the castle to us, and told us that the Constantines must take it, someday. When we finished we'd sneak out the back door and play in the alleys, and he'd talk business with his peers. We own a quarter of the shop, our investment funded Desiderio. Thus it came to pass I met the king when he was but a prince, riding round outside the royal district, in Primavera Circle."

Speaking soothed her fear. She went on.

"My father had permission from old Ambrosius the Eighth. Not a promise, but the chance – if I could turn the boy's head, he was mine, and I his. That's how sad the royal purse is. My father sat me there and waited. I didn't know. He loved me and he thought the world of me, so he thought the handsome prince must feel the same. And he was right."

She smiled into the darkness.

"I suppose if I'd been a few years older I'd be the widow of Ælius Pellucidus. You're with him now, somehow, aren't you? You're here, but you're also there.

"You and Diophantus are walking around in a golden mist of love, but you have nothing in common. He's an alley rat and a warrior. You're something very much like a princess raised in a library. In a few years, when the mist clears, you'll find you don't really know each other. Listen to me, Claire. *It doesn't matter.*

"I was raised in a cruel house, taught that nothing is to be given away. I learned crafts and calculations. Manfredi was raised on a horse, hunting, fighting, leading men. He has the careless generosity of his kind.

"Our marriage is like a garden. When we began, it was a garden for the two of us, with each plant in its right place, and all things pleasing, and we walked in our garden in happiness with one another. Then life intruded, and the life of a king intrudes more than most. Each absence parched our garden. Each child we lost burnt some of it. Each of his women and their children tore plants from the living Earth. After the catastrophes that man and crown and life inflicted on our garden, Ambrosius and I would plant fresh plants in fresh soil. Our garden is not the same garden, nor so pleasing as it was. But it is still our garden. If we survive the perils of this hour, we will plant again. We will set it right."

Antonella was silent a while. The wolf clacked along beside her, Bitsy Boots fast asleep on his mighty back. She put her hand on the boy's head, felt him rising and falling with the pace of the beast.

"Living with Marcus will be more difficult than loving him. Tend your garden. That is all that matters."

The cold came closer to her, as if to embrace her. Then it left. It didn't blow away; it simply left. Antonella walked a great distance further, her hand on Domenico and Domenico on the wolf.

Finally, Antonella thought she saw a patch of brighter dimness ahead. She couldn't be sure. Sometimes she blinked and lost it. Other times she saw it and it seemed to grow. While she was squinting into it, she came to it: a wall lit by starlight. She was at the end of Exile's Tunnel.

## XXX

Clouds scudded up from the north in the evening, and the setting sun lit up their mountains and valleys, briefly revealing that catastrophically gigantic world that overlies our own. Then the sun fell behind a violet escarpment of cloud in the west, and bands of orange spread across the sky. They ripened into reds and crimsons, and the first stars showed in the clean dark overhead. The king had his attendants dress him in a fine robe and crown. Though these clothes lay heavy on him, he still felt light when he walked across the ward, as he'd felt at midnight, lighter even, unbound even from regret. As he climbed the stairs one last time to the ramparts, he thought of his wife and only son, escaping from this ruin.

He came up to the wall-walk. His eye fell on the waiting graviculae. He'd labored so to place them, and now he wouldn't use them. For the best. Let those still living, go on living. The cold wind that had troubled him all through this siege was constantly at hand now, so much colder than the day. He kept looking after it, as if it were a man; but he saw nothing.

He took up the city horn he'd left here in the morning, and blew loud blasts upon it, in public codes that even ill-schooled Barbarossa must understand:

Three short: *Florence city*

Long-short: *the royal district calls*

Five long: *Constantine*

He could have simply shouted down to Barbarossa, but he used the horn instead. Now the whole city watched the king, alone upon the royal district wall.

He looked into the west, at twilight falling on the Campus Iucundum, where some fraction of the Redheads kept his Wardogs penned up. He looked at the impenetrable wall of mighty Florence. He looked at the dark forest of steeples. Home. He watched the shadows deepen on the streets of the city, on the warrior nobles waiting. He looked down at the rest of the third morax, their torches blazing, filling Primavera Circle in their angry thousands.

Now he came forward from the crowd, one eye bandaged: the raging man, the Crimson Knight.

The king roared, "Barbarossa!"

Barbarossa roared back, "Ambrosius!"

The king said, "I –"

Then the light of the risen sun blinded him.

# 47

## COLD HEAVEN

SHE HAD EXPECTED to find him. She had expected to find him a dead skeleton, crumpled in his armor at the base of the withered oak. This was nothing to the majesty confronting her.

The room was of a yellowish white stone. It seemed large and sunlit, but she could not tell the extent of it. The oak filled it. It was the strangest oak she'd ever seen, its trunk was twenty little trunks or more, ruffled here and there with shelves of yellow mushroom. From this giant base shot mighty branches, which rose a little while then dipped, reaching, splitting, splitting, reaching, brushing ceiling walls and floor, till they filled the room with tangle, like the staircases below. Every branch of this enormous tree was bare but one, that grew thickly with green leaves, and now she looked, she saw they were flat leaves and needles both, she knew not how.

At the neck of this leafy branch, where it split from the trunk, there hung a naked man. He was crowned with a garland of leaves and needles, and his long blond hair fell forward and covered his face. It was the same fine honey-gold as the hair of his nephew Prince Domenico. His ribs swelled over his hollow belly, as if he had just breathed in. The fur below was brown. His feet were purplish-blue; his fingers very thin, and bloody at the ends. Blood had frozen where it trickled from a wound on his breast, and another on his flank, dark against his pale pale skin.

His hands were dotted with the smaller, rounder snails of the upper reaches. Dense black mosses furred the girdle of his hips; dusty orange lichens patched his ribs. Several folded shelves of yellow mushroom grew from off his flesh.

Notwithstanding its terrible palor, his body was young and lithe and strong. He seemed intensely beautiful to the patricia. Death made Ælius Pellucidus somehow *more*. Lustfully surveying his muscles and his fine hair and his sex, his wounds and all the living things that grew in him, she had a strange thought – *This is a complete man*.

All these things she perceived immediately, the brilliant patricia, then she groaned: she was somehow back in the world, and connected again to her palanquin. Therefore a wave of thunder rolled from her, and it gave her a cramp, sharp and gripping like a menstrual cramp, and she bent wincing with the pain. When the wave rolled past and she stood again, she registered the cold.

The summit of ai Ctesiphôn was cold, and not just cold, but mortally cold. The cold of the higher stairs dropped here to an intolerable lunar cold that stung the eyes and scoured the skin and cut the lungs. The air was very thin and the edges of Claire's vision darkened. Gingerly she turned the way she'd come, and found the entrance gone. Scanning through the branches of the giant oak, she saw no exit from this awful cell. She couldn't see around the mighty trunk, but she already knew: the window of the summit that had lit her entry into Florence – this window did not exist inside the tower.

Breathing lightly of the homicidal air, she padded through the brutal cold toward Ælius Pellucidus. She saw the rope he hung from was his shredded clothes. His Florentine medallion lay on his breast, the medallion he'd followed through the maze. His armor was piled below his foot, and with it the red sword, Sibyllam Cumis, its rosy metal stained at the tip with his own blood.

In her cold-dazed mind she pictured it: the quick-witted boy had found his way up to the summit of ai Ctesiphôn. Trapped inside, he'd seen no end but what he chose or what he didn't choose. Shivering, he'd tried to stab himself but his nerve had failed him. So he'd torn his clothes to strips and knotted them together. Then he'd hanged himself – but no, but no, *the garland, Claire*, how did he make a garland of green leaves and needles from a dead tree?

No, the reckless youth who stormed the tower was not the man who died here. She stared up toward that shadowed face; she touched his hard shin; she fought a mad impulse to climb him, to press every inch of her to every inch of him, to warm his sex against hers and coax a living child from his dead seed. The reckless youth became a man. When he met the tree, the oak tree of the kings of Florence, something passed between them, and he became more than he was. The tree offered him living sprigs, and he accepted them and wove himself a crown. He left the kingdom of the world to his brother, and chose this – what was this kingdom? He threw away his weapon and his armor, he shed his clothes and made a new garment from them, he sacrificed himself on the tree. The life of Ælius Pellucidus flowed into the branch he hung from and it bloomed; he bloomed; his death was living. He hung living from the dead tree, and the tree lived again where it touched him.

Tears welled in the eyes of the awed patricia. She blinked and they froze in her eyelashes. They rolled from her eyes and froze on her cheeks. Her teeth chattered terribly and she feared they would shatter. An agony of pain pierced her brow, and her blood throbbed against the cold. She turned her head, squinting in the splintered sunlight. Her gaze met a long sprig, growing from the mighty bowing branch beside her.

*Was it always there?*

A world scoured of pettiness; the home of final things.

She reached, as if compelled, for the sprig. She picked a little bit of it, and turned it over and over before her icy eyes. Its green leaves were not lobed like the other leaves, nor were they needles; they were ellipses, pointed at the ends. Shaking, she stared at it. *Am I to do what he did? Tear my gown until my lovely fingertips are bloody, then hang myself?* She looked up at the naked branch, dead but for the sprig. *Am I of your blood, O Tree?* Her gown glowed red. The tree beckoned her toward some insight, some insight –

*No! This is not my task, this is not my path, I will not walk it, I will not hang, no!*

Her organism rebelled, and she rebelled. She was not a king of Florence, the tree was no blood of hers.

*I am the last daughter Reason bore; I rose from Zanzibar and to Zanzibar I must return.*

But even as she thought it, she recognized the Florentines were wrong: this tree was not theirs, it was overwhelmingly more. She slipped the sprig-end in her white gown and turned her back on what the branch offered.

Resolving to escape ai Ctesiphôn, she took stock of her situation. She could not survive this cold. If she failed to find an exit, she would freeze. She'd stand there, a stony pillar of a woman, until somebody found her and retrieved her. She'd stand there forever.

The agony of cold was unstitching her, but she dreaded its replacement. Here it was coming – here it came – yes, the trembling and the pain washed back out to sea, and in their place: warm quiet. She'd read about the fearful warm embrace of fatal cold. A soft grogginess filled her head, and she wished nothing more than to curl up at the foot of Ælius Pellucidus and sleep. The cold was trying to seduce her with its comfort, tender and deep. Her reason slowed, her eyelids fluttered. She stood still, staring dully at nothing.

A tiny weightless image of Ælius Pellucidus danced before her eyes. He came into the summit of ai Ctesiphôn, the hotblooded youth who beat up lonely Beno Tiresias. So puffed up with his beauty, so pleased he'd solved the stairs. Now he found himself trapped here with the oak tree and the murderous cold. The sleepy patricia asked herself, *How long did all this take?* Sure he had warmer garments than did she, and his frame was girt about with insulating muscle. But no mortal could survive this place for long. The quaking would have shook him from the start. In a minute he'd have understood it was the end of everything for him – the end of everything he had and was before. *How long from a spoiled peacock to a priest, nearly a god?* Only minutes, it took only minutes. He saw, he understood, he acted. The life of Ælius Pellucidus was transformed and redeemed in its last five minutes.

*I will smell the sea again. I will roast again beneath the western sun. When my fury is soothed, it will be the desert wind that soothes it. The striped ramparts will fill my eye; the embrace of my mother will fill my heart; the happy republic will fill my soul. I will return to Zanzibar.*

Five minutes. If the barbarian prince Ælius Pellucidus could save himself in five minutes, then she could as well. Standing softly in place, wrapped in her blanket of mock-warmth, she grabbed her slumping reason by the shoulders and shook it. Her reason blinked in its fatigue, as deep and silent as a winter's night. She shook it again, and it scanned the summit of ai Ctesiphôn. All mazes have a path.

*Think Claire!*

Her limbs were slow and heavy, but her senses sharpened. She felt little warmths touching her. At first she thought they were false warmths of the cold, but no – real warmth touched her. *There are warmths in here.* Little puffs of warm air saved the room from total cold. She squinted through the cold, through the nest of branches. She stared through freezing eyes at the air itself, because she saw a ripple in it, like air rising from the desert floor, in the savage heat of noon, outside the walls of Zanzibar. Yes, there was a ripple to it, but it was very strange, and she recognized it for the technology of those who built this tower. The ripples were straight lines up and down, shimmering here and there, and where they shimmered – little puffs of thick warm air, air of the world, swirled through the thin air of the summit. A grim hum filled the room. She only heard it now. *What Art made this thing?*

She stared into the straight lines, up and down. They winked into place, and stood a little while, and winked away again. *How is this room connected to the world?* It had no exit, yet she felt her bond to the palanquin, she felt the ceaseless thunder. *How am I in the world?* Then she saw it. Of course it had an exit. But the exit was not in space. *O you poor poor prince, you could not have known. If you'd known, would you have claimed your living crown?*

The girl tinkered time, and time slowed and unfolded for her. She teased time apart like the backbones of an animal, setting them before her in a row. She looked between them and saw: Florence. Ai Ctesiphôn had gaps, and in the gaps she saw all Florence passing by. In the fast present, the room was solid. But at the tiny scale of real time, it occurred at intervals. For each flash of its solid presence, it cycled through each point in Florence. This was an astonishing feat: expanding the spacelike dimension of time, up to the scale of a man, of a tower... Ai Ctesiphôn may as well have been the same size as the city. Astonished, Claire thought, *When I chased ai Ctesiphôn, I misunderstood the tower. It's not that it's always* somewhere, *it's that it's everywhere* sometimes. It wasn't like a normal tower. It didn't always exist.

A warm damp breeze of Florence blessed her skin and filled her aching lungs. The pain of cold returned as her body shook free from the sleep of freezing. She shivered in hyperbolic time, and shook her arms, and her hands and cheeks stung, but she warmed and lived and Florence shimmered in her eye like sunlight on a brook.

She watched the city passing and, by pressing on time's wheel, she persisted in the places that she wished to see. These scenes were stilled in the unfolded present: flames hanging in the air at

Shepherd's Gate – Barbarossa's soldiers underneath their hides – the queen, looking at the faded heroes on the tapestries, alone in the great hall – moonlight glowing in the colonnaded courtyard where she'd spoken with Aeneas. It was the very day she'd stepped into ai Ctesiphôn. In her four days in the tower, the world had passed from afternoon to night.

As she roamed the city, the smooth brow of the sky furrowed. The storm approached. It was that same horrendous storm that had stolen her from Zanzibar. It tracked the scent of time unfolding, and it smelled her now. She stood motionless inside ai Ctesiphôn, time laid out around her, staring up into the madness of the storm. It whirled without quite coalescing.

Then, as if disappointed, it dispersed.

She smiled, delighted and relieved. The storm couldn't see her inside the tower.

She went back to her search through Florence. It took a while but she found whom she sought: the king. He was up on the wall-walk, tying a rope through a hole in a stone. In the quiet of the night and hyperbolic time, the patricia looked at his unseeing face. She hadn't seen him since he'd spurned her, but he'd sent the quinces on, and she knew he wasn't angry any longer; nor was she. *It is you, my chosen lord. You weak, wise man. You are descended of great blood, and you are a credit to your blood.* She reached to caress his cheek. But her place on the wheel of time was not the same as his, and there was no reaching across the void that separated them. She knelt on the wall and studied him, his gray hair pale by moonlight, his forehead lined with care, his eyebrows nicked with scars. She marveled at the younger brother grown old, and the older brother young still, young forever, in his cold heaven, in the summit of ai Ctesiphôn.

Pressing on the wheel of time was a new skill for the patricia, and it took her some practice to accomplish it in normal time. She returned to the bright and terrifying cold, focusing her reason and her will, and soon she slipped her fingers through the cracks in time, spreading ai Ctesiphôn apart like curtains, roaming Florence as events unfolded there. She kept up with the king, and stood with him as he labored on the wall-walk. She heard his benediction. She saw him lose the queen. She saw his troubled sleep and the miserable days that followed. She resolved to enter in the world at the moment that would save him. It cost her terribly, in cold and thirst, but when she numbered all the powers in Florence, she had failed to count ai Ctesiphôn. It threw in with her, and she was loath to waste the boon it gave her when it showed its ancient door. Therefore she waited on the moment. When Ambrosius summoned Nederick Frederick, like the queen she knew the time was near. But she didn't know exactly when.

As evening was falling the next day, the king led Marcus to the place apart, and she learned exactly when it would be time.

Alone with Claire's savior and champion, Ambrosius said, "Tribune, I'm afraid I have to ask you to save Florence again."

Marcus said, "My lord, tell me."

"You must survive this day and get to the estate of Judge Salvatorio. The queen will meet you there. Go into hiding. Barbarossa intends war with Genova. Start rumors of a rebel army and paralyze him. Then raise it. Raise an army. Return to Florence and do to him as he's done to me. Unseat the usurper. Sit as regent till my boy is of an age to rule. Raise him up, Diophantus, and pass your virtues on to him."

Marcus's jaw dropped. He said, "But – but – how? What?... Why would you trust me?"

"Lawless Rhegium."

Silence.

"You know?"

Claire frowned. *Lawless Rhegium? Is that a person? A place?*

Ambrosius said, "When Tarquin menaced Claire, you tattled on him, Marcus. As soon as Cleon heard, he told me."

"Why didn't you seize me then?"

"My boy! It was only then that I relaxed – that I believed you truly didn't seek the throne."

Ambrosius stopped while Marcus pondered it. Claire saw a smile dancing around the edges of Marcus's lips. Then Ambrosius spoke again.

"So you'll understand why I trust you with the throne *pro tempore*."

"It would be such a burden to me."

The king crowed, "*I know!*"

Marcus's smile bloomed and he laughed. It tugged at Claire's heart, seeing the two of them in harmony.

*If we all live I will tell you both how sweet it was, so rich a happiness, to meet you and to know you.*

Then Marcus said, "Wait – why are you telling me this now?"

Ambrosius sobered up and said, "We may have us a little battle tonight. If it happens, you will lead the Thousand. Don't be too much the hero. As I said, I need you to live. For my part, I expect to die."

*Tonight.*

She returned her whole self to the freezing cell to fetch the one thing that she wished to take with her. But as she reached for it, she suffered an insight, and almost wished she hadn't. It was this: that the spacelike waves of time had overtones, like musical notes. Ai Ctesiphôn wasn't the size of Florence at all. Its faintest, highest overtones must brush the edges of the universe.

Zanzibar, be it never so far, was much closer than that.

It took her only a few moments, listening to the music of time, and she found her shining city, so far in the west, where the desert meets the sea. It was before morning in Zanzibar, the quietest hour of the night. A giant moon hung over the city. The sight of home filled her heart with a joy and ease so pure she could scarcely sustain it. Claire wandered Zanzibar: the moonlit streets, the marble halls, the soaring spires and bridges.

Finally she found her. Her mother was out on the strand, facing the uncharted sea. Her mass of gold-red hair gleamed beneath the moon. Claire could tell from her posture she was thinking not of her daughter, but of her husband, missing all these years. Claire stood behind her like a shadow.

Abruptly, Reason straightened and turned. Those eyes, the same gray as Claire's, brilliant even in the night, stared straight at Claire. She half-smiled.

"Oh Claire, you've done it."

And she held a hand out. Claire extended her own hand toward Reason. Her mother must already have known the art of pressing on the wheel of time. Effortlessly, she reached across the void. Reason took Claire's hand. But as soon as she touched her, she hissed, and sandwiched Claire's hand between both of hers and rubbed it vigorously.

"Baby, I hate to think of you so cold, inside that terrible machine."

"Can you see me?"

Her mother squinted at the place Claire was standing and said, "Something less than seeing, and more than having faith."

Claire stared into that beloved face, the overwhelming beauty and protection of it; into the face of home.

"Lean into the wheel, Claire. Once your center of gravity shifts, you'll step onto the sand, right here, with me."

Claire pressed her lips together and her chin dimpled like a child's. Ai Ctesiphôn had made it known to Claire she could only enter once. Zanzibar or Florence, she had to choose.

Her mother let go her hand. She wrapped her arms around herself. She said, "I see."

Choking, Claire said, "I'm going to have to go the long way around."

Reason shut her eyes.

Claire let go that high harmonic, the note of home in a sea of time, and came back into the summit of ai Ctesiphôn. The light dazzled her; the cold savaged her. She reached for the one thing she had meant to take and grasped it. Every trace of her mother's warmth fled. The cold of the object seared her hands, but she held fast to it. She knew the tower wished her to have it. It had two wishes for her, but she could only receive one. She chose this one. She was ready.

When the king climbed the ramparts in his finery, she climbed with him. She stood on the wall-walk with King Ambrosius, unseen, unheard, no more than a puff of freezing air. She pressed harder on the wheel of time, so hard as she might. Her mass shifted from the point she stood at, in ai Ctesiphôn, to the point she pressed upon. Thus she left the tower and came back into Florence.

# 48

## A MAN MAY KEEP WHAT HE CAN DEFEND

KING AMBROSIUS SQUINTED into the brilliant sun and shadowed his eyes with his hand. He was utterly disoriented. The sun had already set – what was this sun? As the edges of his vision cleared, he comprehended a splintered light at the summit of a giant blackness. His reason caught up with his eye, and he recognized ai Ctesiphôn.

He had never seen it so large. Half of Florence vanished underneath its foot. It swallowed most of the Via Floribus. It straddled the Liliana at all five bridges. Its near wall brushed the backs of the warrior nobles, and its far wall must have climbed Serapetine Hill. *My city! My city is gone!* The sky behind it was the violet of evening, and its bulk was utter darkness. But a terrible sun glared from the window in its summit, as if it were a larger sun, or closer to the Earth. Its rays were splintered by the oak, the withered little oak of Florence's puny kings. The sun shone on Ambrosius, where he stood on the wall-walk of the royal district, facing the army of the Crimson Knight.

The king stood and did nothing. He could think of nothing to do. He understood nothing. Nothing at hand made sense, measured against the tower of the city. It was only a gust of cold air that moved him, a vivid, hostile cold beyond endurance. He turned, still squinting, to its source, and saw a shining figure.

*This is the new world.*

It was a woman. Standing in the shaft of light, she seemed to him herself made from the light. She was a river of light, in the shape of a woman, ablaze in an ocean of light. Slowly, slowly, his streaming eyes picked details from the light. The woman wore a red gown – no, a white gown – tied about her hips and waist, beneath her breast and at her throat by threads and bands of gold, and her plaited hair was a gold almost white in the overflow of light upon her. In despite of her brilliance, she was not entirely of white and gold. Her eyes were a gray like storms and metals, and they looked to him, smiling tenderly.

King Ambrosius whispered, "Claire?"

She nodded and looked down, and he saw what she held. Needles of frost bloomed and counter-bloomed on its red blade.

He whispered, "Sibyllam Cumis?"

She looked back up to him. Clouds of freezing air poured off her. He saw every whirling mote in the brilliance.

He spoke softly, saying, "Where did you come from?"

She answered quietly, in a grating voice gone long unused. She said, "My lord, I never left your side." She swallowed around her cold dry throat. She glanced briefly toward the fearful tower, adding, "I was inside ai Ctesiphôn, and ai Ctesiphôn is everywhere." The king felt his legs go soft beneath him. Claire looked down at Barbarossa's army, standing all in awe. She looked across to the warrior nobles. She scanned the streets and windows of the city. She assured herself they saw her, every Florentine. Then she knelt. She held up the pale red sword and offered it to the king. Her throat had warmed and she spoke in her terrible strong voice. It was not loud, but it crackled the air around her. The silent city heard. She said, "My lord, I have climbed ai Ctesiphôn and sat beneath its tree. The tower chose me for its messenger. It returns to you the red sword of the Ambrosii."

On the Epicondyle, Reburrus saw and heard her put the lie to his account of travels in the tower. He covered his face with his wounded hands. But he also took the first step toward that plan his friend foresaw, just before the end, when it was too late to speak; the plan with a happy outcome.

In the street, noble Valerius Corvus turned to venerable Decius Mus. Each saw his thoughts writ on the face of his friend. They softly hurrah'd their force and turned, northwest, toward Shepherd's Gate.

Atop the royal district wall, Ambrosius heard the clatter of their horses. He turned and looked, but didn't parse it. He saw all Florence, spread below him, watching. He whispered to the kneeling patricia, "Why aren't they looking at the tower?" She smiled up at him and said, "It does not look the same to them." He said, "And the light?" She said, "The light is the same for all." She stretched her arms toward him, and he relented, and took the sword.

His arm hitched and he almost dropped the sword; the coldness of the hilt was nearly unbearable. But he recognized the feel of Sibyllam Cumis. The texture of its grip, its light weight, the point of its balance – they summoned his childhood. His heart filled with grief for Ælius Pellucidus. He brought the sword near his face. His breath melted the frost, so that droplets of water ran down its blade, as if it were crying. Almost without sound, he spoke to the sword, repeating a childhood formula, "What do you want?"

He remembered a voice, Ælius Pellucidus pretending to his child brother that the sword was speaking. Across a lifetime, his brother's voice whispered back to him, "I want to die."

The sun went out. Blinking around his tears, Ambrosius looked to the west. The tower was gone, the streets were intact, and there was only night, falling on Florence.

He murmured, "I was so tired of killing, Claire. I had hoped to surrender without a battle."

Claire asked him a second time, "Do you have the heart to go on being king?"

Ambrosius looked down at his city.

Beyond the Redheads and their barricades, the warrior nobles shifted on their horses. Restless, blood warming. He knew his species. For them, the miraculous return of Sibyllam Cumis was a sign from the gods.

He saw movement in the windows of the tenements. The Florentines were watching.

The peace with Genova was his. He had a right to enjoy the new world. He had a right to his name and his land and the fame of his deeds.

He shouted down to Primavera Circle, "You've seen what I saw! Will you put down your arms?"

Barbarossa howled, "I saw the foreign witch give back your own sword. Why would I yield?" His voice was higher-pitched, almost panicked. His army murmured around him.

From the windows of the tenements the reckless burghers chanted, "Hail Claire! Hail Claire! Ave Ambrosius! Ad gloria Florentis!" and they rained refuse down on the startled Redheads. All Claire's days selling fruit – all her days feeding the poor – the city had given its heart to the patricia.

Ambrosius grinned a ferocious grin. Suddenly he saw how to undo the man through his commoner's idea of honor.

Ambrosius filled his lungs and shouted, "As you will, you shave-cheeked upstart! I challenge you to single combat! Each man picks his arms and armor!"

There was a long pause below. Barbarossa clearly recognized how much the red sword excited the warrior nobles, how it had shifted the balance of interests. And the burghers were choosing the king over him and his loutish Redheads.

Barbarossa conferred with his commanders. They nodded, and he nodded, and Barbarossa yelled back up, "I demand the warrior nobles attend and witness!"

He'd want them there to witness it, to acclaim him king – or was it really to be Antonio?

Ambrosius shouted down, "I accept!"

Barbarossa yelled, "I will fight you if you can make your way to me! You have a thousand in there? Let them face a thousand of mine!"

Not as much the hothead as he played. Winning a single combat might prove his honor to the warrior nobles, but winning a contest of main force would teach them to fear the Crimson Knight.

And he damned well knew the Thousand, less those who had gone home with the peace, was about six hundred.

Ambrosius roared, "I accept!"

Barbarossa bellowed, "The warrior nobles to Primavera Circle, at Golden Gate! Witness battle for the throne!"

The third morax started clearing the barricades.

Ambrosius shouted, "I'm coming for you Barbarossa! Are you ready? Get ready, you wounded dog!"

He stalked to the back-side of the wall-walk and shouted down into the ward, "Diophantus, prepare the Thousand as you will!" Marcus looked up, seeing Claire direct, and the two of them looked at each other a moment. Then he shouted up, "Aye, my lord!" and trotted off. Ambrosius shifted his attention to his staff and called, "Fetch my battle-stuff!" A runner departed.

Ambrosius turned to Claire and said, "In case I don't come back, tell me quickly – you've seen Ælius Pellucidus?"

Claire said, "I have."

They heard clanking below, on each side of the royal district wall.

Ambrosius sadly asked, "Did he die a fool?"

She seemed unsure how to answer. Barbarossa shouted something; both of them ignored it. The king's armorer shouted, "Which shield?" The king called down, "Dirty Leonidas!" He looked back to Claire.

She said, "No, my lord. He is not dead at all."

Ambrosius said, "H-how? He lives?"

Claire quickly clarified, "No, no, he is not living either. He lives in the tree, and all things live in him. His life gives life to the tree. That tree – my lord, Florence had it wrong. The lost sword was a mark against you. But the withered tree is not. The tree is not the tree of kings."

Ambrosius cocked his head at her and stared. He said, "What is it then?"

Claire said, "It beckoned me, but I did not follow where it offered."

He repeated, intently, "What is the tree?"

She looked back at him and answered, "It is not yet time to say."

A thrill of awe ran down his back. *She was in the land of the gods.*

She said, "If you live a good long life, then when your time comes round, I will return to Florence, and blaze you a path to that holy tree."

Tears made his eyes bright. He knew he'd never climb the tower with the young patricia, but her offer stirred him to the marrow. Stealing moments he did not have, he cupped her cheek and studied her. In the blaze of light, she'd been more confident, more present than he'd ever seen her. Now she wasn't lit to brilliance, she looked thin and tired and shadowed by some unnamed grief. There was a dark bruise on her chin, and another on her breastbone. Her skin was cold like the skin of the dead. She looked up to him as his youngest daughter might have looked, if she'd lived.

He said, "I will never doubt you, Claire. If I fall, you must forget my name – if Barbarossa wins, pledge fealty to him. He brings the Constantines in train, and they will send you home. For now, get you to your room and tell the maids to fetch you up some hot soup and a bath. You're falling off your feet."

Then he let her go. She touched her cheek where his hand had been, then dropped her hand. She murmured, "What I've given up for you." He tilted his head, confused. She spoke solemnly to him.

"I will do the things you say, but not yet. I know you've sent the queen away, and I've heard a champion should have a lady cheer him in his combat. Will you let me stand for the wives and daughters of House Ambrosius?"

Ambrosius said, "If you stand for me, this may change how Barbarossa deals with you in victory."

She said, "With him or against him, I will make my way to Zanzibar. But it doesn't matter – he will lose, and you will win."

"If I let you stand, you bind yourself to House Ambrosius in kinship, love, and honor."

She took his great scarred hand in both her icy hands. She said, "My lord, I am your girl."

*If she is with me, who can defeat me?*

Movement behind Claire. Ambrosius shifted his gaze. He said, "Lady Varo, will you prepare her?"

Claire turned, startled. Lady Varo made a graceful bow: one leg back, one forward. A bend of the knees. Hand on breast, shoulders forward, head down. The bow of a woman of the warrior nobles.

Then she stood and said, "Absent the queen, the most fitting lady for the cause."

A tremor shook the exhausted girl.

Lady Varo went on, "But you look like a plucked chicken. Let's fix you up."

Claire extended a hand, and Lady Varo took her hand and held it. They looked at one another, then Lady Varo led her down the stairs. Claire kept one rigid hand locked on the stone railing.

Ambrosius turned from them and took a minute to breathe the two smells up here: the stink of Florence, his clean grassy district. Then he started down the stairs.

The sword of his family was warming in his hand, and his back fingers ringed it firmly now. It was a long one-handed sword, not remarkable except in its color and its shape and balance. His arm was short, his hand was weak, the last time that he held this precious sword. Now he was a man, and it was the right size for him, just the right size, as it was for all the men of House Ambrosius. Testing, he swung it as he walked, and recognized the path it cut across resisting air. It made his right arm into a long arm with two elbows, stiff or supple as need be, and beyond the last elbow sharp murder only.

At the foot of the stair, his dresser and his armorer and their men waited for him. Ambrosius held up the sword to hand it over. In the firelight he saw its tip still dripping – blood, fresh blood, newly melted. *My brother's blood, whose else could it be?* He kissed the tip of the sword. He tasted the metal and the salt.

*I take this for your blessing, Ælius Pellucidus. I pray we will meet again at the end.*

He handed the sword to his armorer. The armorer received it with reverence, setting it in place among the pieces that he'd brought. The dresser and his men removed the crown and robe. They undid the fancy lacework and removed the finely colored dresses. The cold night wind passed through the king's white underclothes, but the cold of it was not like the cold of Claire, and he scarcely noticed. The dresser and his men departed, hastening from the madness coming at the gate.

The armorer asked the king what armor he preferred, and the king answered, "Full metal." The armorer raised an eyebrow, but directed his men: they dressed Ambrosius in heavy infantry armor, of a style long abandoned. They only had it handy because the king had always shown a fascination with old arms. The armor was bronze from head to toe except the leather soles of the boots.

It was very heavy, and stifling inside, and one had to finish fighting quickly before collapsing from exhaustion. When they had the breastplate on, the armorer asked Ambrosius if he wanted the neck guard. Ambrosius considered. With it on, he could look neither up nor down. What need had he to look up and down on the level street? Better to survive a blow to the throat. He stretched his neck for the guard.

With each weight added, his heart rose. Antonella's wooden room was not his only home. He had one other. Now he was returning to it. He thought, *Constantine, you should have waited four summers till I ran out of money. This? This is what I love, this is what I was born to do.* With a resignation equal parts sweet and bitter, country miles from his wife and son, he thought, *I am coming home to war.*

He looked in the face of his armorer. The man was his own age and the son of a noble house. He'd been a horseman in the second morax, early in the king's reign, till a fall broke his leg and put an end to warring for him. He understood the battle-excitement writ on the king's face and smiled at him, indulgent and envious. He lifted to the king's left arm Dirty Leonidas, a battered round shield with a big spike in the middle. He slid the padded bronze armlet on the back up the king's forearm till it caught. Now the shield would only leave him with his arm. He offered to the king's right hand Sibyllam Cumis, and the king's right hand took it. With his own hands he lowered the bare domed helmet onto Ambrosius's head. King Ambrosius the Ninth of Florence became what he had always been, a man of bronze.

Sweltering, half-deaf, three-quarters blind, he watched the Thousand raise the crushing panel behind the gate. They were using it all wrong – or rather, they were using it their own way. Marcus must have planned and practiced this. His men set it up with the hinge vertical, opposite the middle of the gate. Arranged this way, it was a little taller than a man. Three ranks of men filed around the front of it. The rest remained behind. A fighting team in front and a pushing team in back. Marcus was going to form an arrow. Behind the panel, Ambrosius would walk protected to his contest. Such a shame this brilliant deserter would never get a chance to lead a real war.

Over the stink of metal and old sweat, he caught the scents of honeysuckles and of thunder. He turned. The beautiful patricia stood with him. She wore a jeweled breastplate and cape. She had fronds in her hands and flowers in her hair. Black ringed her eyes and her lips were blood red. Back straight, shoulders back, a posture that could not be learned, only bred. A champion's lady.

The lightness that had lifted him was vanished now. He felt packed with vital force. He felt so overfull of living he could scarce contain it in his organism. He nearly vibrated with it. He was not so war-drunk that he overrated his chances: likely he would die. But his death would be a death to earn the blessing of his father and his father's fathers. He felt them at his back. From the shining land of heroes, they whispered to him, *A man may keep what he can defend.* The gate groaned open. With joy in his heart, he went out to fight.

## XXX

*I AM THE tip of the arrow.*

While the gate slowly parted, Marcus rolled his shoulders and shook his ankles. He shifted his shield to test its weight. He judged the wobble of his spear. Raised his grip a little, then leveled it. He touched his elbow to the hilt of his sword. Locked shields with Taranto to his left and Brindisi to his right.

There they were, the Redheads. Hooting and stamping their feet. They saw his men but not his panel. They weren't quite clear on the shape of this fight. One blast of the city horn, from Cornelius at the far right: best he could do for him, let him play the spotter. The blast told him the gates were wide enough now.

"*ADVANCE!*"

The Thousand lumbered forward, only as fast as the massive panel allowed. As they advanced, the men behind the panel began to close it around the upright central hinge. It took on the shape of an arrowhead. The fighters in front let it push from behind, shaping their ranks to it. Two blasts of Cornelius's horn: *stop closing.*

The Redheads ran at them, hot with arrogance. The clash was furious. Shield shattered shield. Marcus snapped his spear off in their middle man. He reversed it and swung the lead-weighted butt. It smote the man behind, flying aside with him. He pulled his sword and stabbed through shield-gaps, again and again. His line held. Of course it did: the center of it was bronze. His men fought with their back to a wall.

His arrow walked forward, shoving Redheads aside, trampling those who fell. He took a savagely painful blow to the shin and a nasty clang on the side of his head. He walked forward.

Now the Redheads showed the weakness of arrogance: without immediate victory, they wilted. Pressed aside by his arrow, their lines wobbled. They tripped each other and got turned around. Finally they split apart and their front ranks tried to flee and got mixed up with their rear.

Almost without realizing it – certainly before he was ready to be done – Marcus found himself facing the Crimson Knight.

Their gazes held an instant. Barbarossa shouted, "*You!*" and lunged forward.

Marcus's shield was half-gone so he flung up his sword to turn aside the blow. But the blow landed a little short.

Both men stopped, startled.

Then Marcus grinned and said, "Enjoy your combat, one-eye."

He and his friends stepped aside.

Three blasts on the city horn: *release the hinge.*

## XXX

THE TWO HALVES of the crushing panel swung apart, opening a path between them. Ambrosius surveyed the disarray of battle, wounded men and fallen. Mostly Redheads. Men were backing up to make a square. A flash of motion showed him a plume half sheered off: Marcus slipping around to the side, to escape and survive as he'd been told. Behind the Redheads, warrior nobles, astride their fine horses. He couldn't look up to their faces, but a good king knows his crowd. He registered their amusement at his armor. He registered their awe at the fierce patricia.

There was Barbarossa.

The big man wore the same leather armor with the gold shapes painted on it that he'd sported in New Forest. It was a little tattered at the edges now, and the gold was duller. His helmet bared the middle of his face, showing his bandaged eye, his cheeks ruddy with rage. He carried a door-shaped shield that covered him shoulder to thigh, and his long sword.

*He's younger, his armor is lighter, and I have aged so much since the end of the war. He'll move much faster than I can. I pray you, Master Rabbit, bless my scheme.*

Barbarossa took one look at King Ambrosius in his full bronze suit and laughed: "Is that the king hiding in there? Is this the face of honor?"

Ambrosius rumbled, "Honor is shown to the honorable."

That dropped Barbarossa's face. Noticing Claire, he snarled, "And the witch."

Ambrosius said, "Claire of Zanzibar stands for the lady of House Ambrosius. Where is your lady?"

Barbarossa spat, "Who cares for a woman?"

A cold voice answered him, "The merit of a warrior noble is demonstrated in the quality of lady who stands for him."

Wry Ffidius, not joking at all. Barbarossa twisted, looking up to survey the mounted nobles. A row of stony men. Perhaps they were not pledged to the king, but they were far from being his. He thrust his chin out at them, and got nothing for it. He turned back to the king.

Ambrosius said, "Till one man dies, or submits, or is so overcome the other ends the fight."

"Agreed."

Ambrosius gestured to Claire and said, "Stand you safe aside." She nodded and moved back from the square, standing by the two giant Stonebreakers who followed Marcus around.

*Where is Antonio?* Ambrosius hadn't seen the pretender. He scanned the hushed crowd one last time, then let go the world beyond this little fighting-ground. There was nothing but to start.

Clanking in his bronze, Ambrosius paced his end of the square. The paving stones of Primavera Circle were smooth and flat and well-maintained. The soles of his boots gripped them handily. His mind was clear and his arms were fresh. His legs were weary from climbing up and down the wall-walk all day for a week. He tested the dance of his foot, and his foot danced for him, but he could tell it was fight-euphoria, and if the fight outlasted it, he'd have nothing left. *Will I die here, on the paving stones of Primavera Circle, right outside the castle gate?* Barbarossa paced across from him, shoulders tight, neck forward, stiff with rage.

Each man drifted in. Each extended his sword in front of him and checked his distance. Barbarossa wagged his head right and left. *That bandaged eye.* They paced again, but closer now. Ambrosius waited, and soon enough Barbarossa lunged. *Good, his passion overwhelms his reason.* Ambrosius dodged and parried, the two blades clashing. He felt the ring of Sybillam Cumis like music in his arm. He and Barbarossa reversed places in the square.

Then Ambrosius tested Barbarossa, leaping forward, sword high, cutting across and down. Barbarossa flung his shield up and blocked it. *He can defend.* The weight of the armor dragged Ambrosius past his attack. He caught himself and balanced and turned.

They went around and around, engaging with each pass. Barbarossa was faster but sloppier, wasting motion on showy swings. Ambrosius measured every step and cut.

Barbarossa wore out his shield arm, blocking Ambrosius's vicious attacks. Ambrosius preserved his own shield arm, absorbing most of Barbarossa's wide blows with his bronze suit. He felt his ribs bruise, and his arms.

There was a sound of horse and many foot, heavy enough to intrude upon the fever-dream of combat. Barbarossa paused and looked around. Ambrosius scanned as well. He couldn't see beyond the Thousand and Redheads packed tight on all sides.

*Set it aside, Manfredi. We'll solve it later.*

He turned his half-blind gaze to Barbarossa. Barbarossa gave up riddling the sound as well. He squinted at Ambrosius, sizing him up and plotting his aim. The Crimson Knight advanced with a stomp and suddenly swung around and up. Ambrosius raised his shield, but not as fast as Barbarossa swung. He was aiming for Ambrosius's head. His sense of distance was off: he struck him in the throat.

The neck guard stopped it with a clang. Ambrosius's jaw snapped shut and he felt a molar crack. He stumbled back against his line of soldiers. Convulsed with coughs, he steadied himself, holding his sword out to ward off Barbarossa. When his breath calmed, he advanced a step and stood impassively, a faceless wall of bronze, watching Barbarossa, making Barbarossa work.

Barbarossa growled and paced diagonally, first one way, then the other, seeking an opening. Ambrosius saw the moment he recognized he couldn't win with cuts. It had to be a stab. But it would take a mighty blow to stab through bronze. A downward blow with his whole weight. He had to knock the king down first. Barbarossa was smart, but not subtle. Ambrosius watched him reason it through. *He's right. If he can knock me down, my own bronze will hold me down. I'll be his to finish as he likes.*

Barbarossa changed the way he fought. Instead of shying out of range, he started looking to advance and hold. He was aiming for a shoving match.

He circled one way toward the king, and the king circled the other way. Ambrosius made little testing swings with his sword, but Barbarossa slowly closed the distance. A couple times Barbarossa saw an opening and lunged, but Ambrosius dodged away, or bounced him back with the edge of his tilted shield.

Barbarossa slowed, exhausted, considering his next move. But it was much worse for Ambrosius. Throbbing tooth. Sweat stinging the eyes. Raw lungs, aching legs. One ankle ready to go. *I can't complete this. I don't have enough left.* In a battle years before, he'd fallen on his hands, so hard his collarbone had detached from his breastbone. He'd felt a hideous tearing in his breast. Now he felt it again; he felt his spirit start to detach from his organism. Dizzy, he scanned the scene. Redheads, Thousand, horses, armor. A general clamor like a pack of angry dogs.

He spotted Claire but almost didn't recognize her. Her irises were ringed entirely in white. Her nose was raised in a furious snarl. Her mouth was wide and her teeth gleamed and he could see right down her throat. He realized it wasn't general clamor he was hearing. It was her terrible strong voice. She was cheering him, as she had pledged to do.

The agony of detachment fled and his spirit came back to him. Life filled his limbs. His bronze felt light. *I will fight this. I will win.*

He looked to Barbarossa. The unsubtle man was out of ideas. His tactic wasn't working and he had nothing else. Again they circled and again Barbarossa found an opening. He lunged, and this time –

– this time Ambrosius saw the angle he was waiting for. He set himself and leaned hard forward, so that their shields were face-to-face.

*Why do you think I lured you into a shoving match, Barbarossa?*

The big spike in the middle of his shield struck Barbarossa's shield.

*I've never fought a man who asked himself what the spike was for.*

The spike pierced Barbarossa's shield clean through and held it. Their shields were one.

Barbarossa didn't understand. With a grunt, Ambrosius wrenched his left arm up. So many blows he'd taken, keeping that arm rested. Now it easily overcame Barbarossa's exhausted shield arm.

Both shields rose. Instantly Ambrosius reached across with his supple long right arm, backhanding his sword as he moved. He carefully poked Barbarossa between the sections of his leather armor. A sharp bronze poke in the right armpit, as deep as a finger.

Barbarossa screamed and dropped his sword. Ambrosius dropped his shield arm, and the falling shields showed him Barbarossa's face, eye wide, flesh pale, lips distended and dripping drool. *You are young and fast, but I am old and wily.*

Ambrosius wrenched his shield left, and Barbarossa's shield flew off his arm. Barbarossa dropped into a crouch, leaning right and keening, wrapped around the hole in his armpit. It was a disabling wound, not a fatal one. Ambrosius stood crooked over him, left side weighed down with shields. The crowd went silent. Ambrosius spoke.

"You are overcome. I end the fight."

Barbarossa looked up at him, wobbly with pain, realizing Ambrosius wasn't going to honor him with death in battle, that he'd never planned to.

Ambrosius said, "One of my men come for the shields. Another take my helmet. A third my neck guard." Three came and did as he commanded. His scalp was slick with sweat, his face was dark with bruises, his ear was dulled with the echoes of clangs. He stood straight, the king of Florence.

He looked around the crowd. Redheads, Thousand, horses, armor. His eye settled on the beautiful patricia. Tears streaked her black eye-paint down her cheeks and she bounced up and down on her toes, as if she couldn't calm herself. He bowed his head to her, and she put trembling hands over her blood red lips.

Looking up, he scanned the faces of the warrior nobles. His kind: handsome, haughty, ancient of line, all the way back to the founding of Florence. To them he spoke next.

"You witnessed my fearful days, and did not raise a hand. I gave you cause, but not sufficient cause. For your perfidy to your king, you will henceforth pay a tenth part of the taxes you collect into the royal purse. I will be grateful to consult with you in spending it upon the interests of the state."

He spared a thought for their tenants. They'd just tax them more.

"This applies to the amount you taxed this year. Any greater taxes go to me eight-to-one."

If they had combined, they could have cut him down right where he stood. But there is a glamor to the man who just won his battle, and the king knew his crowd.

"The Family Dinner is canceled. You have not earned a seat at my table –"

He looked around for Corvus and Mus. *My friends, where have you gone?*

"– perhaps, in time, you will. Meanwhile, the war captives are nearly home from Genova. You will celebrate their return with your brother Florentines."

There was cheering from the tenement windows.

He squared his shoulders toward them all. He raised the red sword above his head.

He shouted, "Who is your king?"

Some of the burghers cheerfully shouted: "You are our king!"

"Who is your king?"

Now all of them, hollering: "You are our king!"

"Who is your king?"

The warrior nobles began cheering and shouting.

"You are our king!"

He brimmed with life, was overfull of life. Tonight he could do anything.

He shook the sword. He roared at his city – at his nation.

"I am Manfredi Ambrosius, Ninth of the House of Ambrosius! I am the Lion of Andamer and the Grief of Tyana! I was the prince of war and, by grace of the exile, I have brought you peace! I am your king!"

From the tenements: "Hail Ambrosius! Hail Ambrosius!"

Amid the noise, Ambrosius heard words from below. It was Barbarossa. The king dropped the red sword to his side. Silence fell.

Barbarossa was saying, "And I?"

Ambrosius said, "You will face Judge Salvatorio, and he will try you, and you will be executed for a common criminal."

Barbarossa stood unevenly. He hunched around his armpit. He faced Ambrosius and raised his left arm and pointed at him with a shaking finger. He looked around at his Redhead army. He opened his mouth and thundered, "Advance!"

Ambrosius thought, *I'm a fool.*

The Thousand stiffened. The Redheads tensed. Then the sardonic voice of Ffidius called out from back in the crowd, "Mister Crimson Knight, O Mister Crimson Knight – a word?"

Barbarossa turned, staring rage at the mounted nobleman.

Ffidius went on, "I am on a horse, and you are not. Shall I report you what I see?"

Barbarossa growled, "Out with it, you skinny fop."

Ffidius said, "Rufus Quintus Ffidius, if you please. From where I sit, I can just make out the mouth of the Via Floribus. I see the king's faithful friends, noble Valerius Corvus and the venerable Decius Mus. Behind them the street is none but Wardogs. What do you think, usurper? Do you think Corvus and Mus took their force while your back was turned, and busted up your prison camp upon the plain?"

He opened his mouth and thundered, "Advance!"

Barbarossa's eye bulged. For a moment, he seemed to grow, to become fiercer, harder. Then he deflated. His shoulders sagged, his good arm went slack. He howled, "Second form!"

Then he turned and ran.

He sank into the mass of the third morax. He drew men in his train, as if they understood where they were going. Tens, then hundreds, then thousands ran.

Ambrosius thought on it a moment, then said, "O you clever dog." He'd assumed Barbarossa wanted the warrior nobles for witnesses in case he won. But he also wanted them at this square in case he lost. If they were at the square, they weren't blocking all the streets out of Primavera Circle. It was simple enough for his men to avoid the Wardogs too, confined as they were to the Via Floribus. They could take Via Lata, wide and empty, all the way to Shepherd's Gate.

Confusion reigned outside the district gate. Ambrosius shouted to his men, "Somebody come get me out of this ridiculous armor!"

## XYX

THE WOLF SNUFFED and Antonella untied Domenico and gently lifted him down. The giant beast padded off into the woods. Antonella carried Domenico the last few steps, out from the concealed entrance to the place Ambrosius told her. She startled them there, the loyal men with their horse and carriage. She told them where she had to go. They helped her and the boy up, the drivers took their seats, the armed riders fell into place, and the tiny caravan turned north. Their path would take them between the city and the Campus Iucundum. They didn't have a choice, the villa of Judge Salvatorio lay in the wealthy suburbs northwest of Florence.

When the king had led them to Exile's Tunnel, they'd taken a particular curving stair down to a cellar. The stair seemed to frighten him. She looked around but saw nothing fearful: just the yellow glow of a rushlight, and water trickling down the wall.

Ambrosius had never looked so old as he did just then. He stood on the stair as if stunned, and finally he murmured to her, "Don't let our blood vanish from this Earth." She'd leaned in, so that her lips touched his ear, and whispered, "I will not let them kill our son." It was words and she knew Fate held them all in the palm of his terrible hand. But she was his queen, and she saw him find strength in the power of her will. He shook himself and continued down the stair.

Now it was clear cold night beneath a half-moon, and they'd met no one on the plain. They were nearing the fatal leg, the passage between the walled city and the fortified camps. The camp of the Thousand was a ruin before the hulk of the warehouse. The camp of the army was a fearful sight: a glowing haze hung above it, the belly of a column of smoke. As they rounded the camp, the burst gate came into view – beyond it was white flame. Antonella squinted at the guard towers. She couldn't make out the enemy at this distance. They would see her, or they wouldn't. They would raise a cry and follow, or not. Her carriage was crossing the palm of Fate.

## XXX

PRIMAVERA CIRCLE WAS quiet now. A waste of dead and dying, of rubbish and abandoned materiel. Ambrosius and the Wardogs prowled it, searching.

*Where is Antonio?*

They took prisoners as they found them. Those who resisted were put to death. It was unclear if Antonio had fled with the Crimson Knight. The king had an intuition he had not.

He and his line of men advanced south, then east. From the smoky gloom a man approached, hands raised and empty. He had a big head and broad ribs. He was filthy and wore rags and looked like a fat man who had lost weight recently. He looked like a ghost.

The man said, "Did it make a difference for your cause, the single combat?"

Ambrosius couldn't quite recognize this man, but somehow felt he had reason to trust him deeply, to trust him with the life of family. He said, "It made the difference between victory and defeat."

The man let out a long breath.

Ambrosius said, "Do I know you?"

The man said, "I am Novacila, the groom of your cousin Temet Nosce Ambrosius, magister equitum of Florence. I walked his ill-starred path upon the Via Circumflorentia. In road and field and forest I stood by his side. I was there when the Crimson Knight, in his great wrath, destroyed them, yea, destroyed them all. I only am escaped alone to tell thee."

## XXX

It took Antonella a while to catch the sound, because the carriage rattled and the horses' hooves pounded on the hard-packed soil of the plain. But when she heard it, it filled her with icy fear. There was a thunder approaching: a faint rumble soon resolved itself into footsteps and voices and clanks and hoofbeats on stone and soil. What was this? Where? The bulk of the city hid the view on her left. Irresistably they rode on toward the giant noise, and finally they came around the curve and saw:

An army was pouring out of Shepherd's Gate. They were infantry at a fast march, with sparse cavalry riding circuits up and down their flanks, protecting them. An enormous army, advancing into the broad flat Campus Iucundum. Antonella knelt on the floor of the carriage and removed the cushions from her seat and swung the bare wood up. She lifted Domenico from his own seat and settled him in the concealed compartment. She stole one last look at him, dim in the shadows, then shut the seat and put the cushions back on it and sat down.

The front edge of the army sent a team for them. As they approached, Antonella's caravan slowed. The team was on foot but there was no outracing the force they represented. Antonella called out to one of her armed riders, a man she'd known and trusted twenty years, "The prince is concealed in the seat. Do not let them have him." The man heard and nodded. The caravan halted as the team neared. Antonella climbed down and shut the door of the carriage behind her.

The team arrived. One of them held a guttering oil lamp and when he raised it near the queen's face, he saw who she was and anxiously begged her to wait. They sent a man running back to the army. Presently he returned with company. The second man walked fast but gingerly, hunching right. Antonella recognized his big shape.

She said, "What do they say on Serapetine Hill?"

Barbarossa looked hideous, pale as a plague victim, sweating so that the bandage on his eye was drenched. In a growl he said, "Who have you got with you?"

She said, "It is only I, cousin. The king sent me to seek refuge with Judge Salvatorio while he –" She stopped. "What is going on in Florence?"

Barbarossa grat his teeth, "Your man's won, cuz, and we've lost."

She didn't answer.

He looked up at her from underneath his brow and sheepishly admitted, "Single combat."

Soft Antonella couldn't quite swallow her delighted laugh, and Barbarossa took it. They were family. She stepped close to him, and he spread around her. The warmth of family.

He said, "The patricia's back. She says she was in ai Ctesiphôn. Came back with that sword to prove it. She stood for you, lady of the combat."

Antonella pictured it. *If she hadn't just saved my son, I think I'd poison her.*

Barbarossa concluded, "There's nothing for it, so I'm leading the boys to safety."

Behind him the army continued to march, their leading edge already vanishing into the dark woods north of the plain.

Now he looked down where she stood close to him, with an evil look in his one good eye. He said, "I think we'd better take a look in that carriage of yours."

Antonella looked up at him and said, "I'm quite sure it's empty, Ineto Picolomini." And she moved slightly, so that he could see the gleam of her short sword at his gut.

He let it hang a long, long time, underneath the moon, his soldiers marching past. Then he said, "Alright, if you can't trust family, who can you trust?"

This gave her an idea. She said, "Barbarossa, where is my brother?"

He looked at her sharply, shame-faced. She went pale. She stepped back, sword bare for all to see, and shrieked, "*Where is Antonio?*"

He cringed before the sound of her voice. His men watched him shrink. In a low and deadly voice she said, "O you wretched coward." And she slapped him.

His men drew their swords, but he held up a hand. Tears started from his one bare eye. He turned to her again and started, "I – I –"

Her own tears starting, the queen implored him, "Barbarossa, what have you made me do?"

He reached for her, and she swatted him away. She turned, wiping her tears, and said to the rider she'd spoken to, "My good man, your horse, give it me. Get in yon empty carriage and ride on. Continue to Salvatorio's as we had planned, but bring the judge back to the city. He is needed in Florence."

The rider dismounted. Antonella turned back to Barbarossa, pointing her sword to ward him off.

"Go," she said, "go and live, you sniveling dog. May the gods forget we were kin."

His shoulders shook, but he did as she commanded, fading with his men back to the third morax in headlong retreat.

The rider climbed into the carriage. The queen shut the door on him and slapped it. The caravan rode toward the third morax and waited unmolested for them to pass. Antonella did not look after it, didn't peer after the carriage, where her heart lay sleeping underneath the seat. She mounted the horse and heeled him around and pounded toward Shepherd's Gate. She pressed past the soldiers and entered the city, clattering south at a gallop toward the Via Floribus.

## XXX

When Antonio was a boy, drinking honeyed milk with Antonella, he'd liked Desiderio very much. He remembered him as a robust man with giant forearms, his thick graying hair tyed back, a twinkle in his eye, with a laugh that filled his establishment, founded on a Constantine loan.

During the siege, at loose ends and anxious, Antonio drifted to the place he spent so many childhood afternoons. It turned out Desiderio was still alive. He was old as a cricket now and mostly lay in bed upstairs, dozing in a nest of blankets, while his daughters ran the eatery. The third morax left Desiderio's alone. For the first few days the men could still get snacks there, and after that, Antonio's word protected it.

While Barbarossa raged and plotted and gave orders, Antonio sat at his old table in Desiderio's, drinking wine and asking himself how he'd gotten mixed up in this. Cleon wasn't a part of it, and Cleon was the one who was really good at planning big campaigns. Barbarossa's father Ineto Tacitus kept trying to get to his son in Primavera Circle, but the army had orders to hold him off. It made the old lion look pathetic.

From the moment Lovers' Gate swung shut, Antonio was convinced it would end in tears. Nobody wanted his opinion, but for once he was right and they were wrong.

He didn't know what happened tonight at Golden Gate, but he'd seen the men stampeding. He'd retreated upstairs and found Desiderio awakened by the din. His teeth were worn to stubs, his flyaway hair was bone-white, and his eyes were filmed with cataracts. His lifelong good cheer was stained a little bit with madness now. Antonio sat beside his bed, and, for what it was worth, confessed.

He said, "Desiderio, I don't know what I've done. I've wasted my life, and nobody thinks much of me. Maybe they're right. I'm not much impressed with myself either. I don't know what's going on out there. I think Barbarossa was defeated, or he's forgotten me, or something. I don't know where to go or what to do. I'm very afraid."

Desiderio stretched forward and felt around and patted Antonio's knee with his furry hand at the end of his bony arm. Then he told Antonio a strange story about an eyeball with wings that flew across the sky to visit god, who turned out to be a bigger eyeball. When Desiderio got done he leaned back and smiled encouragingly, as if it were clear how anyone would be heartened by this story. Antonio didn't really understand the point of it. It sounded like the kind of thing that Tarquin liked. But he made some appreciative noises, and Desiderio raised his hands benevolently. Then his head turned to the side, and he listened to the shouts echoing in the street, and the lines of his face grew drawn and still. Antonio quietly left him there.

When he got down to the empty dining room, he looked at the men running past outside. They seemed fewer now, and panicked, and there were horsemen chasing amongst them. He saw a spear go through a man with a ghastly noise, and the man fall on the paving stones, a flopping dead thing. He didn't think he could bear to go out in that street. So he put on his winter cloak and headed for the back door he and Antonella used to use when their father's conversation bored them and they slipped out to play in the alleys.

He opened the door and had a fright: his way was blocked by a figure.

The figure was unlit, but it cut a sharp black shape from the moonlit wall of the building opposite. Now he looked, he'd have known that shape anywhere.

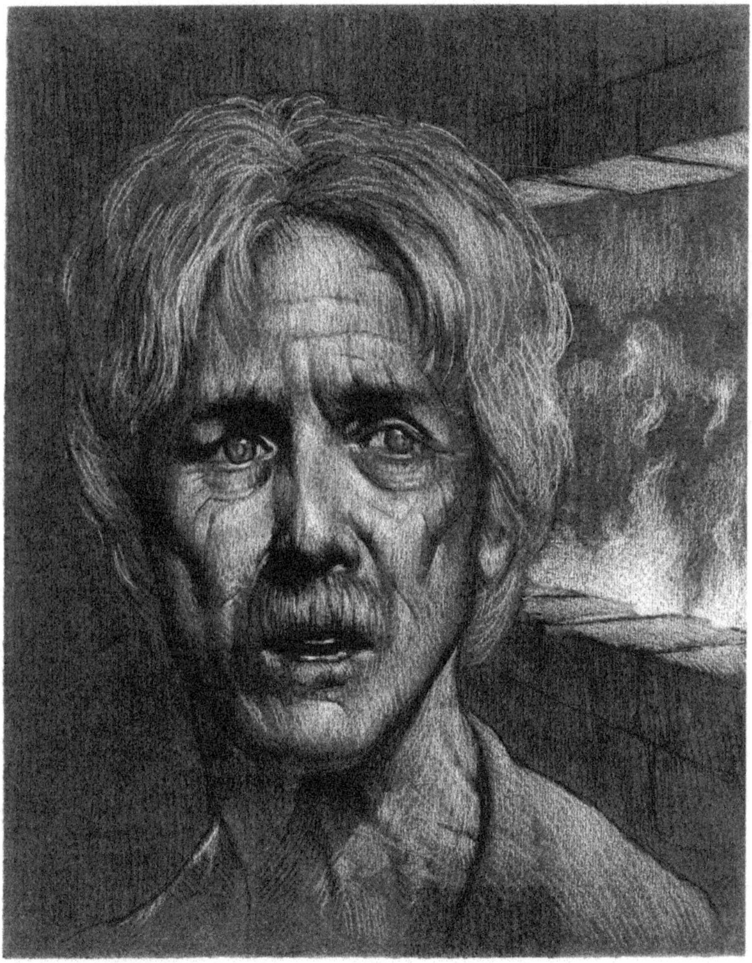

He listened to the shouts echoing in the street,
and the lines of his face grew drawn and still.

"Hullo sis," he said.

"Hello brother," soft Antonella answered.

They stood there a moment, he bristling and she serene. Presently a flicker lit her face. Men with torches had entered the shop from the front. He caught the tiniest downward motion of the queen's hand: *stand back*. She saw them and commanded them, but her eyes never left his.

"Will you let me pass?" he asked.

"You will not pass except through me. I am Florence. Will you pass through Florence?" And he felt her hand catch his. They had not held hands in many, many years. It comforted him. His shoulders slumped, and he let out a breath. Then he squared his shoulders and let go the queen's hand. She lowered it slowly.

Antonio finally knew what to do. He turned and faced the king and his men.

"I submit me to the justice of Florence."

He showed that dignity which had so often failed him when he had any hope.

They all left Desiderio's together. Antonio looked up once but the smoke hung so heavy he couldn't see the stars.

## XXX

Epida cried, "Where is she? Where is she?" and the other maids told her Claire was already in her apartment.

Epida ran to the apartment, drawing breath to greet Claire as she opened the door. But the scene inside confused and horrified her. It looked as if a giant monster had half-eaten the beautiful patricia. Epida's heart pounded and her reason raced to comprehend what she was seeing. Claire looked over at her and raised a finger to her lips: *quiet*.

Epida stood and watched, and gradually she pieced it together. Claire was sitting on a bench in her empty chamber. The monster was a wolf, a great old wolf with brown fur. Claire was somehow suckling the wolf.

Epida stood there like a statue of stone. Finally the wolf stepped back from the patricia. He turned, muzzle dripping milk, and looked at Epida with his golden eyes. He growled as he passed her, and clacked softly down the hall. When he was gone, Epida let out a gasp of fright and sank to the floor. Claire sat slumped on the bench, eyes living but somehow alien. Her nipple was dark and her breast was swollen and covered in scratches and bruises.

## XXX

CLAIRE WAS SORE and cold and hungry and thirsty. Water was the easiest thing, so she drank first. The taste of it shocked her – it was the same sweet fresh water she'd licked from the stones inside ai Ctesiphôn.

She said, "Where is this water from?"

Epida said, "It's siege-water. It's from Tristana, the second river, the one that runs through Florence underground."

Epida fetched her some hot soup, and she ate a little, but her starved belly rebelled, so she let it go. Epida drew her a bath, and knowing her strange ways, stood to leave. She paused at the door, and Claire could see she needed an embrace. But Claire had nothing left to give and finally, the girl left.

Claire meant to get up and go to the bath, but her breast ached and she hunched over it and endured the ache with clenched teeth. When the ache passed, she stood and barred the door; only then did she take off her gown. If a mortal had seen her, he would shortly have died.

She found the green sprig from the withered oak in a fold of her gown. She padded over to Trypsomayne and tucked it away with her half-coins of greeting. Then she climbed into the bath. It felt scalding on her frozen skin, but soon her skin warmed, and the bath became bearable, then suddenly it was delicious and life rushed back into her. With life came fatigue, and she nearly fell asleep. Her reason drifted and she felt the ghosts of her mother's hands in her hair, washing her hair when she was very little. Some days she still wheedled her mother into washing her hair, she enjoyed it so. Then she thought of her mother, tonight, out on the strand, grasping her own frozen hand, rubbing a little warmth into it. *I've chosen the long way around.* A pain transfixed her, an indescribable sadness, with all the intensity of childhood. She remembered feeling it before: when her father had gone. Now she was feeling it on her own behalf. *It's I who have gone.* She objected to the sobs she felt against the back of her mouth. Not now. It was not time to cry. She blew breaths out quickly, denying the pain and sadness, so that the pain and sadness turned into a debt she owed her heart. *I'll pay that later.*

Finally she dragged herself from the bath. It was cold in her room and she quickly dried and dressed herself and stumbled up to Trypsomayne. She burrowed in the covers till she was as snug as a mouse in his mouse-hole. Her eyes fluttered over the metal stars above her head, and her long strange day passed before her eyes. She considered the bitter fact of ai Ctesiphôn: enough technology was here already, thousands of years before, to send her instantly to Zanzibar. *How were the tower builders and their crafts so thoroughly forgotten?*

With a falling sensation, she asked a better question: *What does Zanzibar take for granted, as the Florentines take ai Ctesiphôn for granted? There must be traces everywhere of mighty beings who have come and gone. What am I missing? Is there a giant shape in the sky that nobody notices? In the heart of man?*

*Have there been other Zanzibars?*

*Ay, many, and there will be many more.*

Tantalizing thoughts spidered past on their impossibly long legs, then she was asleep.

# 49

## THE APOTHEOSIS OF THERSITES

CLAIRE WOKE IN the middle of the night. She had the clear and certain insight that when daybreak gave their streets back to the frightened Florentines, they'd come braying for revenge against the Constantines. What they did next would define the moral character of the Florentines. This was their hour of choosing.

*Can't I just rest?*

"Epida!"

She heaved herself out of bed and fastened her gown properly and took the bar down from the door and opened it, just as Epida, dazed and tussle-haired, raised her hand to knock. They looked at one another, and their composure collapsed like sandcastles. Claire wrapped Epida in her arms and said, "Oh Epida, Epida, I'm sorry Epida," and Epida in kind nearly squeezed the breath from her.

When they'd pulled themselves together, Epida said, "What disturbed you at this hour?"

XXX

Thersites surveyed the mob. If he didn't talk them down, nobody would.

The mob surrounded the Counting House, the Constantine establishment on the south side. It was a brick building which formerly included a wooden stable. The mob had torn down the stable and piled the scrap around the building. They were looking to light it.

Thersites clutched Claire's letter to his chest. One of his apple boys had delivered it before dawn. He was not sentimental about objects, but this one object was dear to him, and he figured he'd carry it the rest of his days. In a clear and simple hand, she wrote him of the trouble she foresaw, then went on:

*...Look beyond this present turmoil. I know you have no sons of your own, but I also know your costermonger army are, to you, like sons. Consider them, grown up, and their own children, and their children's children. What kind of Florence will we leave them, Thersites? What kind of Florentines will they be?*

*The age-old war is dead. The attempt upon the king has failed. Now the time of choosing is at hand for the Florentines. Will they choose vengeance and the mob? Will the streets run red with the blood of factions? Or will they choose justice and forebearance and the dignity of free men?*

*Help them, my teacher and friend. Help them lay a foundation, mighty in its virtue, for tomorrow's Florence. No man can instruct them better than you.*

So here he was, down off Serapetine Hill to face the mob at the Counting House. They were packed together, bumping shoulders and angry. Anything could start the violence. He considered how to begin. At a lull in the murmuring, he banged his staff on the ground, and opened a tiny window of quiet.

"Friends! Brothers, sisters, Florentines!"

They turned at the sound of his shrill, squeaky voice. Some of them laughed a little. All the Florentines knew Tiresias.

"I beg you'll give me quiet, fellow citizens, to speak my piece."

They looked put out, but they held their tongues. It was a start. Nobody knew better than Thersites, veteran of the third morax, that when men shout together, they'll forgive themselves anything.

"Thank you."

They murmured and fell quiet again. Some of those on the far side of the Counting House sidled around the corners to hear what he had to say.

"The Sower of Peace sent me here today."

He held up the letter, and the mob seemed very impressed.

"She asked me a question, and it is a question I want to ask you: what will become of Florence? We are at the end of the age of war, and the start of the age of peace. What do we want to become?"

The mob muttered angrily at him. He saw Constantines watching from the windows of the second storey. The winter sun shone on him, the ugliest man in the third morax. The cold wind played with the few hairs left on his head.

"Are we animals who greet afront with violence? Or will we be a proud free people?"

Somebody shouted, "Death to the Constantines!" and others cheered. Thersites nodded toward this voice and answered it, "Perhaps. We are not milk-drinkers, Florentines. But neither are we beasts. We mustn't be. I beg you choose the middle path of wisdom."

Somebody else shouted, "What do you want, Tiresias?"

Thersites bowed his head to them and said, "I want you to submit your fury to the judgment of Salvatorio. Let him decide the remedy. Thus will Florence smite the guilty and spare the innocent."

A third man shouted, "Don't you hate the king and his men?"

Thersites raised a hand and said, "It's true I've hated kings. But I was young, and it was a different king. I do not hate this king. When we cried out for peace, he cut the throat of war. His father didn't do it. His brother couldn't. Only this king.

"Now there is a different, better question - do I hate kingship? Yes I do. No kings! No kings! I am a democrat."

They cheered him, but in a shocked and sarcastic way.

"Kingship is only as good as the king, Florentines. Likewise democracy is only as good as the people. You are not ready. I am not ready. But today we can work on getting ready."

Somebody asked, "Ready for what?"

He said, "Ready to govern ourselves."

There was an abashed silence. Then some of the crowd began to disperse. Others clapped Thersites on the shoulder and shook his hand. A ring of men remained around the Counting House, and their leader said, "We will wait on Nederick Frederick's men, Tiresias, but we will wait all orderly."

The crowd exclaimed: a door of the Counting House opened, and Cleon walked out, the older brother of Antonio and Antonella, the erstwhile partner in mischief of Barbarossa. He was unshaven and red-eyed. The shoulders of the crowd grew tense, but Cleon made his way to Thersites and said, "I will go to the castle with you, Thersites, and face what I must from the judge." Thus the crowd cheered a Constantine the day after the siege. Before the door closed, they caught a glimpse of dreadful Tarquin, and the old men and the women and the children. They did not come out.

When Thersites saw that the people listened to reason, and showed dignity and self-control, it was as if a splinter were removed from his soul, a splinter that had reddened it since Ælius Pellucidus humiliated him before the third morax, and the third morax mocked him. Right away, the lifelong inflammation of his soul began to heal. He was a new man, a happy man. Light shone through his ugly face, and those there with him saw it.

The fever that had gripped Florence since the end of the war finally broke.

XXX

Salvatorio heard the cases. Of the Constantines, only one old man and two of the younger generation had fallen in league with Barbarossa and Antonio. The old man and one of the youths were killed in the fighting. The other youth was missing and appeared to have escaped with the Redheads.

Salvatorio handed down his sentences: dragging by a team of horses for Antonio, on the Via Floribus from Serapetine Hill to the Epicondyle. The ground that he had sought to rule would break him. Surprisingly, he had a sentence for Cleon as well: "You, who were your cousin's partner in all things, were blind to this. Therefore will you be blinded by the blade." To the rest of the Constantines he meted out a brutal fine, forgiving the war-debt of Ambrosius. They counted themselves lucky, except Tarquin, who had an unmeasured pit where his soul should have been.

Salvatorio left the remainder of the third morax to the king to do with as he saw fit, as a military matter and not a civil one.

## XXX

Claire wanted to visit with Antonio in his dungeon, but he spent his few remaining hours in quiet conversation with Reburrus. Thus the ichneumon, comforting the usurper, spat in the eye of the king.

Claire decided to visit Cleon instead. She wished to set things right with the Constantines. She felt the fate of Florence, and her own, rested on their shoulders. Though the king was her ally, it was Constantine resourcefulness that would get her home. But they were not an easy family.

When the cell door whined open, Cleon wearily turned his head. He was haggard with grief and fear, waiting for the hot blade to the eyeball. Seeing Claire, he seemed to her to read all her hopes and plans. His nostril flared, but he calmed himself. She stood and waited. Finally he spoke. He said:

"A riddle, Claire. A floor, tiled in the old temple style of squares of yellow limestone and dark red granite. The floor - flooded. Not deep the flooding, but deep enough. It covers a household god, and a sprig of lilacs tied to the foot of a dead finch. It covers some gold and silver coins, and the wedding rings of Coelestin and Iolanthe. It covers a slingshot, and a scroll with all the wisdom of men writ on it. It covers a clear circle that bends light to let a blind man see. It covers an antler and a candle, a candle and a hoof. And a little blood is spilling in the fine clear water, pinking it like wine too heavily mixed. The riddle: what day have I described to you, Claire?"

Claire leveled the pale gray of her eyes on him and said, "O Cleon, you have described the last day of the world."

Startled at her swift reply, he said, "How did you answer this riddle?"

She said, "How else would all the things that men hold dear drown in the temple, unless no one remained to save them?"

Cleon looked shrewdly at the beautiful patricia, wrapped in her cloak and lit by the winter afternoon outside a high window.

He said, "I think you plan to live a thousand years beyond me, Claire. I think you plan to watch even the memory of Constantine dry up and blow away. But the end comes for you too, and after the last day, as you told us in New Forest, even the gods will be forgotten."

A darkness bloomed in the eye of Claire, and she strode to him and seized his hand, finding it soft and cold and slightly damp. She held it in both of hers, that were warm and rougher than they'd been.

"Trust me in this, O Cleon. I am mingled now with Florence. Even if I get me back to Zanzibar, I stay mingled with the Florentines. Therefore when the wall of fire comes, or black water, or the shrieking winds, or the flailstones, and all men say, 'Woe are we, it is the last day,' even on that day Florence cries out to me, from the mouths of the living and the dead Florence cries out to me. And on that day what is left of me hears the cry of Florence, and I return to you, so that when all things are dispersed, my atoms mix with yours. Let there be no tongue to speak it nor heart to mark it, yet still my atoms mingle with the atoms of the Florentines, on that last day. I swear you this is true."

He took back his hand and cradled it as if it stung. He smiled a strange smile at her, that was like the pride of someone wounded.

He said, "It will be midnight for a long time yet, O Claire."

She nodded and took her leave.

## XXX

THEY DRAGGED ANTONIO in the morning. The logistics didn't really make sense: they rode him in an open carriage to the west end of Florence, just so they could drag him east again. The king and queen waited for him at the foot of Serapetine Hill.

While they waited, the king turned to the queen and asked her, "I still don't understand – how did Barbarossa mix Antonio up in this?" He could tell that Antonella had trouble composing herself to speak. She said, "When we were little, Antonio was very impressed with Ineto. He wanted to play with him, but Ineto was older and only wanted to play with Cleon. I'm sure Ineto came to him and said, 'Let's play together,' and my poor brother..." but she couldn't finish.

Here was the carriage. Antonio stepped down, pale but composed, still displaying the dignity of despair. As he walked toward them, Antonella noticed his fingertips brushing the stone walls, the brick walls, the metal bars, the vines, and the bushes, savoring textures, just as he did when he was four years old and she was three; and she hid her face and sobbed. This was her last sight of him. He looked to the king, and the king nodded his permission, and he came up to the queen and kissed her brow, and she put a hand on the back of his neck and held him there, and then she let him go. Thus she didn't watch them bind him, or whip the horses; her last sensation of her brother was his kiss.

The horses dragged Antonio the length of the Via Floribus. Claire saw him pass from where she stood at the foot of Piccola Strada. The sight was so terrible she hid her face in the broad chest of Marcus. When she turned back to the Via Floribus, Antonio was well past and the crowd around them was moving on.

Antonio lived until he reached the crooked paving stone at the corner of Via Strocchia, that trips everybody. It tripped his head, and put an end to his suffering.

Far to the west, the queen lifted a mop along with the mayor and some of the Constantines, and they mopped the trail of blood from the Via Floribus. This is a very old custom in Florence, and the mayor and the family always take part. The trail was narrow at first, and then it was wide a while and very tacky and red, and then it thinned again, long before it reached the end of its route. The thing the horses delivered to the foot of the Epicondyle could hardly be called a man any longer.

## XXX

THE KING HAD intended to order a decimation of the captured Redheads. But then his Wardogs made their report, and he went out to the Campus Iucundum and saw for himself. His Wardogs had never abandoned him. They'd died in their hundreds, attempting to break out.

The king ordered the Redhead captives out to the edge of the forest on the far side of the plain, digging a trench for the dead of the second and seventh moraces. When they got done, he had them all put to the sword.

It was not a great number, no more than five hundred. The rest had escaped when Barbarossa fled. Ambrosius sent scouts after them, up Ligusticum Steet and Balearicum Street and Ibericum Street. But there was no sign of the Redheads. Finally, Nederick Frederick thought to send some vigiles along the Cartenna Trail. They found evidence that thousands of men could march it after all. But the litter ended where the trail met Cartenna Creek.

They'd entered the creek and walked on its shallow bed. Now they were long gone; where, nobody could tell.

Thus the Crimson Knight, whose attempt on the throne was such a disaster, led perhaps the greatest retreat in the history of Florence.

# PART VI

# The Tomb of John the Pilgrim

# 50

## THE PYRE

CLAIRE LAY ON the ground cloth and looked over at the trees. It was a sunny day and the forest was turning. One tree was a luminous yellow, and another a dazzling red, and a third an orange unimaginably rich. Claire's eye was filled with the beauty of the leaves and her ear was lulled by their rustling in the wind. On heavy gusts, leaves would shimmer down and settle in drifts on the forest floor.

There could be no joy more thorough than these colors, and yet they made Claire sad. Her passions filled with a serene melancholy, and her thoughts turned to the passage of time and the dissipation of things that were.

She recognized that she was feeling a new set of feelings, alien to a daughter of the desert.

*This is autumn.*

She settled onto her back. The leaves left her gaze and she looked at the sky. It was a clear and brilliant blue. At the center of its dome, her eyes played tricks on her, and the blue seemed to flow and curl in upon itself in an endless chain of shimmering horns.

She was wrapped in a blanket, and the sun was warm on her

face. She shut her eyes. Her eyelids glowed red and orange in the brightness, and the horns went on curling at the zenith of her view. She stretched, lazy as a cat.

Half-dozing, she heard the carriage approach. She heard Taranto and Brindisi stand and crunch over to it. Voices, calm. She blinked and sat up, suddenly dizzy. She threw aside the blanket and stood. The wind was cold, but so moderate a cold didn't bother her much, not after the summit of ai Ctesiphôn.

The carriage door opened. A man stepped down. He wore a fine coat woven with gold and crusted in jewels. But it was unbuttoned and beneath it was a simple white frock, somewhat worn. He said, "Claire, patricia of Zanzibar, thank you for arranging this."

She said, "I am your servant, Khrysanthos Pindar, king of Genova."

## XXX

One week earlier, horses foaming at the mouth and black with sweat, riders entered Florence to report a train of Genovan carriages, golden scrollwork gleaming on their dark bulk. They rolled out of Rusadir on the old king's road, and it seemed they'd never stop. All day long the carriages rolled from the forest.

Then the endless train was four days off, then three. Florence city swelled: visitors filled all the public houses, all the rooms to let, every patch of grass, every alley, crook and hollow. On the ancient blood-stained hooks by Traitor's Gate, boys and girls hung garlands of winter-blooming lilies and cornflowers and carnations.

Ambrosius summoned Claire to the jade office. He had with him the queen and Lady Varo, both in black mourning-wimples, and Salvatorio Elegans Sestertius, chief judge of Florence. He encouraged Claire to bring whomever she wished, to lend her succor in her trial. She brought Diophantus, still limping from his battle-wound, and the maid Epida.

Ambrosius sat back silent and let the judge put the painful questions. He hated this, but he was king of Florence and he had his duty.

Salvatorio grimaced and said, "O Claire, know this, we impute no guilt to you in anything. But Florence requires answers."

Her face white and still, Claire said, "Ask me what you will."

The judge said, "Your belly remains flat, but your breast is swollen. Are you with child?"

Claire had been wearing a shawl over her bare breast since the end of the siege. She reached up now and unclasped it and drew it aside. The king gasped. Her breast had fading scratches over it, and it was yellow and purple with half-healed bruises.

Antonella blurted, "What *happened* dear?"

Claire said, "A wolf came to your aid in your flight from Florence."

Salvatorio turned and stared at the queen. Antonella said to Claire, "I spoke to you in that hour."

Claire nodded and said, "The wolf came at my word. I called upon an ancient alliance. Under its terms, the fearful beasts will lend assistance. In return they must be fed as soon as they ask."

Antonella put her hand to her mouth. Ambrosius said, "I don't understand."

Epida said, "My lord, she suckled the wolf. I was there. I saw. It was the very evening you defeated the Crimson Knight."

Ambrosius sat back, aghast. Antonella put her hand on his wrist and said, voice unsteady, "She saved our son."

Claire clasped the shawl again. Salvatorio looked over at the king, and the king nodded.

The judge turned to Diophantus and said, "Have you lain with the patricia?"

Without adornment or elaboration, Diophantus said, "No." He didn't look at Claire. Like a shadow, Claire softly repeated, "No."

Salvatorio glanced at Lady Varo, then addressed Claire. He said, "There remains the question of your menses."

Claire said, "I have heard that women in the world find their menses timed to the moon."

The king said, "We are not ignorant children, Claire."

Claire calmly answered, "It is not the same for the women of Zanzibar. Perhaps you have some famous comets in your annals?"

The judge said, "We have seen our share."

Claire said, "Among these mysterious bodies, there is one that returns. He is a great comet, and we call him Trebizond, for the city, Étienne's city, my lord. When he will return, no sage can predict. But he will return. When he shall blaze again his path across the sky, then all the Zanzibari women will bleed. Our menses are timed to this Trebizond, as your women's are to the moon."

In the king's ear rang the words of Reburrus: *She is a thing of her god, made hastily of living clay. She will lack a navel or a womb, menses or bile.*

There was a long pause. The green gloom of the office seemed to brighten, then dim. Judge Salvatorio began, "In regard to the questions of the swollen breast, the sexual intercourse, and the absent menses –"

Ambrosius stood and said, "In regard to these questions, Florence is satisfied with the Zanzibari's answers."

## XXX

ON THE MORNING of the day, the Florentines saw a column of dust advancing across the plain, the black procession raising it still hidden in the haze. They called the greeting celebration in the square of Gracious Ambrosius II, just inside of Traitor's Gate. The watchmen stood on the ramparts shouting down reports, and inside the open city crowds gathered. The king and queen and prince arrived.

The Family Dinner was canceled, but Ambrosius sat Corvus and Mus beside him on this day of peace. He clapped Mus on the shoulder and said, "I –" but then he lost the thread of how to say what he wanted to say. He looked each of his friends in the face and said, "I understand you had to wait. You do not do your duty to Florence if you prop up a weak king."

They nodded, and he said, "But there is a price to pay."

Younger Corvus looked to older Mus, and older Mus said, "We have meditated on it, and we too understand."

Amicus, the crippled hunting dog, nudged his way into their company, and the king rubbed his head. Ambrosius looked back up to the nobles, with such a look that their wounded hearts were soothed.

## XXX

CLAIRE STOOD BY the open gate with the king and his party. While they waited, a bard charmed the crowd with a bawdy tale of Master Rabbit, the trickster god of the low religion. The tale captivated Claire, like all the folktales of Florence. She found out that Master Rabbit was an ancestor of Tacamo's. Therefore Tacamo, a penniless vagabond, was part god. This sort of thing happens more often than you'd expect.

When the bard finished, the pickpockets got back to work. The vendors with their beer and nuts and little cakes renewed their circulations. Everybody heard the jingling of ten thousand golden bells on the Genovan train, and the thunder of hooves.

Claire's sweeping eye saw the coaches enter the city, rolling slowly west on the Via Floribus, looking set to fill it all the way to Jubilee Gate. Claire studied the faces in the open windows of the coaches, but they remained strangers to her. To the Florentines, they were faces longed for day by day, their memory dying day by day, framed in those windows. The swollen crowds cheered in the square of Gracious Ambrosius and all along the street. Householders and their servants threw petals from the upper windows. Tears ran down their faces and all unwilling their every limb was shaking, and their laughter had a panic to it, so intense was their relief: the war was over in Florence, and the war was over in Genova.

The doors of the coaches opened. The throngs surged. There was a melee, almost like the melee of war, as the captives sought their people, and their people sought the captives. Claire's eye followed individuals a while, but the feelings she beheld were very strong, and did not belong to her. The focus of her eye frayed, and her gaze flickered without resting. In fragments, she saw everything. Mothers wept at the sight of their boys. Husbands and wives reunited. Ancient fathers clasped sons already gray. Brothers embraced sisters. Finally there was simply motion, joyful motion. These were human beings who had been apart, and it hurt them to be apart, and now they were together again.

Her return to Zanzibar must echo these scenes. Surely it must echo these scenes. Claire shuddered with her loneliness and closed her eyes.

## XXX

SHE MOVED AMONG the Florentines as if slipping between drops of rain, her gown ever dry. Her brow was smooth, and her gray eyes calm, and she had a smile for any who smiled at her. She drifted west along the Via Floribus. Those who met the ones they loved stood where they met. But the day was not generous to all. Lonely multitudes drifted west, and Claire drifted west with them. They gathered in little pockets throughout the city, at the corners of dining tables, under trees in public squares, at the cobbled banks of the foul Liliana, and hung their heads together in bewildered sorrow. By evening they had all reached the west end of the city. They gathered in the square of Serene Ambrosius the Fifth, just inside Jubilee Gate, with the gambler's towers to the north and south. The Genovan coaches rattled past, on their way out to park on the Campus Iucundum.

In the square, Claire found evidence of the wisdom of her own Ambrosius, the Ninth. His attendants conveyed her to the platform of the gambler's tower of the south. From there, she surveyed a tall pyre, standing prepared in the center of the square, with a large effigy of a man upon it. The gathering crowds, first of the bereaved, who stood near the pyre, and then of the joyous, who took places in the back, filled the square. The cold night wind blew aside day's curtain and showed the stars.

When the square was full and the crowd waiting, torch-bearers came out on the platform of the gambler's tower of the north, and the king and queen and Bitsy Boots followed them. In his voice of command, that led armies in the field, Ambrosius spoke to the crowd.

"The peace is complete. The captives have returned. Those who were to be made whole today are made whole. Those who were not to be made whole today will never be made whole again. Tonight the whole and the bereft gather at the pyre of the one who did not return.

"O Florence, I have ridden in the wilderness, and stood watch by pyres that howled through the night. I have burned up friends and family upon them. Youth and age alike have I burned upon the pyre, men I loved and boys I led I have burned upon the brutal pyre. Honor and the wounded heart demand the pyre.

"Florence gathers here to light the pyre of the one who did not return. We make the end of it. Abandon we dashed hopes. All Florence celebrates, and all Florence laments. Your joy is the joy of all. Your suffering is the suffering of all."

The crowd kept sober, in a speaking voice repeating, "Florence. Florence," and the warrior nobles repeated it with them. The chant was loud only because it was spoken by the many. Those in the front quaked, and could not speak. Claire expected the king to order the pyre lit, but instead she felt heat approach her back. Torch-bearers suddenly surrounded her, and the crowd turned to look up to her.

Ambrosius said, "Behold Claire, the patricia of Zanzibar. She delivered Florence; she sowed the peace. To her we owe the boon. When springtime comes, Florence will deliver her to Zanzibar."

Now the crowd shouted, saying, "Hail Claire! Hail Zanzibar! Hail Claire! Hail Zanzibar!"

Claire surveyed the thousands hailing her and her republic. She swayed, and the palace of her memory set a scene before her eye.

Some summers before, she had gone with her mother to a ceremony commemorating those who died in Guerra Domestique. It had been early in the war when Claire's mother achieved the rank of general. Reason's half-sister, the maiden huntress, fought beside her, and their vicious, beautiful half-brother was a leader on the other side. During the Wild Nights, Claire's mother caught her half-brother and flung him in a bronze pot in an abandoned warehouse by the port. He would have died there too, but one of her mother's own staff, seduced by his beauty and moved by his sobs, told his confederates where he was. When Claire's mother found out, she put the staffer in the empty pot, and sealed it.

The ceremony of commemoration took place at the hall of the dead. Claire's mother wore her old armor to the ceremony, the full panoply: greaves and heavy leather skirt, manteau segmenté and cuirass, shoulder guards, the plumed helmet with the famous gash in its side. Claire held her hand as they walked quietly there at dusk. She met her mother's gaze once, then avoided it. The helmet covered her cheeks, and the nosepiece hid the center of her face. In the failing desert sunlight, all that was left were her gray eyes, that glittered, and her teeth, that dazzled white. This was the aspect of her mother that scared Claire most. Not the rages or the black moods or the confusions, but the glory. She was terrifying to Claire in her warlike aspect, resembling her legendary companions: the lion, the wolf, and the owl.

The hall of the dead was lit up with pans of fire, their flickering light catching the names of the dead incised on the far wall. Claire and her mother made their way through the crowd. The crowd fell back when they saw who approached. The breezes from the crowd powered the bellows, a mechanical contrivance that cleared the air when the hall was full. It irregularly boomed and sighed, so that Claire felt herself inside the hot damp lung of a monster breathing in its sleep.

They reached the wall of names, and Claire's mother stood with her back to Claire, tracing letters with her fingers. They were just names to Claire, barely legible, but to Claire's mother each told a terrible story: this one held the street, and this one threw himself on the fire, and this one met a hail of spears, halfway across the river. These were Claire's mother's people, her friends from her own generation. Claire's mother's hand shook, tracing the names on the wall, as if it hurt her to touch them, as if each letter were an open wound, as if she went on asking, *Can it be true?* Claire imagined her compatriots, from the Académie and Angoulème and Café Null, all sent down to darkness in the flower of their youth.

Then Claire's mother lifted her arms and pressed her hands to the sides of her head. The crowd stirred, watching her frozen grief. Finally a spasm passed through her, and she lifted off her helmet, so that her thick mane caught the firelight and made a tangled red-gold halo round her head. Slowly she turned to Claire, who stood behind her. Claire saw her beautiful face in the dim light, and her glittering eyes. Her cheek was dark with grief, and her lips were swollen with it, but she did not cry. Claire saw again the broken thing in her mother, a world, a broken world hidden in her. She knew this face of her mother and had learned how to love it, to care for it.

Her mother looked at her and shook her head. Only a tiny shake, but it said all: *Do not seek to console me.* Claire's blood ran cold. Then Reason spoke, and the whole crowd heard her speak. They listened to everything the general said, the general who crushed the enemy of Zanzibar.

She told her youngest daughter, "On two things you may depend, O Claire: on goodness, and on war." Claire's arms stiffened and her stomach clenched, for she who so loved peace took this for a curse, the worst and most inevitable curse. From that day, she began seriously to seek her father, to plan to really drag him back from the limits of the cosmos.

Claire returned to the world, and received on the platform the crowd's chant of "Hail Claire! Hail Zanzibar!" She saw those who were made whole holding up those who would never be made whole. She began to doubt her mother's curse. Perhaps there might be goodness and an end to war at last, at least in this precious corner of the wide uncertain world. She felt a pain in her womb, such as she had felt at the end of her dream, that first night in the valley of the world. She spoke again in the strong voice, which rang like a bell and could be heard everywhere.

"Yes, let us have no more of war. Let brother sit with brother by the fire, and recount fading memories of war, and laugh."

Each forceful word was like a blow against the wall of her womb. *I shall have to bear myself, if I want to get born.*

She called in a piercing voice, "No more of war, O Florence."

The pain crested and passed. She blinked and shivered. It was as if she'd broken the surface of the waters and could breathe quick air at last. She saw herself in the glimmer of truth: her left hand was red, where she clashed with Reburrus, and her right hand was red, where she clashed with Barbarossa. But her breast was white, and shone, where she had sown peace among the nations.

"I have brought you peace," she called, who so loved peace. She stood apart from her mother now, a separate woman. Her shining white breast cried out in rage and adoration.

*Mother, I have brought them peace! There is peace beneath the sun!*

But she knew her mother couldn't hear her, all the way in Zanzibar.

XXX

Claire said other things, and forgot what they were; she didn't have a lot of training in public speaking. She remembered that she said some words of gratitude, and some of humility; some words of celebration, and some of consolation. Then she stopped speaking, because she had said what they needed her to say. The king ordered the pyre lit. Claire noticed an ichneumon did it, but not Reburrus.

That was the first she ever saw of Idomeneo Lucan.

Claire walked down the winding stair inside the tower, and after she got a hold of herself, she went out the door. When the Florentines saw her, they parted, as the Zanzibaris parted for her mother. But when she came forward, they closed around her, as if she were one flesh with them, and beloved. Thus she stood with the Florentines, and faced the pyre with them. They sang a lullabye of their people, and she swayed with them in the light and crackle of the fire, and learned the sad words of the song:

Beloved, beloved,
Your man has gone to war,
He has gone to war,
The champion of the city has gone to war.
Beloved, beloved,
Your man came to the field,
He fought the beast of the field,
The champion of the city slew the beast of the field.
Beloved, beloved,
Your man came to the sea,
He fought the serpent of the sea,
The champion of the city slew the serpent of the sea.
Beloved, beloved,
Your man came to the mountain,
He fought the monster of the mountain,
The champion of the city slew the monster of the mountain.

Beloved, beloved,
You wait in the road for your man,
He defeated all his enemies,
The champion of the city won the war.
Beloved, beloved,
Go to your man in the orchard,
He lies buried at the foot of the apple tree,
The champion of the city never came home.

# 51

## THE PILGRIM AND THE EXILE

MARCUS WALKED THE patricia back to the royal district, but when they were nearly there, he said, "Come," and led her to Desiderio's. A girl waved to them from the kitchen door, and they heard the muffled sounds of lodgers upstairs. The main room was almost empty. Marcus steered Claire toward the same table they had eaten at, when she'd spied ai Ctesiphôn through the little window, and he'd kissed her for the first time. Three men sat at the table. It was dark, but Claire recognized the great shapes of Taranto and Brindisi. She couldn't make out who the third man was, the one between them.

Marcus said, "The carriages secreted us a visitor."

Claire reached the table and saw his dark hair, his twinkling eyes.

King Pindar said, "Hello Claire."

XYX

WHEN SHE GOT back to the royal district, she went straight to the carriage house and her gold palanquin. This was the only place no

Florentine could breach. In it, she was alone from the world. She needed to sit there and breathe.

She felt what Pindar begged of her was more than she could bear. But she recalled again a thought, and placed it now: she thought in the storm, when she was still most of herself –

*I could save you. You could save me.*

She slouched in her seat and stared at the thirty-two clock. She was still frightened to open it. Her eye followed the six hands, meting out sidereal time.

She was not recovered from her efforts. Battered, bruised, alone. *Why? Why must I do more?*

She thought of Aeneas, of everything she would have given for him to have lived. For Epida to have got her husband. Once again, the vision of his dying face reminded her of Angoulème. She heard the thunder of wheeled youths on the boardwalks, the squeal of children on the shore, the crash of waves come off the bright, bright sea. *Why does Aeneas remind me of this place?* She was finally too tired to resist, and abruptly saw the thing she didn't want to see, never wanted to see again: the dead girl.

Among the visitors to Zanzibar, there used to be a certain type of older man. Perhaps he did not know his type until he got there, or perhaps he did. These men were attracted, like the needle to the lodestone, to Angoulème. They sat on the benches there, and hopelessly admired the youths screaming past. Now some of these youths, boys or girls as the case might be, would stop and talk with them. Perhaps they'd come to an agreement and gold would change hands. They would share an afternoon or two in the rooms to let beside the sea, with the sunlight filtering through slats, warm rooms, damp salty skin, glowing ceilings, and the crash of waves. It happened, and some said it was disgusting, and others said it was in the nature of things and nothing worse than poignant; adulthood does not come for free. This was at a time when the harsh initiations of adulthood were not yet universally agreed upon in Zanzibar.

The thing Claire wished to forget happened when she was a little girl, and had only been in school a couple years. Her mother liked to keep her out of class sometimes, and the two of them would spend the day adventuring around. On one of these stolen days, they went to Angoulème. They got their sugared ices and walked far out along the northern verge, past the boardwalks, to the inlet where the water calmed and the land grew spongy. They found a girl youth there, where the bulrushes grow, hair plastered to her face. Her fingernails were splintered and her neck was broken. She was the strangest color: every place she wasn't bruised, she kept her vivid tan, but her flesh was white beneath it, so that the color of the tan seemed brittle and impure. Claire had seen dead cormorants and rats, but she did not see death clearly till that afternoon, in the awful moment before her mother clapped her big strong hand over her eyes, and hoisted her up on her mighty shoulder, carrying her out from there at a pounding run. They found a member of the Sûreté-Metro. The massy gates of Zanzibar were shut. With one mind, the city hunted down the ragged visitor who did this thing, did this thing to a girl youth of Zanzibar. They crucified him and flung the cross out on the waste for the jackals. There were no more older men of this kind permitted into Zanzibar thereafter.

Seeing her again, Claire realized it was the possibility that she would meet this fate, alone and unprotected, that must have tormented her mother – must torment her still – now her baby girl was gone. The guilt and anguish of it overwhelmed the young patricia; she sat upright and her eyes darted and bulged. She bit her fist to stifle her shrieks.

*I have to get home! I have to get home!*

## XXX

Now it was a sunny day and King Pindar, wearing his last fine coat and his worn smock, climbed down from his carriage. Claire greeted him. He greeted her.

He looked over the curious little building at the edge of the wood. He said, "What is this thing?"

It was hunched and asymmetrical. It had a staircase up one side that led to nowhere. There was a doorway in the front which opened on a wall.

Marcus said, "This is the tomb of John the Pilgrim."

King Pindar said, "Is he the one we call Eiuenos il Waidhor?"

Marcus frowned and said, "I think that's his name, in the old language."

Claire said, "It is."

They both looked at her.

She said, "One human tongue."

Marcus grinned. Claire said, "Who was John the Pilgrim?"

Before Marcus could answer, a man on horse approached. He arrived and dismounted and strode to King Pindar. He said, "Khrysanthos, what happened?"

Pindar shrugged wryly, but real sorrow weighed on him. He said, "Sit with us. I'll tell you." King Ambrosius sat. Claire opened her basket and offered charred walnuts and slices of quince around. For a moment they sat and ate, four friends on a sunny autumn day.

Then Pindar said, "I've heard the tale of late events in Florence. Your problem, as I understand it, was a faction – a powerful faction – which objected to the peace so angrily, it decided to unthrone you."

Ambrosius said, "It's a fair summary."

Pindar said, "Something similar occurred in Genova."

Ambrosius struck his brow.

Pindar said, "And yet I lacked a Claire and her Thousand." He looked ruefully at Claire and Marcus.

Ambrosius said, "Who was it?"

Pindar waved his hand dismissively. "One of my sons. He has his allies. Here's a difference between your land and mine – nobody knows."

"Knows what?"

"Knows it happened. The king goes unseen in Genova. Lysander does not wish it known he's overthrown me. Also, he has no idea where I've gotten to. A king unseen can escape unseen."

Ambrosius reflected on this. Then he said, "Will he start the war again?"

"It will take him a year. The nation is exhausted and the people wouldn't follow him yet."

He blurted it without thinking.

Suddenly, they were not four friends sitting together any longer.

All three looked at thoughtful Ambrosius. Finally Claire said, "My lord..."

Underneath his war-notched brow, his pale eye rolled to her. But it didn't see her, not exactly.

Marcus said, "You told us Thousand about the friends, who trusted one another even unto death."

Ambrosius said, "It's just a story. I'm sure they tell it in Genova as well."

Pindar looked at him, face white.

There was a long, long silence. Then Marcus turned his back on the kings and spoke to Claire.

"John the Pilgrim came to Florence from the east, from beyond the valley of the world. Consider the great cities, like Florence and Genova. They stand five hundred years. Generation after generation living in them. And then, one day, they fall. Some mighty enemy puts everybody to the sword. A scattered few survive.

"John the Pilgrim came from the last generation of a great city. We do not remember his city's name. Every man, woman, and child was slaughtered when it fell. John survived. Alone he came to the valley of the world. Alone he crossed the fertile plain. Alone he came to Florence, a pilgrim, and made a new life here. He made friends here. He taught Florence the worship of great Pantokrator. He lived and died here, and through him, Pantokrator blessed Florence and took Florence for His own. This is the house of John the Pilgrim, the first ichneumon, a gentle man.

"He was the opposite of you, Claire. You are an exile; you have a home to get back to. He was a pilgrim; he left nothing behind him and made a home where he went."

Marcus turned to Ambrosius and spoke, his voice tight with fury.

"Pantokrator and Master Rabbit have blessed you. You have a great land, a brave queen, and a fine son. You have the love of your people and the faith of your army. You have the living god for your lady champion. You have peace. You tell me that the two friends were just a story. This is the new world. You have friends."

Ambrosius looked at him, then at Pindar. He expected to see Pindar frail and sunken, but instead, he swelled. His breast grew broad, his flesh firm. It was as if every dark color of Genova flowed from him, shimmering like the feathers of a peacock. Even ruined and alone, he was nothing less than king. Voice steady and powerful, he said, "Must you be what you are?"

Ambrosius stared into the eyes of his opposite, his friend.

He said, "No. I can choose again."

Pindar held out a hand. Ambrosius took it.

Ambrosius said, "What do you need?"

Pindar said, "I need Claire."

## XXX

THAT FIRST NIGHT at Desiderio's, he'd explained what he wanted from her.

"When the dark of winter is narrowing at last, the Genovans will celebrate Thesmophoria. It is the one day of the year the king shows his face to the people. He takes his place, and the queen of the dianae acknowledges him –"

"Dianae?"

"The ladies of the court. They choose among themselves a Queen of Thesmophoria."

"Ah, I see."

"She places the crown again upon the king's head and anoints him."

"O Pindar, what has this to do with me?"

"On that day, Lysander plans to reveal himself king. I need you to come to Genova with me and win yourself the part of Queen of Thesmophoria. Then you will reverse the plot: three months hence, you must crown me and return me to the throne."

Claire actually burst out laughing, but there was something hysterical about it. She calmed herself and said, "Forgive me, my lord. I have *just done that* in Florence."

Pindar showed his teeth and Claire recognized he was a man whom it is dangerous to amuse. He said, "I've had an account of your adventures here, and it is not the same at all."

"Educate me."

With a glance at Marcus, Pindar said, "Florence is a simple place. When the king has an enemy here, they kick each other in the shin until one of them falls down."

Marcus sneered, "How do you perfumed Genovans do it?"

Pindar smiled and bowed his head and said, "With words and secrets and maneuvers."

Claire said, "The sorts of skills a woman can master as well as a man."

Pindar said, "Precisely so. This is what I ask of you: turn up in Genova and make yourself at home. Confuse the logothetes and make each think some other one invited you. Infiltrate the court. Win over our idle nobles. Circle the false king without allowing him to catch you. Dominate the dianae. Unfold the secrets of the up-and-down castle. Never allow anyone to guess your mission till it is too late to undo it.

"We may fight subtle wars in Genova, Claire, but they are not make-believe. The stakes are equal to those in Florence – victory or death."

XXX

SHE'D BEGGED A day of him, to decide.

She wandered Florence. She wasn't seeking company and didn't find it. But an absence tugged at her. She realized she'd always seen ai Ctesiphôn in Florence. Every day, near or far, big or small, she'd seen it. Now she didn't.

*The tower offered me two gifts, didn't it? Florence or Zanzibar.*

A thought tickled the back of her mind. She thought of the sprig from that dying tree, hidden away in Trypsomayne, but then she forgot what she'd been thinking, as if waking from a dream.

*What color was my gown?*

She stopped suddenly, hunching around herself, around a hole in the center of her.

*It was red, true red, my red. I was all of myself.*

She comprehended that Ambrosius was wrong, when he said all parents recognize their children. Her mother wouldn't recognize her if she came home less than herself. She'd be cast out of Zanzibar.

*I have to get back in ai Ctesiphôn!*

The tower had offered her two choices – Florence or Zanzibar. Surely it was only two, and she had chosen one, and now ai Ctesiphôn had gone.

The patricia stood and breathed in shallow gasps, face frozen in an awful mask of anguish. An abashed crowd gathered around her, and only a child had the bravery to approach her and ask what was wrong.

## XXX

CLAIRE SET TWO objects down upon the table in front of Pindar, covering them with her hand. Then she uncovered them.

He looked down: the two half-coins of greeting. He looked back at Claire. She looked only at the coins. She pointed at the divided rectangle on the silver coin of Florence. She studiously said, "Ai Ctesiphôn."

She pointed at the golden coin of Genova.

"What's that?"

Pindar looked down at the figure on his coin, like a branching tree or the veins of a leaf. He looked back up at her. She faced him, eyes fearfully bright. He had the most disorienting feeling, as if he'd known her several years already, long before he'd met her in Andropolis.

He said, "That's the other Ctesiphôn."

## XXX

So this was her last evening in Florence.

She headed east along the Via Floribus, arm in arm with Marcus, walking slowly to match his limp. She saw the city with the clarity of departure. She heard afresh its noises, of commerce and of industry, of hustle and bustle, of life – the music of cities, everywhere the same, the music of Man.

"I've fallen in love with your Florence, my champion and savior."

He squeezed her arm and she enjoyed the warmth of him against her, his taut muscles, the syncopated rhythm of his gait.

"I want to go with you."

"You can't."

He couldn't. She had to sneak into Genova. She was taking three tenmen of the Thousand across the frontier, all of them Genovans. She couldn't hazard Florentines.

"In the springtime we'll adventure into unknown lands." Her voice caught. "You and I, together."

The stink of the Liliana grew as they approached it. The Via Floribus was emptying and a round peach moon was rising over the royal district. She looked at the moon and said, "Tonight was to be the Family Dinner."

Marcus beside her murmured, "It would have been my first. The first in the line of Diophantus. Ah well."

He finished his seedcake and tossed the wrapper in the Liliana as they crossed the bridge. Claire wrinkled her nose and said, "You know something all the really advanced cities have?"

"What's that?"

"Clean rivers."

## XXX

HE TRIED TO show her all his pickpocket tricks before he left. It was adorable, really: he conceived her a spy in Genova, and needing spycraft. This happened to be one set of skills where she could beat him. For every one of his hidings in shadows, she could wield invisibility itself.

She considered her mission more a matter of diplomacy. As she conceived it, she was meant to balance a plate on a pin. Each player was a morsel on the plate. She had to weigh each player and place him, to keep the plate from overturning. The price of failure: war – the expedition home – her head...

In the dead of night, she returned to the carriage house and sat in her palanquin. It was time at last to confront the golden thirty-two clock. She glared at its face, its six hands and revolving numbers. She glared at its many spines. She'd tinkered it together in her kitchen workshop while her mother baked the fish. Claire watched it tick, then finally took it in her hands and turned it over. She'd been terrified before to look inside it. Now she was resigned. She opened the clock.

It was exactly what she expected: she saw a nest of wheels and springs and rods and pallets, of couplings, clicks and rollers. The revolving magnets balanced the five escapements, and the marching gears measured sidereal time.

She had no idea how it worked.

*I am not that which I was.*

# 52

## HOW TACAMO BECAME A VAGABOND

CLAIRE TOOK SAD leave of Trypsomayne. She took from it the green sprig of the oak of kings, leaves still moist and fresh, and hid it inside her palanquin.

Half-coins clinking in her gown, she climbed down from the palanquin and handed it off to the cart team. One cart for supplies, and another for the massy palanquin. The sun was not yet up and her breath misted when she came out of the carriage house. The king wished the city not to know when she had gone, or where, or how. She met the Genovan Thousand on their horses and they made their way to Traitor's Gate. The city guard opened it at the king's command.

She faced the queen, but felt a little hand work its way into hers. Looking down, she saw Bitsy Boots; his face was full of woe. She squatted to face him.

"Are you going to die, Auntie Claire?"

"No."

"Will you come back?"

"Yes."

He shambled forward and wrapped his arms around her. He buried his face in her hair and huffed great little-boy breaths of her smell of honeysuckles and of thunder. She felt his tears on her scalp. Finally she had to extricate herself. She kissed his brow, then looked him in the eye and said:

"Wolfrider."

She saw how he liked this name. She stood and faced the queen.

The queen grasped her hand and said, "You make me miss my daughters, Claire." Claire said, "You make me miss my mother." They embraced.

Finally she traded hugs with the king. She felt the strength of his arm. She thought of the sight of him, so grand in his bronze armor, swinging his red sword.

*You don't comprehend how fine it is, wry Pindar, a warrior in his element.*

She said, "When I come back to Florence, will you have somebody teach me to fight with swords?"

The king stood back from her and gripped each of her shoulders and looked her in the face.

He said, "I'll make a deal with you. I will arrange it, if next time you go up ai Ctesiphôn, you bring me back the scabbard of Sibyllam Cumis."

Claire's eyebrows rose and she said, "Oh! I'm sorry, I didn't think of that. Yes, if – if I go back in there, I'll fetch it."

*Will I somehow go back in you, ai Ctesiphôn?*

Marcus turned up with a small flask and a spoon. She was so happy to see him, so enormously happy to see him one more time.

He offered her the spoon and said, "I've brought a present for you. Taste this."

She took the spoon and he tipped the flask over it and poured her a little soup. It tasted hideous and she spat it out. She said, "What *is* this horrible present?"

He laughed in the dimness.

"Revolting, isn't it? I tasted it once. Portable soup. It comes from a solid block and it keeps forever. We'll bring it with us in the springtime, when we take you home."

"Well, now you've got to taste it again."

"What – why –"

She put her arms around him and kissed him. The royal family was watching, but she didn't care. When she finally let him go, he breathed one word in her ear: "Dawn."

The start of new things. The hour of departures.

The sky in the east was turning pale. Claire climbed up into her gold palanquin. The driver switched the team. Claire left Florence.

*So many friends I left without farewells. I left the city like a rat. I entered it the trophy of a king and I left it like a rat.*

They met Pindar and his staff upon the Old King's Road, just as the sun was rising.

## XXX

MARCUS WAS PUTTERING around the warehouse, feeling empty and aimless, getting in the way of Cornelius and his crew. When he heard commotion at the front, he hurried over right away – anything to distract from his unhappiness.

Attendants led a man inside. The man's head was swaddled in blood-stained bandages and he stumbled, as if in pain. It took Marcus a minute to recognize blinded Cleon Constantine.

He said, "Embezzler, tattle-tale, traitor."

Cleon bowed and said, voice hoarse, "Deserter, thief, rebel."

Marcus couldn't help smiling. He said, "What can I do for you today, Constantine?"

Cleon said, "I heard Claire has left the city. I need to speak with her. Tell me how to find her."

Marcus went tense. Sensing the chill, Cleon said, "I mean her no harm, I swear it."

Marcus waited a long time. He looked to Cornelius at his desk. Cornelius shrugged faintly: *this man is harmless.*

The royal family was watching, but she didn't care.

Marcus said, "Information isn't free."

Cleon grimaced.

"Name your price."

"What did you learn about my missing Stonebreakers?"

Cleon sighed. Marcus could see how it hurt him to give away his secrets.

"Two of them made it to lawless Rhegium. Our mutual friend received them. He kept up his end of the deal; I don't know where your men are now."

"And the third?"

"I have a strange story of a man found living on the riverbank, perhaps forty-five years of age. He had an Andropolitan wife, much younger than he was, and they had a brood of little children with them there."

"Ah, this must be my Valens."

Cleon's jaw dropped. He said, "How could you guess so unnatural a thing?"

Cornelius flashed his brilliant white grin. All these years and he'd somehow kept his teeth.

## XXX

FULL DAY NOW, and the mix of feelings, crestfallen and hopeful, of an open road.

Claire looked back, scanning the impenetrable wall of Florence, tall as a mountain and wide as a plain. At this distance it was a low line on the horizon, grayish yellow. The road was empty except a carriage far back in the distance.

Claire shifted in her seat and something disturbed her. She reached beneath a cushion and touched skin. She yanked her hand back and threw aside the cushion. She stifled a shriek.

It was a hand there, a human hand. A left hand, old and brown and wrinkled as a walnut; capable and hard. Severed cleanly at the wrist, a cut no crueler than it had to be.

Tears started to Claire's eyes. There was a divot in the thumbnail, with a little ridge to each side, just as she remembered it. The knife's path, a fixed habit of Libra's flesh.

*Somebody ha' killed my priestess.*

Then cold terror overlaid her grief.

*Reburrus was inside my gold palanquin.*

She stuck her head out the window, gasping for air. She looked back toward Florence, and it was as if an evil glamor hid it from her. On the empty road, the carriage approached. It was a very fine carriage. Men were shouting from it.

*Don't let him get near me! Don't let him near me!*

Several of the Thousand fell back and conversed through the carriage windows. Then one of them rode up to Claire. She was nearly frozen with fear.

The rider said, "A blind man says his name is Cleon Constantine, and he must speak with you."

Claire let out a bark of relief. The rider tilted his head at her. Claire said, "I will speak with him."

Part by part, the train halted. Claire left Libra's hand and climbed down shakily from her palanquin. She smelled cold water and wet soil in the ditches either side of the old King's Road. Wind tussled the bleak winter grass, and crickets creaked. Riders climbed down from the fine carriage: a woman, two lads under seventeen. When they stood on the ground, one lad said, "She's here," and the other said, "Come, *Pater*."

An unsteady figure climbed down from the carriage. Bandages covered the top of Cleon's head. They showed dry brown stains where his eyes had been. He draped his arms over the lads, one on each side. The woman set her hand on his back and guided him toward Claire. Claire tried not to imagine his empty eye sockets. She found something hideous to the idea of an eyeless man still living. What is he but a chattering skull?

Claire said, "I'm here, Cleon Tertius Constantine."

He said, "Claire, this is my wife Næva. Our sons Juventus and Florian. My loves, the Sower of Peace." His voice was ragged, as if his throat were sore.

Claire could hardly listen to him. Fear gnawed her gut and grief clutched her heart. She nodded to the woman and her boys. She said, "I'm for the road, Cleon. Why have you come out to meet me?"

Cleon said, "I've heard you like stories of Tacamo, and I wanted to tell you one."

Claire felt the evil glamor drifting toward her. She said, "What story of Tacamo would you like to tell me?"

Cleon raised his arms from his sons' shoulders, then dropped them to his sides. The blind man took a step toward her unassisted.

He said, "I want to tell you how Tacamo became a vagabond."

This was proceeding with the logic of a nightmare. She said sternly, "Let's have it then."

Cleon licked his dry lips, and scratched at his stained bandages.

He said, "When Tacamo was a little boy, he had a little-boy-sized bed. His mother pushed the bed against the wall. She warned him not to pull it away from the wall, because he might fall behind the bed. But he did it anyway, and sure enough, he fell behind the bed. He found there an entire land, with farms and towns and roads and people. It was so exciting, he wandered off to explore, and before he knew it, he was lost."

Sunk in a hideous sense of the inevitable, Claire said, "How did he get back out in the end?"

Blind Cleon leered at her a minute. Then he said, "He didn't."

Claire said, "I don't understand."

Cleon said, "I think you do understand. Florence is the land behind the bed of Tacamo. That's why he's a vagabond. He's still searching for the way back to his mama."

And suddenly, the nightmare ended. The black terror broke, and Claire was human again. Her company was human company, and her feelings merely human feelings. She knew exactly what Cleon wanted, and she was ready to give it to him. She began to bawl.

She let him hear her crying entirely uncontrolled. She wept so hard that her grief mimicked hysterical laughter, and she became confused whether she was laughing or sobbing. She covered her face with her hands to hide her shame and shook and wept. Cleon began to cry as well. She heard and dropped her hands and leaned her brow to his, she pressed her brow to the brow of the mutilated wretch. She rested her hands on his shoulders, and he rested his hands on her shoulders, and they pushed each other down and held each other up. When she regained language, she wailed, "I want my mama! I want to go home!" and then she lost language again, and went on crying, wetting his bandages and his cheeks. He howled, "I want my brother! I want my cousin! I want to see!" though he had no means of shedding tears and his crying was a raw sound in his throat. Thus they wept together, over all the sufferings they suffered, both those the world piled on them, and those they brought down on themselves.

It went on a very long time, the two of them sobbing like children, right there in the middle of the road. Finally Claire calmed down and put her hands on each side of Cleon's head and said to him, "You must cauterize your eye sockets, and pack them with a paste of honey and wine, thyme and calendula. You belong to me now, Cleon Constantine, and I will need you, and you will need me." She let him go, and he stood himself up weakly, and his two sons steadied him.

Claire turned away from the Constantines and climbed back in the gold palanquin. Her gut was at ease and her heart was calm. Patricia, student, graduate – mortal, goddess, exile - she tenderly covered Libra's hand with her own. The soldiers took their places and the train began to move again. It gathered speed on the old King's Road, riding east, away from Zanzibar.

# AFTERWORD

Thank you so much for reading *Railroad to Zanzibar I: The Exile of Zanzibar*. I'm grateful for the time and energy you've invested in it, and I hope it rewarded your effort.

If you enjoyed it, I would humbly request a favor from you – could you leave a review? Posting reviews to Amazon or Barnes & Noble or wherever you bought this book – and to Goodreads – really makes a difference in the fate of the book.

Thank you! I hope to see you again for *Lucky Angel*, the second volume of *Railroad to Zanzibar*. Thesmophoria turns out to be very much not what Claire expects.

# ACKNOWLEDGEMENTS

I have it on solid authority that you should learn to write novels by writing a lot of bad ones until you write a good one. I took an alternate path and wrote *The Exile of Zanzibar* eight times. It took seventeen years.

As with any project this large, I owe enormous debts to many people. My heartfelt thanks go to my family: my wife Charlotte Sears, who has always wanted for me to accomplish whatever would make me happy – my son Boaz, who believes, perhaps more than I do, that I am an author – my father Maynard Maidman, who helped me place my ideas in literary and historical context – my mother Ellen Maidman-Tanner, who interpreted and evaluated the story visually – my stepfather Mike Tanner, who applied an expert-level passion for fantasy to his critique and support – my stepmother Janice Warren, who believes the absolute best about me and my work – and the irreplaceable Chris Speck, who helped trim the waves of text down to a *story*. Each of you has made it possible for me to get here.

Surrounding this nucleus I am so happy to offer thanks to a constellation of friends and acquaintances whose contributions have been crucial: Mike Johnson and Jess Roberts and Jeremy Boxen and Jackson George and Seung-Yoon Lisa Lee and Jason Fisher, for a lifetime of faith and love – China Miéville, for believing in me from the start – Greg Bear, for allowing me to borrow an excellent neologism from his novel *City at the End of Time* – Ljiljana Babic, for reading with a sympathetic eye and forcefully seeing what I hadn't yet managed to express – Simon Kavanagh, for a deep structural criticism which profoundly transformed and improved the manuscript – Kathleen Rooney and Martin Seay, for your unstinting encouragement and support – Kimberly Brooks, for being my guardian angel – Rachel Stout, for generously stepping in as needed with professional advice – Jennifer Quintenz and James Berry, for helping me lift this project at the very beginning – and Merav Hoffman, for materializing in the eleventh hour and carrying it the rest of the way with me. Though I don't know them personally, I am very grateful to Brandon Sanderson, Dan Wells, Howard Tayler, and Mary Robinette Kowal. Their long-running podcast *Writing Excuses* taught me worlds about writing.

In a category all his own, I thank Dr. Samuel Peralta for, astonishingly, archiving a copy of this novel on the surface of the Moon. I never, ever thought such a thing could happen. Thank you also to Didi Menendez of *Poets and Artists*, who has supported my work for years and through whom I met Samuel, and to Astrobotic, the trailblazing company that built the Griffin Lunar Lander.

I offer my deepest thanks to my visual art community, too numerous to name here, for your friendship and company in the uneven pursuit of a creative way of living. You thought you were encouraging me in painting and drawing, but you were encouraging me in writing as well.

Finally, this book did not physically happen in a vacuum. Over its seventeen years, I did most of the actual writing in coffee shops and forests. I am grateful to these creative spaces: Stir Crazy on Melrose, in Los Angeles, and the Coffee Bean & Tea Leaf on Hillhurst, also Los Angeles – the Cup A Joe on Hillsborough Street in Raleigh, NC – Café Grumpy in Greenpoint, Brooklyn – and

Uptown Coffee in Kingston, NY. Thanks also to the City of Kingston Department of Parks and Recreation for maintaining Forsyth Park, and all the trees for growing there. I have spent such happy hours in these places, reading my favorite book by writing it.

# ABOUT THE AUTHOR

Daniel Maidman is an author, artist, and art critic. His art is included in the permanent collections of the Library of Congress Department of Prints and Drawings and a number of American art museums. His art and writing on art have been featured in *The Huffington Post*, *ARTnews*, *Forbes*, *W*, and many others.

*The Exile of Zanzibar* is his first novel.

WWW.DANIELMAIDMAN.COM

CPSIA information can be obtained
at www.ICGtesting.com
Printed in the USA
BVHW042006190523
664530BV00002B/6

9 798987 59780